UNEXPECTED VENGEANCE

UNEXPECTED VENGEANCE

By Timothy Neal James

Published by
MIDNIGHT EXPRESS BOOKS

UNEXPECTED VENGEANCE

ISBN-13: 978-0692400180 (Midnight Express Books)
ISBN-10: 0692400184

Although I've borrowed names and physical characteristics from those in my life, by no means are their true personalities reflected in this book, nor are any of the negative attitudes of my story related to anyone I know.

Published by
MIDNIGHT EXPRESS BOOKS
POBox 69
Berryville AR 72616
(870) 210-3772
MEBooks1@yahoo.com

UNEXPECTED VENGEANCE

By Timothy Neal James

DEDICATION

Dedicated to my stepson, Michael, and to my biological sons, Jeremiah and Phillip.

And a special dedication to June and Jimmie James, my Mom and Dad.

I'll love you always.

AUTHOR'S STORY

As a small child, I heard my grandfather brag about being employed by DuPont for over fifty years. He never missed a day stamping out heels for boots on a press his entire life. He took great pride in this accomplishment. The whole idea scared the crap out of me. At that very impressionable age, I decided that I couldn't, and wouldn't, fall prey to such a mundane existence.

Sticking to that early life decision, I've spent the last forty years working at different careers, usually changing every fifteen to thirty months. It sounds crazy, I know, but I've done everything from dipping ice cream, to performing minor surgeries, and have excelled at each and every one of them. These jobs include, but are not limited to teaching elementary school, counseling the criminally insane, operating construction companies, running heavy machines, drafting blueprints & designing homes. I've helped to develop fiber optic cables for communication systems, worked in pediatrics, endocrinology, bariatric and as a general practitioner, etc. You name it, I've done it. Of course, most of these positions required college, which I've spent a large chunk of my life attending. I've also taught myself how to play guitar and sing. This led to composing a few songs. I've had my poetry published and have acted in a few movies like Scarecrow, Dark Harvest, III and The Burning Dead.

The book you have in your hands is my first attempt to add "novelist" to my ever-growing list. I hope you have as much enjoyment reading this story as I had in creating it.

Thank you so much for your time.

Timothy Neal James

CHAPTER 1

The Sun had just begun to expose its beauty through the surrounding oak trees, when Sara rolled over and struck the snooze button for the fifth time. This time with enough hate behind it to cause the small bedside clock to malfunction; the little light illuminating its face blinked twice before going out completely. Staring at the damage, she laid there like a drunken wino after a three-day binge; her mind clouded with the green monster of jealousy. She knew lots of people in her social class who could stay in bed until noon. Why couldn't she? It wasn't fair!

Finally, surrendering to reality, and with a groan resembling that of a grizzly bear, she lazily forced herself up into a sitting position near the center of the large bed. Lifting her arms straight up over her head to stretch, she took on an uncanny resemblance to Buddha, sitting on a shrine. The morning light filtering through the window blinds and spilling over her voluminous mid-section added to the illusion of being in a Chinese Temple.

After running her tongue over the roof of her mouth, she was unfavorably reminded of the cheeseburgers and chocolate pie she'd consumed just before retiring. Mixing that with her morning breath, she found herself disgusted and assaulted. "Yuck! Maybe I should have brushed my teeth last night," she said to the empty room, and then thought, *"Maybe I'll find the time later."*

With great effort, she lumbered herself to the edge of the king-sized mattress. As she erected her gigantic three hundred pound bulk to a standing position, the bed frame sang a happy chorus of joyful squeaks that were accompanied harmoniously with the tormented groans produced by the hardwood flooring.

As she began to walk, her thighs made an audible and irritating swish as they struggled, with each foot-dragging step, to occupy the same space. Already finding a need to rest, she stopped to sit on a six foot wooden bench that she mostly used to pile her clothes on. Sitting there, she began to get angry. On the floor were the socks she had kicked off last night, and her lazy husband had failed to pick up. Worse, they were the ones that she wanted to wear again, requiring her to have to bend over and retrieve them herself; something that had proved to be physically impossible a hundred pounds ago. Thinking maybe she could wait until her husband came into the room, she began to relax.

"When he gets here, he'll not only pick them up, he'll kneel before me and slip them on my feet. Next time, he'll think twice before failing at his duties," she said to herself, smiling at her supremacy.

However, after ten minutes had passed without him showing, she began to get angry again. She was suddenly very aware of something soft that she felt next to her substantial backside. To her delight, it was a half-eaten donut.

"Now how did I miss you?" she said as if talking to an infant.

"Come to mama!" With a single bite, the pacifying morning snack vanished along with her temporary good mood.

Her thoughts were suddenly drawn back to yesterday's traumatic evening, and the memory caused her to shudder. Two of her shows aired at the same time. Not just once, but twice. Even with T-Vo, it took well past midnight to catch up. And to make matters worse, her smart-assed husband Tim asked if he should roll her over every hour or so to keep her from getting couch sores. It was so rude. He knows that she is fat only because of her overactive thyroid. Just because he's some high and mighty neurosurgeon at Vanderbilt didn't give him the right to judge her.

She began swinging her arms in an attempt to get up. The bench cried out for mercy as the glue desperately fought to maintain its integrity.

"To hell with socks, I'll go without any. That'll show him," she said, and then under self-examination she spoke under her breath, "Ten hours of television a day really isn't that much. He can kiss my ass!"

On the third try, managing to stand, she swayed her way into the master bathroom, plopping down on the toilet, covering it completely. When finished with that task, she got to her feet. Looking at the sink, she wondered if she had the strength to brush her teeth and maybe wash her filthy rear-end. The thought made her cringe. Being a diabetic, it was just too much work.

Instead, she proceeded to dance back and forth, painfully inserting her size fifty-two extra-wide stretch-frame into a pair of under panties that were half that size. The effort caused little beads of sweat to form on her pimply forehead, her body odor reaching the point of repulsiveness.

Either oblivious to or through some disturbed, neurotic absence of concern about her obnoxious aroma, Sara returned to the bedroom unwashed. Once again finding a need to rest, she sat back down on the bench and began scanning the large sleeping chamber with disgust and thoughts of unjustifiable rage. The bed sheets were a tangled mess. A week's worth of empty Mountain Dew bottles covered her nightstand, and her clothes were like multicolored carpeting that covered most of the floor. For the life of her, she couldn't understand why her cheapskate husband wouldn't allow her to hire a maid, especially knowing about her weak back and heart.

"He just doesn't care!" she spat angrily.

Her disposition only degraded when she went to get dressed. Most of her clothes, even the brand new things, no longer fit. She began throwing and tearing at her stuff like the spoiled brat she'd always been, refusing to accept the fact that her lazy body was getting fatter by the day. In her mind, she blamed Tim. He must have screwed-up the laundry again; shrinking all of her clothes.

"Idiot!" she screamed sharply and returned to her attack on her wardrobe.

Thirty minutes, twenty colorful metaphors, and four new medical inflictions later, Sara was finally dressed for work. Breathing like a charging buffalo, she stomped down the hallway in search of someone to vent her anger upon.

In the kitchen, Tim was preparing their five-year-old, Michael, for school when she arrived. The joy and laughter being shared over some father/son antics came to an immediate halt the second their eyes met Sara's infuriating glare.

There was no way at this point to understand her problem, and the tension was so thick you could cut it with a knife. However, after years of the same kind of morning ritual and hypochondriac related complaints of fabricated burdens, they wouldn't have expected anything less.

Sara dropped herself down with a crash on a twin of the wooden bench in the bedroom, uncaringly causing an avalanche of her week's worth of carry home items. Stuff she could easily put away; like her purse, book bag, coat, gloves, hats, and many other articles she discarded there every time she entered the house. But she never bothered. She was always running a little late for her mid-day shows, usually Oprah.

Nowadays, Tim cleaned the house from top to bottom on Sunday. Today being Friday, the bench was full. Her huge rear-end barely found room in the place of the fallen items. She pretended not to notice the mess, and Tim didn't say a word, not wanting to hear about her arthritis, or some other fictitious disorder that would hamper her ability to perform the physical labor it would require in order to pick up her things.

Like a vicious predatory beast, Sara locked her eyes on Michael, her first victim of the day.

"Who dressed you?" she barked, knowing full well it was her

husband. This way she could strike twice with one blow. "You look like some homeless street orphan," she added.

It never really mattered what the boy wore. It was always ugly, unthinkable, or the stupidest things she'd ever laid her eyes on; no matter who picked it out, unless it was her.

"And," she went on heatedly, "There's no way on God's green Earth that you're stepping foot out of my house with those cheap looking shoes on your feet! Do you understand me?"

"But mom ... ", Michael replied before thinking, and then took a step backward when he saw the animosity clouding his mother's bulging eyes like a mad dog succumbing to the insanity of rabies. Redness began spreading over her fat cheeks like the Sun rising over a vast open desert.

"Go do what you were asked Michael," interrupted Tim, elevating his voice slightly. Sara's mouth dropped open and a scream that resembled an elephant, or ironically, a large pig, escaped her lungs. Michael froze with perplexity. Was his mother's heightened anger still directed at him or at his dad for having the audacity to interfere with her role as queen?

Sensing his son's confusion, Tim raised his voice further, "Now! Son," he said, snapping Michael out of his daze.

Thankful that once again his dad had saved his hide, Michael made a dash for his room. "Yes sir," he said, using the longer route through the formal dining room for his escape. He may not have learned yet to keep his mouth shut, but the education that he received from getting within reach of one of those ham-sized arms of his mother will last a lifetime. Knowing that if she were ever mad enough to get up, he'd pay dearly. So, he ran as fast as he could.

"Stop running in my house! Do you hear me?"Sara screamed at his back.

"Yes ma'am," he replied though he never broke his stride.

Once satisfied that Michael was far enough away as to not

overhear, Tim turned to his wife, "What's wrong now?" he asked, even though he didn't really care.

Sara rolled her eyes in disbelief, her mouth dropped open in shock at her inability to fully comprehend how stupid her husband could be.

"Blue jeans with a long sleeved shirt?" she barked with disgrace, "and those shoes have Velcro, and not strings," she continued with her flabby arms flapping in the air. "He's not a damn baby, and I'm sick of treating him like one. My God, Velcro! Looks like I've got to do everything around here myself! Can't you do anything right, even once in a while?" she asked, with little droplets of spittle launching from her mouth with every word.

Tim acted as if he were listening; he was not. He had learned years ago how to block her out. Using the 'What's wrong now?' question as a trigger worked well. He knew it always opened a spillway for a flood of anger and incomprehensible complaints. But by asking the fateful question, she could finish her ranting and raving before Michael returned, saving him from his mother's self-gratifying, self-glorifying fits of inconsequential and misguided tantrums. She rambled on for approximately ten minutes.

Trying to be unnoticed, Michael entered the room quietly and seized his backpack before desperately darting for the back door.

"I'll be in the van dad!" he yelled over his shoulder once he felt that he had successfully made his escape. Wrong. Once again, he found himself frozen at the sound of his mother's voice.

"Not so fast," she said with her usual hatefulness. Then, with a difference of night and day, she added in a tone as sweet as an angel, "Give mommy some lovin' baby doll."

Michael's expression turned to one of hopelessness. He looked as though he was being instructed to eat a dog turd sandwich at gunpoint. Slowly, he walked toward his mother's arms like a prisoner on the way to the gallows. Uncertainty had him locked in its grip. He couldn't tell if he were to receive a smack or a sloppy smooch. Like a rattlesnake strike, he placed a kiss on her cheek and then vanished from the house with all the speed that his youthful body could produce, unconsciously wiping his lips with the back of his hand to remove what he envisioned to be an invading army of fat cooties.

After watching Michael cross the backyard and climb onto his trampoline, and taking a couple of nerve-calming deep breaths, Tim turned to face the biggest mistake of his life. *'Well, here goes. Time to go to war.'* he thought to himself. He dreaded speaking to this impossible abomination.

With most married couples, what he was about to request was nothing more than a simple honey-do. But not with this lazy, self-centered human deformity. Everything manifested into a knock-down, drag-out battle to the death. He had to constantly remind himself of just how much he loved his son, and how that kid alone kept him married to this preposterous she-beast before him.

"I need you to pick up Michael after school today," he said, firing the first shot; committing himself to the conflict. The look of unadulterated panic fell over Sara's face like a shroud. Her eyes widened like a deer caught in the headlights of a speeding semi on a country road. She quickly searched her memory. All she had to do today was lock-up a store because it was behind on its taxes. Had she already made an irreversible confession to the fact that her day would be over by noontime? Could she now lie convincingly enough to persuade her husband that things had changed? Maybe she could come up with a new ailment so severe it could discharge her from the responsibility of fulfilling his request.

"Damn it!" she shouted when nothing came to her mind fast enough to ring true, "I've got six hours of Oprah on the TiVo to watch or it's going to erase itself," she said pleadingly, and then became shocked when she realized that Tim clearly didn't appreciate how critical her situation was.

She started rocking back and forth, angrily trying to stand. Upon her success, she approached her husband as if her five-foot, two-inch height could somehow be intimidating.

"Why can't you do it like every other day?" She spat savagely.

"Well," Tim began while thinking, if he could find her neck, he'd snap it like a twig. "It may not be ranked as high on the list of momentous importance as your plans, but ..." raising his hands, palm up as if displaying them to his mother for inspection before coming to the supper table. "Dr. Johnson, Dr. Kempler and myself have a pre-surgical consultation with young Brandon Millichamp's parents. Hopefully to diminish some of their fears and reluctance concerning the encephalic invasive surgery we've scheduled for their little boy," he said, remaining as calm as a saint.

Sara butted in, "Well, that couldn't take all day. And even if it did, why couldn't you excuse yourself and go get Michael? It's not like it's going to change the outcome of this ... sick kid," she added sarcastically.

Her complete lack of compassion for others infuriated him. *'God help me not to kill her,'* he silently prayed while gritting his teeth.

"I know you don't care about anything except increasing your dimension and that stinking television, but I've got to convince these people that I can remove their child's brain tumor without leaving them a vegetable or a ... ", Tim stopped when he saw Sara roll her eyes uncaringly and bored like a girl listening to the same old fatherly speech. Tim no longer attempted to hold his tongue, nor retain his anger. "Look you putrid, over saturated hunk of lard, make damn sure that Michael gets picked up from school on time," he said, now pointing his finger at her. "Or pack your hidden stashes of chocolates and roll your cellulose extended ass out of my house," he added with genuine conviction and then slammed the door behind him.

Tim was still entertaining homicidal thoughts when he saw Michael running in his direction which calmed his soul. 'What the crap! Let the ham and bacon do it for me,' he thought to himself.

"Come on Pooter! Let's get you to school," He said lovingly.

They both climbed into the van and they burst into laughter as soon as their eyes met. Once again, the morning routine hadn't changed their relationship.

"I really love you buddy," Tim said.

Michael pointed his index finger at his dad and winked, saying, "Right back at ya dad."

As they drove away, Tim told Michael a Bible story related to a love like theirs. Genesis Chapter 16-22.

♦ ♦ ♦ ♦ ♦

Unconcerned over any damage she may cause to her new Chevy, Sara jerked the steering wheel, causing the car to enter the parking lot too early, forcing the right-front wheel to strike a large concrete curb. The sudden impact caused her to spill a small amount of cappuccino, which then mixed with the crumbs from her morning fried pies, down the front of her blouse.

"Damn it!" she screamed angrily in frustration. Not over the expensive auto repair coming, but the price of her shirt would have to come out of her own pocket.

Rechecking the address on the tax form, she verified the place as the establishment that she was in search of, and she wasn't surprised by the look of the building that it was behind in its taxes. Like thousands of other convenience stores across America, the windows were covered with advertisements in both English, and in Spanish, selling beer and cigarettes at low, low prices. Equally common was its cement parking lot full of potholes with an occasional lump of asphalt here and there, where numerous attempts at inexpensive repairs had failed miserably. Oil stains blackened the center of each parking space in an almost mathematical flow of proportional design. It was as if visiting automobiles had marked their territory with their own personal scent. Moving closer, millions of small particles from the deteriorated concrete pelted the side of the car, which sounded like rain on a tin roof. That sound mixed with the sound of the recently ruined tire, infuriated her.

"Why my husband buys these cheap, forty thousand dollar cars is beyond me," she griped to herself.

Sara pulled into a spot as close to the door as possible so she wouldn't have to walk very far. She turned off the engine and just sat there, reluctant to open the door. She knew the heat of the day would quickly rob the interior of her precious, cool air conditioning that she so dearly loved, and how hot it would be upon her return. Leaving the car running is not an option because that would mean that she would have to stop for gas on the way home; costing her time and money. This way, her clueless husband could go back out after he gets Michael ready for bed, using his money and his time for gas, while she rested.

The thought made her smile, "He's too stupid to see past my excuses."

Inspecting the storefront once again, she couldn't understand how any self-respecting person could shop here. In her opinion, it should be condemned. Movement inside the store suddenly interrupted her thoughts.

She had been optimistic that no one would be present, making this a simple task. All she would have needed to do was to place a chain on the front door with a pad lock donning a sign that read: 'Closed by the order of The Department of Revenue,' and then leave. However, the job just became more difficult. Having someone inside meant extra work, and there is nothing that she hated more. Now she'd have to enter the building and inform the inhabitants of her intentions. Her face flushed with anger.

"More work," she spat. "God help them if they think that they're going to get away with that!"

20

Striking out in a rage, Sara slammed her huge leg into the driver's door causing it to fly open with a crunch as the hinges hyper-extended. Most people with a new car would pamper it, but not Sara. It wasn't her problem.

With a great effort, she liberated her immense abdomen from behind the steering wheel and sort of rolled to her feet. Ten punishing steps later, she aggressively entered the store. A small piercing alarm beeped to enlighten the proprietor of a prospective customer.

The exterior, as bad as it may have seemed, was obviously maintained much better than the dilapidated interior. The place reeked of cheap cleaning products and incense. The floor tile looked as if it had lost its color back when our Lord Jesus walked the Earth. And there was a trail worn a half-inch deep in the sub-flooring that lead up to the check-out counter. Behind it stood a man with a dark complexion. He was smiling, exposing a mouth-full of larger than normal, yellowish-brown teeth that are common to the people of India.

"Welcome, traveler, to my humble place of business. How may I be of service?" he asked with a sultry accent, bowing his turban-covered head.

"Whatever! I need to speak with Almond Ass-car," informed Sara with an insulting tone, as if speaking the name left a bad taste in her mouth.

A bewildered look came over the man as all the color drained from his face. How did this woman with a butt as large as a bull camel, know his name?

"Why does your journey bring you in search of this man?" he asked almost under his breath.

Sara held out her chubby hand displaying a badge and identification.

"Does this answer your stupid question?" she asked rudely.

His shoulders dropped as his eyes locked on the gold and silver shield, and for a fleeting second, thought of lying. Instead, he sadly confessed, "I would be the one you seek. I am Armand Astarr."

Sara waddled her way behind the counter like she already owned the place.

"Who cares," she said. And then as if rehearsed, "Under the authority granted me by the Great State of Tennessee, I am hereby calling for a cease and desist of all retail functioning associated with this establishment."

With that said, she lost her professionalism and returned to her natural hateful self.

"So get the hell out so I can secure this trashy property!" All the time she spoke, her sausage-sized finger pointed to the exit door; a holier-than-thou smirk on her face.

Armand moved close to a small set of shelves with a dingy dish towel covering its front like a curtain. He then began fumbling around for something hidden within, never taking his eyes off the fat American.

Sara's first thought was that the man was trying to find a gun, and it made her become frightened. Her mind raced over the fatal mistake she had made by not having an armed escort as required by law. She wished for another chance to do the small amount of extra work of calling someone in, and not be so lazy.

Seeing her fear, Armand quickly removed his hand to show her it was empty.

"I was only after the tax money that you require," he informed her, and then pointed back to the covered area. "Allah be praised; may I please?" He requested.

He then noticed that she had become totally oblivious to him, and preoccupied herself with some far away thoughts. Following her line of sight, he could see that all of her attention had been diverted to a fresh tray of doughnuts.

Armand turned toward the glass tray while speaking delicately, "If it would please you, I would be greatly honored to present you with one of your choice."

Sara looked like a child on Christmas morning. "Well, maybe just a few," she replied.

Armand removed the glass cover and presented the treats as if to royalty. Catching on to his play-acting, she accepted them with the curtsy of a queen.

Satisfied that he had tranquilized the situation by pacifying the she beast, Armand returned to his stash. This time withdrawing a bag-full of money that he dumped out on the counter top. Sara's eyes went from displaying pure joy and contentment, to one of scorn.

"I can't accept that without my supervisor's approval," she lied. She could, but once again, that would require more work.

Armand desperately searched his mind for an answer that would allow him to keep his door open. He was just about ready to give up when a glimmer of hope came over him as he watched the huge woman lick the icing from her chubby fingers.

"If you could please call the person in charge, I would again be humbly in your debt and honored to present you with another one of these wonderful treats," he said, waving his hand over the service dish as if he were a game show host. He lifted the lid to hopefully allow her access; she just stood there staring at it stupidly. Armand was sure he'd made a big mistake trying to bribe a tax enforcement officer. Sweat formed behind his ears; his intestines cramped painfully.

"Or more if it pleases you," he added with a nervous little laugh, which snapped her from her trance. She actually lunged, almost knocking Armand over in the process of greedily filling her hands. The first doughnut entered her mouth even before she grabbed a second one.

"Yum, mmph," she moaned, as if filled with sexual ecstasy.

"Well," she said between bites and reaching for a third. "Go ahead and count the money out. I'll clear it with my boss later."

Chocolate covered most of her chin and encircled her lips like the pictures we've all seen of a child's first introduction to a birthday cake.

"I'll need two thousand, five hundred dollars in order to leave you open," she advised, spitting small chunks of dough onto Armand's shirt. Then she pointed an icing covered finger toward the cash like he'd forgotten where it was. "Go ahead," she mumbled through a mouthful of un-chewed confections. Then she noticed the sweet stuff on her finger nail. She pulled it back toward her face slowly until her eyes crossed to look at it. She then struck at it like a hungry shark.

Armand stepped back in shock and fear for his life because his clothes had enough dough on them to arouse the beast's predatory instincts. He continued to watch in horror as Sara gulped down every last doughnut like a ravenous dog.

A few minutes later, while Sara was busy licking the crumbs off the platter, Armand counted out the money into five nice piles onto the counter.

The door opened and once again the store was filled with that high-pitched beep. The new patron's eyes widened as they came to rest on the large amount of currency. The room's atmosphere filled with the feeling of uncertainty. All three tensed, awaiting an unknown outcome. Unsympathetic of the message of mistrust that she projected, Sara quickly snatched-up the money, stuffing it into her purse.

However politically incorrect or impolite it may have been, it was easy to understand, stereotypically, how this new customer would elevate mistrust in anyone. Clearly he was of a rebellious nature and it had gone to extremes. Silver-plated rings in an overabundance, dangled from every accessible surface his ears had to offer. Others of various shapes and sizes penetrated his eyebrows, lips and nose. Cheep tattoos littered most of his visible skin. The clothes he wore were obviously four-times larger than he required, and as black as funeral attire. His hair was a colonnade of six-inch green spikes which pointed skyward down the center of his head.

Seeing the way the fat woman reacted sort of rewarded his ego, and he subconsciously expanded his chest, over emphasizing his dimensions.

Armand broke the tension that hung in the atmosphere like a thick fog. "Welcome friend. How may I serve you?" he asked.

The punky customer replied with a fake sounding deep voice, "Marlboro Reds, in a box."

Armand was tempted to request some form of identification as required by law, but wanted this kid gone as soon as possible.

"That's four dollars and twenty-three cents, please," he said. Then half turning to face Sara, and with his nightmare of the American Dental Association smile, he added, "That includes tax."

Because of Sara's normal unsociable and childish attitude, Armand's attempt at levity enraged her. She spun her huge girth away from him, upsetting a display of novelties, mostly key-chains and lighters, causing a hundred dollars worth to hit the floor. Unconcerned with the damage, she stormed from the store, knocking the young customer painfully into a rack of magazines. If, like she had claimed to Michael a million times, she had eyes in the back of her head, she would have seen both of Armand's hands in the air. His middle fingers extended vertically in the traditional American salute that we've all seen on the roadways, proclaiming: "You're number 1," or possibly some other meaning entirely.

After struggling to re-insert herself into the car, Sara started the engine. "How dare they treat me that way," voicing her superiority, and adding, "They should grovel at my feet like the dogs that they are."

The coolness of the air conditioner helped her to calm down and she began to relax. In doing so, she rolled her bottom to one side so as to pass a little gas. The rattle would have made a beer-drinking, chili-consuming, truck driver blush with shame. Sitting there trying not to gag, and waving her hand in an attempt to disperse the stench, she caught movement in her peripheral vision; the sight somehow shocking her temporarily. There was that punk kid staring at her with demonic eyes, causing her hair to stand on end. Panicking, she jerked the shifter into reverse and then slammed the accelerator to the floor. Once the car was pointed in the right direction, she threw it into drive, never letting up on the gas pedal. The rear tires squealed like beaten dogs as she rocketed out of the parking lot. Relief came over her like a fresh morning shower as she watched the place disappear in the rear-view mirror.

◆ ◆ ◆ ◆ ◆

Pulling up another few car lengths closer to the school, Sara's stomach started to rumble. Unsure if the dozen doughnuts were unfavorably mixing with the fried pies and cappuccino, or if she were again hungry, she decided to eat something again soon, just in case.

Then her lower abdomen rattled internally. She raised her hind end to one side and pushed. Her face showing her effort. A long, slow flatulent made her feel better, but the idea of lunch still pricked at her mind.

Moving up a few more spaces, she started to get irritated. She hated sitting in these lines with common parents that were waiting to pick up their brats. Once again, it was Tim's fault.

"I guess his stupid job is more important than mine," she said sarcastically to the empty car. Then she hit the steering wheel with the palm of her hand. "Come on damn-it! Some of us have things to do!" she yelled at the people in front of her. Once more her mid-section called to her demandingly. Her thoughts again went to food. She knew that she would get something to eat as soon as she picked up Michael. That is if she didn't starve first.

Michael was right where he was supposed to be, and Sara pulled right up next to him. He quickly opened the door and jumped in with his backpack in tow.

Instead of saying 'hi honey' or 'how was your day', Sara spat at him rudely, "Hurry up, your letting all the air out!"

The new-car smell had been replaced by something obnoxious, so Michael covered his nose. 'Talk about a weapon of mass destruction', he wanted to say; but wisely kept his comment to himself. He felt a little perturbed at his dad. But only because he had to ride home in a manure truck, and listen to his mother complain all the way there.

♦ ♦ ♦ ♦ ♦

Sara pulled into the bank's parking lot between McDonald's® and Arby's®. This way she could drop Michael off, allowing him to run across the road to his favorite place to eat, while she used the drive thru at hers, saving precious television time.

After obtaining her sack-full of artery-clogging, grease saturated, decaying animal flesh, she headed back for Michael. One burger and two fistful of fries later, she arrived. A little nervousness had been prickling at her subconsciously. Some people might look down their noses at a person dropping off a five-year-old by himself, but *they can mind their own damn business,* she thought, because she was in a hurry; Oprah had already started. If trouble did arise, she carried a badge. And in her mind that raised her above most. It was easy to see that she was talking herself into getting angry again.

Pulling up to the usual prearranged spot, the front passenger door sprang open with a bang. "What the hell is wrong with you?! Jerking my ... ''she started yelling. Then she realized that it wasn't Michael, but the punk from the store and he was pointing a gun in her direction.

"Give me that bag you fat pig!" he yelled abruptly. Thinking the gunman was after her lunch, Sara frantically grabbed the bag, causing the intruder to do the same, resulting in a tug-of-war. The punk wanted the money, and Sara wanted her food.

As if in slow motion, the gun discharged, filling the car's interior with an ear-shattering explosion and the smell of rotten eggs from the sulfur-laced smoke. Sara's arms fell limp as her lifeless body slumped against the driver's door. Behind her, the blood spattered window spider webbed outwardly from a hole caused by the bullet after leaving what used to be the back of her head. Shocked over what had just transpired, the would-be-robber turned to flee, only to come face to face with a small redheaded boy and two very large Hendersonville police officers. Apparently, someone had called the law concerning a five-year-old boy being left alone in a restaurant.

The next thing the young rebel knew, he was face down in a discarded Happy Meal®, and a heavy knee was in the center of his back pressing the air from his lungs. The clicking sound of handcuffs signaling the end of his life of freedom.

CHAPTER 2

Michael laid on his bed, staring sleepily out the window. There, a couple of deer grazed lazily on the front lawn. Today marked another anniversary of his mother's death. Witnessing the murder had upset him in ways most people could never understand. He knew the killer had only taken her body and not her soul, but it had scarred Michael for life.

There were many nights when it all came back, haunting his sleep. Sometimes his dreams placed him in the car when the bullets flew. Others included him being the victim. Last night was absolutely one of the worst. It had seemed so realistic. He had sat up in bed, sweating and grabbing his chest to obstruct the blood flowing from non-existing wounds. Teetering between REM sleep and reality, he could feel his vital fluids oozing out through his fingers. It took a good five minutes for the panic to fade, and for his heart to return to a normal beat.

And like many nights similar to this one, he'd lost control of his bladder. Dad said it was medically common for boys his age, but it was still embarrassing. Michael knew better, but he couldn't bring himself to explain the real reasons behind his accidents. Even though he was only eight, he had been psycho-analyzing these nightmares as to why they were progressively worsening as the killer's release date grew nearer. Dad already had enough on his mind. He acted as if everything was hunky-dory. However, Michael could tell that something deep inside his dad had been murdered the same day as mom. It got worse the day they laid her to rest. On top of everything else, the court system had only given the killer a few years on account of his age. When the creep turns 21, he'll be freed with no criminal record or supervision. That was the main reason for Michael's elevated apprehension, fabricated fears, and thoughts that terrorized his sleep.

A familiar noise from the hallway alerted Michael that his dad was on the way in. The door opened slowly and Tim walked in.

"Wake-up Pooter, time to get ready for school," he said affectionately using Michael's nickname.

"Can't I stay home today dad?" Michael groaned. "I feel sick," he added while putting on his best 'feel my pain' face and using the protruding bottom lip that had been filling his toy-box for years. Tim raised his right eyebrow speculatively.

"Maybe I should give you a quick examination and a shot of B-12. That should do the trick," said Tim.

"No dad!" Michael yelled, then toned it down quickly. "I just need to rest. I'll … be okay tomorrow," he said, just knowing that he was about to hear the 'I received a perfect attendance award in medical school' speech.

But, to his surprise, he didn't. Instead, his dad said, "Well, that's a real shame. I've got tickets to the World Championship Karate Tournament for tonight. Not to mention a little surprise afterward." Tim shook his head back and forth to show his disappointment. "Well, maybe next year," Tim said, adding as much displeasure to his voice as he could. "I'll call and cancel. You get some rest. I'll be back shortly."

Miraculously, Michael was cured. He sprang to his feet in a run. "Dad Wait!" he yelled, taking three or four steps in mid-air. He stood there flapping his hands with excitement.

"Feeling better I see," Tim said knowingly. Michael turned as red as his hair. "Well hurry and get ready; I'll start breakfast," Tim said and left the room.

Michael stood there dumbfounded. He couldn't believe that nothing was said about his futile attempt to deceive his dad.

"Oh well," he said as he walked over to his walk-in closet to pick out his clothes. A lump formed in his throat, and a tear ran down his cheek. It still felt weird to wear whatever he wished. For some odd reason, he missed being yelled at over his clothes every morning.

Once dressed for the day, he entered the bathroom. The reflection stared back at him from the wall mirror with its big blue eyes and freckles. Its red hair laid haphazardly over its ears and forehead. Looking at himself, he couldn't understand why the kids at school teased him. According to dad, he was as cute as a bug's ear. But the 'Mr. Perfect' types with their blond hair, like Brad Davis, always had hurtful things to say. Not only to him, but to all the kids that were less fortunate than he.

"If I was bigger, I would …," he said to his image while throwing a punch, "POW!!"

The bravery quickly changed; replaced by a nagging anxiety. School was cool, but the bullies made it frightening. At least once a week, and sometimes more often, Michael was their target of choice. This included being pushed around, called names, punched and sometimes kicked. And even though he retained a brown belt he'd earned at a neighborhood karate studio, Michael still didn't have the heart to fight back. The fact that he was tiny for his age didn't help matters either.

Finished with combing his hair, he ran down the hallway, ready to eat.

Sitting at the table always gave them time to discuss personal things. This morning was no exception.

"Still having trouble with the bullies at school, Pooter?" Tim asked like he was stating an already established fact. Michael's eyes widened. How did his dad always know what was on his mind?

"Yes," Michael admitted. Tim nodded his head slightly with understanding.

"Are the karate classes not helping you learn to defend yourself? Should I check into another school?" he asked.

"No, I mean yes … well, yes and no. Top Gun is a great school … it's just … well," Michael tried to answer, but couldn't quit find the right words he wanted. He lowered his head in a hurtful submission, feeling shame. "I'm scared" he finally admitted with tears welling-up in his eyes.

Tim gently reached over and grabbed his son by the arm, and pulled him closer as he stood-up, picking Michael up in the process. Michael was small and frail in his daddy's arms, and Tim was thankful for that. His little one could still fit so perfectly, and could be held for the duration necessary to comfort his boy through most difficult situations. Or to disperse any sadness that befell either of them. Each depended on the other like a lighthouse on a stormy sea. If every father and son relationship were as strong, and full of love as this one, the world would already be God's promised new Earth. Although Tim wanted this moment to never end, he knew it must.

"Michael honey," he said, pulling away just enough to see his buddies watery blue eyes. "Listen sweetheart, there's no shame in being afraid of someone or something. We've got to realize why we're frightened before we can face those fears. These mean kids are probably just as scared of you and don't know how to handle it. As I've told you before, if you don't stand-up for yourself, it will never end. I'm not suggesting that you get in a fight. I'm saying that most bullies are like stupid dogs; they will only chase something if it's running away. The second it stops and faces them, they'll tuck their tail and cower away. Other times, you need to simply out-smart them. If you really want to confuse them, be nice. Return their meanness with kindness." Realizing that he had gone overboard with a bad case of verbal diarrhea and had already lost his son's attention, Tim tried a simpler approach. "Sticks and stones may break my bones ...,"

Michael finished it for him, "... but words will never hurt me." Trying to put on a brave face, Michael smiled. "But it is sticks and stones, and they are hurting me. I could fight back, but wouldn't that make me as bad as they are?" he asked.

"No buddy. It's quite different as long as you're defending

yourself." Tim explained. Michael thought about it for a minute or so before responding. "But the teacher doesn't see it that way, and will paddle everyone involved."

Tim shook his head saying "If that happens, I'll be down there knocking some heads together. Nobody touches my boy! I won't allow it!" He boasted.

Michael hugged Tim lovingly. "I love you dad." He proclaimed.

"Well duh," Tim jokingly replied, returning the embrace, and then asked, "You okay now sweetheart?"

"Well duh," Michael answered, making a goofy face.

"Then let's get your red-headed hind end to school." Tim said as he hugged Michael again.

On the way to school, they sang along with the Brooks & Dunn song 'I Believe'. Michael acted out the part that goes "I raise my hands, bow my head."

After the music ended, Michael began repeatedly begging for enlightenment about the earlier mentioned surprise. Finally, to appease his son, and to find a little peace, Tim gave in.

"Okay you rotten little fart," Tim yelled.

Then laughed when Michael said, "I knew you'd give in."

Tim made a fist and shook it at Michael, "One of these days boy, I'm gonna ... ''

Michael just sat there with a 'yeah right' look on his face and said, "Well, HELLO ... the surprise?" he prompted.

Tim lowered his head like a scolded child in confession. "After the tournament tonight, Jack Lee, the world's number one expert in martial arts, has agreed to have supper with us."

As Tim had expected, Michael was clearly disappointed over the insignificance of the surprise, and it showed on his face. Tim let Michael stew for a moment, and then went on.

"Oh yeah, by the way, I almost forgot this part. He also has agreed to give you private lessons in the art of ancient eastern fighting. But I knew the 'eating' part was of greater importance," he joked, then waited for some kind of response. When none came, he looked over at Michael and was pleased to see his son's mouth gaping open in shock.

"Really? And for true?" Michael asked, forgetting his proper use of the English language.

"Yup, really and for true," Tim answered teasingly mocking his best friend.

"I love you; you're the greatest dad ever!" Michael said with enthusiasm.

"How could I be anything else with the greatest son ever born, and of course, I love you too." Tim replied.

They pulled up to the school's drop-off area and Michael sprang from the van.

"Bye!" was all he said before slamming the door behind him.

Tim watched as the love of his life disappeared into the crowd of children. He missed the little guy already and a lump formed in his throat. He'd rather die a thousand deaths than to have any harm or sadness ever befall his son again.

CHAPTER 3

It was one of those incredible nights that Tennessee seems to hold a patent on. Truly, no other state could offer a more perfect atmosphere for a walk. It was calm and comfortably warm with a gentle breeze caressing their skin like butterfly wings.

Tim was thinking as he and Michael moved at a lackadaisical pace, that it was a shame that many people were indoors missing the beauty of the night. The event arena was over a mile away from where they had parked. They could have found something closer, but these times of unhurried togetherness meant the world to them. It also gave them time to gaze at the starry heavens, revealing a mysterious and endless universe. The idea that anything was possible in God's creation of space always kept Tim awestruck, and he continually encouraged Michael to open his mind to the extraordinary experience of mental exploration and imagination. Whether consciously or not, these little treks provided ample time for education; short periods of thought and reflection.

Coming to one of Nashville's river front parks allowed them a momentary break, and time to play a game of trying unsuccessfully to skip stones across the Cumberland River, the current being too strong.

Hoping that by sharing his inner demon, Michael would do the same. Tim revealed something that was bothering him.

"Michael, there's something that's been eating at me like myoblastic cancer for the last two weeks." Tim admitted.

"What is it dad?" Michael asked with genuine concern reflected in his voice.

"Well, do you remember the last time that we attended the fellowship dinner at church?" Tim asked.

Michael scratched the side of his head while thinking and said, "Yeah, I remember, why?" he replied.

"It's...," Tim started to explain, but was having trouble holding back his emotions. "You were running on all eight cylinders and I had asked you over and over again to calm down." Tim continued while removing his handkerchief to blot the moisture that was forming in the comers of his eyes. "I allowed myself to get angry and lash out at you by grabbing your shoulder.'' Michael moved close and put is arms around Tim's waist.

"I remember, it really hurt," he said, starting to get emotional himself. Tim tilted Michael's head back and placed a kiss on his son's forehead.

"I'm really sorry Pooter; I had no right to hurt you like that. And if I could pay with my life to take it back, I would in a heartbeat. That, or any other pain, that I've brought into your life, please forgive me. I love you more than you could ever imagine. I swear, I never wanted to harm you," Tim said, then just held on to his son.

"I know dad," Michael replied gently.

After about three minutes, Tim pushed Michael back gently. "We best get moving or we'll be late for the show," Tim said, taking Michael's little hand. They left the park to the night owls.

Twenty minutes later, they arrived at the arena. The lights from the city diminished the twinkling of the stars, but the fullness of the moon still illuminated the night brilliantly. Conversation soon became impossible as they stood in line waiting for admittance with hundreds of others. Music blared from the building with overloud and unnecessary announcements. Most were advertising the event over huge loud speakers. Tim mused to himself that it must be for those poor morons who couldn't comprehend why they found themselves standing in this line, or to inform others that this wasn't a line for the soup kitchen.

All this excitement was beginning to get on his nerves, but after looking down at the glow of exhilaration on Michael's face, it was worth it. He would have stood neck deep in excrement while freezing rain and hail soaked him to the bone just to keep that look on his son's face. "Thank you God for this child," he softly prayed. "Love you!" he yelled, hoping to be heard. Michael gave his dad the thumbs-up sign and then returned to his realm of innocent, childlike wonder and happiness.

It didn't take long for them to reach the seats assigned to them once they entered the building. One look at the tickets and they were immediately escorted to front row, V.I.P. seats by a very apologetic young man wearing a black T-shirt with the word 'STAFF' written across the back of it. The guy couldn't seem to say sorry enough for letting such important people stand in line with regular admissions. The special treatment made Tim feel uncomfortable, but Michael was eating it up. In Tim's opinion they were, after all, just like everyone else. Apparently though, when the world's number one karate expert gave out invitational tickets, the possessor of them became a member of the elite. So for Michael's sake, tonight's royal treatment would be tolerated.

After taking their seats, they could tell by each other's faces that they were surprisingly comfortable. And the only people with a better view of the stage were the judges. Michael's seat had been stacked with cushions, borrowed from somewhere, to level his line of sight with that of his dad's.

Ten minutes passed and before the show began, Dr. Peppers® were served to the both of them. The crowd simultaneously went from a roar, to blissful silence, and the announcer took center stage.

"Hello Nashville!" he began, and the place erupted in applause, accompanied by hoots, hollers and whistles.

Michael jumped up and down with his hands in the air, joining the mob.

The speaker continued after everyone began to settle down, "Welcome to the world's greatest display of martial arts from around the globe. Plus, tonight you will see the battle of all battles to determine who will be crowned 'Champion of the Universe'!" Once more, the place exploded with noise. "It now gives me great pleasure to introduce to you, the one, the only, the world's greatest, number one fighter and martial arts expert of all time ..." By now the man on stage was yelling into the mic in an attempt to be heard. "Ladies and gentlemen, I give you ... Jackeeee ... Leeeee!" The arena became a mad house that didn't seem like it was going to stop short of a riot.

Jackie took center stage like he owned the place, then stood there like a king before his subjects, allowing his people to enjoy themselves. After all, that's what they paid for.

Satisfied that the audience was ready for the show, Lee raised his hand in the air. Then like Moses parting the Red Sea, he moved it over the auditorium, quieting everyone in its wake.

"Thank you one and all," he began. "Before we go any further, I would love to have the honor, if you will allow me, to introduce to you one of tonight's V.I.P.'s and tomorrow's 'Champion of the World!' Ladies and gentlemen of Nashville, Michael Stephen Clark!"

The spectators went crazy with applause. Then simultaneously, with Jackie's pointing finger, a spotlight illuminated Michael's seat. "Come on up here young man!" Jackie prompted. At first Michael refused to move, but with a little coaxing from Tim and the audience, he gave in and reluctantly climbed onto the stage under a thunderous roar of cheers. As Michael took hold of Jackie's offered hand, Jackie somehow threw himself into the air, landing unmoving on his side. In all appearances, Michael had just used a lethal move on the champ, filling the air with an unnatural hush. The application was so perfect; the illusion even pulled Michael into its deceit.

Placing his hand over his mouth, Michael sympathetically knelt down to comfort the fallen hero. After a short pause, he stood back up with the microphone.

"Let the show begin!" he yelled with childlike enthusiasm. The place went ape wild as Michael, like a rock star, sublimely dove off the stage into his dad's waiting arms.

The stage filled with ten, perfectly choreographed ninjas dressed in white. Swords flew with razor-sharp precision, honed over a lifetime of practice and concentration. It appeared that one slight misjudgment would be fatal. The blades moved so quickly, most of the time you had to watch closely to make sure that they were even there.

Next came an awesome spear handler, so well trained, one would believe that the guy was born with one in his hands.

Nun chucks followed, impressing Tim greatly. It started with four small boys of oriental decent. Each looked to be around five years of age and had already mastered their art. Soon they were joined by four eight year old girls. The whole time never missing a beat. Then two teenagers and two adults entered the program.

Tim couldn't believe the accuracy and was thinking that these people must practice together every waking moment.

By this time, the cold drinks had finished their internal processing, and the call of nature had become more of a howl. Tim had to literally drag Michael to the restrooms, complaining all the way that he didn't need to pee.

"Come on dad, we'll miss the show," Michael repeated. However, the truth became clear the second they entered the men's room. Michael started dancing around fanatically, not able to hold it much longer, and close to urinating on himself.

"I'm sorry. I was wrong. I see now that you really didn't have to use the restroom," Tim said sarcastically.

"Well, I guess I did," Michael responded as he stood on his toes to reach the urinal. Then, before he even terminated his urinary flow, he turned in a hurry to leave, dampening Tim's pant leg.

"Thanks," Tim said, giving the boy a hard look.

A couple of minutes later, they headed back. The main corridor was filled with teenagers; most of them standing in small groups. Some of the boys were showing off their karate skills. Others were fabricating exciting stories of fights in which they had been triumphant. Kicks and punches were added as visual aids. It was clear to Tim that their training had come from video games, or Texas Ranger re-runs. He had to smile.

All of a sudden, Michael stopped dead in his tracks. Tim, being preoccupied with the comical surroundings, and less than a step behind Michael, almost trampled his son. Instead, he managed to slide-dive off to one side, landing painfully on his shoulder. A rare and uncharacteristic anger took its grip on him. There he was lying in discarded drink cups, candy wrappers, cigarette butts and what looked like a year's worth of tracked-in dirt. His first reaction was to pull his son down into the filth, allowing him to share in the humiliation. But the terror on Michael's face quickly replaced his bitterness with love and concern. Immediately he scanned the area in search of the danger that had just paralyzed his child.

Seeing nothing out of the ordinary, Tim got to one knee in front of Michael, placing both hands on his sons shoulders and asked, "Michael! What's wrong son?" but received no reaction. "Hey! Michael!" he tried again, raising his voice slightly, and then gently shaking the boy in an attempt to reach him. "Michael!" he said once more, this time just short of a yell.

Michael's blue eyes suddenly came into focus on his dad like he had just now realized the man was there, and then tears filled his eyes. Tim took Michael into his arms and held him. Everything else around them disappeared. Even forgetting that he was kneeling in trash. The only thing he wanted to do was comfort the love of his life. Whatever was wrong couldn't be corrected until he knew the problem. But first, even though it was eating him alive with worry, Tim knew his son needed this time. And if it took all night, crouched in this dingy hallway, that's what would happen.

A young woman asked if they needed any help, and Tim just shook his head no. Everyone else did little more than stare, perhaps trying to imagine what was going on.

An insurmountable amount of time passed before Michael released himself from the safety of his father's arms, leaving the front of Tim's shirt soaked with tears.

While wiping his eyes with the back of his hand, Michael mumbled as if caught in a dream, "I just saw the guy that shot mom."

Though he had spoken with nearly incomprehensible speech, it was clear as a bell to Tim. It made the hair on his neck stand on end. No wonder his son was scared out of his wits, Tim thought.

"Are you sure, sweetheart?" Tim asked.

Michael finally looked directly at his dad. "The judge said he'd release the guy when he turns twenty-one, remember?" he asked. Then added as if stating a fact, "That was last week dad."

Understanding rolled over Tim like a tidal wave. How could he have been so blind? All the nightmares, the increased bed-wetting and insomnia; his responsibility to identify the needs of his child was a complete failure. Now in hindsight, it had all started to worsen around the release date. Apparently, Michael had been conscious of the approaching time and had been living on edge.

"My God honey, I'm so sorry. Please forgive me," he pleaded.

Michael looked lost.

"For what, dad?" he asked specifically.

"We'll talk about that later son. All I care about right now is you. Are you alright?" Tim asked. Michael nodded his head in response, so Tim continued. "Do you want to finish the show or head for home? It's totally up to you sweetheart."

Trying to see if any danger still lurked in the shadows, Michael took a quick look around before answering. "Let's go ahead and finish the show," he spoke with apprehension.

Tim could tell that Michael was only doing what he thought was best for his dad. The same reason he hadn't said anything about his stress over the last few weeks. Their roles had switched. Michael had become the protector, leaving Tim to feel stupid, despite his education. He promised himself to open his eyes, not just his mind, from this day forward, relying less on his 'book-smarts' when it came to his red-headed gift from God.

After they were once again seated, the competition had begun between rival dojos from around the region. It turned out that the only thing that they had missed was the demonstrations of defense using everyday items like newspapers, umbrellas and purses. It was fun watching the beginners with their amateuristic attempts to look good. However, every time Tim looked over to see if Michael was enjoying himself, his heart ached to find the boy's attention diverted from the stage.

Instead of watching the performers, Michael kept searching the crowd for his walking nightmare. Seeing this, Tim made a mental note to contact the detective in charge of Sara's murder, to see if the killer had in fact, been released. Not that he didn't trust Michael's recognition of the creep, but with the type of psychological trauma the child had been suffering, he may have seen somebody close in description, letting his mind misidentify some stranger. *'Oh well. So much for relying on heart instead of intellect,'* he thought to himself.

The exhibition was getting overly repetitious. One more intermediate three-point battle would be intolerable, and Michael's eyes were growing heavier by the second. He had even given up his vigilance and was fidgeting with his shoestrings. The crowd seemed to be losing their interest as well.

Then, as if reading everyone's minds, the stage cleared, and the lights went down. Everywhere voices could be heard questioning what the change might indicate. The spotlights came up like the rising sun, accompanied by the sound of a marching band, filling the arena with renewed excitement.

Returning from where he'd almost been forgotten, the announcer took center stage. "Now for the event you've all been waiting for!" he yelled. "Ladies and gentlemen of all ages! The World Championship free style battle of the best of the best! Let the war of all wars begin!"

Everyone was caught up in the rush of the excitement and went hog wild. A boxing ring slowly descended from the ceiling area over the audience, floated forward before coming to rest on the stage. The effect was pure magic. To top off the performance, the ring already contained the champion and his challenger, standing face to face, ready to begin.

For the life of him, Tim couldn't see how he hadn't seen the ring sooner, or how Jackie and this other fellow had entered the ring unnoticed.

Both combatants were introduced, and descriptions of their professional history and physical sizes were shared with anyone who could still hear over the crowd.

Within minutes, the match was underway. Jackie was clearly the superior fighter of the two and could have finished the competition within seconds. But the people paid to see three rounds, and money always talks. Strike after strike, kick after kick, the cheers grew louder and louder.

Nearing the end of the last round, Tim caught a very subtle signal from Jackie's corner, instructing the champ to finish the match. With less than three seconds remaining, he did just that, using a fake punch followed by a lightning fast round house kick, turning the challenger's lights out.

While waiting for the reigning champion to shower and dress, Michael ran tirelessly up and down the isle of the auditorium with all the energy that God grants the youth.

Tim did his best to give chase for a little while, but forty-eight is a long way from eight. *'If people my age were blessed with that kind of stamina, our hearts would burst in our chest,'* he thought. So he contently sat and watched as Michael played. Like most doctors, Tim was required to carry a cell phone with a twenty-four hour beeper. Someone somewhere always had to contact him. People never had a set time specific for emergencies. Having a few minutes on hand, he decided to check for messages. Finding none, he dialed Bill Edison's office number, and to his surprise, it was answered on the third ring.

"Edison," is all the policeman said.

"Yes, this is Dr. Timothy James. The reason I am calling is my son Michael is under the impression that he saw his mother's killer here in Nashville tonight," Tim said, and then paused to allow a reply. When the officer remained silent, Tim went on. "It scared the crap out of both of us ... , are you there?" he asked uncertainly.

"Um-hum," answered the policeman.

Tim continued, "I just wanted to assure my son's safety by confirming the man is still behind bars. Otherwise, you would have to contact us like you swore you would."

The detective automatically started making excuses. "Well, *um*, Dr. James, it's like this, a well, *um*, David Watts was, well you see, he, *um*, was released on, well, I was going to call you when ... " Tim cut the detective off in mid-lie.

"You were going to call! When? When were you going to call? After we came home one night and found the son-of-a-bitch sitting at our dining room table? What the hell?" Tim yelled into the phone.

The bumbling detective still tried to cover his butt. "Sir, please calm down. Mr. Watts is supposed to be out of the state. And I assure you as soon as we locate him, my men will put the fear of God into him. I promise he'll never be a bother to your family again. I swear to you."

44

Edison made Tim so angry, he almost crushed the phone in his hand unconsciously. "You mean to tell me that you morons don't even know where this jackass is? And now you have the balls to make more promises! We've seen how reliable those are you imbecile! And again you swear! You worthless sack of shit!" Tim finished sharply. Then disconnected before he got angrier, if that was possible. He already had to fight the urge to throw his phone across the arena.

Michael hopped down the aisle smiling up a storm, took one look at his dad and his world of fun spun out of orbit.

"He's out just like I said, isn't he dad?" he asked nervously.

All they could do is stare at each other and wonder who was going to scream out of frustration first. Even if they could find some words to express their feelings, the truth was right there in their face. The huge arena became as enclosed and suffocating as a coffin.

"You guys alright?" came the voice of Mr. Lee, who had walked within three feet of them unnoticed, causing both Tim and Michael to jump. "Woe! Hold on there, big guy, settle down. I don't feel like getting thrown again there fella,'' Jackie teased as he threw a slow punch at Michael's chin. Then seeing that his friends were in a semi-trance over something he'd walked into. Lee spoke again, "I'm in the mood for pizza. Who's with me?" he asked comically, hoping to elevate the situation.

Tim finally came to his senses. "I'm sorry Jackie. How are you my old friend?" he asked, extending his hand.

Jackie accepted the greeting. "I'm starving," he answered, and they both laughed.

Trying to be one of the big guys, Michael offered to shake as well, and the champ acted reluctant. "You're not going to pull some deadly move on me are you?" he asked, putting a big smile on Michael's face, who only shook his head 'no'. Still pretending to be unsure of his safety, Jackie accepted Michael's hand.

"Well, let's get moving," Tim instructed. And they made their way to the exit, stepping out into the beautiful night air. They hadn't made it very far when Michael remembered his promised lesson with the champ. So, no matter how hungry, tired or reasonable Tim or Jackie tried to be, Michael insisted on receiving his private, one-on-one training, and now.

Knowing Jackie's great rapport with children, Tim finally just stood back to watch the fireworks begin to fly. Knowing the whole time that when Michael's bottom lip came out, it was curtains for his friend. A memory came back to Tim of how Mr. Lee had spent twenty-four hours a day at Vanderbilt's children's ward where his only son, Tiger, lay dying in the intensive care unit. Tim had been the surgeon to perform the operation, attempting to remove a massive brain tumor from the little boy. But the cancer refused to yield its desire to grow, even if it meant killing its host, making any other attempts unsuccessful. Then after the death of his son, Jackie had continued to visit the children's ward weekly, lifting the spirits of other young patients. His love for them was obvious. And that's how they had met. Even though Tim had been unable to save Tiger's life, Jackie and he had become close friends.

While Tim was lost in reminiscing thoughts, Michael and Jackie debated back and forth like candidates running for public office, voicing points and counterpoints like pros.

Tim was unsure of how they had reached an agreement, but they had. The deal was for Michael to receive a quick lesson now followed by more extensive instruction in the near future. Tim kind of wished he'd paid more attention. It would have been interesting to see the face-off Jackie just had with his above average, non-yielding little boy. One thing was for sure, Michael had risen triumphantly which didn't surprise Tim even a little bit. The three of them returned to the building. The youngest with a smile from ear to ear.

◆ ◆ ◆ ◆ ◆

David Watts sat in the stolen van with Paul Dickson and his

other new criminal associates, Onezean Otey and René Caldron. They had been watching the exit doors intensely. Nervously waiting for their target to emerge. All four had been incarcerated on various levels of criminal charges up until about a month prior to tonight's intended crusade. Undoubtedly, not a single one of them had learned their lesson. David's new gang was about to commit the ultimate crime against the sixth commandment of God and mankind: First Degree Murder. It wasn't the primary objective of the evening. They originally were only going to shanghai the proceeds from tonight's karate event. But after David spotted that red-haired kid who testified, repeatedly pointing at him in the courtroom, Watts had, in his twisted, felonious mind, received a bonus. His initiation of a homicide to the gang had mixed results. Paul was psyched-up, but the other two, not so much.

David couldn't wait to face that high and mighty doctor or his brat son without being handcuffed. He smiled to himself as his mind's eye displayed their expressions as he pulled the trigger, ending their lives the way they ended his.

Sitting in the front passenger seat, Paul, the blond-headed boy, had the best view, so he was the first to see their quarry emerge. "There they are! Let's go!" he yelled, causing everyone else to jump, obviously too caught up in the rush to think clearly. Paul grabbed the door handle, apparently intending to run across half the parking lot, charging at the victims.

Onezean, the handsome black guy, and apparently the only smart one, grabbed Dickson's shoulder before he was able to open the door far enough to activate the dome light.

"Wait fool! You go stampeding at those people like a wild injun trying to cap folks we'll never see five cents of that cash. And that's the only reason I'm here, so cool it," he demanded authoritatively.

Paul settled down in his seat and pulled the unlatched door tight. "Sorry man, you're right," he admitted, then pointed at the arena. "Crap man, there's someone with them," he announced, drawing their attention forward.

"De-cost of one more bullet spleet four-way eees cool wit' me," René said comically with his Spanish accent. In the group's sick and criminal minds, they found this extremely humorous and they all laughed like a pack of jackals around a fresh kill.

Paul chuckled so hard that he couldn't help letting go a few short blasts of digestive gas. The smell was so foul that the other guys began popping him on the arm and calling him filthy names.

"Crap man look, they're going back in," Paul said, thankfully turning the burden of being the center of the gang's abuse back to the doctor and his son. "Maybe we should stop them now man," he said, getting excited once more.

Onezean spoke up once again, and in David's opinion, too much like he was the boss. "Let them go, like I said! The money comes first! After we get it, you guys can sit here all night waiting on that kid for all I care. Me and Caldron will be ghost with the cash."

The tension between them quickly elevated to an unfriendly level, and the pent up animosity was about to reach its boiling point. But before the impending battle could begin, the van filled with another odor. This time, it was the pleasantly sweet aroma of top-grade quality marijuana. René had fired up a nice sized joint. Always seeming to know the right time and method of calming the guys down. Within minutes, their minds were filled with chemically induced fantasies of wealth and fame that would be theirs after tonight's outing was over with.

◆ ◆ ◆ ◆ ◆

Tim's beeper signaled a possible early end to the night's entertainment, and Michael's face showed his disappointment. However, he knew that his dad's job was saving lives. It was hard sometimes. But year after year of seeing his father jump up and leave at all hours of the day and night, it never surprised him anymore. Truthfully, it never got easier, but the understanding came with time. What he didn't expect was what happened next.

"You two need to excuse me for a minute," Tim said, wriggling his phone in the air as a gesture of explanation. "Go ahead with your lesson; I'll be right back."

Michael's face lit up. He'd never thought of that. His dad must really trust Mr. Lee to leave them alone like this, something he never did. Matter of fact, his dad was over-protective. He watched with disbelief as his dad disappeared back through the exit door. Then turning back in the direction of the stage he said, "Let's get it on."

Jackie smiled. He really liked his new apprentice already. Michael reminded him so much of his own son, Tiger. Together, they half ran, half walked back to the boxing ring.

◆ ◆ ◆ ◆ ◆

Outside the night was still perfect. Dr. James stepped to the side of the entrance way where he began the series of phone calls that ceremoniously followed these never-ending emergencies.

Standing with his back to the wall, casting a shadow that resembled the Marlboro Man, minus the hat, gave him a panoramic view of the huge parking lot surrounding the arena. Of the four thousand parking spaces, only five were occupied. The owner of the beautiful, black, four-door BMW was obvious due to the 'Rest in Peace Tiger' sticker on the rear bumper. Three of the others were nondescript. However, the last one, for some reason, stood out like a sore thumb, and its mere presence made Tim anxious. It appeared to be around a 1996 or 1997 Dodge work van, complete with roof racks carrying ladders. That alone singled it out and gave it a sinister aura. People never bring a work van to events like this, where they will be left unattended and easy prey for thefts. Plus, its motor was running. From where he stood, Tim could see the exhaust emitting repetitious puffs of white smoke.

As he watched, the vehicle started to move in his direction, almost taunting like a predatory hunter closing silently in on its kill. The effect was quite mesmerizing. Somehow time had stopped. Nothing else seemed animated except what Tim believed to be impending evil.

"Hello ... Hello! Is anybody there?" Came the voice of a woman over the cell phone, sounding a little irritated. Tim suddenly realized that his hand had gone numb from holding the tiny electronic device so hard.

"Yes, I'm sorry. This is Dr. James. I received a page," he said.

"I was about to hang up sir," came the female voice a little calmer. "You need to call the children's intensive care unit at Vanderbilt. It seems that little Taylor Anderson has fallen into a coma. They informed me that it doesn't look good for the poor kid," she said softly.

Still halfway in a daze, Tim hung up without realizing that he'd done so. Didn't even say goodbye or thank you. Not because of rudeness, or any kind of superiority complex, but on account of his thoughts being preoccupied with the sinister van. And now they were with young Taylor and his family. An overwhelming feeling of guilt filled his heart. Here he was out on the town enjoying life, while a three year old angel under his care fought for his every breath.

Tim lowered his head, "Where are you tonight Heavenly Father," he asked, and then started rhythmically tapping the phone on his forehead, concentrating. Knowing full well he'd done everything humanly and medically possible. Still, every time he failed he'd beat himself illogically and unmercifully with doubt.

"Sir, are you alright?" someone asked in a very deep voice from right next to Tim, snapping him from his trance. He quickly looked up to see two armed security guards standing right in front of him. Both appeared able to hunt grizzlies bare handed and could have very well been a father and son team. Each carried four large bank style money bags.

Either under-trained or overconfident in their duties, they failed to notice the white van creeping up less than twenty feet to their left. This lapse in judgment and inattentiveness cost them their lives. The forehead of the younger man imploded as his head snapped violently backwards, breaking his neck, and spraying blood and brain matter onto the blacktop. Without its life force, his body slumped down into a kneeling position, never to rise again. The older guard simultaneously dropped the canvas bags and drew his weapon with the lightning fast reflexes of a person half his age. The action was brave but futile. His body was immediately escalated two feet into the air from a gunshot blast to his midsection. He didn't even hear the shot that took his life, mercifully succumbing to the reaper before landing ten feet away, facing up, his eyes staring lifelessly to the heavens. His gun discharged on impact, the bullet striking the van's bumper with a metallic ping. The sounds of the explosions began rebounding off the surrounding buildings, each blast increasing in decibels to an ear-shattering boom that echoed across the large open parking lot like thunder.

The carnage proved greater than the gang of unseasoned criminals expected and they were clearly troubled over the situation. This was real. They had killed before on their 'Play Stations' and 'X-Boxes', but this scenario didn't come with a reset button. These people were really dead, and the huge amounts of blood drove home the point. The violence held everyone present in its grip.

Being used to blood and injury, Tim's mind cleared quickly. He threw all his power into a jaw connecting punch, knocking two of the pimple-faced blonde's teeth out, dropping the punk like a sack of potatoes. However, it also broke the trance of the other three. Onezean reacted first, striking the doctor in the temple with the butt of his shotgun, causing Tim to buckle at the knees. René stepped up and put the barrel of his gun between the doctor's swelling eyes. "Adios amigo," he said.

The sound of the hammer clicking as Caldron pulled it back was the loudest thing Tim had ever heard, and it seemed to be in slow motion.

"Wait, he's mine!" yelled David, who stepped forward and moved René's gun gently away with his left hand. In his right he held a .44 caliber Smith & Wesson. Squatting down, he placed his weapon under Tim's chin, roughly using the barrel to lift the doctor's head, forcing Tim to look him in the eye. "Remember me?" he asked with a smile that could only belong to a psychopath.

"How could I forget a piece of subhuman shit like you?" Tim replied and spit in Watt's face before smiling himself. He was scared out of his mind, but wasn't about to give these creeps the satisfaction of seeing it. He was immediately awarded for his bravery by a strike across the face from the .44's barrel. Blood sprayed from the impact, splattering the wall behind him.

Disgusted, David wiped the spittle from his face with the palm of his free hand.

"Shoot him man, let's go!" came the voice of Onezean.

Having someone tell him what to do really pushed David's buttons, so he spun in Otey's direction. "Don't boss me around! I'm in charge here! You two grab the money and put that idiot Paul in the van," he instructed. Then he got a crazed animal look in his eyes, and once again focused all his hate on his kneeling prey. "Just to let you know Doc, I'm gonna kill that uppity red-head of yours before I leave," he said, then laughed insanely.

The threat to his son caused Tim to lunge forward, driving the top of his head into David's testicles, doubling the creep over in pain.

Onezean and René had finished loading the still unconscious Paul into the van when they saw Tim's attack. Shaking his head in disbelief, René stepped back out of the cargo door and fired two rounds into the doctors chest, dropping him in an already growing puddle of his own blood. René then stooped to assist his fallen comrade by helping him to stand.

Suddenly the arena doors burst outward ...

◆ ◆ ◆ ◆ ◆

Standing in the center of the stage, temporarily forgetting his student, Jackie Lee froze and tilted his head to elevate his ear. As if doing so would somehow increase his hearing by capturing some elusive sound. He was unsure if he'd heard a gunshot, or something more probable like a car backfiring. He looked down to solicit his young friend's opinion on what the sound could have been, only to find an empty stage. When he looked back up, Michael was at a dead run for the exit doors and had a good lead on him. "Wait!" he yelled, trying to persuade the kid to stop. When that didn't work, Jackie began to chase.

Michael had no doubt as to what the sounds were. He had heard it three years ago and in his sleep almost every night since. The only thing on his mind was the safety of his father's arms. Totally oblivious to the voice calling behind him, or the immediate danger waiting less than twenty feet away, he continued to press on as fast as his little legs would allow.

Being in good health and very athletic, Jackie closed the gap between them within seconds. Fear of the unknown pushed him supernaturally to his limits. If graced with a split second more, the pursuer would have overtaken the perused. As it were, they both crashed through the doors side-by-side, face-first into a cloud of smoke mixed with the pungent smell of spilled body fluids.

One step outside the door, Michael slipped in a pool of blood, falling. It resembled the act of sliding into home base.

◆ ◆ ◆ ◆ ◆

Attempting to ease the pain, David held his injured manhood with agonizing pressure. If it wasn't for the assistance of his friend, he wouldn't have been able to stand. The banging door drew his attention. There before him was the source of the hatred that had irrationally grown during those three long years of incarceration. Deep inside he always knew that going to prison was inevitable, but he needed someone to blame, and this kid was that someone. He pointed the .44 caliber at Michael's head and began frantically pulling the trigger, but like magic, his target disappeared.

Through the smoke, David saw his first bullet splinter the door's frame. The second striking a Japanese man square in the chest, and the third just above the same man's right eye, sending him stumbling backward through the door and out of sight.

Michael lay less than a foot from his dad crying and screaming, "Daddy!!" The sound of approaching sirens was barely audible over his wailing.

Finally standing on his own, David redirected his aim at what he thought was the only remaining member of the James family.

"How sweet," he said, drawing Michael's hate-filled teary eyes in his direction. "You'll be together again soon," David continued with sarcasm then pulled the trigger, receiving nothing but a 'click' as the hammer fell on an empty chamber. His eyes widened in disbelief. "Damn!!" he yelled, turning around and seeing René still standing there. "Shoot that lucky little punk!!" David angrily shouted at him.

René looked from David to the crying child and back again. Somewhere deep inside, he still had a heart. "It's over. You've killed his ma-ma, and now I've killed his pa-pa. Let it go amigo. Look at him. It is enough." he said while turning away disgusted with his association with a madman.

A voice came from behind them.

"Leave him fools; can't you hear the law-dogs?" Onezean yelled from the van and started to pull away. Locked in rage and unable to resist his inner demons, Watts grabbed René's gun, turned and fired the pistol at point blank range at the red-headed little boy, Hitting the child and spinning his small body from the impact, knocking the kid across his daddy's body, their blood mixing together as it pooled on the blacktop.

Close by, the van squealed as its spinning tires fought for traction. And the group of new murderers began their lives once more as fugitives.

◆ ◆ ◆ ◆ ◆

Tim forced his eyes open to see his precious son's tiny blood-soaked fingers only inches away. With all his remaining strength, he placed his hand over that of Michael's. "I'm sorry son," he said through red frothy spittle. His only thoughts were of how much he loved his child, and how badly he had failed to protect him. The light grew dim and then went out. He was dying without knowing what would become of the love of his life.

Unexpected Vengeance

Chapter 4

Somehow, for reasons unfathomable to our internal mental justice of right from wrong, or why Murphy only applies his law to honest people, the fleeing van left from the north side of the parking lot less than a second before a regiment of police cruisers converged on the scene from every other direction imaginable. All coming to a screeching halt within a dozen feet of each other, their sirens simultaneously silenced, leaving the night as quiet as a morgue. The buildings, trees and anything else visible in the surrounding area displayed an incredible light show of red and blue.

As if choreographed, the police officers exited their units, using the doors as shields to protect them from a possible threat, yet unseen. After a few minutes of assessing the situation, a single hand signal from the highest ranking police officer gave clearance for others to advance, which they did carefully. All the while, their service revolvers remained trained on the menacing shadows near the entrance doors.

The first victim they reached was clearly with the Lord. However, protocol requires a two-finger check for cardiovascular activity. A swiping hand gesture across the officer's neck indicated to the rest what was already obvious.

The next one was likewise deceased.

Slowly, the officers approached what appeared to be a man face down with a small child lying across his back. The police officer was shocked at the amount of blood, and he assumed that these two had also failed to survive. But once again, the rules must be followed to the letter. To his astonishment, both still clung to life with weak and unsteady pulses.

The situation drastically changed from a slow paced investigation, to an expeditious rescue. Radios began filling the quiet night with electronic static and excited voices. Tons of information was being rapidly exchanged between the officers and their dispatcher. Medical services were requested stat, along with the need for the county coroner.

With that complete, the hardest part of the job was initiated—the waiting game. Most policemen hated the stand down and do nothing part. But under these circumstances, there was little else they could do. They would have to hold until the arrival of the ambulances and the chief investigator of the crime scene.

Unfortunately, the SWAT team would need to secure the area before any of the aforementioned personnel would be allowed to approach the victims. Survival chances for the wounded decreased by the second.

The minutes dragged by for ten-year veteran James Garrett. He just couldn't divert his eyes from the blood-soaked, red-headed child that laid only fifteen feet in front of him. Guilt began to work on his gut like bad seafood. Here he was hiding behind a car from an unseen danger while a child slipped further and further into an early grave.

"Damn it!" he yelled after reaching the breaking point of his tolerance. He slammed his fist on the trunk of the cruiser, drawing the attention of his fellow officers. Staying low, he broke cover and advanced on the young victim. From somewhere behind, a loud voice repeatedly instructed him to stand down.

Ignoring those orders and the regulations ingrained in his soul, he maintained his pace.

"Fire me!" he said over his shoulder.

Knowing at this point that a gun battle would mean certain death, James bravely holstered his revolver despite any danger and then gently lifted the little boy into his arms, being rewarded by a painful groan. 'Thank God!' He thought, knowing that life remained in the tiny body.

"Grab some blankets!" someone yelled as Officer Garrett ran back to the safety of the units.

Like army ants converging on a discarded piece of hard candy, the policemen frantically worked to control the child's bleeding and to provide some semblance of comfort to the fallen youth.

Garret knew that he had done the only thing that he could have lived with, and was glad of it, no matter what the consequences to his career. His heart however, was still burdened. He hadn't said anything to the other officers for fear of being overheard by the little one. But when he lifted the kid, the older victim held tight to the youngster's hand. It wasn't until recognition came through the most tortured, pain-filled eyes that Garrett had ever seen, was that grip released. Then the man's eyes showed some relief and clouded over again before returning to unconsciousness. A sight that officer James Garrett would never be able to forget.

That must be the boy's father, he thought, standing there rubbing his chin. His mind's eye replaced the victims with himself and his son and that was all that he could take. Aggressively, he grabbed the mic from his unit. "Where the hell are those buses?" he yelled angrily through tears that his emotions could no longer retain.

♦ ♦ ♦ ♦ ♦

After receiving a full report, the chief investigator's anger quickly faded over Officer Garrett's actions. After all, it may have saved the child's life. But he still made a mental note of the incident and would forget it ever happened, unless of course it somehow came back to him.

The first set of paramedics had already removed the child from the area. Their lights and siren were quickly fading in the distance.

Still wrestling with his internal emotional roller coaster, James Garrett turned to the SWAT leader and asked, "How much longer until we can help that man?"

"Less than an hour. Once we clear the roof, we can begin the interior sweep to secure those doors," responded the team commander while pointing his finger at the nearby exit.

Garrett still saw the torment in the downed man's eyes. "Bull Shit!" he said, then grabbed his nightstick from his car and basically marched through the police line, past the downed doctor, and did not stop until he reached the double doors.

Everyone watched in admiration as Garrett slipped the wooden weapon through the door handles, temporarily disabling them. He then turned around and walked back.

Before the chief could open his mouth to criticize his officer, Garrett removed his gun and badge, handing them over.

"I QUIT! And I'm going home to my son," he said, and walked into the night.

The realization of what had just happened astonished everyone. It was so simplistic, everybody wondered why it had not been thought of sooner, the SWAT team clearly felt embarrassed as they stood up, as if the childhood war games they had been playing had just came to an abrupt end.

The medical personnel were impressed over Garrett's quick thinking, and after exchanging understanding looks, they descended on the remaining victim.

When detective Edison arrived, his recognition of Michael Clark echoed the earlier phone call in his mind, assuring him that the man lying face down in his own blood had to be the doctor.

Watching the night unfold, two things drummed on his mind like a marching band. One, If he had responded to the doctor's call sooner, would this massacre have been avoided? And two, was this going to end up biting him in the ass? After all, a young child may be dying tonight along with a very prominent citizen of Nashville. Plus, two members of someone's family lay mangled and lifeless only a few feet away.

He really didn't feel anything for the victims. His true concern was his pension. *'Maybe I can get lucky and steer this investigation toward robbery and away from revenge,'* he thought. Of course, he was positive that scumbag David Watts committed this horrendous crime. But as long as he could keep that name from coming up, he knew he'd not be under someone's thumb. The thought made him smile. Like most self-righteous cops, he believed that the law should be strictly enforced and never broken – unless, of course, it came to one's self or family. Then it could be bent.

♦ ♦ ♦ ♦ ♦

For any child involved with a serious injury, Vanderbilt's Children's Trauma Center is the best in Nashville. While in route there, one of the paramedics radioed ahead to inform the hospital staff of the inbound patient's status, which included blood pressure, respiration, drugs administered and unfortunately a bad prognosis.

The ambulance had barely come to a stop before the medical team had Michael on a gurney, rushing him through the entranceway. Again and again his vital signs were checked and rechecked.

Somehow, through an unintelligible barrage of voices, a delegation of pre-surgical tests were ordered. Multiple view thoracic x-rays, blood-typing, any and all medications on board, plus many others that would be gibberish to a layperson. With the efficiency and resemblance of a fast moving assembly line, Michael's rolling bed shot down the hall. His shirt was removed in seconds with razor-sharp precision. Needles from every direction found new homes in every available vein that his tiny arms could offer. Light shot across his vision as someone forced open his eyelids with their thumb and forefinger. Within minutes of arriving, Michael's appearance went from a bloody mess, to what resembled a science fiction movie; one where a mad scientist strived to bring his experimental creation to life.

Michael was moved to an operating table with one quick pull on his sheet. The room immediately became bathed with intensely bright lights and strange sounds. Close by, a mechanical pump hissed as it forced oxygen through a tube someone had forced into his airway. A vacuum hum accompanied by a slurping came from yet another tube somehow introduced down his esophagus. Beep after beep emanated from a machine monitoring his heart beat via wires attached to his bare chest. And above him, three bags of fluid dangled from a metal tree, feeding him saline, dextrose and plasma, one drip at a time.

By the time Dr. Johnson finished scrubbing up for the task ahead, the radiology technologist had finished and was displaying the films on a lighted view box next to a transfuser.

While he studied the pictures, the doctor held up his hands, as if in praise, as an assistant adorned his hands with latex gloves. Analyzing the situation gave him great concern, and it showed on his face, seemingly aging him ten years. "The projectile, after entering the dexter superior pectoral, proximal to the bursa, has shattered the clavicle," he explained, pointing at the black and white images. He then trailed the bullet's path with his finger before continuing. "It's forced it way down, severing the sub-clavicle artery supplying the arm. Then lodged itself inter coastal, collapsing the pnumenary cyst." He stopped speaking to contemplate his options. "The lung and that artery must be the first repairs if this child is going to live," he said to his surgical assistant, who only nodded her agreement.

"He's one hundred percent under doctor, but we had better hurry. His pulse is weakening," informed the concerned anesthesiologist.

Everyone circled the table to begin. "Oh my God! This is Tim's little boy," the doctor said in a shocked voice. "Someone find out what's going on here, and make sure that Dr. James is informed immediately!" "Scalpel," he added, and a small knife was slapped into his open hand.

The first incision was made starting near the center of the chest, running approximately six inches toward the arm. A trail of already depleted blood followed the surgical instrument's path. The next incision lapped the first, coming down from the shoulder, stopping just short of Michael's nipple. His future scar would appear in the likeness of the cross that Jesus died on.

After the doctor separated the subcutaneous tissue and dissected the pectoral muscle, it became clear that there wasn't enough of the target artery to repair. Another operation was required in order to borrow a vein from Michael's leg. This meant more preparations, time and blood loss, creating a greater trauma to the already over taxed patient. Forceps were applied to the severed artery to stop the bleeding, but it also further endangered the arm. This was a major concern to the doctor. However, the loss of a limb was preferred to losing a life. Twenty minutes later, the hemostats were removed and once again, life flowed back into the starving, oxygen-poor tissue. The damage to the lung required another half hour to seal and re-inflate.

While contemplating the need to amputate the arm, all hell broke loose. Every machine's alarms and buzzers went off simultaneously, demanding attention.

"Doctor, I've lost the pulse. Respiration is at zero; we're losing him," said the anesthesiologist excitedly.

"Paddles," yelled the doctor. "Two-ten," he instructed. And the assistant handed him two round discs with rubber handles. "Clear!" he yelled once more, the sound came from the electrodes and as before, flat lined.

"Two-eighty damn it! Clear," *buzzz* … nothing.

The assistant gently took the doctor's arm, speaking for the first time. "Sorry sir, we've lost him. Time is ten forty-six. Do you want to call it?" she asked.

They all stared at the doctor for directions, but his eyes were locked on the tiny, lifeless boy. "Hell no! Three-twenty! Clear!"

◆ ◆ ◆ ◆ ◆

It was obvious to the paramedics that the man lying face down was not going to survive being transported the second his shirt was cut away. Two large ruptures were all that remained of the left shoulder blade. Fragments of the shattered scapula, mingled with massive amounts of coagulated blood, looked like the aftermath of an active volcano. A small amount of vital fluid still trickled from the wound unmercifully, as the heart desperately tried to fulfill its obligation to maintain life. How they could still even locate a pulse astounded them both.

Each went to their appointed task, futile as it was, with professional vigor.

Morphine is normally administered under these circumstances to ease the pain of death, however, there wasn't enough circulation remaining in the man to distribute it throughout his body, so the idea was discarded.

Human compassion on the other hand, was something that they could still offer. Keeping the man warm was another. Jimmie Coleman, the more seasoned of the two, removed a wool blanket from a nearby stretcher, and spread it on the blacktop. Dark stains instantly began to form from human discharge. "Help me to roll him onto this," he requested of his partner.

The front of the victim became another confirmation that death was imminent. The other medic, Robert Hunt, pulled the blanket up to conceal the concave entry wounds. As he did so, the victim's eyes opened slightly, and his mouth began to move, trying to form words. Robert leaned forward on his hands until his ear was as close as possible to the man's lips.

"What is it friend?" he asked sympathetically.

"Ma ... Michael, my sa ... son," the downed man asked just barely above a whisper.

"They've taken him to Vandi. He's fine," Hunt answered with conviction, even though he had no idea if it were true or not.

The man smiled for a fraction of a second, then his eyes became fixed and dilated, and the angel of death claimed another soul for its eternal journey. Time: ten forty-six.

♦ ♦ ♦ ♦ ♦

"Go ahead Alpha team, over."

"Yeah, SWAT leader, the exterior is clear and secure. Holding for Delta team, out."

"Roger that, over."

Officer Joe Latimer lowered the microphone from his mouth as he surveyed the area, mentally summarizing the situation. In front of him lay the remains of three Nashville civilians. Purely out of respect, two had been covered with sheets. The third, being almost torn in half and eviscerated, required two plastic tarps. The ever- growing splotches of red on the white cover and the lifeless man still on his knees, as if in prayer, had Joe on edge.

Alpha team's report had given him some relief, but delta was still inside the massive building, checking every nook and cranny for an undetermined number of armed killers.

Joe was responsible for each and every member of his unit; no loss was acceptable. And the minutes seemed like hours.

Thankfully, the sound of faraway traffic broke the tomb-like silence, returning some realism to the otherwise unrealistic evening.

To Joe's left stood Bruce Edison, finishing what appeared to be the last of a hot dog. How anyone could eat in the presence of all this carnage was beyond Latimer's comprehension. And Joe couldn't discern the food's origin. Either the pompous fool carried his midnight snack in a pocket, or it had somehow materialized out of thin air. He leaned toward the first. Especially the way Edison dressed. If not for his visible detective badge, the man could easily be mistaken for a homeless vagrant.

Joe never did like Edison, and every time he saw him, he was reminded of why. But right now there was a job to do, and personal feelings would need to take a back seat to professionalism.

"Let's get one of your guys to get that night stick out of those doors detective," he said. "If my men flush out some kind of human garbage back up to that entrance, it'll be like cornering a wild animal, and someone might get bit."

Officer Dale Primm, a thirty-four year old, fifteen year veteran and chaplain of the force, accepted the task without hesitation. At six-two, he was an easy target, but his personal safety always came second. Holstering his weapon as he approached the exit, one quick jerk on the baton and the doors were once again operable. Swiftly turning around, not from fear but from proper training, he ran back to the safety of the squad cars.

"Good job Primm," came the voices of Latimer and Edison in unison.

"Nothing to do now except wait," Joe added. Then he turned toward Edison and said, "If you're waiting for an injection, twenty-minutes seems like seconds. But if it's a gun fight you're expecting, a minute becomes forever." Edison only grunted.

"Delta force to team leader," the radio came to life.

"SWAT leader go. Over."

"Clear to point zero. Hold your fire. Over."

Latimer let out a sigh of relief and raised his arms to get everyone's attention. "Stand down men!" he yelled, and a hush of relief fell over the officers like rain on a hot summer day.

Pistols were re-holstered, jackets were removed and stored in the cruiser's trunks along with shotguns and rifles.

Delta team streamed from the exit, simultaneously removing their equipment as well. Some were thankful for the uneventful, altercation-free mission, while others were clearly disappointed over the lack of action. These opinions were obviously ordained by age; the older the officer, the greater the complacency.

A tall, balding delta team member walked directly over to the commander. "Sir, we have another man down," he said, thumbing over his shoulder at the doors that had been the primary focus for the last couple of hours. Joe shook his head in disbelief. "Damn! Let's get the medical team in here," he said.

The paramedics were reloading their bus close enough to overhear the conversation and immediately responded. However, once again, the condition of this victim warranted no medical attention.

One look and Hunt almost lost the pizza he'd eaten earlier. His legs felt like two sticks of Jell-O. He had seen plenty of gunshot victims and mutilated bodies over the years to be immune to the effect of carnage. Even the man torn in half out front didn't impact him as horrendously as this guy. This poor man was sitting up right; the whole back of his head was missing from just above the hairline. The open cavity was empty of brain matter, allowing light to shine through the eye sockets. One of the eyeballs hung over the cheekbone from strands of muscle. The other was missing. Small chunks of gray matter glistened from the carpeting and the nearby seats. Getting closer, Hunt stepped on something that popped. Checking the sole of his shoe, he found the missing eyeball. And that was the limit of his control. He quickly turned away before falling to his knees to throw-up violently.

Jim Coleman quickly covered the corpse with a sheet before he lost it as well. Then offered greatly appreciated assistance to his partner. The two men rushed from the building in search of fresh air.

♦ ♦ ♦ ♦ ♦

The medical examiner had finished his job of removing the bodies shortly after the crime lab had taken a thousand photos.

Some distant traffic from unsuspecting commuters filled the morning with noisy congestion, and the sun gave promise of a beautiful day. That is, to everyone except those whose lives had been changed forever by last night's criminal activities.

Time of death for each victim was estimated to be between the hours of nine and eleven PM. A more accurate time was to accompany the autopsy report within five working days. Officer Mark Cash was posted in the parking lot to turn away curious onlookers or morbid thrill seekers, and it made him uneasy.

Yellow tape had been stretched between barricades surrounding the crime scene with the words "METRO POLICE" printed on it. White chalk outlines of human silhouettes had been etched in the bloodstained area marking the places of the fallen ones.

Mark knew that within another week, all signs of this horrible crime would be washed away by the rain., mercifully shielding those who were not involved. Right now, his concern was the noon-day sun. Once it started baking the spilled body fluids, it would lure every stray dog for five miles. Making the task of maintaining an undisturbed crime scene almost impossible. And explaining the loss of evidence to the District Attorney could make this assignment one that ends careers.

Cash removed his hat to wipe away the sweat forming on his forehead. "Great, it's going to be a hot one," he said, then looked down to spit. In doing so, he found a half smoked joint and a scrape of legal looking paper. He carefully picked the items up and slipped the blunt into his shirt pocket. The paper, however, he took the time to read. For now, it really meant nothing to him, but it could be a piece of evidence that the crime lab may have missed. After all, it was just a learner's permit for some guy named David Watts. 'Who knows,' he thought to himself, then pocketed it as well. Then he heard the dogs coming closer, making him anxious.

"I knew I should have gone into music like Uncle Johnny," he said to the empty lot, looking up at the blue sky and slipping off into a daydream of being on stage with his band, a thousand beautiful young groupies screaming his name.

Unexpected Vengeance

CHAPTER 5

The light was excruciatingly bright, radiating like the sun, but didn't hurt his eyes. It also appeared to be so intensely hot that it would blister your hide to the bone, yet actually felt cool and pleasing to his skin. It was unimaginably dangerous, and inconceivably compelling, extraordinarily frightful, and lavishly peaceful at the same time. Within lay a feeling of purified love that consumed him, body and soul. However, a need to look back, away from the light was an overwhelming internal battle of will power, which he couldn't deny.

Turning effortlessly required only thought, and Michael found himself hovering weightlessly as a cloud over his own body. From there, he could see his blood running from the incisions they had made in his chest and leg. Plus his left arm looked like a pin cushion full of needles. Everyone in the room acted panicked. Michael wanted to tell them that he was fine and that he no longer felt any pain. But for some reason, they couldn't, or wouldn't, listen. They kept trying to make him return to his mangled and painful body. "Quit!" he yelled over and over. "Please leave me alone."

Not wanting to watch them any longer, and needing an escape, Michael thought himself back into the light. Immediately, his emotionalism vanished, leaving nothing but a peaceful feeling of tranquility and calmness.

Ahead of him, he heard joyous voices. There were people talking and singing. One of them was his dad, so he willed himself faster. "Dad!" he screamed.

"Just a little farther, sweetheart," came the voice he knew better than anyone's.

"Dad, where are you?" he yelled again.

The light lifted like dissipating fog. And standing in the mist was the only father Michael ever knew. The feeling was greater than mere words could ever express. Next to him was Jackie Lee and a small boy who appeared just as elated as Michael.

Tim dropped to his knees before opening his arms out to his son, who shot into them like a rocket. The hug was bone crushing and if ever ended, would be too soon.

Everywhere he looked, Michael saw people that he recognized, even though most of whom he'd never met. And they all loved him. He could feel it emotionally as well as physically.

"Isn't this fantastic honey? Look at me! I feel twenty-one again," Tim said as he spun Michael over his head like a feather. Then he handed him to Jackie.

"Hello my young friend. This is Tiger," he said as he pointed to the child next to him. "And this is Michael." The boys smiled. Somehow, they already knew each other.

Everything was just how dad said it was going to be when mom died Michael thought.

"Dad, Where's mom?" he asked scanning the area around him. But before Tim could explain that she was close by, Michael's feet turned a pinkish mix resembling sand and smoke, that worked its way upward. Like a genie returning to its bottle, Michael's very essence was being vacuumed back the way he'd come.

"Dad!" he yelled with a panic stricken voice.

"No! Please no!" Tim called out. Having no idea what was happening, he dove forward, grabbing his son's arm.

"Dad, I'm scared!" Michael screamed as he continued to disappear. Then, desperately clinging to Jackie, as well as his dad, he faded to almost nothing, dragging some of each spirit with him.

Tim held on as tight as he could until his hands were empty. "Please God no! Don't take him! I love him so much," he pleaded, as he fell to his knees again, this time in despair.

Michael felt himself flying back through a tunnel of stars, faster and faster until he approached the speed of light.

All at once, the strange sounds of medical equipment returned, along with unspeakable pain. "Dr. Johnson! We did it! I've got a heartbeat, and blood pressure is back to within tolerance!" announced the anesthetist excitedly.

Everyone else cheered and clapped over their returning patient.

Michael's eyes popped open for a split second, and a single tear rolled down his cheek.

'Could I have been dreaming?' He thought not, but couldn't clear his drug-filled mind. Then mercifully drifted back to sleep before any decision would come.

"Okay everyone!" said the doctor. "We saved a life. Now let's see if we can save an arm. We'll celebrate later"

Unexpected Vengeance

CHAPTER 6

The breath from the two officers had lightly fogged the windshield, but not quite enough to block their visibility. The street stretched out before them like a glass-coated runway due to the rain, which was in the process of evaporating off the hot blacktop.

At two o'clock in the morning, the world seemed so isolated and unreal. If it wasn't for the movement of a small white cat on the prowl and the sound of distant thunder, Private Jerry Cox could almost convince his imagination that the world had ended or that everyone else had been lifted up in the rapture, except for him and his coworker.

This was his first stakeout, and his nerves were wound tighter than a banjo string. Plus, he really had to pee.

"What time is it Sarge?" he asked louder than he meant to, abruptly breaking the stillness of the night and causing his superior officer to jump from being startled out of some faraway place his mind had taken him to.

"Damn!" said the sergeant while trying to keep any more coffee from spilling from his cup. He then over-dramatically raised his hands, as if gallons of boiling liquid had just drenched his crotch.

"Its five minutes since the last time you asked. Will you just relax?" he inquired. Then turned his attention back to the house they were assigned to watch.

Jerry was reluctant to speak again, but his bladder was now screaming hard-core, head-banging rock and roll in his gut.

"Sergeant Hayes! I've got to pee like a Russian racehorse!" he explained. To emphasize his point, he began pushing down on his private area with both hands.

To the Sergeant, this gave Jerry a boyish quality, and his first reaction not to care vanished. His heart had softened for the rookie. He remembered how his first time had been and how long it had taken him to learn to ignore the call of nature.

Not wanting to draw attention to the unmarked unit, Hayes extended his arm just far enough out the window to pour out the remainder of his drink. Then he handed the empty cup to Jerry.

"Here, go in this," he said smiling like he had done Cox a great favor, professionally handling the problem.

The younger patrolman accepted the small, white Styrofoam cup like it was covered with red fire ants. The expression on his face made the sergeant want to burst out laughing. But somehow he held it in long enough to say, "Go on, hurry up. If something goes down," he pointed at the house they were watching, "you don't want to be caught with your pants down."

Jerry looked up from the container, "You've gotta be kiddin' Sarge," he said, holding it up in the air between his thumb and forefinger. "I'd never be able to, plus, right now I could fill this tiny thing ten times easily."

"First off, call me Tom while we're out here, second, we're on a stake-out. That means we need to blend into the night. That's done by not drawing unwanted attention to ourselves. How do we do that, you may be asking yourself. The answer is by sitting very still," he explained and paused for a second. "If that learner's permit that was found at those murders is from the killer, we'll need the element of surprise."

Jerry felt a little more comfortable and confident now that he was on a first name basis with his sergeant. "Think of it this way Tom, can you picture me throwing cup after cup of hot, steaming urine out the window? It would look like we'd sprung a leak, no pun intended, and I'm frantically bailing water to stay afloat."

The mental picture was the frosting on the cake. Hayes couldn't help bursting into contagious laughter, which quickly spread to

Jerry.

Both of them immediately rolled-up their windows to contain the sound of their uncontrollable roar. A full performing orchestra would draw less attention on this lonely and seemingly peaceful road.

It only took a few minutes for the summer heat to re-dominate the car's interior, demanding its release by causing discomfort.

Resisting the need to continue chuckling, both officers re-opened their windows. The damp air was as refreshing and cool as a dip in a crystal clear pool. Each took deep breaths of the wonderful smelling ozone, which always accompanies storms this time of year. Then they sat quietly for a few minutes with their own thoughts.

"Sarge, I mean Tom," said Cox. Hayes looked over at Jerry, who was sitting there fidgeting with some arrest warrants.

"Yeah. What is it kid?" he asked. Their eyes sort of locked on each other, and the seriousness on their faces was intense.

"I've still got to pee," Cox said, and was immediately rewarded for his confession with a shower of spittle. His partner had once again lost his composure.

This time, there wasn't any reason to close the windows. Tom had accidentally elbowed the horn, blasting the sleeping neighborhood with the rudest of wake-up calls. Their cover was blown.

"Well, you might as well ... " Tom was trying to say through his laughter, "go up there ... and ... " he caught his breath, "ring their damn doorbell, and ask to use their bathroom!!"

Both men howled at the silliness of the situation with tears rolling down their cheeks. If anyone had seen them, they'd think they were witnessing two stoned law enforcement officers after sampling some marijuana from their latest bust.

As soon as the Sarge could see through his watery eyes, He

turned the key in the ignition, and the huge Chevy 350 police interceptor engine rumbled to life.

Holding his hurting belly with one hand, and his crotch with the other, Jerry continued laughing so hard, he was sure he was going to wet himself. He struggled to ask a question.

"Where are ..." he began and stopped to wipe tears from his eyes. "Where are we going?" he finally inquired.

Hayes rubbed the moisture from his face as well. "I need some coffee, and I guess you still need to pee. No reason we can't leave now, is there?" he asked, putting the cruiser in drive and pulling away from the curb. They were both oblivious to the fact that an inconspicuous feline wasn't the only watcher as their police car moved slowly down the mailbox-lined street.

◆ ◆ ◆ ◆ ◆

The interior of the sparsely furnished house seemed void of color in the darkness, and the smell of stale weed mixed with body odor dominated the room. A small pie-shaped sliver of light from the street shined across the right side of René's face, illuminating one of his dark eyes and the stubble of his unshaven chin. He felt confident that the small opening in the curtain wouldn't be detectable from the street.

Onezean turned in the chair he'd occupied for the last paralyzing hour, his body aching from the lack of movement. "What are they doing?" he asked just above a whisper.

René lowered his thirty-eight to his side while turning to face his comrades. "They laugh as locos Diablo's," he mused, shaking his head with disbelief. "I can't figure out these locos gringos," he finished, once again taking up vigilance at the window.

Paul sat rocking back and forth like an autistic child. Even though he'd been instructed repeatedly to remain still, he couldn't. Fear was consuming him.

"Man! They know we're here! We've got to start shooting, man!

Oh man, we're done for!" he ranted, getting closer and closer to a full-blown panic attack.

David sat to Paul's left, holding a butcher knife he'd borrowed from the kitchen earlier. He was contemplating cutting Dickson's throat if he didn't settle down. It would be better than letting his voice give them away.

"If they knew we were in here, they would've already kicked down the door," he said.

Paul, not listening, only turned his swollen, black and blue face in Otey's direction.

"Man! You guys shouldn't have killed those people! We're going to the chair!" he cried.

Watts couldn't take it anymore. He pulled the blade out so Dickson could see it in the dim light.

"I'm sick of your whining. There's no way they know crap!" he demanded.

The weapon in David's hand resembled a machete when he raised it above his head to strike. Whether he intended to use it or not would haunt Paul for the rest of his life. Luckily, the voice of René caused the confrontation to halt like pushing pause on a DVD player.

"They're leaving," he announced, louder than he had intended. The tension drained out of the group like going down that first hill on a roller coaster, relaxing everyone over their temporary reprieve from justice.

Except Paul who still awaited his leader's judgment to spare his life, or to terminate it like he had done the James families. He could picture his friends giving the thumbs down signal in his mind. Before he had time to beg for mercy, the would-be executioner lowered the huge blade, then tossed the deadly tool on the hardwood floor with careless disregard to any damage or the noise of such an action.

Onezean reached for the lamp beside the chair, turned the switch with a click, and the room was instantly alive with color and contrast. The look on his face displayed that he was obviously not in agreement with David's decision to grant amnesty to a sniveling coward, he was actually considering raising his shotgun and killing both of the white trash before him. The thought of splitting the cash two ways instead of four sweetened the idea.

"Why didn't you go ahead and kill that slime ball? You know he's going to wind-up sending us all back to the joint!" he said, and then turned his head toward René in search of agreement, receiving it by way of a nod of Caldrone's head.

Watts spun quickly and violently on Otey. A look of pure evil radiated from the demon behind his eyes, and it made a cold chill run up Onezean's spine. Never before had he feared another man. But right now, he felt like he was facing the devil himself.

"If I wanted him dead, that's exactly what he'd be. I would tear his heart out with my bare hands," David said while demonstrating, "and take a bite out of it while he watched." The act turned into a fantasy as pure demonic joy continued to darken David's face.

No one could say a word; the performance turned their blood to ice water.

After a short time, Watts returned from his psychotic episode and back to his self-appointed job as leader of the small band of criminals.

"This slime ball," he said, pointing at the still cowering Paul, "as you called him, was my cellie for three years. We have a bond of honor, just like you and that spic," he explained, stopping long enough to allow any comments over his choice of words. When none came, he continued. "Plus, if you'll stop long enough to think things through, how long after they found his body would it take to connect it to us through our records?"

80

He made his point and then shrugged his shoulders. "If need be, I'll feed his ass to the dogs myself, but only when I say so!" he said, turning on Paul again, slapping him as hard as he could. "Understand me Dickson?"

Through forming tears, Paul squeaked out a "Yes sir!"

Watts turned back to Onezean and René.

"How about you guys?" he asked roughly. Both Otey and Caldrone could swear they saw flames behind David's eyes.

"Yeah, we hear you. He's your problem, not ours. But don't get me wrong. If we go down because of him, I'll put a bullet in his brain, permission or not," confessed Onezean.

David felt as if he were being challenged over the role of alpha male. Tension grew between them like an over taxed rubber band. Their hands tightened on the grips of their firearms. The slightest wrong move and someone's body count would grow.

A not so distant dog began barking wildly, ending the standoff. Once more, they were comrades facing a common foe.

Otey quickly hit the switch again causing the darkness to consume them.

"René, check the street!" commanded the reigning leader.

Responding quickly, Caldrone had to rub his eyes to help them adjust to the different lighting. Then he scanned the front yard and street from his already established guard post.

"It's one of those mucho grande limos," he said, beckoning his friend to his side with a small hand gesture.

Onezean took a position by the window and moved the curtain a crack. What he saw shocked him.

Two huge black men in dark T-shirts exited the luxury automobile and then just stood there like ebony statues, their hands crossed at the waist, muscle after muscle bulging from head to toe.

To Otey, these men looked like overstuffed mythological gods. At six-two, two hundred twenty pounds, he still felt small in comparison to these seemingly unreal giants. "What the fu ... " he was going to say when the phone rang, one time, cutting him off in midsentence.

All four of the room's occupants locked their eyes on the communications device as if it had sprouted wings and was about to take flight. No one could move. It seemed as though the contraption had somehow hypnotically anesthetized them. Then it happened again, and fear engulfed their faces as they shot looks back and forth, trying to find an answer in each other. Eight eyes the size of silver dollars shined in the otherwise gray room.

Time came to rest for an agonizing five, very disturbing, minutes before Mr. Alexander Graham Bell's invention filled the house with its attention grabbing sound again. This time it didn't quit. It was clear to the gang of thugs that whoever was calling knew of their presence and expected an answer.

"Answer it!" Watts demanded looking at Paul.

Dickson's face turned white as snow, which made him look like a ghost. His head started unconsciously shaking back and forth.

"Why me?" he asked, which sounded more like a plea than a response.

David raised his hand over his left shoulder to back-hand the blond-haired boy. "Because it's your phone, and because I said so!" he yelled.

The high-decibel chimes were getting on Onezean's last nerve. He cocked a shell into his Remington before pointing it into the white kids' face.

The open end of the double barrel looked like two open manholes to the already traumatized Paul. He wanted to faint, but he knew if he did, he may never wake-up again. So he reached for the receiver nervously. It rang again, causing him to jerk his hand away as though it had burned him.

Otey thumbed back the hammers with a *click-click*.

"If it rings one more time," he said, and his message was received loud and clear. Dickson finally grabbed the hand piece from its cradle.

"Hello?" he squeaked, sounding like a child of around three years of age.

"You have five minutes to send out your leader, or everyone in the house dies," said the deepest voice that Paul had ever heard. Then the phone went dead. Not just hung-up dead, but disconnected, never-to-speak-again-dead.

Paul hung up slowly without even realizing that he had done so. He looked as if Jesus Christ himself had called to say hello. After a few quick glances at the other three, He unsuccessfully tried to escape reality by burying his face in his hands.

The group didn't let him. "Well?" came the voices of Otey and Watts in harmony. "Who was it?"

Paul lost no time relaying the message, though he was uncertain why. Whether from fear of his so-called friends, or in hopes of being rid of His Excellency, preferably forever.

He looked David in the eyes, "It was the guys out front," he explained, paused to swallow his fear, then continued. "They asked for you personally to come outside. They asked for you by name. They said they'd kill us all if you do not comply," he said, changing the message slightly. Because if he hadn't, he would've instantly became the new leader, the one forced to die in the unknown confrontation awaiting beyond the front door.

Some of Watts' abrasive bravado drained away, and was replaced by fear, temporarily emasculating him. This exposed the youth hidden beneath the surface by years of hate and anger, giving him an almost childlike quality. He hopefully scanned the others for support and immediately understood the situation. He'd made his bed, as the old saying goes.

"I say we let them try coming in," he said, extending his chest to appear fearless.

"No wanna amigo. These have many," René said from over beside the window. "De weapons," he added, then whistled lightly while shaking his head in disbelief.

Watts crossed the living area to view the street for himself. The sight was stolen right out of an old gangster movie. The sidewalk was saturated with large men carrying automatic weapons.

"Oh my God," he said. Now he was a believer in the Lord.

From back on the couch, came Dickson's frightened and timid voice.

"They said five minutes man. We've got about two left, then we're all dead man!"

Onezean whirled around and turned the shotgun onto the confused leader.

"Out you go boss," he said, waving the weapon toward the front door. Realizing that he had no other choice but to comply, David walked to the entranceway.

After opening the door halfway, he yelled, "I'm coming out!" Before he stepped over the threshold, he raised his hands up over his head. The first thing he noticed was the clear sidewalk. All those men had vanished into the shadows from which they had materialized only seconds ago. The next, was the biggest human being he'd ever laid eyes on, who stepped in front of the door, blocking David's view of everything except the behemoth's massive torso.

The gigantic and unexpectedly gentle face broadened with a brilliant, white smile. "Put yo hands down fool. This ain't no western," he said, comically rolling his eyes, then added, "White boys."

The titan took hold of David's arm at the bicep, covering it completely from shoulder to elbow.

Watts knew his captor could pull his arm off with ease and then beat him to death with it. So, he allowed himself to be lead off the porch, down to the open door of the limousine, where the iron grip was released.

"Get in," came that deep voice again with pure conviction that it would be obeyed.

Doing as instructed, Watts climbed in with the enormous fellow in his wake. The seat could normally hold three adults in luxurious comfort, but David found himself wedged between two gorillas, and he was cramped to the point of suffocation. Each breath was a chore, laced with the smell of leather and expensive cologne. Across from them sat a thin light-skinned man of around thirty, dressed in what appeared to be a ten thousand dollar suit. Gold and diamonds shined from rings that the man wore on every finger. His left hand rested on his slim, crossed legs, holding an unlit cigar, his right hand held a martini style glass, which was filled with an unknown clear liquid.

"Mr. Watts," he began, speaking over perfect teeth. "Let's make this quick. The police will be returning soon, and I'd rather not have to deal with them this evening, so ..." he now pointed with his cigar. "Let's get started, shall we? You and your group stole a large sum of money from a business that is under my protection." Watts was shocked.

"You have the wrong guy ..." David started, but wasn't able to finish lying. Pressure was applied to his ribs by the oak-tree-sized arms of the goons on either side of him. The inability to draw air caused his chest to ache painfully. After only a few seconds, that really seemed like hours, the burden was released. Air filled his lungs, and understanding filled his mind.

The well-dressed man took a sip from his drink as if nothing had happened. "My name is George Woods. You will call me "sir". Have you heard of me?" he asked.

David looked as if he'd seen a ghost. "Yeah, I ha ... aaa!" Another squeeze came a lot harder than the first one.

George shook his head. "We must always remember to use our manners," he instructed.

The very effective reprimand ceased, and David gulped for air as if he'd stayed under water too long, almost drowning.

"Mr. Watts, we're wasting time. Please try again. Have you heard of me?" Woods asked a second time.

With his newly found respect, David spoke as properly as he could. "Yes sir, I have. You're the boss of the biggest gang in Nashville." George got a shocked and comical look on his face. He just stared at his prisoner, as if trying to comprehend something new.

"Gang?" he finally said.

David expected to be crushed to death for his elaboration. Why hadn't he just said yes sir and left it at that. He began squeezing his eyes shut in anticipation of the coming pain that didn't come. Instead, he felt the seat start to jiggle. Opening his eyes again to discover the two next to him laughing to themselves.

Woods also had a smirk of levity on his face.

"Gang? How barbaric," he said, waving his smokeless Cuban as if to clear the air. "Mr. Watts, I'm the leader of a massive organization. The position that I hold requires constant vigilance over the city in which I rule. Every so often, however, an isolated insubordinate, or an outsider, unknowingly jeopardizes the harmonic balance that I hold so dear to my heart," he said while touching his chest with a doubled up fist, then went on with his speech. "When these inconsistencies in conformity transpire within my brotherhood, the perpetrator usually pays with his life as well as the lives of his family."

David's stomach turned sour. He actually had to squeeze his butt cheeks together to keep from messing himself. And he felt the sting of urine as it dampened the front of his pants.

Mr. Woods took another small drink and then he held the glass up in admiration, using the act as the perfect form of psychological torture, just by giving his captive ample time to fill his imagination with the worst of scenarios.

The smell of fear and the sight of perspiration beading up on David's bloodless, pale forehead told Woods that he had David right where he wanted him. Now the punk would do anything to leave there alive.

"That brings us to you and your cohorts. I can't maintain order while simultaneously allowing this infraction to go unpunished," Woods said.

That was it. David's pants turned dark from him completely losing control of his bladder.

"Please!" he began to beg through tears already soaking his face. "We didn't know. We had just got out of the joint and needed a score. Please sir, don't kill me!" he sobbed.

George rubbed his chin, pretending to consider his options. "Well … if you and your men will agree to a tax on the money you stole and a fee for my protection, I think we can come to an understanding."

Some of the color returned to David's face.

"Anything sir!" he said, then looked at the ceiling as if to give thanks through prayer.

"Well good. I'll expect fifty percent as tax and another ten for my services and assistance in keeping you alive under my security," explained Woods, waving his hands to dismiss the conversation and that there was absolutely no room for negotiation.

The car pulled to the curb and stopped. David hadn't even realized that they had moved till that moment. He was thinking over the amount that he'd have to pay, and like a moron, tried to pull a fast one.

"Thank you sir. Five thousand dollars it is," he said. White hot pain shot up his spine as the shaved gorillas professionally squeezed pressure points in his arms and legs.

Anger rose in the lord of Nashville's face, like dropping a lobster into a pot of boiling water.

"Mr. Watts, Are you some kind of damned fool?" he asked, moving in closer and then raising his voice. "Or do you take me for one?"

The goons grabbed David by the hair and forced him to his knees in the floorboard.

George's eyes drilled holes through David's.

"How do you think that we found you so quickly?" Woods asked before violently slapping Watts across the face. "Or how I know who you robbed?" he went on. This time, backhanding David. "And how do you think I found that out? Or why you shot that doctor, his wife and the kid?" he spat before adding another strike. This one splitting Watts' lower lip, slinging blood onto the far window. The sight of the crimson fluid and seeing it run down the door panel of his two hundred thousand dollar car caused him to pause. Then he pulled out a Glock nine-millimeter from inside his coat, placed the barrel against the forehead of the kneeling punk and chambered a round. "I know to the penny how much you scored. And that lie just cost you another ten grand. The next one will cost you your life," George said, letting the gun finish speaking for him. With his face covered in disgust, he continued. "One of my police officers will be at your house at precisely 1:00pm to collect my sixty thousand. If you're not there, you're dead," he stated, motioning to the door with his pistol.

David was pulled to the door by his hair, then kicked to the sidewalk. The pain was so intense from the large boot contacting his lower spine that all he could do was roll around in agony. The morning dew that had settled on the grass soaked through his clothing, providing some comfort to the many bruises forming on his backside and all four extremities.

◆ ◆ ◆ ◆ ◆

Both officers looked up from their relaxed positions, where they had been leaning against the hood of their unmarked cruiser, their conversation being interrupted by the sound of a moving vehicle and catching sight of an extra large automobile turning the corner. Thomas Hayes straightened up and watched with intense interest as the limousine moved away down the otherwise abandoned street. "Will you just look at who we have here," he said to himself with disbelief.

From the opposite side of the unit, Cox followed the sight that held his partner's full attention.

"What is it Sarge?" Jerry asked, instinctively placing his hand on the revolver strapped to his side. He didn't receive an answer. As a matter of fact, nothing else was said until the luxury sedan was out of view.

Hayes finally broke his silent trance. "I'll be damned," he mumbled, a look of astonishment covering his face. He turned to his partner, but didn't act as if he were seeing him. His mind was running a thousand miles an hour. Slowly, he took a sip from the steaming white cup. The coffee must have helped to clear his mind from contemplating some elusive thoughts. Shaking his head slightly, he spoke again. "Can you believe that," he asked, then shook his head again. "Get in! We've gotta go!" he ordered, climbing in behind the wheel and leaving the trash on top of the car for the younger officer to handle.

Cox quickly dispensed with his duty of clean-up guy, then rushed to his place in the cruiser, hoping for action.

"Are we going after them? I'll call it in!" he said. But before he could reach the mic, Hayes smacked Jerry's hand as if he were a small child about to touch something hot. The atmosphere between the two changed instantly.

Tommy's angry eyes locked on Jerry's. Astonishment and an

objectionable mask came over his face, "were not here, remember? We're on stake-out three blocks west," he said coldly while putting the car in gear.

Cox sat in complete silence, trying unsuccessfully to comprehend what had just happened. Had he done something wrong? Was it stupid to react the way he'd been trained? Whatever; he needed some answers. Loss of friendship or not.

"Sir, what about the limo, sir?" he asked with as much military conformity as possible. His manner of speech and the tone of his voice were perceived as it was intended.

Feeling sorry for his behavior, Hayes tried to save the friendship.

"Sorry kid. I didn't mean to snap at you like that," he confessed, extending his right hand, offering an explanation. "It's just seeing that devil's car. The best thing for you to do is forget that we ever saw it."

The two shook hands and some of the animosity drained away.

Cox couldn't let it die.

"You know you'll have to do better than that," he informed his sergeant. He then started thumbing through a stack of reports for something to do with his nerves.

Hayes hesitated, but only for a second or two. The rookie would find out sooner or later anyway. Might as well be now. Maybe this way he could avoid in the future what so many officers, including himself, fell victim to.

"That, Jerry, was the boss of our fair city," he explained, thinking that he'd provided a clear enough picture, but obviously didn't when the reply came.

"That was the Mayor?"

Hayes thought Jerry's innocence was refreshing. However, it was time to grow up. "This is the real world kid. That man owns the Mayor. And most of the force is on his payroll. For your safety, you should just take my advice and never mention this guy again. Okay?"

They rode back to a small rise on a side street across from the stake-out, giving them a view of the target house from another angle. They were hopeful that their last circus had been forgotten and that there weren't any curious onlookers. Maybe they could return to the shadows unnoticed.

As soon as Hayes turned off the engine, Cox reached and tapped his arm, then pointed up the road.

Following the direction indicated by the rookie revealed a white male between the ages of eighteen to twenty-five, either drunk or injured trying to stand.

Cox believed that the individual was in need of medical attention, so he reached for his door handle with full intentions of fulfilling his oath to protect and to serve. However, before he could exit the unit, the Sarge grabbed his arm.

"Hold on partner. He fits the description of our man," he said, pulling out the clipboard for a quick inspection. The picture being illuminated under Hayes' hand-held pen light was a perfect match for the now erect person coming their way. "That's him alright," Hayes said. "Let's see where he goes."

As the pair of law enforcement officers maintained their silent visual, their primary target turned east, rubbing his rear end and limping because every step obviously caused great pain. Next, the object of their assignment made his way agonizingly slow to the house under surveillance, climbed the steps in torture, then disappeared through the front door.

Cox turned to his superior officer, confusion written all over his face. "Shouldn't we have arrested him before he got inside?" he questioned with both of his hands held out, palms up.

Hayes unhooked his mic and held it across his thigh. "We're just recon. Detective Bruce Edison needs verification on this suspicious character's location. As far as I know, he's not wanted," he explained, then thumbed the transmitter button. "One-eighty-one to control," he said, then static filled the car.

"Control. Go One-eighty-one," came the voice of a very serious sounding female.

Hayes wiggled his eyebrows at Jerry to show that every man thinks of sex when they hear a woman speak. "Mary, it's me. Sergeant Hayes. Would you be so kind as to patch me through to Edison?" he requested, and again the fuzzy noise dominated the interior.

"Sure Tom, go tach two, and I'll see you at supper," she responded, with a friendly and more relaxed tone.

Hayes turned the dial on the dash-mounted radio to the required number before replacing the microphone to its three-pronged holder. He then leaned back to wait for the call from the detective.

"Sir, why are we sitting on this creep if he's not wanted?" Cox asked, clearly agitated over his wasted time.

"Grunt work kid. Some gold-badge wants us to sit, we sit," he waved his hands in the air. "You heard the old saying, shit rolls down-hill. Well," he pointed at Jerry and then back to himself, "we're the septic tank," he explained, then laughed at his illustration. "I think this mission is, in reality, to cover a screw-up by the brass, probably Edison himself. That's the reason I have just called him."

The radio crackled, "One-eighty-one come in."

"Speak of the devil," Hayes said as he reached over and palmed the mic. "One-eighty-one. Go."

The voice of the detective was blunt and to the point, "Report!" he demanded.

Tommy rolled his eyes while flipping his middle finger at the communications device. He hated everything about Edison, but had his job to consider.

"We have confirmation on David Watts. Plus, we have strong evidence of G.W.'s involvement based on visual, over," he reported professionally.

The voice of the detective came back sounding somewhat frightened.

"Holy Mother of God," he said. "You get back to the station. We need to talk. And by the blessed Mary, tell no one else!" he ordered. Then nothing else came over the speaker, except the low frequency of open air waves.

"You're welcome jerk!" Hayes barked, tossing the mic onto the dashboard. The spring-style cord attaching it to its base reached its limit, pulling the hand piece back until it dropped to the floorboard, elevating his anger another notch. "Catholics!" he spat.

Cox was irritated as well, but for different reasons. He felt that he had been used, and from all indications, illegitimately.

"I don't get it," he said, looking for answers.

Hayes looked at Jerry with understanding.

"All right but first, call in and let them know that we're on our way. Then I'll explain what little I know while we ride."

Cox could tell that the sergeant had no intentions of retrieving the fallen transmitter, so he bent down to get it himself. The moment his head dropped below the horizon of the dash, he found himself in the bowels of hell. It sounded like a cannon went off just inches from his head, causing his eardrum to become racked with excruciating pain before discontinuing to process information to the brain. The second gunshot blast was followed by tiny bits of windshield glass, bone fragments of his partner's skull, and gray matter. All raining down Jerry's back. Even though he could no longer hear himself, he knew that he was screaming.

The sergeant's lifeless body fell limp across Jerry's back. Blood poured from the decapitated torso down through Cox's hair and into his face. It felt like he was drowning in it. How many more shots were fired was unknown to him in his state of deafness. Red-hot pain flared as lead stabbed into his right thigh, followed by a more painful punch to his left butt cheek. Then the worst one, which drilled into his lower lumbar near his kidney. He knew he was being repeatedly and systematically shot. The shooter's amateuristic aim was slowly moving up the body in search of a kill zone. The realization of this horror ran through his mind, along with thoughts of Jesus, his wife, son, the dog, truck payments and pizza. His thoughts came like a million bats taking flight from the mouth of a cave. He spat to clear the warm fluids still running down his face. Because of the way that he was positioned, the next bullet impacted his spine, then made a blazing trail to his lung, stealing his breath. Knowing his life was over, his fear drained away, and he willed himself silent, and began to pray for his family. The pain subsided and darkness wrapped him in it's comforting embrace.

CHAPTER 7

"Michael ... Michael Clark ... can you hear me? Come on, wake up child! It's been over a week now ... Michael! Try to open your eyes son ... can you hear me?" the hopeful doctor prodded encouragingly.

Michael opened his right eye slightly. Then like one of those creepy dolls whose eyes open at different times when you hold them upright, he forced open his left. His desire to return to the world of the unconscious was strong, so he allowed the heavy lids to reclose, succumbing to the blissful darkness.

"Michael! Look at me!" The doctor continued diligently.

The sternness of the voice elevated Michael's awareness. This time he opened his eyes as wide as he could. Fortunately, the nurse had completed her given instructions of closing the curtains and turning down the lights. But even in the darkened room, the smallest amount of light stung like bee stings. He tried blinking to calm the assault, but even that became painful. *'Someone must have filled my eyes with sand,'* he thought.

"That-a-boy!" came that distant voice again.

Michael finally focused on the speaker.

"Doc...tor John ... son, where ...?" he tried to ask, but the sandman had also covered his tongue. It was dry as toast.

"I'm glad you recognized me," the doctor admitted as he reached for a Dixie cup with a straw bent over its edge. "Here. Take a sip," he offered, then held it to Michael's parched lips. "Slowly," he warned.

It was the best tasting, most refreshing water that Michael had ever drank, and he wanted it to last forever. However, after a small swallow, it was removed from his unsatisfied mouth. This made him angry, that is, until the doctor offered to have a nurse bring him some crushed ice to chew on. Be a good boy in church and you'll get a new toy, dwarfed in comparison to this promise.

Michael's like for Dr. Johnson disappeared quickly when the man shined a tiny, intensely bright light across his already sensitive pupils.

"Ouch! What are you trying to do, overload optical nerves? Why don't you take your fingers and poke some holes in my sclera's!" he ranted, then stopped himself.

"Where did that come from?" the doctor asked.

"I don't know. I'm not even sure of what I said." Michael admitted, exhaling a nervous little laugh. "Maybe I overheard my dad say it."

Mentioning Tim made them both go silent and clearly saddened. Michael's eyes floated with tears.

In an attempt to steer his patient away from talking about his dad and having to divulge that he is deceased, Dr. Johnson said, "Listen, in a couple days, when you're a little stronger, I'll take you down the hall and introduce you to a young man about your age. And I'm sure I can arrange ice cream for the both of you. How does that sound?"

Michael could see through the attempt like it was made of glass. *'Come on Jim, we've known each other for years, ever since college. Why are you talking to me like a child?'* he thought, and it scared him. However, to keep from disappointing the doctor, he smiled and said, "Sure, that would be nice. Thanks." Michael tried to wipe his eyes with the back of his hand, and in doing so, noticed his right arm was immobilized and bandaged from his neck, down to his elbow.

Following Michael's line of sight, the doctor smiled. "It's fine buddy. We got blood back to it just in time," he said happily.

"Thanks again Dr. Johnson. By the way, what's his name," Michael asked.

Jim was lost for a second, and it showed on his face.

"The boy down the hall," Michael prompted, as if now he was the one speaking to a child.

"Oh," Johnson said, realizing how silly he must have looked. "His name is Brandon Millichamp."

Once again, Michael felt as if though someone else spoke through him. "Have his parents consented to the tympanic, minimal evasive procedure?"

This statement made the doctor come to his feet, and Michael's eyes to widen with shock. "I think my dad must have told me that too," Michael said. Somehow, that didn't ring true, but it was the only explanation within reach.

"Yeah, it sounded like him," was the doctor's response as he turned to leave. "I've got to go now, rounds to make," he added.

"Okay, thanks ... *umm...* Dr. Johnson, are you gonna miss my dad?" Michael asked, starting to cry. "Now that he's dead," he said through a flood of emotions.

"I was going to talk to you about that after you've recovered. How did you know? You've been unconscious since you arrived. Who could have told you about that?" Jim asked.

Michael smiled through the tears. "When you were poking and cutting on me with those metal things, and all that blood," he said, cringing at the thought, "there were wires all over me. I watched for a little while, then I just couldn't anymore, so I followed this bright light that came through the ceiling," he paused to look up. When he looked back down, his eyes were full of tears again. "That's when I saw my dad, Jackie Lee and his son Tiger. I knew that they had all died because we were all together in a cloud full of love. It was so peaceful." His face turned angry. "Then the pain returned, and I just sort of fell asleep," Michael finished, clearly disappointed in being brought back.

They both stared at each other. The doctor in awe, and Michael as if he was unsure he even believed it himself. Now, it did seem impossible. Johnson's education and logic kicked in.

"That sounds beautiful. But let me explain something that I hope you'll understand. Sometimes, as humans, we want something so bad that our minds play tricks on us," he explained, and put on his best sympathetic face and began again, speaking gently. "It's true. Your father and my good friend is no longer with us."

'Horse manure,' came to Michael's mind from somewhere, making him jump, which paused the doctor's speech.

"Are you alright?" Johnson asked.

"Yes sir. Gas bubble I think," Michael lied.

"Well, relax. You'll be fine," Jim promised, and then went back to his explanation. "Your dream is, and has to be, coincidental. The brain releases a chemical substance that reduces pain naturally. As much pain as you were in, you must have been overdosed, making this realistic dream a false reality," the doctor finished, but could tell that his young patient didn't buy his story, and still looked emotional. That's when the doctor asked himself why he couldn't keep his mouth shut. What would it hurt to allow Michael to believe the fantasy if it comforted him temporarily. Once again, he stood to exit the room. "I'll return as soon as I can. Now get some rest," he ordered.

Michael's voice caused the doctor to pause yet again.

"I was with my dad," he said as a rhetorical response, then closed his eyes to sleep.

Dr. Johnson watched for a second, and then let the door close behind him.

Alone in the room, Michael whispered, "I wanted to stay there with you dad."

Tim's voice was clear. It was as if he were standing next to the bed. "I know you did sweetheart, try to sleep now. I'm right here." Michael quickly opened his eyes expecting to see his dad and searched the room excitedly. Finding no one, his heart became heavy and he wanted to cry again. However, as he felt himself drifting off to sleep, a smile brightened his face. Somehow, he could hear his dad singing their favorite song. *I raise my hands, bow my head. I'm finding more and more truth in the words written in red, Oh I believe.*

Michael chuckled softly, "endorphins my rear end," he said, but didn't know why. "I love you dad," he mumbled as he gave-in to the sedatives, drifting from an uncertain reality of consciousness, to the peacefulness of sleep.

I love you too, son.

Unexpected Vengeance

CHAPTER 8

Michael was a little more than excited when the nurse showed up. She was there to transport him to the therapy room on the other side of the hospital. The thought of being someplace else, anyplace else, was thrilling. He'd felt like a prisoner of the intensive care unit for over a month now. The hardest part was watching summer days slowly pass by. His only view of the real world was a window at the end of the hall. And if his door was closed, he didn't even have that.

His mind could play in the endless sunshine, but his injured body remained stationary. And his arm had been immobilized by a medieval torture device these dungeon masters had disguised as traction. Just being freed from that thing was a blessing, even though it rekindled some forgotten pain.

At first it was frightening to see how thin his arm had become. It was bluish in color and looked as if it belonged to a stick man. Plus, it refused to respond to any commands. But his dad's calm and reassuring voice gave him comfort. Dad promised that the therapy, in time, would return him to normal.

Tears stung his eyes the second his wheelchair crossed the threshold into the brightly lit hallway. His emotions were mixed and confusing. For the most part, fear pecked at the back of his brain like a wood pecker, another part, even though he thought he hated every agonizing second of the post-surgical trauma unit, he, for some incomprehensible reason, was going to miss it.

The nurse informed him that his belongings would be moved to another room. One where he could still be watched, but not as aggressively. More of a place to rest than the poking and prodding of the I.C.U.

The ride down the hallway was exhilarating, and Michael felt like a newborn baby seeing everything for the first time. Never before had he paid such close attention to the smallest of details - the colors, the taste of fresh air, the smell, and even the symptomatic design of the lines in the tile floor.

As the elevator door opened, it made an amazing swishing sound along with a musical bell, just as has been witnessed thousands of other times in hundreds of other buildings. But, this time he really appreciated how beautiful and clear it was. He thought of a country song he'd heard on dad's favorite station, "I hope someday you'll get the chance to live like you are dying." *'Or in my case,'* he thought, *'like you just died and came back for second chance.'*

The ascending ride only lasted about a minute before the doors opened up, facing a huge wall of windows that separated them from a courtyard paradise. He had a better understanding of how the blind in the Bible must have reacted when given back their sight by our Lord Jesus.

"Stop, I want to go outside," he ordered.

The elderly lady just pushed on like she hadn't heard.

His anger flared. "I said stop!!" he yelled, reaching down with his good hand, levering the brake, causing the wheelchair to spin like a top, taking along the medical aid with it. As she fought to stay standing, Michael sprang to his feet, at first almost falling on his face due to a slight case of vertigo. He didn't realize how weak he'd become.

The woman in white turned as red as a chili pepper. "You rotten, ungrateful child! Get back in that chair this instant!" she ordered, while pointing at the chair like an Army drill sergeant.

Michael simply turned away, totally ignoring her demands.

"Lady, I'm going outside. I'm not a prisoner here, and this isn't supposed to be a concentration camp," he said, moving to the door. "Ten minutes of this Garden of Eden, and I'm all yours," he finished, and stepped outside into heaven on earth.

It seemed more exquisite than he'd first imagined. Of course there were only a few trees, but never before had any grown anywhere in the world as eloquently, or with such perfection.

A few black and yellow birds must have agreed with Michael's interpretation, and had made the little paradise their home. The leaves rustled in a gentle breeze, making them dance with delight. There was only one thing that Michael could compare his joy to, and that was when he had visited the cloud of love.

"Dad, he whispered. "I'm glad now that I came back. I'm sorry, but think of all of the really cool stuff that I would have passed up if I'd stayed."

Still a little shaky from his ordeal and lack of energy, Michael took a seat on one of the two, moss-covered benches that the paradise had to offer. Immediately, he could tell that they were hardly used for more than ashtrays on which to put out filthy cigarettes. His mood started to deteriorate. The sight of hundreds of discarded cigarette butts around his feet stole even more of his joy.

He turned to watch the people inside fly by, each trying to line their pockets at the expense of never experiencing life's simple treasures, like this tiny garden. *'Everyone should have the chance to die,'* he thought. *'That way when they have returned, they would appreciate what God has given us.'*

Two women then entered the courtyard and destroyed what remained of his serenity by lighting-up. The smoke drove the birds away, and Michael back inside to the impatiently waiting transporter. He sat down, giving the woman his sweetest smile.

"I'm ready when you are," he said.

The nurse shook her head in disgust.

"Well-I-never," she responded, returning to her required task.

Seconds later, an automatic door with THEAPUTIC SUITE 104 written on it slid open to reveal a large room with multicolored mats on the floor. To Michael, it looked like a playground had given birth to a gymnasium. Only two things in the room didn't scream, PLAY TIME!

The first was a large padded table, presently occupied by a man of around twenty-five years of age. He was doing something obviously painful to his legs.

The second being the mean look on the face of another guy coming Michael's way.

"Mr. Clark, I do believe that you're late. Unacceptable!" he said, his reddish skin grew brighter with each word. He then pointed his nose upward as his eyes locked onto the nurse, obviously accusing her of negligence and insubordination.

His superiority was not lost on her.

"Don't look at me! Talk to Tarzan here; ask him about his little jungle safari," she said, giving the chair a last little 'He's all yours' shove before throwing her arms in the air, spinning on her heal and leaving the room in a huff.

Michael watched as the extra-wide backside of the woman disappeared through the automatic door before turning his attention to the reddish-brown haired man standing in front of him. The guy's arms were crossed at the chest, and he had a no-nonsense-will-be-tolerated look on his face. Michael tried his "aren't I cute" face, but it had no effect on the dude, so Michael raised his hands palm-up, shrugging his shoulders.

"What?" he asked.

The tall therapist leaned forward just enough to be intimidating and tapped his nametag with his fingernail.

"My name, as you can see." he stopped and squinted his eyes. "You can read can't you?" he inquired, obviously trying to insult Michael's intelligence. Michael only nodded, so the man went on with his ill-mannered introduction. "As I was saying, my name is Elmo Baker Jr. And I find no humor in this fact," he said, dropping his hands to his hips, pausing long enough to allow Michael a chance to screw up before continuing. "Some may find unacceptable amusement during therapy sessions by saying things like, tickle-me Elmo, dancing Elmo, etc."

A small chuckle came from the sublime man over on the table, and the therapist's neck line turned even redder than normal.

"That just cost you ten more minutes of leg raises," he barked over his shoulder, which was answered by a heart-felt groan of pain. "And you young man," he said, refocusing on Michael, "you will have to work extra hard to compensate for your tardiness." He pointed to a small desk. "If you please," motioning with his thumb to get moving.

He looked to Michael as if he were hitchhiking, and he was tempted to tell him to hop on, but instead, allowed Elmo to help him to the workstation. There, he was handed a small blue ball with a circumference of approximately 4 inches.

"Place it on the desk, palm-down," Elmo instructed, demonstrating the movement. "Squeeze and raise the arm until the ball is at least six-inches off the table, without bending your elbow. Let's start out with twenty repetitions if possible."

Michael rolled his eyes at the easy task that he'd been given. Then after the fifth repetition, he was thankful the therapist hadn't said eight-inches, or twenty-five repetitions.

Mr. Baker seemed delighted with the pain on his young patient's contorted face. "Good. Next time, be here when directed," said the sadistic Elmo with a smirk, letting Michael know that he was being reprimanded. Then he turned on his other victim, clearly being tortured under the ruse of health care. "Your ten extra minutes starts now, funny man," he said as he moved across the room to a small hallway. "I'll get your whirlpool ready."

Before stepping out of sight, the therapist took on a very serious look. "Don't think that I won't be watching for slackers," he said while pointing at both of them with two fingers and then to his own eyes, then back again. Then he closed the white panel door behind him.

Both Michael and the other patient let out a sigh of relief; neither even realizing that they had been holding their breaths.

They started to giggle quietly like children after mom and dad had sent them to bed.

Michael was the first to speak. "Hey, are we allowed to talk? Or does the warden not permit fraternization between the lab experiments?"

The comment made them laugh aloud and immediately, the door that Elmo had closed only seconds ago flew open, which stopped the chuckling instantly. It was as if they had been misbehaving and had been caught in the act.

The therapist scanned the room with bulging eyes, like an overzealous sentry, or a king trying to detect the source of disobedience or unorthodox behavior within his kingdom. Finding no violation of the rigorously enforced rules, which he himself had sanctioned, he returned to his unseen duties.

"We almost bought the farm that time kid," said the man lying on the table. And once more, they allowed the humor of the situation to overcome them, only this time with a little more control.

Michael watched as his developing friend tried to lift his legs off of the table; even an inch or two looked like a struggle, and quite painful.

"If you don't mind me asking, what happened to you?" Michael inquired, as he clinched his teeth with effort, trying to achieve his required exercise.

Without taking his eyes off the ceiling, the man thought of an answer. "Well kid, I don't mind one bit. It's just that it's quite violent and not really appropriate to talk about with someone your age," he said while continuing his painful exercise. "What about you and that arm? Did you throw a fast-ball a little too hard or what?" he asked.

"Eighteen, nineteen … twenty. Whew! That was tough!"

106

Michael said, giving himself a moment. "No, nothing sport related at all. I'm a surviving victim of attempted murder. A guy shot me with a .38 at point-blank range. I'm lucky he didn't use the .44 he had just unloaded in my dad's chest. But you're right, we shouldn't talk about it or the fact that the same animal blew my mother's brains out in front of me three years ago," he finished, wiping a tear away that had found its way down his cheek.

Michael noticed that the man was no longer moving and was staring at him intensely.

"Oh my God kid, I'm sorry. I heard your name when you arrived, but I didn't put two and two together," he said apologetically, then searched his mind for something comforting to say. Nothing would come to him. How could anyone find the words? "You're that Michael Clark, Dr. James' boy aren't you?" he asked and accepted a nod from Michael's head as an answer. Maybe sharing his burden could help. "I too, am a victim of a shooter. If it hadn't been for the department's requirement of Kevlar, I wouldn't be here either. Sometimes, I wonder if it would have been better to have left that vest at home that night," he said, feeling sorry for himself. "Then I wouldn't be going through this," he added, pointing at his toes as he tried to lift his heels. "I don't know if I'll ever be anything more than a crippled ex-cop."

A realization of how the same kind of violence had destroyed a large part of their lives filled their hearts. Their thoughts created a dark mood that was very depressing and hung in the air like smoke, but it also created a bond between them.

"What's your name?" Michael asked, trying to pull himself away from the need to cry.

"Me? Oh, my name is Jerry. I used to say, 'Officer Cox,' but only time will tell if I ever do again," Jerry answered.

"I'm sure you will,'' Michael responded encouragingly. Then they both became silent for a few heartbeats, which Michael could feel and hear in his chest. "Who shot you," he asked reluctantly, as his curiosity got the best of him.

Jerry Shook his head, either to clear it, or to express his failure to understand.

"I wish I knew buddy. My sergeant and I were on some bogus stakeout for the brass. Next thing I know, it's the fourth of July," he stopped long enough to wipe his eyes, trying his best to hold back his own tears. "And my headless partner is lying on top of me, I'm screaming at the top of my lungs and being pumped full of hot lead. I'll never forget the way it burned through me like a worm headed for the center of an apple," he finished, then turned to face the wall, ashamed of the moisture he could no longer contain running down his chin.

Michael nodded with compassion and comprehension. "I know who shot me and murdered my family. Someday I'll find the trash and kill him! I'll find them all. But first, David Watts is going to die."

Jerry snapped his neck back around. "What did you just say?" he asked. A look of astonishment covered his face.

Michael could tell that Jerry hadn't missed a word, but wanted to hear that name one more time.

"I said David Watts!"

Cox couldn't believe his ears. Even hearing it the second time. He rolled himself up to his elbows. "Michael, this is crazy, but that's the name of the guy that we were watching the night I was shot."

They stared at each other in awe. "You're shittin' me," Michael said.

The room closed in on them, becoming the center of their universe. "Thirty-eight," they said in unison as the realization that their injuries could very well have came from the same gun. And there was a very high probability, from the same monster.

They look at each other again and spoke at the exact same time as if rehearsed.

"David Watts."

Michael released the rubber ball unconsciously. It rolled off the desk and bounced unnoticed across the floor where it soon joined the dead silence of the room.

◆ ◆ ◆ ◆ ◆

As is the case with most American hospitals, Vanderbilt's floors shined like polished glass. The walls were mostly bone-white. And the smell of disinfectant made its presence known with each and every breath.

Despite all the signs and arrows giving clear directions to all possible destinations, Anita found herself totally disoriented; lost within the medical city. She couldn't remember if the last directory had said follow the blue line to the red one, or had it said the yellow.

At eighty years old, thin as a beanpole and standing in the center of the corridor, she became a beacon of distress, so it took only seconds to draw the attention of a Good Samaritan.

"H... Hel ... Hello. Are you o... okay?"

Anita felt some relief from her despair. Standing next to her was a thin black man of around twenty-five who was holding the hand of a beautiful young lady of around five.

"Well," Anita began, while blushing from embarrassment. "I seem to have lost my way," she admitted nervously. "At my age, I do well to remember to put my pants on in the morning."

The thought of that made the little girl giggle. And the musical sound made Anita relax.

"What's your name?" she asked, while looking into the youngsters' big, black eyes.

"My name is Kenyelle Crowe Ma'am," she answered with a small curtsey.

"Oh how sweet child," Anita said, placing her hand on the girl's forearm. "Hello Kenyelle, my name is Anita, but everyone knows me as Giggy."

Hearing the silly name, Kenyelle laughed aloud with that cute childish laughter that warms one's heart. "Ha... Ha... Hi ma'am, mm ... mm ... my n ... n... name is Ca ... Ca ... Coray," said the man with a bad stutter.

Anita looked up and took the hand extended in front of her.

"How do you do Corey? Would you be so kind as to point a finger in the direction of the doctor's personal offices? It could help save an old woman's sanity," she asked.

Corey could tell he already liked this woman. "Why sh ... sh ... sure. Fa ... fa... follow the b... blue line," he said, then tilted his head toward the hallway on the left.

"Thank you for being so helpful Corey," Anita said. While turning to leave, she spoke to the child again. "Bye-bye sweetheart."

"Bye Giggy," said Kenyelle, laughing again at that funny name.

Corey and his daughter watched as Anita started to walk off in the wrong direction. "Giggy!" they yelled at the same time, causing Giggy to turn back around. Both of her new friends comically pointed to the left.

Anita put her hands to her chest like she was holding her heart. "Well I never, must be as dizzy as cooter brown," she said and finally walked away, this time in the right direction.

It didn't take long before she found herself standing in front of yet another directory board. Dr. James Johnson's name was fifth on the list; a small arrow next to it pointed to a carpeted hallway, finally ending her search.

Her knock on the dark wood paneled door was answered quickly by a male voice. "Come in please."

Anita opened the door to the small office. It was just big enough to hold a highly polished walnut desk, a few shelves containing medical books, and a high-backed leather chair with two matching smaller ones for guests.

You must be Mrs. Anita Box," The doctor said as he stood and offered his hand.

"That I must," she replied with a bright and honest smile, then accepted the doctor's hand. "How do you do?" she said.

Once she released his hand, the doctor motioned for her to have a seat on one of the smaller chairs. She complied, sitting on the very edge with her legs together like a proper lady, her purse standing erect on her lap. She resembled a frightened school girl before the principal, timidly awaiting her reprimand.

"The reason I asked you to stop by my office first is I have some concerns about Michael I wish to discuss before … " the doctor was saying, but the look of shock on his visitor's face caused him to pause. "No, no, no … " he began again. "Michael is healing just fine. He's a strong little boy physically. I see no reason for anything less than a full recovery." He gave her a professional I know better than you smile before placing his hands around a coffee mug on his desk. It was obviously empty, but still seemed to pacify him with its presence.

"Well then, I don't understand," Anita confessed. The doctor looked up from his cup, returning from some faraway place that only he could go, to find a very confused looking woman.

"Would you like some coffee?" he asked, as if he hadn't heard her.

Anita was getting a little angry, especially when the doctor turned the mug over to poor out the last drop. "It's Maxwell House®," he added.

"No thank you Dr. Johnson. I'm here to talk about Michael!" Anita said.

"Please Mrs. Box, call me Jim," Johnson replied.

"Okay Jim, fine. You may call me Anita. But, what about my great-grandson?" she said, trying to remain calm.

Feeling defeated over his offered drink to justify having one himself, he pushed the cup aside. "Back to Michael; like I said, it's not his physical health, it's his adaptability to reality that concerns me," he said and then paused to allow his statement to sink in.

"I'm still not sure what you mean. Michael seems fine to me. He acts happier than he's been in a long time," she explained.

"Bingo! That's what I'm talking about," Jim said, pointing his finger rudely at Anita to emphasize his point. "I've dealt with hundreds of post-trauma patients over the years. Not once since graduating from Harvard ..." he waved his hand at his diplomas that were hanging on the wall before he continued, "have I run across the form of acceptance of a loss that this child expresses, both through his emotions and his actions. It's not natural to be so calm and understanding after the death of loved ones. I can mention his dad and of course he tears up, but not in my opinion from sorrow. It's more like ... I don't know," he said, rubbing his chin in thought. "It's like the idea brings him to the kind of understanding we doctors get after years of dealing with death. It becomes another part of life. He's only eight-years-old. It doesn't make any sense," he finally finished and began messaging his forehead between his thumb and index finger as if he were suddenly suffering from a migraine.

Anita sat through all of this, watching the doctor struggle with a problem that he couldn't answer. Something that he clearly wasn't used to.

"Michael and I," Anita began, "have been spending a lot of time talking about his future. He will be coming home to live with me." She paused to see if the doctor had something to elaborate on or question, and felt a little anger rekindle when he seemed distant, ignoring her with everything but his eyes. Anita started speaking again because she had no idea what else to do. "Michael doesn't really accept that his dad is gone. Of course I try to explain, but he doesn't agree that mommy and daddy are with Jesus. I mean ... well ... he does say his mother is, but that his dad never left, and they still talk to each other," she said, as she looked up from where she had been unconsciously twisting her purse-strap into a knot, finding a bewildered look on the doctor's face.

Johnson turned his head to scan the documentations, reflecting on his life's achievements, as if trying to find an answer hidden within their frames. "Well, that's another part of my concerns. You know that he believes that he was on a cloud with people ... " James was saying as he turned back to Anita. Now she was the one with a look of confusion. She was actually looking at him as if he were crazy. "Let me start over," he suggested, making a pleading motion with his hand.

Anita nodded that his suggestion would be favorable. "Please do."

Dr. Johnson nodded. "Michael told me the minute he was conscious in the recovery room that while he was being operated on, he had what we refer to as an out-of-body experience. In his state of mind, he claims to have floated or flew, if you will, over the room. He then says that he went through a tunnel of fog. There, he was met by Tim and some others who welcomed him with love." Once again, he used his hand to draw Anita's attention to his college degrees. "Of course with my education, and in the opinion of the scientific community, that is not possible."

Anita was really starting to dislike the doctor's vanity, but remained civil. "Michael doesn't lie, and science says a bumble bee can't fly," she informed him, catching herself in a rhyme, which caused her to smile. She continued with a little less anger in her voice. "God works in mysterious ways and some are beyond our comprehension," she said sarcastically, while waving her hand at the doctor's fancy paperwork shrine.

Jim clearly caught the implications of her mockery. "I assure you Mrs. Box, Michael only believes this fantasy because of the chemicals which his brain released in order to tranquilize his body against the great trauma that had been inflicted upon it. As I've explained to him as best I could, there is no after-life."

Anita's eyes grew big as pie plates. Enraged, she stood up and slapped her hands on the desktop. "You did what?" she said, with her face only inches from that of the doctor's.

He recoiled as if he were about to be struck, which was actually quite possible. "Please! Mrs. Box!" he stammered, putting his hands in the air as if to surrender.

Anita lifted her hand, pointing a tiny, frail finger in the frightened doctor's face. "Listen here you over-educated, self glorifying pompous ass!!" she said, just getting started when there came a knock at the door.

"Come in. Please come in!" Jim said quickly, extremely thankful for any form of interruption.

The door opened just enough for a very pretty, young nurse to poke in her head. "Doctor, the patient is ready sir," she informed him over bleached white teeth.

Exceptionally pleased for his salvation, Jim waved the visitors in. "Yes, Yes, come in, come in," he begged.

The exquisite looking blond opened the door completely and stepped into the room, revealing the young person that she had with her. Totally incapacitated by the beauty of the nurse, Michael didn't even notice anyone in the office.

The red of Anita's face went from the burn of anger, to a glow of love instantly. "Michael!" she called out.

Michael's head snapped around at the sound of her voice. "Giggy," he yelled. Violating hospital rules, he jumped from his wheel chair and ran into his great-grandmother's arms. "Oh, Giggy! Can we please go home now? I'm sick of this place," he admitted between hugs and kisses from which he was being smothered.

"Yes sweetheart. And the sooner, the better," she said, taking Michael's hand. "Say goodbye to the doctor honey."

Michael raised his hand in the air while giving a peace sign. "Peace-out Doc. Thanks for everything," he said, turning to leave. Just before reaching the door, he stopped and turned back. "Oh yeah, about Brandon Millichamp," he said.

The doctor looked sad. "Well Michael, I'm sorry to say ... he just wasn't strong enough to survive the operation. We lost him," he admitted, shaking his head with despair.

Instead of reacting in a saddened manner, Michael grinned. "I know that. He left yesterday. Anyway, tell his mom and dad he's fine and not to cry. He's in a really cool place waiting on them. Dad said they'll all see each other again," he finished and smiled. "Let's go Giggy. I'm starved!"

This time it was the doctor's voice that halted their departure.

"How did you ...? Never mind. But you'll have to ride. I can't let you walk out. Sorry, hospital rules," he said.

"Only if Giggy can drive!" Michael said, jumping into the wheelchair. He then looked at the young nurse, put his thumb to his ear, his pinky next to his lips as if talking on a phone. "Call me some time," he said, then winked while simultaneously making a clicking sound with his mouth.

Anita's face flushed with embarrassment.

"Oh Michael," she said affectionately, swatting at him as one would shoo a fly.

Anita, side by side with the nurse, pushed the eager child down the hallway, or as Michael perceived it, THE RACE TRACK!

Once alone in his office, Dr. Johnson's mind reeled as he considered everything Michael had said. 'What have you done to me Michael Clark?' he asked himself while shaking his head with disbelief. A new thought emerged. Should he relay Michael's message to Brandon's parents, even though it contradicted everything he believed? What could it hurt? Did he need to change his way of thinking? His life? All these thoughts had him doubting his education. He looked down to where his hand busied itself while he searched his mind. It shocked him to see that he had written the name Jesus ten times. That was the last straw. He got up to leave. His destination: The hospital chapel, where he intended to do something that he hadn't done in years. Pray.

CHAPTER 9

Michael was really nervous entering the classroom. Not only because it was his first day back to school, but he was also late. That meant standing in front of the classroom while explaining his tardiness, giving the other students, especially new ones, ample time to examine every move he made and every word he spoke, scrutinizing every aspect of his character down to the smallest of details, unconsciously forming a first and lasting impression. The realization that he would even have such a profound thought added to his anxiety.

He entered as quietly as he could, hoping to avoid detection. The attempt was useless. The noisy third graders went from a monkey-cage roar, to a funeral parlor silence, stopping him in his tracks. All eyes fell on him like a speeding locomotive. Even the teacher stared at him with uncertain anticipation. She clearly was new at her job, and was unsuccessfully trying to control her unruly bunch. And Michael's mere presence had accomplished what she herself could not. For some reason, having been shot makes you a celebrity for all to see.

"I'm Michael Clark," he said, breaking the silence, stepping forward. He extended his left hand to allow the woman to accept the tardy slip he held.

"Well Michael, welcome to my class. I mean our class. My name is Mrs. Tellmen," she informed him, then pointed in the direction of an empty desk. "I've assigned the class alphabetically, so that second desk in the third row is yours. Please have a seat and we'll all get started."

Michael just stood there as if he'd left his body. The teacher wondered about his failure to move.

"Is there a problem Michael?" she asked, sounding very concerned.

Michael seemed to focus, but in his eyes, he didn't look like a child. "I anticipated, hypothetically of course, that you may require some elaboration regarding my uncharacteristic tardiness. After all, I received awards for perfect attendance all through college, as well as medical school," he answered, then clamped both his hands over his mouth to prevent any further uncontrolled articulation. He then noticed how green Mrs. Tellmen's eyes were. Mainly because they were bulging out of her head, staring at him in complete amazement.

"Excuse me?" she said dumbfounded.

Michael felt ridiculous. His instinct told him to flee. He'd never fit back in now, and tears started to burn his eyes. But then the entire class started laughing, not at him, but with him.

The teacher smiled, knowing that she'd been the butt of some joke that she just didn't understand. "Very funny young man. However, before Harvard, you'll need to finish third grade. Go have a seat Dr. Clark," she said. Once again, the students gave in to the giggles, and some added a thumbs up.

Michael felt relieved and quickly walked to his seat. To his delight, he was between two very pretty girls. Both had taken a liking to him already. It showed in their smiles. *This isn't going to be a train wreck after all,* he thought. However, scanning the room, he locked eyes with none other than the hate-filled face of his almost forgotten playground rival, Brady Davis, who doubled his fist threateningly. Catching the boy's intentions, Michael mocked the action and mouthed the words "Bring it on big boy!" Then wondered why he'd do such a thing? What had happened to his fears? His thoughts were then interrupted by the word "test."

The teacher was walking between the rows of desks, placing blank forms in front of each student. The looks on the children's faces indicated their surprise as well. On her second trip, everyone was given three booklets of questions face down. Then she returned to the front of the room, raising her hand in order to stifle the groans and grumbles.

118

"These tests are not intended to be graded. You will not see them on your report cards. They are just to allow the school, as well as myself, to better understand where you stand personally with your education. It will help show the areas you'll need to have extra help in," she explained, then looked at the clock. "You will have one hour to complete each booklet. After the second one, we will break for recess, then we'll finish the third. You may begin," she said, and the room filled with the sound of rustling papers and more groans.

Michael turned the first booklet over along with everyone else. It was a collage of mathematics, reading comprehension, as well as basic spelling. He grabbed his pencil with intentions of beginning, but he couldn't. For some reason, the directions at the top of the page kept demanding his attention. He scanned the room for an ally in his confusion; however, everyone else busied themselves with the task of filling in answers. Why do these instructions mean so much to me? he wondered. Unable to resist their call, he laid the pencil aside and began reading the top of the page again. The fifth direction stated: Before you begin, read all the questions thoroughly. Feeling it was a waste of time, Michael complied anyway. A few minutes later, at the last of one hundred questions, he was happy that he'd listened to his inner voice. It read: 'Do not answer questions one through ninety-nine. Answer only question number one hundred.' The question was, "How old are you?" He simply filled in the blank, and then looked at the clock. He still had over forty-five minutes left. Obviously, this test was to see if the students would follow directions, nothing more. And he had passed with flying colors while everyone else was still trying desperately to beat the clock.

Michael raised his hand and it wasn't long before Mrs. Tellmen looked up.

"I'm sorry Michael, I can't answer any questions during a test," she explained. And Brady snickered, pretending to sneeze the word "stupid."

Michael only looked at him and smiled.

"No questions," he said with confidence. "It's just that I'm finished with the first test."

The teacher clearly didn't believe him by the way she walked up and took the paper for inspection. Her arms dropped to her side looking shocked.

"Nobody's ever caught the reason behind this exam. How did you know?" she asked.

"I just read and followed the ..." he began to answer before she quickly cut him off.

"Shhh!" she warned, putting her index finger to her lips. Everyone was watching. "Back to work class. Time is running out," she said, then turned back to Michael, turning his next test over in front of him, and then wrote the time on its top. "You might as well start on this one. I'll let you know when time is up," she said, and then returned to her desk, once again looking over Michael's answer sheet. His earlier statement echoed in her mind. Medical School? She quickly dismissed the thought, returning to her work.

Michael inspected the test in front of him, hoping for another hidden agenda. Nothing. He started thinking about how hard it was going to be over the next hour, having to actually do these problems. Especially the math. He always hated that the most. Looking up at the clock again to see how much time he had left, he immediately calculated the remaining duration, and how much of it was to be allowed for each question. He could see that the ratio provided inadequate sums, leaving only an eighty-five percent probability that he could even finish. He had to shake his head to clear those runaway thoughts. Why was he wasting his time on nonessential, nonproductive mathematical hypothesis? This thought shocked him "What the ... " he said out loud, drawing the attention of the class again and embarrassing himself in the process.

Under the quizzical stares of his classmates, he began the exam.

Somehow, he knew the answers before he'd even finished reading the question, shooting through the booklet like crazy. He checked the clock again. Seeing it still graced him with fifteen minutes, he decided to work on the third exam. At first he was thinking that he should first ask the teacher, but that would once again draw unwanted attention, so he dismissed the idea.

As with the last test, he flew through the answers, proving his earlier calculations of probability to be incorrect. Just as he completed the last question, the teacher spoke.

"Pencils down class. Time's up."

There were plenty of groans and slammed pencils from the frustrated third-graders as Mrs. Tellmen checked the room for compliance.

"Please bring your answer sheets and your first booklets to me," she instructed.

The children clambered to their feet, working their way forward.

"Place the booklet here," she pointed, "and answers here."

Everyone did as instructed, except Michael. He just stood there looking bewildered.

"Oh Michael, I've already collected yours. Don't you remember?" she asked, as if talking to a three-year-old.

"Yes ma'am, but ..." Michael replied, holding the last two exams out in front of him like a gift. The class started to mumble how stupid Michael was for not understanding such simple instructions. Brady even pretended to sneeze the word "stupid" again.

Mrs. Tellmen stood up quickly, pointing her finger at the class.

"That's enough," she said sternly, then turned back to Michael and lightly patted the papers he held. "We'll all work together on these two after a short break," she informed him, then looked at the clock. "I'll stop your time on number two, and you can begin again when the rest of us do."

Thinking she had handled the situation, Mrs. Tellmen sat back down to start marking all the papers with Fs because the lesson would have no meaning without negative consequences.

"Mrs. Tellmen, I've already finished," Michael said nervously.

The teacher's head popped up in amazement. "You've finished the second test already?" she asked.

Michael began to rock back and forth on the balls of his feet. "Well, no," he confessed.

"I didn't think it was possible given the time ...," she was saying when Michael interrupted her.

"I'm finished with both booklets, number two and number three."

Mrs. Tellmen jumped back to her feet. "What?" she barked, grabbing the papers from his hand. "That's impossible," she added while quickly checking over the exams, she discovered every answer was completed. "Don't you want to recheck your work," she offered, thinking he must have just filled in anything to get done.

"No ma'am, I do not," Michael replied.

The whole class was now watching in awe.

"Go sit down then," she said angrily, waving him away with the test papers. She sat back down to correct Michael's papers first. That way she could force him to do them right the next time. She'd teach him to try to pulling the wool over her eyes.

"Class, you can begin the next booklet," she said, then began going over Michael's answer sheet thoroughly. It took her almost as long to review his work as it had taken him to complete it in the first place. Both exams scored one hundred. She couldn't comprehend how he'd done it, but she knew he had cheated.

"Mr. Clark! Come up here and bring your worksheet," she ordered.

Michael got a knot in his stomach when he looked down at the empty piece of paper on his desk. He hadn't used it at all.

"Yes ma'am," he said, then timidly walked to her side.

The teacher took one look at his blank work sheet and went off.

"That proves it," she yelled, slamming the paper down in front of her, drawing the attention of the class. "Back to work!" she spat, re-directing her anger. Only Brady found the situation comical. Mrs. Tellmen glared straight into Michael's eyes. "Okay young man! The truth! How did you cheat?" she demanded.

Michael stepped back in shock.

"I didn't," he replied.

The teacher grew angrier.

"Empty your pockets!" she ordered him.

He did as directed. The only thing he produced was a gum wrapper.

"Roll up your shirt! Now!" she went on. He did and she checked for hidden crib sheets, finding nothing.

Michael started to tear up over his own anger starting to surface.

"I'm telling you, I didn't cheat!" he said sternly, then pulled his shirt down really hard before crossing his arms. "This is classified as character assassination and slander. I demand an apology this instant for your inappropriate and unprofessional behavior," he said.

This was the straw that broke the camel's back. She came around her desk with murder in her eyes.

"You demand nothing in this classroom," she growled through clenched teeth, pulling up a chair. "Sit!" she ordered. Then she marched over to Michael's desk and searched its contents. It didn't take long. It was completely empty. She then checked the surrounding area. Still finding nothing, she stomped like a spoiled child back to the front, then slammed herself down into her chair like a teenaged drama queen. "I don't know how you did it, but you had to cheat!" she accused.

Michael looked at her as if she'd grown a third eye.

"I assure you to the contrary," he said calmly.

Mrs. Tellmen jerked open her desk drawer and produced two copies of the test.

"Alright smart guy! How about you just do these again?" she suggested with her holier-than-thou attitude, handing them to Michael.

"Gladly," he responded. Accepting the booklets, he turned to return to his desk.

"No sir! You'll do them right here where I can watch!" she said, knowing that she'd out-smarted him.

Michael sat back down with unbelievable confidence.

"May I borrow your pen?" he asked, holding his hand out to accept the unoffered ballpoint. Reluctantly, she gave it to him. "Thank you, may I begin?" he asked politely. At the nod of her head, Michael started redoing the exams. The answers came to him faster and easier than the first time. Most were stored in his memory.

Mrs. Tellmen watched in amazement as the child zipped through the questions. She could see that he wasn't cheating and it caused her some anxiety. How could she apologize in front of the class? If she did so, she'd risk losing control of them. But how could she not?

Eight minutes later, Michael placed the pen down gently on the answer sheets and pushed himself back from the desk.

"Would you be so kind as to check those to confirm their

correctness?" he asked, crossing his arms and legs.

Mrs. Tellmen was clearly uncomfortable when she pulled the answer sheets into a viewable position. There was still forty-five minutes until the rest of her class would finish, so there wasn't any saving distractions close at hand to end the confrontation between her and the overly confident red-head.

Once again, it had taken her longer to review his answers than it had taken him to do them. The first had a perfect score and she started to feel a weakness in her intestines. This was a bad situation that could only get worse. She had already been warned to approach Michael with a gentle heart because of the trauma involving his family's death, and now, here she was not only angry at him, but calling him a liar and a cheat. *'This could turn out very bad for a new teacher like me,'* she thought.

The second test proved to be perfect as well. She lowered the papers to her desktop before facing Michael, who had stood up and placed his hands on his hips. His looks reminded her of her father when he'd catch her in a lie. Plus, Michael was tapping his foot, adding to a fatherly image. She actually felt intimidated.

"Well, I'm waiting," he said, staring right through her. The roles had changed, she was now the one who felt like crying, and she could feel every eye in the room on her.

"Please," she squeaked. "Go have a seat. We'll talk about this later," she requested, obviously whipped. "Please," she asked again.

Michael started to comply by heading toward his desk, and then stopped. He turned back around to face his teacher. He looked more sophisticated than his years could have ever produced.

"I do believe you owe me a public apology before an audience of my peers. After all, the verbal contamination of my true character was on display before my fellow students." Michael no longer tried to retain his newfound intellect. "No other configuration of appeasement will be accepted or tolerated," he announced, then stood there in perfect silence. It seemed that even the birds outside held back to hear the outcome of this statement.

Mrs. Tellmen looked around the room in desperation. She quickly decided to pull Michael aside and walked up to him, grabbing at his arm. Not understanding her intentions, Michael stepped aside, causing her to miss. She tried again. This time he knocked her hand away with a sweeping block without even thinking about it.

The teacher's anger went all the way to her top floor.

"That's it young man! Get your smart butt to the principal's office this second," she ordered while pointing to the door. "I'll see you there and we'll see who owes who what!"

Michael calmly started for the door. "I believe the proper English usage would be 'Who owes whom'," he corrected. Just before he stepped into the hall, he paused to face her one last time. "You are correct; a confrontation between us is inevitable. However, for now I shall not dignify your egotistical dialogue any further, so good day to you!" he said exiting the room, leaving a very angry teacher at a loss for words.

♦ ♦ ♦ ♦ ♦

The hallways were completely empty because all the classes were still in session. Michael left the third grade wing and headed for the principal's office as instructed. The silence of the locker-lined corridor helped to clear his thoughts. The reality of what had just happened started to surface. *'What have you done?'* He asked himself. *'Michael Clark, have you lost your redheaded mind?'* Wondering if he may be forced to leave school forever.

'You just have to tell the truth. You've done nothing that I wouldn't have under the same circumstances,' came the voice of his dad. That one voice that he'd been hearing since he awakened in the hospital.

"You mean what you did do. That was you in there, not me, dad!" Michael said aloud, and then quickly looked around to make sure the area was still void of others. *'Well, I'll be there to help again if you need me,'* responded Tim in Michael's head.

"Help? You call that help? Doing my test isn't help. Look at the trouble I'm in already!" he responded.

"Excuse me young man, who are you talking to? And why are you not in class?" someone asked from behind.

Michael snapped his head around at the sound of the unfamiliar male voice. There sat a dark skinned man of around thirty years of age. The rubber tires on his wheelchair rolled silently on the floor, which explained how he came from nowhere without detection.

"What? Oh, I'm talking to my dad and it's rather personal!" Michael answered rudely, still peeved at his dad.

The man moved his chair around to a face-to-face position with Michael, and then folded his hands across his lap.

"Sorry I interrupted you. My name is Mr. Williams. I'm the school counselor here at Madison Creek. And you are?" he asked.

Michael failed to answer. He was mesmerized by the man's handicap. So much so, he missed the extended hand that was being offered him. Realizing what he was doing, he looked up quickly.

"Uhm ... uh, I'm Mr. Clark, I'm a student here," he said and then remembered what had happened about ten minutes ago. "At least for the time being," he added.

"Well now, Mr. Clark is it?" Mr. Williams asked respectively, already liking the young man. "I tell you what, even though it's against school policy, you can call me Trevor," he offered with a bright smile, hoping to gain trust.

"Then you may call me Michael," Michael responded

pleasantly.

With the barrier of being strangers now broken, they released each other's hands and once again Michael's curiosity focused on Trevor's artificial limbs.

Following the boy's line-of-sight, Mr. Williams spoke.

"Shotgun blast," he said.

Michael looked up to meet the counselor's eyes, obviously embarrassed about staring.

"I'm sorry ... what?" he said.

"I said shotgun blast. I noticed you were trying to imagine what could have caused me to lose my legs," Trevor answered, then knocked on his prosthetic to emphasize his coming explanation. "I was shot by a drug addict who wanted my wallet worse than I did. Instead, he took my legs off right below the hips, which severed my right femoral artery," he said while making a chopping motion to indicate where they had separated from his body.

Michael contemplated the violence of the act, shaking his head to express his failure to understand how people could be so cruel to one another.

"Man that sucks," he said, then pulled his shirt up over his head to expose his bare shoulder. "A thirty-eight hollow-point, close range, broke my clavicle bone and scapula, severed my sub-clavicle artery, deflated my right lung, then lodged itself between my ribs, where it has set up residence." Then he pointed to his scar. "And this is my cross of Jesus to remind me of why I'm still breathing," he said, pulling his shirt back down.

It was unspoken, but obvious, that the human drama caused by violence, had drawn these two into a bond of friendship, as well as fellowship.

"Well Michael, looks like we have a lot in common," Trevor said, offering his hand again, which Michael accepted.

"Run along to your class now, but if you ever want or need to talk, come to my office," Trevor said.

"Maybe I should come with you now. I've sort of been ... thrown out of class," Michael said, shrugging his shoulders.

"On the first day back? What happened?" Mr. Williams asked, looking very concerned.

"Let me tell you when we get there. It's a long story," Michael requested.

The counselor thought that would be a good idea. Then used his hand to indicate that Michael should lead the way. So like a picture-perfect Norman Rockwell painting, they headed down the hallway, two unfortunate members of an elite group of survivors. A membership that grows larger as social morals decay, separating us from God.

Michael had just finished telling his new friend the story of his clash with Mrs. Tellmen word-for-word. He had been very animated with his movements as the story unfolded, making it a theatrical performance that displayed skill and talent.

The whole time, Mr. Williams analyzed each expression and term for the sound of truth. In his professional status, he was trained to spot a lie, and nothing this adolescent said came across as false. Even when he stopped Michael for a reiteration, the story never changed or wavered from the child's recollection of facts.

"Well, that's quite a first day," Trevor said once Michael had finished. "So where do we go from here?" he asked, tapping out a beat on his desk.

Michael did the same thing and they both laughed. "Well, I guess I should get to Mr. Watson's office before they call out the National Guard. I'm sure by now I'm missed," he said, then got up to leave.

"No, no ... have a seat. I've already spoken to the principal. He knows you're here," Trevor said, underestimating Michael's deductive reasoning.

Michael looked shocked as well as hurt.

"Is there something wrong?" the counselor asked. "You look troubled."

Michael turned red.

"Yeah you jerk, something's wrong! The only way you could have told Mr. Watson that I would be here, is to have done so before we met," he said, and looked down at his shoes to keep from crying. "That means you knew all along. So our friendship ... my trust in you ... you planned this charade before we even talked in the hallway. How could you? Did you really even get shot, or was that just another part of your diabolical trickery? You suck! And I'm leaving!" Michael said and reached for the door.

"Hold on ... hold on please, you're right. I did come looking for you. I'm sorry ... really, really sorry!" Mr. Williams admitted.

"I will agree with you on that point," Michael answered sarcastically. Trevor raised his hands pleadingly.

"I didn't realize how this was going to work out. Most children your age are inaccessible when confronted by a dominating and strange adult. They can actually internalize their feelings for weeks making it almost impossible to communicate with them or help them to come to grips with their problems. Please forgive me," he requested and lowered his hands in submission, feeling shameful. His voice dropped to a sorrowful tone. "I had no idea that we'd become friends, but I assure you that we are and we have the scars to prove it," he said, and rolled his chair closer to Michael to close the gap between them, offering his hand of friendship again. "You can trust me Michael. No more lies, no more misleading you," he promised.

'Man, this guy is a world class con man,' Michael thought.

But in his head was Tim's voice. *'I think he's sincere son. Give him another chance.'*

Michael turned his head to one side, staring suspiciously at the counselor.

"No more lies?" he asked.

"No more lies," Echoed Trevor. "Friends?" he asked as he yet again offered his hand.

Michael spit in the palm of his own hand and waited for Mr. Williams to do the same, then shook with him. "Only on a trial basis. We'll be watching you."

The counselor was wondering what Michael meant by "we will be watching" but didn't want to ask.

The sound of a metal-clanging bell ringing throughout the school building drew their attention. It was soon followed by the pounding footsteps and chattering voices of hundreds of happy children headed for the playground.

Michael looked out into the hallway, then back.

"Can I go to recess please?" he pleaded, and then produced a pouty face.

Mr. Williams was pleased to see that Michael still retained some child-like innocence somewhere deep inside.

"One question first," he said.

Michael started to dance around with anticipation.

"What?" he replied desperately, once again looking out at the quickly emptying corridors.

"What do you want to do about this morning? Would you like to try Mrs. Tellmen again, or would you prefer being transferred to another class?"

Michael stopped fidgeting, clearly concentrating on his future. To the counselor, Michael looked as if he were listening to someone speaking wisdom in his head before answering.

"In the best interest of my future, I'd like to take a high school equivalency test now and a college placement test in a few days," he said.

Mr. Williams started to laugh at what he initially believed to be "Michael Humor", but stopped instantly when Michael didn't laugh along with him.

Displaying a mature confidence, Michael responded.

"I assure you sir, no form of levity was intended. My ambition is to incorporate my time into a more sophisticated plateau of education. The fundamentals administered on an elementary level represent an absence of mental challenges, thus creating an incalculable quantity of negative indifference, clearly annihilating my idealistic future. You would concur, would you not?" Michael asked, looking down the hall again.

Mr. Williams had a dumbfounded look of astonishment dominating his face.

"What?" he asked. "Ah..ahh ... okay, I'll see what I can do. Go play. But come back here after recess," he said, as if in shock.

Michael shook his head at how silly Mr. Williams was acting, and then ran down the hall.

"Great dad! Now I've got Mr. Williams to deal with as well," he voiced.

'I had nothing to do with what just happened. I've been quiet the whole time. It appears that you can will my silence and I'm gone,' Tim said.

Michael was glad to hear that theory. He was starting to believe that he'd never have any time for himself or get away with any childhood antics. The thought made him smile. He burst through the back door into a beautiful, sun-shiny day. The lure of green grass and the sound of children playing forced his legs into overdrive.

◆ ◆ ◆ ◆ ◆

The playground covered an area of just over two acres. Both sets of monkey bars crawled with energetic children burning off their bowls of sugarcoated breakfast cereal. Michael was slightly disappointed; the monkey bars were his favorite. Next came the swings.

"Oh man!" he said, watching the last of the twenty-four available seats become occupied.

The extravagance of the schoolyard began to lose some of its appeal and his enthusiasm along with it. He turned to see a large number of kids standing in line for a chance at the only slide. Others simply ran back and forth in one form of shenanigans or another.

Michael's shoulders dropped, clearly displeased about being held up by Mr. Williams until all the cool stuff was saturated with other children.

Slowly, he began walking toward a row of park style benches, disgustedly kicking the mulch with every step. After inserting his hands into the front pockets of his pants, he dropped himself down on the closest seat and began swinging his dangling feet.

'What's the matter buddy?' Tim asked.

"I don't know. It's like the magic has gone from this place," Michael answered, then looked up at the passing clouds. "They're so beautiful. Are you on one of those clouds dad?" he questioned with a whisper.

'No honey. I'm not sure how to explain my whereabouts. When you need me, I'm part of you. When you don't, I guess I spontaneously cease to be,' said his dad's voice from inside his head.

"That's weird!" Michael responded aloud, and then scanned the area to make sure no one else caught him talking to himself before he continued the conversation with his dad.

"Dad, I told Mr. Williams to give me the appropriate tests to show how smart I am and will get me out of school sooner."

'There's nothing wrong with a little ambition and being intelligent son,' Tim pointed out.

"I know dad, it's just that … it's your intelligence, not mine. I feel like I'm cheating," Michael confessed.

'Think of it this way son, everything we learn in life comes from someone else's experiences, education and ideas. They share their knowledge with us through textbooks, lectures or even word-of-mouth and it becomes ours to use, improve and pass on. Somehow, your mind is absorbing my wisdom. Overall, I'm teaching you what I've learned just like I would be doing if I were there. It may be incredibly fast, but it's not cheating,' Tim explained.

Michael thought about it for a few seconds, then smiled.

"Cool!" he said, "But what about the yucky stuff with girls?" he asked.

'Just shut me out if something comes up that makes you uncomfortable,' Tim suggested.

"Dad, why do I feel so differently about things? I never used to just sit during recess," Michael asked, then lowered his head to look at the dirt on the tips of his shoes.

'I guess with wisdom comes maturity,' Tim answered.

"That sucks," Michael said.

'Yes it does son, it really does,' Tim replied.

Michael sat quietly contemplating everything that had happened to him over the last few years. *'Maybe I should write a book,'* he thought to himself. *'People would love to read all about my pain and suffering, the violence and survival, spirits, the After Life and …'* His thoughts were interrupted by the sight of Brady and three of his derelict band of self imposed desperadoes coming his way.

"And here comes chapter thirteen," he said.

'Don't worry son. I'm right here with you. Together we'll
134

outsmart them,' Tim boasted.

"Thanks dad, but you've got to have a brain to be able to be outsmarted. These four lack the necessities. What I need is Jackie Lee," he admitted.

The voice of the karate champ filled Michael's mind like opening a flood gate at the Hoover Dam. *'I'm here young one. Your next lesson begins now.'*

Startled, Michael let out an involuntary yelp, simultaneously jumping to his feet. His heart played "Wipe Out" in his chest.

The group of approaching bullies took Michael's actions as a sign of fear, and quickened their pace.

"Jackie! Why haven't you said something before now?" Michael asked.

'As it is with your father, I cannot be unless required with your open mind,' Jackie explained.

Michael thought of the move he had made so naturally when Mrs. Tellmen grabbed at him. Now he understood how it was possible that he was able to perform it so perfectly, even though he couldn't remember ever learning it.

The ruffians were now within ten feet, so Michael quickly and quietly asked, "Jackie, what do I do?"

Jackie laughed, *'Nothing. I'll fight this one for you. Just open your mind, releasing yourself to me.'*

'Violence is not the answer. We need -' interrupted Tim. But before he could fully voice his objection, Michael closed the door on him, opening fully to the champ.

"Smooth move in class ex-lax!" Brady said, and those with him laughed, boosting his ego and giving him further incentive to puff out his chest and continue with his verbal attack. "Freckles come from eating fried farts in garlic," he added, faking a punch at one of his cronies, egging them to join in.

"We'd rather be dead than red!" one of the other guys

confessed.

Michael only stood there with his hands crossed at his waist until the boys finished.

"Then please grant me the honor and privilege of helping you to achieve your goal," Michael offered.

The laughter came to a halt. Brady had what he came for: an excuse to fight. His eyes filled with hate.

"Yeah right, puke face! Screw you!" He said roughly.

"I'm flattered. However, I must assure you that I do not share your homosexual tendencies," Michael responded calmly, waving his hand as a grandmother would dismiss a bothersome child.

The confused boys quickly looked back and forth at each other wanting to see if any of them comprehended what Michael had said.

"What's that supposed to mean puke face?" Brady asked through clinched teeth.

Michael responded with the patience of a preacher correcting a lost parishioner.

"Well dumb one, if you retained the intelligence God gave a mule to sit down on, you would've understood," he said.

Brady doubled his fist at his side and stomped his feet, looking like a bull about to charge. However, the lack of fear in Michael's eyes caused him to pause. He looked to his comrades for support but they, too, seemed reluctant.

"Get him!" Brady ordered.

The three boys began to circle around their victim like jackals, blocking any route of escape in case their pray attempted to flee. Still uncertain of what to do, and unaccustomed to fist fighting, the boy on Michael's left acted first. He sprang forward in an attempt to bear hug his target. All Michael did was lower his body weight to one knee, causing the attacker to tumble over him, then stood up as the boy was above him, sending the bully into an involuntary spin, which landed him face first on the bench with a loud crack of nasal bone breaking before rolling into the dirt.

By this time, a crowd started to gather and the small confrontation had become the main attraction of a three-ring circus.

The two remaining boys charged at the same time, almost as if choreographed with corresponding dives. Also, as if rehearsed, Michael jumped back in the air, landing on the park bench behind him. The aggressors heads impacted with a hollow thud like two colliding coconuts. Both fell to the ground with their already fallen cohort, forming a human pile of defeated, embarrassed and crying children.

For a second or two, Michael stood over them admiring the effects of his move and smiled. He then slowly and dramatically raised his eyes like he'd seen Clint Eastwood do in the movie "High Plains Drifter", meeting Brady's frightened stare. Fear had transformed the bigger boy's features from an angry demon, to one of an innocent, misunderstood child.

Everyone silently waited with the anticipation of what was coming next. Then Michael descended from his perch in a cartwheel, landing less than four feet from where Brady stood frozen in awe. He then parted his legs like he were riding a horse, cocked his left hand back into a punching position, his right arm straight out in front level with his shoulder in a traditional karate stance. Turning his right palm up, he began opening and closing his fingers, inviting Brady to come closer.

The playground attendant arrived just in time to keep Brady from the embarrassment of getting his butt whipped by a much smaller boy.

"What's going on here?" the thin lady asked. She then looked down at the crying boys who were now coming to their feet, covered with mulch. "And what happened to them? Are you boys fighting?"

Michael lowered his arm and stood up straight. "I didn't touch a hair on their heads. Honestly," he said.

The older woman scanned the faces of all the children before coming to rest on the injured trio.

"Is that true?" she asked.

The boys didn't answer. Instead, they busied themselves with the task of removing debris from their hair and clothing, and using the backs of their hands to wipe away the still flowing tears.

"I said is that true?" she repeated with a louder voice.

The would-be band of marauders looked at each other uncertainly, and then at Michael. If they lied, they knew their paths would someday cross Michael's again, so the newly found respect they had for the small red headed boy made them tell the truth.

"Yes ma'am," they responded in unison.

The attendant raised her eyebrow in disbelief.

"Then you three go inside and get cleaned up before the bell rings. Move it!" she ordered as she refocused her attention on Michael and Brady. "Is there a problem here?" she asked while towering over them like an incoming storm.

Both boys shook their heads as a reply.

The woman crossed her arms over her chest to help emphasize her point. "Good! Let's keep it that way. Comprendé?" she instructed.

This time, both boys nodded, so the attendant turned and walked away, leaving silence and the smell of her perfume lingering in the air.

The second that she was far enough away not to overhear, Brady started in again on Michael.

"You're lucky Clark! Ms. Mary saved your butt! I was about to pound you!" He said, puffing out his chest again to look intimidating, and maybe to salvage his reputation in front of all the other kids.

Brady was a head taller, so Michael had to look up in order to respond. He winked and spoke like a southern bell.

"Why yes, I do declare. I owe her my very life," he said comically, placing the back of his hand to his forehead, like he was feeling faint, and receiving more than a few laughs. "I don't know what would have become of me and father's farm without her," he went on sarcastically, and then laughed at Brady's threat before changing his tone. "Ha! Anytime you feel the need to bully anyone on this playground again, come see me first and I'll beat it out of you. Or, if you ever need to prove something, I'll be here to oblige you. Now go away while you still can," he suggested.

Brady scanned the congregation of students for their reactions. His eyes filled with moisture as he turned and walked away without another word.

The watching children moved in on their new hero. Congratulating him with cheers, pats on the back, and handshakes. They had been liberated from their school bullies and couldn't refrain from expressing their joy. The noise level was high enough to ask a quick question of his inner friend.

"Why didn't we just beat them up?" Michael asked.

'My young friend,' answered Jackie's voice, *'Don't you see how effectively you have crushed your enemy? Fighting could have caused you injury, plus breaking the rules of your school. A true warrior knows when to act with force or to let the forces act for him.'*

Michael did enjoy the way he allowed the attacking boys to defeat themselves. But he still wished he could have thrown at least one really cool punch.

"Thanks," he whispered, finding his way back to his previous seat.

Some of the children dispersed back to their sunshine coated activities. Others, however, were so infatuated over what they had witnessed that they gathered around Michael as if he were about to divulge some divine words of wisdom that had been handed down through the ages.

Not really sure what he was to say or what they expected, Michael started retelling the story of his life and death struggle. He thought about asking for his dad's assistance in the tale, but quickly found it unnecessary. The story unfolded naturally as the truth always does. He did find it more comfortable to leave out the return of Jackie and his dad's spirits because, just as in the case of Dr. Johnson, these newfound friends would think he's crazy.

◆ ◆ ◆ ◆ ◆

Michael had just finished removing his shirt, displaying the scar that would verify his story when the bell rang, which indicated the end of recess.

Children from every direction ran grumbling and moaning to the center sidewalk to line up, just as it had been done for years. This is always a time for pushing and shoving for position. No one wants to go inside, but for some reason known only to elementary aged children, the front is the place to be. And God help anyone who tries to cut in line.

Slowly, Michael strolled up to the back of the line, prolonging the feel of the great outdoors as long as possible. A shadow came up on his right side, drawing his attention. Immediately sensing danger, he spun around to face it. The sun was blinding, keeping the apparition from full view, so he lifted his hand in order to shield his eyes from the brilliant globe, just in time to see an incoming fist. Thankfully, his hand was already coming up; otherwise, he would not have been fast enough to slap away the incoming threat. The block was effective enough to spin the attacker a step to the left, allowing Michael a second to slide into position a little to the right, which removed the aggressor's advantage of invisibility. Now Michael could see who he faced, and it temporarily confused him. It was Brady, only somehow he'd grown a lot larger.

"You're about to get pounded punk! I'll teach you to mess with my little brother," the boy said. Michael now knew that he was dealing with a bigger member of the same defective gene pool that had produced Brady. The family resemblance was uncanny.

From behind, Michael heard the voice of the younger inbred family member. Actually, Brady was so close to Michael's back, he could feel rhythmic puffs of breath on the back of his neck. Brady either was still getting over the earlier confrontation, or very excited about the violence soon to occur.

"Teach this puke face that he can't mess with the big boys Bobby!" Brady exclaimed.

Michael started to laugh at how stupid that sounded.

"What is this, a Brady bunch reunion?" Michael asked, refusing to allow these jug heads to produce even the slightest indication of fear in him, which he accomplished, elevating Bobby's anger in the process.

Michael detected a slight movement in the bigger boy's shoulder and instinctively knew that another punch was on the way.

Like a highly trained ninja, he dropped into a perfect split position a fraction of a second before the projected fist parted his hair.

Bobby had held nothing back, and the sound of breaking teeth was impressive. Droplets of blood and spittle rained down on Michael's bare arms. Then came the dull thud of a body crashing to earth. A half second later, a high-pitched scream filled the air in a combination of eagle cry and that sound the phone company uses to punish us for dialing the wrong number.

Every mouth shut. Every eye turned toward the source of the ear-bursting shriek to find Brady rolling in the grass, holding his mouth with both hands as blood poured from between his fingers. Apparently, he was the unfortunate, and unintended, recipient of his older brother's rage.

Still in a crouching stance, Michael looked on as Bobby's mind filled with the horror of what he'd done to his sibling's ten thousand dollars worth of wasted dental work.

"Well, no more Mr. Perfect! Bet you'll have a hard time explaining this one to your dad," Michael said unsympathetically, which instantly drew the bully's attention back to his original prey. Michael saw Bobby's eyes clear of any human emotion except rage. The boy looked like a bloodthirsty predator; nothing mattered to him now except the kill. Only one other time had Michael witnessed this degree of hate and that was in the eyes of David Watts as he repeatedly pulled the trigger in the attempt to end Michael's young life. Bobby raised his booted foot high over Michael's head, screaming like a wild animal intending to squash a pesky bug.

Michael spun on the ball of one foot, spinning backward with the other leg extended; his foot connecting at the calf of Bobby's supporting leg, sending it involuntarily into the air. The effect was perfect and dropped the big boy on his back, hitting shoulder first. If he were a middle-aged man, it would have broken some bones, most likely his neck. The thud came along with a groaning swish of air as every molecule of oxygen was forced from Bobby's lungs. All he could do now was lay there and gasp, his mouth opening and closing like a fish out of water.

Michael stood up just as Ms. Mary arrived.

"You again?" she asked accusingly.

"Not me!" Michael answered innocently.

The attendant turned her attention to Brady who was rolling around in the grass, blood still flowing, which had already soaked the front of his shirt.

"Oh my God!" she exclaimed, quickly kneeling by the injured boy's side. "What have you done?" she asked, once again turning to face Michael.

Michael pointed at Bobby.

"If you'll examine his hand, I'm sure you'll find contusions in the shape of your bleeder's teeth, or what's left of them," Michael suggested.

Ms. Mary gave a quick glance at Bobby's hand as advised.

"Okay, I can see what happened to Brady. But what about him?" she asked, now pointing to Bobby.

"After he hit his little brother, he decided to kick my brains out. I didn't really care for the idea, so I took his legs out from under him," Michael explained.

Another teacher showed up and quickly took charge of assisting Brady to the nurses' station. While she escorted the bleeding, wobbling and crying child away, Ms. Mary took Bobby by the arm in order to help him stand. At first, all he could do was place his hands on his knees and try to control his breathing, but that only lasted a few minutes before returning to normal. However, his anger wasn't extinguished and he actually growled at Michael as he came at him yet again.

Ms. Mary tried to hold onto Bobby's arm in an attempt to restrain him. To the amazement of everyone watching, Bobby pushed her to the ground and continued toward the object of his hatred, clearly out of control.

He began throwing punches, the first being a haymaker that went wild. The next was a jab that Michael caught mid swing.

Now that Michael had control of Bobby's arm, he pulled it in a downward motion, forcing the boy to bend forward. Next, he wind-milled his right foot over the locked arm, landing the sole of his propelled foot on the right side of Bobby's jaw, returning the leg in the same fashion by a snap of his knee. This time, the top of his foot connected with the bridge of Bobby's nose.

Michael released the grip on his opponent's arm, stepping back to see if his attacker was finished. He wasn't. Bobby took a quick look at the woman still trying to get to her feet, shook his head to clear the pain and blood, which flowed freely from his nostril, then proceeded to charge like a raging buffalo.

Ducking under another punch, Michael stepped to one side of the aggressor and struck the boy across the chest with an open hand, straight-arm strike. Bobby's feet continued to move forward, but the rest of him did not, which once again slammed him to the ground with a sickening thud. He recovered quickly and rolled over into a push-up position.

Michael tried to reason with him.

"Stay down Bobby before you force me to really hurt you," he advised.

Bobby grabbed two hands-full of dirt before standing, and then stood there breathing like a locomotive building up steam.

"I'm going to kill you Clark!" he yelled while throwing the dust and debris in Michael's face and attacking with a barrage of ineffective punches.

Thinking he'd better put a stop to Bobby's assault, Michael performed a simple front kick to the boy's chin, stopping Bobby in his tracks. The "big boy" began teetering back and forth, his eyes losing focus as he lost consciousness, and finally fell forward like a great oak being taken down by a lumberjack.

Michael stepped in and caught the boy before he could hit the sidewalk where it was likely to split his head wide open. He then lowered Bobby's limp body gently to the grass.

Voices started coming from all directions concerning the fight and the compassion displayed by the victor.

Ms. Mary came over to Michael's side.

"What did you say your name was young man?" she asked nicely.

"I'm Jackie Lee," he responded. "I mean Michael. Michael Clark," he quickly corrected himself.

Ms. Mary looked at Michael strangely. "Okay Michael, or Jackie, you'll need to explain this mess," she said.

"I assure you ma'am, none of this is my doing. You'll have to agree that I fought only in self defense," he explained.

Ms. Marry nodded her head in compliance.

"Yes, I'm aware that you had no other choice. However, the rules are very clear about fighting," she said, then looked over at Bobby. "He very well may be out for a while. Why don't you go on inside. I'll have you called to the office later."

Michael started walking in the direction of the school building. All the children gave him a wide berth. He could see fear in the eyes of every one of them. The realization that he would never fit in now weighed heavy on his heart.

'You had no other choice my young friend. It was either him or you.' Jackie offered up as a form of consolation.

"What about you, dad? Did you think I had another choice?" Michael asked as he reached the entry doors, thinking he was going to hear the intellectual way. But he didn't.

'Choice about what? You put me in the dark,' Tim answered.

Michael found this humorous and began to laugh.

"Boy dad, Mr. Lee and I have a really cool story to tell you," he said.

'What do you mean? Jackie Lee is dead,' Tim said.

"Yes dad, I know. But so are you, remember?" Michael responded.

'Oh yeah.' Tim replied, and they laughed together as Michael made his way down the hall.

♦ ♦ ♦ ♦ ♦

His knock was answered on the third rap by the familiar voice of Trevor Williams.

"Please come in," said Trevor.

Michael entered without speaking and took a seat in front of the counselor's desk. The variation in temperature between the sun drenched playground and the air conditioned office was enough to make Michael feel like he was freezing to death, so he sat on his hands, rocking back and forth in a futile attempt to warm himself.

The counselor had been sitting with his back to the door speaking on the phone. Spinning around, he held up his index finger, requesting a moment longer, pointing at the receiver he was holding to his ear.

Michael didn't see any reason for the hand gestures. He felt his intelligence was being insulted, as if the counselor didn't think Michael understood the concept of being on the phone.

Next, Trevor gave him a thumbs-up, and Michael had a hard time resisting the urge to flip the man a bird. But in his mind, he told himself to dismiss the insults as an unconscious, idiosyncrasy of an intellectually inferior individual. Fortunately, he was looking at the floor when that thought came to mind.

"Whoa Nelly, where did that thought come from?" he asked himself out loud, then quickly lifted his foot, pretending to examine the bottom of his shoe, as if some foreign object clung to its surface. Otherwise, he may have had to explain to Trevor what he was talking about with his boisterous outburst.

A few minutes passed, and the counselor finally said his goodbyes, carefully hanging up the phone. Then he placed his hands on the desk with his fingers interlaced. His face seemed to brighten as his focus turned on Michael.

"Well my new friend, how was recess?" he asked, his smile

146

displaying a real interest.

Michael lifted his eyebrow and his mouth dropped open in disbelief and mistrust.

"Horse shit!" he spat.

Trevor recoiled as if slapped and raised his hands in the air to surrender.

"What did I do?" he asked.

Michael looked the man over for any signs of deceit. Not detecting any, he squinted his eyes.

"I was wondering if you already knew the answer to that question. And if so, why do you continue to underestimate my level of intelligence and insult me with your poor attempts to psychoanalyze responses to inquiries that you already have the answers to," he said, then placed his little finger to his mouth and his thumb to his ear, mimicking the counselor's movements upon his initial arrival.

Catching the drift of his guest's performance, Trevor understood why he was being mistrusted.

"No sir, that was my wife," he explained, pointing at the phone. "She wants me to bring home some hamburgers for supper. It seems that she has had a bad day and now has a bad headache."

Michael could see the frustration building in Trevor's face and knew that he was telling the truth.

"What happened? Was the Oprah show a rerun?" he asked and then laughed.

At first, Mr. Williams looked shocked but then couldn't help giving in to Michael's humor.

"No. I think the presidential address interrupted General Hospital, as well as Days of Our Lives," he mused. The two busted out laughing with each other like two old men bashing their wives.

"Oh my God, no! Please don't let it be so!" Michael added as if shocked. "You better take home some candy and flowers if she missed her soaps," he suggested, and tears started running down his face from laughing so hard.

"I'll be sleeping in the car for sure," Trevor cut in, joining the laughter.

Not that either of them found their statements that funny. It was more like they shared a common pain with every married man in the country.

Trevor was wiping the moisture from his eyes when he realized that he was sharing adult camaraderie with an eight year old.

"How old did you say you were again?" he asked, still not in complete control of his snickering.

"Physically or psychologically?" Michael asked, barely able to open his eyes.

After a few minutes, they were both able to calm down. They sat looking at each other, lost in their own thoughts.

"Well Michael," Trevor began, "I guess we should get back to business. Did you think about what you wanted to do?" he asked.

"Yes I have," Michael said, after getting complete control of himself. "Let me reiterate my earlier statements of desire," he began, standing up and placing his hands on the desktop. "First the GED and then a college placement exam," he said with a smile and waited for a response.

"Michael, you're eight years old. I can see that you're very intelligent; your articulation and vocabulary is way above normal range for a third grader," Trevor said, "But you can't seriously think that you can pass a high school equivalency exam, do you?" the counselor asked, putting on his "I know best," face.

Michael didn't bite.

"Try me!" he challenged without the slightest hint of humor, his blue eyes shining like pools of pure water on a cloudless day.

The next step was the counselors to take, and he knew he'd have to tread carefully. He knew he didn't believe that Michael could possibly be ready to take such an advanced test. But he also didn't want to hurt Michael's feelings, just in case the child really did believe himself to be that smart. Either way, he decided to go step by delicate step.

"Okay. First let's take a look at the exams you took this morning, shall we?" Trevor said, removing the answer sheets from a file that he'd already placed on his desk.

Because the file was already on the counselor's desk, Michael once again felt that he was being manipulated. He unconsciously shook his head. Not enough for anyone to notice, just himself. *'Some habits never die,'* he thought to himself, but decided not to hold it against the man. They really had become friends.

Michael reseated himself and leaned back, crossing his arms and legs to wait for Mr. Williams to go over his work. Finally feeling warm and comfortable, he closed his eyes and slipped off into a dream-filled nap.

Little Brandon Millichamp lay on the operating table beneath a pure white sheet. A black band was wrapped around his exposed right arm, hissing as it filled with air to check his blood pressure. Another device enclosed his index finger, reading his pulse. The side of his head was shaved and the skin was marked where the incision would be made.

A woman of an undetermined age stood behind the table. Like a Muslim woman, her body was covered from head to toe in blue cloth, except her eyes, which were unnaturally red. A green glove covered her right hand, which was extended over the patient. In her palm was a shiny metal scalpel that seemed to emit its own light.

"Doctor, we're ready," she said as a similarly dressed nurse

joined her.

This one held a respirator mask in one hand, and what looked like a vacuum hose in the other.

"Doctor, we're ready!" she exclaimed, joining the chant.

Then came a third person, a forth and a fifth, all holding some strange form of surgical apparatus. They each added to the defining chorus, "Doctor, we're ready!"

The doors to the operating room burst open with a bang and David Watts forced his way in. He was wearing the same black clothes that he had worn the day he shot Sara. He was dragging someone behind him by the collar of that person's lab coat. It was Tim, who came to his knees and desperately tried to reach the table to save Brandon's life. But the harder he pulled, the harder Watts pulled him back.

"Please let me operate or he'll die," Tim pleaded. All Watts would do is laugh like a crazed hyena. His right hand came around from behind him holding the biggest gun Michael had ever seen. Watts placed the barrel to his captive's temple and, somehow, looked out of the dream into Michael's eyes and smiled.

Michael could see a demon as David rolled his head back with a sick demented laugh and pulled the trigger.

"No!" Michael screamed, jumping to his feet to fight off the threat that was no longer there, except in his memory.

Mr. Williams sprang half way out of his wheelchair.

"Shit!" he yelled as his heart took up new residence in his throat. "What the hell?" he added then caught himself before he said anything else inappropriate in front of a student. "What … what's wrong?" he asked, apparently unaware that Michael had fallen asleep.

Still on the edge of reality, Michael scanned the room again for the killer, and then focused his eyes on Trevor.

"Ah, nothing; I guess I must have been dreaming," Michael responded with a trembling voice.

Waiting for his heart rate to return to normal, Mr. Williams spoke again.

"Man! I think I messed my pants," he said, lowering his hands from his chest. "That literally scared the living crap out of me," he admitted. Then, feeling foolish over his reaction and his choice of words, he began to laugh at himself.

Michael tried his best to share in the levity, but the impact of the lethal and pragmatic daydream still had him in its grips. All he could manage was an artificial sounding chuckle, so unreal it stopped the counselor's laughter.

"Are you alright?" he asked. His face and body language exhibiting the legitimate and authentic concern of a true friend, and Michael noticed.

Now that he felt like he had someone who cared, Michael thought about unloading everything he'd kept bottled up for the last four years. But to do so, he'd have to be honest about every traumatic event, thus re-living the horrors surrounding his short life.

However, he was confident that if he shared so completely, he and his new friend would be found hanging from the rafters in the morning. In his mind's eye, he could see the headlines of tomorrow's paper: TWO FOUND HANGING IN DOUBLE SUICIDE!

So, with that thought in mind, he simply said, "Yes."

Trevor gave Michael a "Bullshit" look.

"Are you sure you're alright?" he asked again.

Michael could tell right away that Mr. Williams was going to keep digging until he provided some answers. It was his job to comfort his clients and that need was ingrained. So Michael decided to give a little.

"I just realized something. The crazed monster that is responsible for the deaths of my parents, my friend Jackie and two security guards, indirectly caused the death of some children at Vanderbilt's Children's Ward," he said, pausing to consider the emphatic truth and the impact of that statement. "If Watts hadn't fatally wounded him, my dad could have saved the life of a boy named Brandon." He paused, lowering his head to hide the tears that were involuntarily forming in the corners of his eyes. "I can't help but wonder how many more will parish because of one detestable, non-sympathetic abomination of hell." The grief he was feeling gave over to pure rage. "If I could get my hands on that putrid spawn of Satan, I'd send him back to his father in pieces," he said and doubled up his fists, slamming them down on the desk with tremendous force. His anger seemed to rejuvenate him; he felt really alive and invulnerable. He lifted up his hands and studied them as if he'd never seen them before. Never had he felt this kind of enthusiasm over anticipated violence, or have it grip him so passionately. It was almost inebriating, and he liked it. Looking up, he met Mr. William's shocked and mesmerized stare.

"David Watts and his gang of trash will die by my hands," Michael stated, no longer worried about the consequences.

The incandescent light of the room gave Michael's face the tormented look of someone five-times his age. The sight made the hair on the back of Trevor's neck stand on end. The sensation was from a mixture of fear and sympathy. He'd never seen such determination in such a young face.

The two sat in complete silence for what felt like an eternity. The sound of a ticking clock was like a beating drum.

Michael finally disrupted the stillness.

"I'm sorry." he admitted, then looked down at his hands that were getting redder by the second.

Another few minutes of quiet dragged past. This time, Trevor spoke first.

"Right now, I think we should talk about what you just said. You're harboring way too much anger, hatred and pain. It's not healthy for a person of any age, especially yours," he pointed out as he began to clear his desk, preparing to change their friendly talk into a therapeutic session. This was something that Michael wanted to avoid at any cost.

Understanding the counselor's intentions, Michael desperately sought to redirect the conversation.

"I don't think this is the proper time for history. My future is my primary concern right now," he explained and acted as if the topic depressed him. "Once I get the next part of my life established, I'll be a lot more comfortable in communicating with you about my past," he lied, and felt awful about it. He knew very well that he'd never feel right discussing anything like that with anyone but his dad.

Mr. Williams wanted to argue, but could tell by Michael's expression it would be a waste of time, possibly building a wall between them and closing off any chances of future therapy.

"Well then," he said and pulled the file back to the center of the desk. "I went over the test you took this morning and found something odd I wish to discuss with you ..." he paused and spun the papers around before sliding them in front of Michael. "What puzzles me is this," he said, pointing his finger at the first answer sheet. "See the handwriting? It's typical third-grade," he said and tapped the paper to emphasize his point. Then he did the same thing on the second sheet. "And see here, this is the hand-writing of a college graduate. How ...? If you filled out both, how do you explain the drastic differences?" he asked and leaned back in his chair. Feeling superior, he folded his hands to wait for a response.

Michael nervously leaned forward and retrieved the documents in question. After a minute or two, he halfheartedly tossed them back, taking his own relaxed position in his chair.

"It's quite obvious to me, as it should have been to you. The first set of tests was of course a total surprise. My level of tension, caused by the pressure to complete them on time, and my anxiety over the uncertain contents were all elevated. These factors cause haste and sloppiness," he explained calmly, His analogy coming so naturally, he felt he could fly. "And these second exams," he began again, "I had already seen in their entirety. I no longer needed to push myself. I was very confident and I had little to no stress. It allowed me to create a more legible and tranquil form of script," he explained, and then waved his hand to dismiss the issue as properly handled.

Mr. Williams had no idea how to proceed, that wasn't the answer he was expecting, and it more or less put him on the spot.

"Ah," was all he could think of to say. He quickly busied himself by removing some other papers from a separate file. What he produced were two more test booklets. Only these were twice as thick as the ones that Michael had already completed. "What I have here are copies of our fifth grade placement exams. Would you like to take a shot at them?" he asked.

Michael shook his head, "No sir, I would not. I requested a twelfth grade level. Did I not?" Michael answered. "If I can pass the twelfth grade tests, I'll no longer be required to attend public schools."

Trevor studied Michael's face.

"You can't be serious," he said with a little irritation beginning to surface in his voice.

Michael returned the stare, and the attitude.

"I'm as serious as a cardio infarction with accompanied pneumoniary edema," he answered.

The counselor threw his arms in the air, giving the impression of giving up to frustration, which was clearly evident on his face.

"Okay Michael!" Trevor snapped irritably. "Do me a favor ...

no wait! Humor me. I'm sure you'll find it's not as easy as you think."

Again, Michael mimicked the counselor's drama-queen arm and hand movements.

"Hand the stupid things here!" he said with some irritation of his own, then accepted the test and number two pencil.

Mr. Williams looked up at the clock feeling triumphant.

"We have a little over thirty minutes before we go to lunch, so I'll stop you in time to eat. You can finish when you return," he said.

Michael looked at the clock as well.

"Whatever! Can we get started?" he asked.

"Yes. You may begin," Trevor answered, then leaned back and opened a book, which seemed to magically appear in his hands.

Michael recognized it as a first year college text, Psychology Today, By James Fox. He was unsure how he remembered it. But every page was clear in his mind. He chased away those memories, diverting his full attention to the work in front of him, which he perceived as a waste of time.

The minutes flew by like seconds; Trevor caught a glimpse of the time. He'd almost allowed Michael to exceed the thirty-minute mark. Closing his book quietly and laying it aside, he watched Michael busily work on the blank worksheet given to him for calculating math problems.

"Michael, I'm sorry but we'll have to stop now for lunch. You may ...," Trevor was explaining but stopped because Michael continued to write as if he hadn't heard. "Michael!" he tried again louder.

Michael finally looked up.

"What!" he answered impatiently.

"I said it's time to break for lunch. You'll be given another thirty minutes afterward to try and finish," he explained.

Michael returned his attention back to his paper. Then back to the counselor.

"I'll just take it with me and work on it while I eat," he suggested, and started to get up to leave, but stopped at the sound of Mr. Williams' command.

"No, I can't allow you to do that," he said, thinking he'd proven the test was harder than the child had anticipated, and that Michael was trying to manipulate more time dishonestly. "Don't worry about finishing. I knew you would realize it was a lot more difficult than you imagined. There's no shame in accepting our limitations," Trevor said understandingly.

Michael made a face as if he'd smelled something awful.

"What are you talking about?" he asked.

"The test, Michael. What else would I be talking about?" Trevor said rolling his eyes.

Michael laughed and said, "Oh, this is what else. Do you like it? It's almost done. It's a cross between representational and conceptual forms of art," he explained and handed the drawing to the counselor.

"Yes Michael, it's wonderful. But I thought you were taking the exams," Trevor pointed out, confused again.

Michael followed Mr. Williams' eyes to the papers on the desk.

"Oh yeah! I completed those about ten minutes ago. I was going to tell you, but you were reading. I didn't want to be rude."

Trevor's mouth dropped open in shock. He gathered the questionnaires and answer sheets. To his amazement, they were in fact completed and the handwriting was superb. He unconsciously handed the drawing back to Michael who then returned to his spot to finish his work of art, while the counselor began checking the test answers.

A few minutes later, the lunch bell rang and Michael jumped to his feet.

"I'm outta here! Your picture is finished," he said and darted out the door.

Mr. Williams' looked up, still in shock.

"Okay, come back after lunch!" He yelled because Michael was already moving down the hall. Trevor returned to the exams. He couldn't believe what he was seeing. Every answer was correct. Not one place appeared to have been erased or changed. *'The child has gotten them all right the first time. Phenomenal!'* he thought, and shook his head with disbelief. While doing so, he caught the drawing in his peripheral vision. He picked it up gently and studied it, becoming even more confused. The artwork was incredible. The strange thing was the way it was signed. The name across the bottom was: Timothy Neal James.

◆ ◆ ◆ ◆ ◆

The cafeteria is the second largest room in the school. Everywhere you looked, table after table were crammed with children. The noise level was so intense, if a rock and roll concert was being held in the center of the talking, screaming and laughing youngsters, it would be highly unlikely anyone would be able to hear the music.

Two lines formed in front of some doors in the rear. Hundreds of hungry children would need to be fed in the next hour, so anarchy was a normal part of the daily program.

Michael decided to wait in the shorter line with the fifth graders. He felt slightly out of place with everyone around him being a full head, or more, taller. But this way, he could avoid his classmates. He began to contemplate the many different outcomes that awaited his future. It was hard to think. The racket was interrupting his thoughts and getting on his last nerve. *'Getting out of grade school is going to be a blessing,'* he thought. Now he understood why his dad didn't like Chuck-E-Cheese's. The memory made him smile.

A tap on his shoulder caused Michael to do a quick check behind him. There stood a heavy-set boy twice, Michael's size, with a short military style haircut, giving him the look of a stereotypical bully in search of recognition. On his chest was a nametag introducing him as Donnie Roth. Being the first day of school, the tag seemed appropriate.

The boy lowered his chubby face to look into Michael's eyes.

"Ain't chew 'posta be in dat line wif da west a dem babies?" he said while pointing at the other group of children.

Michael was thinking that this kid is obviously a scholar of English and couldn't help bursting out a boisterous laugh.

"No tanks. Dis un here a be fine wits me," he answered, mocking the butchery of the English language, then continued to chuckle.

The big fellow was unsure if he'd been made fun of or not, so he became quiet in thought.

The silliness of the two attracted the attention of another boy, who turned around to face them. This one's tag acknowledged him as Edward Anderson. He was shorter than Donnie but twice as wide and of a perceptively higher intellect.

"Hey! You're that kid who beat the tar out of those guys at recess. That was really cool. What belt do you have?" he asked.

Michael relaxed a little bit. He didn't detect anything remotely threatening from this new member of the trio. However, his ego started to show in his posture.

'Careful son, pride goeth before a fall,' Tim said, bringing Michael back down to size.

"I only have a brown belt, however, I received personal training from Jackie Lee, the World Champion," he explained.

Edwards face lit up like a neon sign.

"Wow! Awesome!" he exclaimed. Then he seemed to be concentrating on some inner thought. His smile turned into the

158

frowning plea of a spoiled child. One who knew the answer to the next question was no.

"Would you get Jackie's autograph for me please!" he asked.

Michael felt a stab of sorrow for Edward. He liked the boy and had a terrible truth that needed to be revealed. He also had a strange need to hold Edward like a son in need of comforting.

"I'm sorry to be the one to tell you this. But Mr. Lee died the same night my dad was murdered," he explained and offered his hand out to the other boy to show he understood his pain. At first, the reaction on Edward's face was what Michael expected. However, as quickly as it came over the boy's chubby cheeks, it vanished. Clearly, the years of television had desensitized his humanity. After seeing hundreds, maybe even thousands die in living color, death had become unreal. Jackie was just another fallen theatrical hero whose death could be dismissed or eradicated simply by pushing the rewind button on the remote.

"Oh well, can you show me some moves?" asked Edward, and did his best to demonstrate a karate block, obviously already over the devastating news about the Master.

Michael's feeling for Edward went from admiration and fondness, to one of pity. Trying not to show his disappointment or allow the hurt to come out in his voice, Michael lowered his head.

"Maybe later if there's time. We'll have to wait and see," he said and was shocked at how much he sounded like his dad.

The boy named Donnie, who stood behind Michael, had remained quiet until now. Something sparked a need in him to attack.

"Ha! You tink I sposta bleeve dat crap!" he said and moved closer to Michael. "You ain't never meeted no Jackie Lee," he went on and put his index finger into Michael's chest, giving a small but aggressive push. "Jackie be my Onkle and he ain't ded. Takes it backs liar!" he said louder and pushed again. This time harder, a lot harder. "Eyes gonna show jya wat Onkle Jackie done learnt me!" he added and push again.

Michael stepped back and locked eyes with the moron.

"I'd advise you not to do that," he suggested.

Donnie took another step forward and grabbed Michael's shirt collar with both hands.

"Don't tell me what ta doo!!" he ordered, sounding mean, adding a facial expression to match his attitude.

Trying his best to remain as calm as possible, Michael tried again.

"Please Donnie, there's no logical reason for a confrontation between us," he said gently.

Donnie's chest swelled. He knew the eyes of his peers were on him. Plus, he was misunderstanding Michael's request as a plea made out of fear, which cultivated a sense of bravery.

"Last time I gonna tel jya ta takes backs dem lies," he threatened, tightening his grip on Michael's shirt.

"And this is your last chance to walk away unharmed," Michael replied sternly.

When Donnie failed to comply with the final warning, Michael dropped his left arm over both of Donnie's, trapping them. Then he cart-wheeled his right arm over all three while spinning his body to the left. This quickly forced the boy's arms to be jerked forward, destroying his grip and his balance.

Donnie was able to catch himself by taking a few fast steps. He spun around and stood there facing Michael, wondering what the heck had just happened. Shock now covered his face like a Halloween mask.

Michael's posture was full of confidence.

"Have you made your decision yet to stand down? Or do you intend to engage further?" he said, offering another chance to end the confrontation now before someone got hurt.

Uncertainty and fear clouded Donnie's eyes as he weighed his options. He was unaccustomed to rivals, and his reputation was on the line. Of course, pride caused him to make the wrong choice. Stepping forward again, he grabbed Michael's collar in hopes of securing a target in which to launch a punch. To his surprise, Michael took hold of the leading hand and turned it counter clockwise toward the thumb, the pain driving the large boy to his knees. Red hot agony shot all the way to his shoulder. He found himself kneeling there helpless as if giving reverence to a king.

Michael turned the captured hand even further.

"I just knew you would make the stupid choice Watts," he said, applying even more pressure, adding excruciating punishment to the humiliation.

Donnie began to cry out, begging for mercy.

"Please! Please, you're really hurting me! Please stop," the boy screamed through tears.

The pain in Donnie's eyes gave Michael comfort. For some reason, this revenge felt incredibly sweet and he wanted more. Just like when he slammed his fist down on the counselor's desk. David Watts was finally at his mercy.

'Stop it Michael, it's not David,' came his dad's voice. But Michael didn't respond. He was totally alive. *'Michael! Stop it! Look at whom you are hurting son. Open your eyes!'* Tim tried again.

This time he heard the voice that broke his hypnotic state. As suggested, he actually looked at the child at his feet, like he had just realized someone was there, releasing his grip.

Donnie hugged his hand to his chest before falling the rest of the way to the floor, where he curled up into a fetal position and continued to weep openly.

Michael looked around the now quiet cafeteria. Everyone was staring at him like he was a crazed animal. Tears began to fill his eyes.

"I'm sorry everyone. Please forgive me," he said sorrowfully. He then looked back down at Donnie and offered his hand to help him up.

Donnie cowered back and tried to crawl away. The terrified look in his eyes stabbed at Michael's heart, causing him intense emotional pain.

"I swear to God, I'm sorry. Please forgive me!" he asked. When the expression on the boy's face didn't change, Michael turned and ran from the room. Once in the hallway, he yelled down the empty corridor.

"God help me. I'm so sorry. Please!!"

He didn't stop running until he'd exited the building, crossed the parking lot, the playground and entered the grassy area on the far side of the property. There he fell face first into the weeds and cried.

'Michael honey,' came the loving, calm voice of his dad.

But Michael was not yet ready to be consoled, he was angry because of his actions, and frightened at the thought of becoming evil.

"Leave me alone! I'm no better than David Watts!" he screamed.

'You know that's not true son. You're just confused,' Tim explained.

"I said leave me alone!" Michael screamed again and punched the ground, hurting his fist, but he didn't care. What he needed was a good long soul cleansing, a heartfelt cry. One that should have started years ago. He willed his father into silence and let the emotions flow.

CHAPTER 10

Anita had mixed feelings as she drove down I-65. To her, tonight's excursion was crazy, but Michael had insisted on doing his trick-or-treating in East Nashville. On one hand, it was a blessing to see the child excited over the age-old tradition of door-to-door solicitation and of having an opportunity to become his favorite make believe character. This year, his incredible imagination brought to life a world class, four-foot ninja. The costume was made complete with a homemade sword of copper pipe; one that whistled sharply when swung through the air. But why on earth would he want to go to one of the roughest parts of the city was beyond her comprehension.

She had tried and failed to change his mind. Pressing too hard was not an option she would be comfortable with anyway. She just wasn't the type. It had only been three months since she had been called to Michael's school, retrieving a very distraught, crying and dirty-faced boy from the playground. Everyone there was harmonious in there hypothetical belief that Michael was suffering from posttraumatic stress. Time and rest were the only possible remedy. The prognosis was good, but no one could say how long it would take.

Anita could see improvement in Michael every day. It still concerned her however when she'd hear him talking openly to himself. The school's psychologist said imaginary friends were normal, especially in circumstances like Michael's. He also claimed it would soon pass, but to her, it was still eerie. Sometimes, it seemed that it wasn't even Michael that was doing the talking. One day she waited until he was working on the computer, deeply contemplating something he'd found, when she tried a little experiment.

"Tim," she said, and Michael turned around with a faraway stare in his eyes.

"Yeah Gigster," he answered. The hair on Anita's arms prickled as they stood on end. Tim was the only person who'd ever called her that.

"What are you doing sweetheart?" she asked nervously, not one hundred percent sure to whom she was speaking.

"I'm helping Michael track down some police reports were both interested in," he replied, sort of locked in a dream. Then his eyes cleared instantly and a fictitious smile adorned his handsome, young face. "I mean nothing! Just surfing the net," he said, as if trying to convince her he had only misspoken or she'd misunderstood.

Before she could request some elaboration, he sprang to his feet.

"I'll be in the garage," he said, and headed for his private sanctuary beyond the back door. That was another thing that made her worry. If he wasn't on the internet, he was out in the garage practicing karate, receiving instruction from another imaginary friend. Every day, he incorporated something new. Who could be teaching him? Each move became perfect in days, not years like most students of the art.

These were just some of the reasons she reluctantly gave in to the predetermined trick-or-treating route. It was also a good way to get the boy outside. All of her friends said she was crazy to grant a child as young as he such a questionable request. But they hadn't been witness to the strange events, the overnight maturity of this special boy or his outrageous intellectual level and fighting skills.

Even Gussie and Pearl didn't comprehend her decision. They failed to accept her attempts to portray Michael as anything more than a typical eight year old. Last Friday, however, they had received a small preview of the child's metamorphosis. All four were sitting at the breakfast table enjoying a country style meal. The three women talked about everything from church services to price differences in the sixties while Michael busied himself studying Anita's prescription bottles. She kept them on the table as a reminder to take them. It was convenient, plus, most of them were required to be taken with food.

Michael started to complain about the incompetence of the pharmacy.

"How idiotic!" he began, holding two of the containers up to study closer. "Of all the half-wit irrational…!" he stated, as he turned around in order to grab the phone. He dialed the number printed on the label and waited. The person he was calling answered quickly.

"Yes ma'am, you may. Would you transfer me? I need to speak with your pharmacist. Yes, I'll hold," he agreed, then drummed his fingers on the table as he waited. Looking up, he realized the three women were intensely staring at him, so he winked. Then the pharmacist came on the line.

"Yes, this is Dr. Timothy Neal James …" Michael said, then quickly added, " … 's son … " before he continued. "Before I find it necessary to report your negligence to the board of pharmacological ethics and you lose your license to distribute prescription medication, you may find it advantageous to review your record on Ms. Anita Box," he advised, and listened for a few seconds. I'm eight years old if you feel it matters, but it won't justify your incompetence. I tell you what, take a chance. It's your career, not mine," Michael finished and hung up the phone. He gave Anita a malicious, knowing smile, then got up to leave. "I'll be in the garage Giggy. The pharmacy should be calling momentarily," he said and left the room.

The three confused ladies just sat there in dead silence, full of anticipation of what was to come. Even though they had been expecting it, the first ring of the phone made them jump with a humorous jolt followed by nervous laughter.

Anita sprang to her feet and grabbed the receiver. "Hello … , yes, this is Ms. Box," she said, then listened intensely for approximately three minutes, all the while giving involuntary nods of her head and voicing agreeing moans of, "um-hum, okay. Thanks for calling. Goodbye," she finished and returned the hand piece to its cradle, her face turning white as snow. After composing herself, she turned to her friends. "That really was the pharmacist. He couldn't seem to apologize enough for their mistake. Apparently, two of my medications are for the same affliction. By taking both, they counteract each other, aggravating my condition. The physician who prescribed them, the pharmacist, and their fancy computer missed the error," she said, standing there perplexed. "But my great grandson didn't," she added, shaking her head.

No one knew what to say except Gussie.

"Oh my God!" she exclaimed. Whatever was going on in Michael's head was beyond their understanding.

All of these reflections had Anita so lost in memories that Michael's voice was little more than a distant mumble. That is until he almost yelled at her.

"Giggy! Are you going to stop, or what?" He asked.

Anita realized all at once that she had somehow found her way to Fatherland Street. In her dream state of mind, it seemed impossible to have traveled all the way to East Nashville in what seemed to be a short period of time, and to have done so without the knowledge of doing it. She quietly thanked God that she hadn't gotten them both killed.

"Of course sweetheart, I'm going to stop. Don't be silly," she explained, trying to show Michael that she hadn't been daydreaming, maybe not sounding as convincing as she would've liked.

Michael's right eyebrow elevated comically.

"Yeah!" he mocked.

Anita pulled the car over to the curb.

"Honey, I don't see any place to park," she said, turning her head back and forth searching the area. "I don't even see any people around. Are you sure there's a Halloween event in this neighborhood?" she asked, then once more scanned the place for some sign of activity. "I think it's best we go elsewhere," she suggested and started to pull away from the curb.

"No Giggy. This is where he's at," Michael yelled, then caught himself and started again, this time speaking gently. "I mean this is where I want to be," He explained.

Anita looked suspicious. "Where who is at?" she asked.

Michael looked around quickly for an out. He couldn't explain the "he" part without a visual aide. Then he spotted it. "That policeman. See him standing over there by those barricades?" he said, and pointed at the next block. He then opened his door to leave. The sound of the door-ajar alarm was joined by the noise of far away traffic and chilly night air.

The dome light exposed the shock and concern on Anita's face. "Hold on Michael!" she snapped irritably, expecting him to close the door as instructed.

Instead, to her horror, he exited the car while hurriedly yelling over his shoulder, "Pick me up here in an hour!"

A passing motorist blared his horn at Anita's halfway parked car, drawing her attention for a split second. When she turned back around, Michael was gone.

She jumped from her seat and ran around to the sidewalk, uncaringly leaving her door open and the car unattended. Thousands of frightening scenarios attacked her thoughts. "Michael! Michael, where are you?" She yelled at the top of her lungs. Tears began to burn her eyes, and fear consumed her soul. "Please Michael! Where are you?" she cried as she ran in the direction of the police officer standing by the saw horses, hoping to catch sight of the only thing she had to live for. "Officer! Officer, please help me!" She screamed hysterically.

The policeman quickly moved toward her, speaking rapidly into his microphone reporting a developing situation and his location. His boring post had just become lively, and the noise of his radio filled the night air.

Michael remained perfectly still as his great-grandmother passed by. He was less than ten feet away, kneeling in the shadows of two evergreens. He could clearly see the anxiety on her face, and it made his emotions feel like they were fist-fighting in his chest. Just by observing the fear that he was traitorously placing on her was eating him alive from the inside out. He knew it would be a long, hard road ahead to make it up to her, but nonetheless, tonight's mission had to be executed.

The thought of what lay ahead had adrenaline running through his body like greased lightning. His heart pounded like a jackhammer and his stomach soured to the point of regurgitation. The accompanying dread had him reluctant to move, and caused a coppery taste to overwhelm his mouth. "I'm not sure I can do this Dad," he whispered.

'I understand son. I didn't think it was a good idea to begin with,' came Tim's voice. 'Just get up and go to the Gigster. Go home and forget about this act of vengeance. It is the Lord's job, not yours. I want you safe because I love you so much,' Tim added.

Michael thought over what his dad said for a second or two. Then he sprang to his feet in a dead run. "And I love you too Dad," he said as he headed away from his hysterical Giggy. "And that's why I've got to do this for us," he explained.

Michael's legs began to burn like fire as he pushed them past their limit. The faster he ran, the clearer his thought became. The uncertainty and trepidation that had paralyzed him earlier vanished, replaced by an impenetrable courage. The cool evening air had become pleasantly rejuvenating.

Soon the cross shaped scar on his chest became a tingling presence that demanded his attention, so he slowed his pace to a walk and began examining the rustic homes that now surrounded him.

The one he was looking for was right in front of him. The description Jerry had given during one of their therapy sessions was an exact match. It had to be the place. The information on the internet said it belonged to a Metro policeman, but for security reasons, no name was given. The tax site revealed it as an investment property and was currently rented. Michael knew it was a long shot to find Watts here, but it was the only lead he had.

A small amount of foreboding started to creep into his thoughts. If this didn't pan out, all those hours of planning and scheming, the illegal use of the police department's computer system that he'd hacked into in order to set up this fictitious trick-or-treat route, and the emotional pain he had caused Giggy, would all be for nothing. He had to shake his head to clear those mental images.

Determinedly, he climbed the old wooden steps to the front porch, two at a time. The place was a true piece of architectural history and design. The windows and doors were huge in comparison to modern-day slap-them-up prefabs; the kind that are growing like skin cancer across the open plains of this country. No, these homes were made using craftsmanship that was just not seen any more - and from real hardwoods, not laminated trash.

Michael pulled the black ninja mask down over his face, totally hiding his identity. Then he rapped his knuckles on the lower panel of the massive door. The act barely produced any noise but caused a sharp pain to shoot up his arm. The thick wood failed to give even a little bit.

"Man!" he exclaimed, as he admired the hand carvings that must have been cut out a hundred years before his birth, and would most likely be here long after he was gone. He knew it was actually his dad's admiration, and that was comforting.

Doubling his hand into a tight fist, he hammered on the frame.

This time he could hear it echoing through the structure. After tilting his head slightly, he detected the sound of footsteps on a hardwood interior floor.

"Who is it and what do you want?" asked a scared, muffled and an irritated male voice.

Michael rolled his eyes, *'What do you think moron? It's Halloween night and there's a kid standing on your front porch in a costume! Jehovah's Witness! Idiot,'* he thought. All kinds of things came to mind to say, but he resisted the urge.

"Trick-or-treat!" he yelled.

"Go away!" came a more threatening and confident reply.

Michael turned his back to the door and surveyed for curious onlookers. Once satisfied the coast was clear, he drew his knee up to his chest and kicked backward as hard as he could like a mule. The effect was awesome, and the whole front of the house seemed to share in the impact. It echoed up and down the street like a stick of dynamite had gone off.

"Trick-or-treat!" Michael yelled again this time as loud as he could.

The door flew open with a screech from the old and unmaintained hinges.

"What the hell is the matter with you punk? Can't you hear? I said, go away!" said the man who answered the door, then stood in the opening with no shirt or shoes. He looked stoned. After seeing the size of his tiny visitor, the guy puffed out his scrawny chest. "I should stomp your butt for kicking my door pip-squeak!" he threatened.

Tim's voice shot through Michael's mind like electric shock therapy, causing him to jump. *'It's one of them! Run! Run now!'*

The post-pubescent, pimple-faced blond thought he'd put fear in the little ninja, and his features lit up with a diabolical smile that exposed two missing teeth. He also revealed a pistol that he'd been hiding behind his back. Slowly, he moved it back and forth, hoping it would send chills through the candy grubbing solicitor. After convincing himself the gun's effect was maximized, he placed it on a small plant shelf by the door.

'Michael Run! We achieved our primary goal of finding these creeps. Now please leave before they hurt you!' Tim suggested pleadingly.

"Not yet," Michael replied while swinging his copper sword over his head as if he were chopping firewood. The pipe made a swishing whistle, followed by a sharp ping as the weapon found its mark, connecting with the guy's forehead and running downward over the bridge of his nose. At first it appeared to have had no effect. Then as soon as Michael began thinking he'd made a deadly mistake, the guy's pupils became unfocused and a large angry welt materialized between his eyes. He then drunkenly took two steps backward before colliding with a half round table adorned with a large flower vase. Everything went to the floor in a thunderous crash of breaking glass and splintering wood.

The sight of the damage to both the furniture and the novice criminal filled Michael with the same incomprehensible joy he'd felt back in the lunchroom months ago. Only this time it was different. Instead of being demonic and frightening, it felt righteous. It gave him the heart to stand up for his family, administering a little vigilante justice.

In his mind's eye, Michael could envision himself beating the creep, swing after swing. It took every ounce of his willpower not to enter the house, and do just that.

He raised the now bent rod in his hand to admire it. How simplistic, yet effective, it was. The Bible verse Psalms 23:4 came to mind and he smiled; 'Yea, though I walk through the valley of the shadow of death, I will fear no evil; for thou art with me; thy rod and thy staff they comfort me.'

Michael's thoughts were interrupted by his internal partner,

'That breaking glass is sure to bring the other members of the gang. Please take off now Michael. PLEASE!' Tim pleaded once again.

Michael spun on his heal, placing his back against the wall just out of view of the open door frame.

"Let's wait and see who else is here," He said as he raised the pipe to a ready position. Standing in the porch's light, he resembled the logo of the National Baseball League. "If there's too many, I'll split. But if it's just one, he's sure to stop and check on the guy I clocked. That should give me time to get another creep," he whispered.

The night had become as quiet as a tomb. In the distance, he detected an approaching automobile. He had brilliantly manipulated some police orders to cordon off a non-existing block celebration. But there's no way to manufacture trick-or-treaters or participating homeowners, so it could only be a cruiser out looking for him, and here he stood out like a sore thumb. He was also sure that if anyone else had been in the house, they would have moved by now.

'What if they're hiding, waiting in ambush?' Tim asked.

Michael was contemplating what his dad said when his scar started to tingle again. He brushed all thoughts aside and stepped into the house. Using his right heal, he reached behind and closed the door with a finalizing click of no return.

He quickly checked the living area to his left. If a bushwhacker lurked in shadows, that's where they'd be, and hopefully visible in time for him to react.

'Unless it's in the form of hot lead,' Tim remarked.

Michael grimaced with that thought, and his shoulder burned at the memory.

"Thanks a lot dad!" he said, feeling exposed. This had to be how a death-row inmate felt every time he heard the coming of the warden or the rattling of chains.

The unconscious recipient of Michael's revenge started to come around with a painful moan. His eyes cleared slowly as he tried to focus. Then uncertainty covered his face as he tried to determine whether the black ninja was real or a figment of his imagination.

A throbbing, hot pain across the center of his nose quickly returned the recollection and realization of a few minutes ago, along with an uncontrollable burning anger.

"I'm going to kill you! Fu ..." he was saying.

Michael swung his weapon again. This time as if playing tee-ball. The pipe connected sideways across the head of its intended target. The strike was immediately followed by an unimaginable cry of pure anguish and the swelling of another ugly beet-red welt.

"Wow! Now that's gonna leave a mark!" Michael said jokingly.

The presence of levity in the ninja's voice infuriated the crook further.

"What are you trying to do, kill me?" he screamed.

The answer with which he was awarded put the fear of God in him.

"That's totally up to you creep," Michael replied. Then he paused to allow that statement to sink into the man's head.

'Michael! This is the one Watts called Paul, remember?' Tim said.

"Well Paul," Michael said. "Do we have an understanding?"

At the mention of his name, Paul's eyes widened as far as the swelling would allow. They looked as if they were going to fall out of his skull. He now realized the serious position he was in. This couldn't be a child. It had to be a small but deadly assassin.

"Who sent you to kill me?" he pleadingly mumbled through forming tears.

Michael pulled the copper tube back as if to strike again. But instead of swinging, he stomped his foot.

"I'll ask the questions," he corrected.

Paul instinctively raised his arms to deflect the blow, and howled out another yelp.

Michael waited until Paul returned his full attention to him before he continued.

"Allow me to give you a crash course in elementary physiology," he offered, and then pointed to the side of his head, just behind his eye. "This is called the temporal lobe. It's the most important part of the human brain," Michael explained, knowing it was a lie. But he was also confident that this dirt bag wouldn't know the difference if he'd pointed at his belly button. "It's also, for some mistake nature made, the softest part of the skull." He stopped and held the copper tube up to catch the light. "All it would take is a well-placed strike with, um ... let's say a piece of plumbing such as this one," he moved the weapon again so the reflection gave it life. "Death would be absolute; outrageously slow and excruciatingly painful, but definite nonetheless." Michael paused again to allow the new anatomy student time to absorb the lesson. He knew that he'd succeeded completely when urine darkened the front of Paul's shorts. He had to move his foot to avoid the warm liquid running across the floor. "Don't worry Paul; I'll give you your gun so you can use it to stop the pain."

At the mention of the pistol, Paul's eyes shot to the table, wondering if he could reach it before the tiny ninja could react.

Following his line of sight, Michael had no problem reading Paul's intentions.

"I don't think that would be wise, actually it would be suicidal, so don't even think it. Well, unless you're really ready to die," he said like he was Paul's father.

The criminal's eyes returned to his captor.

"What do you want? I'll do anything! Just please don't kill me," Paul begged.

"Good boy," Michael said, then took on a murderous stare. If looks could kill, this confrontation would be over. "Where is David Watts?" he asked through gritted teeth.

"I don't know," Paul whimpered.

Michael raised the homemade sword to deliver a deadly strike.

"Then I guess I don't need you," he said.

"I don't know! I swear to God, I don't know!" Paul yelled and cowered back. "He works for a guy named George Woods now. He doesn't even talk to me anymore," he whined.

Michael lowered the tubing. "What are the names of the other two who were with you the night Dr. James and his son were shot?" he demanded.

Paul started rocking back and forth with nervous energy. He'd known that shooting would come back to haunt him someday.

"I ... " he stammered. "I didn't shoot those people," he said as he began to cry. "It was Onzean Otey, René Caldrone, and David Watts. I was knocked out by the old dude, see," he explained, pointing to his damaged teeth.

The disrespectful comment about his dad almost caused Michael to go ahead and start beating the pee-soaked jerk to death. But again he held back for the sake of more information.

"I know you weren't a shooter. That's the only reason you're still breathing," Michael informed him, then stopped to contemplate how the welts on Paul's face formed a perfect cross like the ones on his own chest. "Where are they Paul?"

The question was answered without pause. The traitor had already flipped on his loyalties. Now it was a matter of self-preservation.

"All I know is after Woods took all the money from the heist, Caldrone and Otey went their own directions. Last I heard, they were living in Goodlettsville," he said more calmly, thinking he was now in the ninja interrogator's good graces.

Michael turned to leave and as he opened the door, he heard a premature sigh of relief from Paul. Standing in the open door, Michael looked back over his shoulder.

"One more thing, which of you four derelicts shot the two policemen out front?" he asked. "One of them was a close friend of mine," he added in a way that said, "I'm here to settle the score!"

The look of pure horror came over Paul's face. Knowing his life was over, he made a valiant, but futile attempt to reach his gun. The second he moved, so did the deadly ninja. Michael spun with all his power into a spinning hook kick that landed squarely on Paul's jaw. It was hard enough to turn the recipient's lights out. However, for an insurance policy, Michael gave him another kick before the creep could hit the floor.

"This one is for my friend Jerry and his family," Michael said and delivered a final sting from the very productive piece of plumbing.

Michael stepped out on the porch again. The fresh air never had smelled or tasted so good.

"It's great to be alive," he said to no one, then turned and looked at the bleeding garbage lying on the floor in his own blood and urine. "At least for some of us," he added.

Once again, a police car was slowly coming down the street. Its searchlight was panning the yards of each house as it drew closer.

An idea popped into Michael's head as he looked back again at the unconscious moron. Reaching back inside with his copper pipe, he lifted the gun carefully from its resting place and slowly lowered it to the floor next to its owner's hand. Then he reluctantly threw his beloved sword into the neighbor's bushes, pulled off his headgear, and walked to the street.

The officer must have spotted him immediately. The spotlight went out at the same time as the ones on top of the car came on. There was a colorful display of red and blue on the surrounding houses. The engine roared as gas was applied. Within seconds, the cruiser came to a screeching halt, and the policeman jumped from his car.

"Michael Clark?" the man asked, in a tone that said, "Don't lie to me I'm the law!"

"Yes sir," Michael replied in his best "I'm just a kid" voice.

"Thank God you're safe! Your grandmother is scared to death about you," the officer explained, then thumbed the transmitter attached to his collar.

After he reported in, the policeman squatted down so he was face to face with Michael.

"So young man, you're a ninja are ya?" he asked, and ruffled Michael's hair. "Where's your trick-or-treat bag buddy?"

'Oops,' Michael thought. Even the best plans have problems. He looked down at his shoes to hide any deceit. "Well sir, there's not too many people into the Halloween spirit this year, so I gave mine to some smaller children," he lied. It felt horrible, but he was committed.

The officer accepted the explanation. He then took out his wallet and handed Michael a five-dollar bill. "Here you go ninja. That was a nice thing you did. Take that and buy yourself some more candy," he said and rubbed Michael's red head again, making him feel even worse.

The cop was nice, but not very observant. *'Hello! Man down! Killer with a gun! Hello! Anybody home?!'* Tim was ranting in Michael's head.

Michael knew he had to do something. He didn't want Paul waking up with that gun so handy.

"Officer," he said as innocently as he could.

"What is it buddy?" the policeman asked.

"It's just that there's a man bleeding on the floor up there," Michael said. "And he has a gun. At first, I was sure it was only a Halloween prank. But now I just don't know," he finished and pointed at the house.

The officer jumped to his feet like a frog in a frying pan, and his demeanor changed drastically.

"Get in here and stay down!" he ordered, opening the back door of his car.

"Am I under arrest?" Michael asked complying, and still playing the role of a confused child.

"No!" the man barked, and slammed the door.

Michael watched as the policeman spoke into his collar mic once again, simultaneously removing his service revolver from its holster on his side.

Within seconds, three more cruisers sat next to the one Michael was in. It was a wondrous feeling watching the officers rush into the house, one of them stood on Paul's hands just in case he tried to reach for his weapon.

The new pain must have revived him. He looked up and out at the units. His eyes locked on Michael and recognition was instantaneous.

One of the cops placed his knee on Paul's neck and forced his arms aggressively behind his back. Then he was jerked to a standing position. No one bothered to search him. Obviously, the only thing he wore was soiled boxer shorts, and they weren't about to touch them.

The whole time, Paul's eyes never left Michael's. Hatred began to grow, along with confusion, as Paul wondered how all this crap could happen to him in one night. He thought, *'A visit from a pint-sized assassin, beaten with a pipe and the cops arresting him. And there he sits not thirty feet away, the witness to a murder that I'm tied to, giving me the middle finger!'*

The policemen finally half-dragged the creep down the steps to the waiting unit. Just as he passed by the window, Michael held up his ninja hood in front of his face, and then dropped it while his tongue was sticking out as he smiled and waved "bye-bye."

Paul's mouth fell open in shock. It was just a child who had beaten him severely.

"That's him! That's the ninja. That's him! That's him!" He kept repeating.

The cop next to him got angry and pushed Paul toward the cruiser.

"Yeah, we know. Trick-or-treat moron! Now shut up and keep moving!" he ordered.

About five minutes later, after Paul was long gone, Anita pulled up to the unit, got out and ran to Michael's door. He crawled out slowly, awaiting his reprimand.

"I don't know if I should beat you or hug you!" she cried tearfully.

"Well, if it's up to me, I'll take the hug, please," Michael replied.

Everyone laughed at Michael's innocence in believing the choice was his.

Another officer walked by with the thirty-eight pistol in a plastic bag marked with red letters that said, EVIDENCE.

Michael's heartfelt warm. He knew that once they ran ballistics on that piece, Jerry Cox, and Thomas Hayes would have some well-deserved justice.

Unexpected Vengeance

CHAPTER 11

The smell of roasted turkey with all the exquisite side dishes still lingered in the air, a pleasant reminder of the day's traditional family gathering.

Michael thought of how hard everyone struggled to abstain from mentioning Sara's and Tim's absence. It was actually comical and made him smile. How brave they all assumed he was, when, in fact, Dad was there the whole time, and they just couldn't see him.

The only real awkward moment was when Grandpa Steve first tasted the succulent bird that Michael had the honor of preparing this year.

"Boy Michael, this is the juiciest turkey I've ever eaten. It's as good if not better than your dad's," he boasted. Then, by the look on his face, it was easy to see that he wished he could digress. Everyone stopped eating and talking at the same time. Their eyes sympathetically locked on Michael, as if he'd just been informed that his puppy died, then into shock as if he'd been loudly flatulent during church over his response.

"Thanks, paw-paw. Dad and I worked on this one together," Michael informed them, then filled his mouth with cranberry sauce in an attempt to ignore their gazes. Other than that, the supper was uneventful.

After dinner was a real bore. All the men crashed on the living room furniture, or as they called it, watched a football game. The women cleaned up, then retired to gossiping, leaving Michael to himself and his computer. A little sadness found its way into his heart. Dad always played with him at times like these. It never mattered how much there was to do, there was always time for him. He really missed that.

Sometime later, Michael's eyes began to burn from the long

hours of staring at the computer monitor. Yawn after yawn threatened to keep his eyes closed with every blink. He was about to sign off when a musical chime indicated the search engine had found a possible hit. He'd already given up on trying to find René Caldrone. It was a waste of time. There were at least a thousand in the Nashville area alone. Many with criminal records or on parole. There was no way to tell which one was his target. The data available wasn't specific enough to narrow the parameters of his search.

Onezean Otey was a different story. There was only three. The first was obviously not the one. He was in his seventies. Likewise with the second who was fifty. That left one, and ironically, he was Onezean the third. Not being very old, most of his records were sealed under the juvenile protection act. However, using a link that Michael had hacked into under the ruse of a special agent with Homeland Security, he found that the Tennessee Bureau of Investigation had a file that provided ample information.

He began scanning the data for anything pertinent to his cause and was shocked at the amount of details the government kept on its citizens. Nothing was sacred.

'See if we can get a picture of him,' Tim suggested.

Michael programmed the system to do as requested, then yawned again, this time from the very depths of his soul, and his shoulders dropped from exhaustion. With both hands, he began rubbing at his blood-shot eyes. The second he removed his palms, he let out a yelp. There he was face-to-face with a killer. The man staring back at him from the screen in living color was definitely the Onezean Otey he was looking for.

The fatigue Michael was feeling turned into hate-fueled anxiety. He pushed the print button so aggressively that the printer misunderstood the command and shot out multiple copies. As if paralyzed in a hypnotic staring contest, he couldn't detach his eyes from that of his new adversary's. His crucifix of scarred flesh tingled as if an army of ants were having a feeding frenzy on his chest.

Finally, Anita yelled from the top of the steps, breaking the coma-like daze.

"Michael honey, I think it's time for bed sweetheart!"'

Michael actually welcomed the intrusion.

"Yes Giggy!" he replied, and started backing out of the system carefully, making sure not to leave a cyber trail. No one would ever believe that an eight-year-old had entered so many supposedly secure sites. Any and all suspicion would surely fall on his great grandmother, and that would kill her for sure.

She still wasn't over his Halloween night escapade. She claimed to be, but he could still detect a tremor in her voice when they were discussing it. Especially once his fictitious tale of the evening had lost its conceivability and innocence causing it to no longer ring true.

The doo-doo really hit the fan the following morning. The headlines in The Tennessean displayed a mug shot of Paul Dickson, adorned with an angry, black-and-blue cross-shaped bruise, missing teeth, and a horribly swollen jaw. Michael recalled hoping the caption said "BEST MASK AWARD," but of course it didn't. Instead it read, "SEARCH FOR MISSING TRICK-OR-TREATER TURNS UP COP KILLER."

The story went on to tell about the extraordinary police work used in the arrest and how vigilance plus old-fashioned surveillance had cracked the case.

The part that busted Michael was a detailed medical report on the beating that the suspect received. A careful search of the area had revealed a piece of copper pipe that had been used repeatedly on Paul's face.

Michael also remembered how he stood there smiling innocently before Giggy.

"I guess some bad guys found my sword," he offered shyly.

Giggy simply stared at him over her glasses in disbelief and Michael knew he couldn't lie his way out of it.

The screen finally cleared and finished its necessary memory storage. Michael arched his back to remove the kinks and raised his arms. He noticed that his shirt was way too tight across his chest.

"That's strange, I just got this one," he said to himself, then pulled it over his head, removing it on the way to the bathroom. He noticed in the mirror that his weight training was paying off. He flexed a couple times.

The enjoyment was short lived, and lost, when he saw the stress in his bloodshot eyes, and the bags underneath them that shouldn't be there for thirty more years.

"I need about a year's worth of sleep," he said to his reflection. "How about you?"

After brushing his teeth, Michael ran upstairs to hug Giggy goodnight.

He wrapped his arms around her thin waist.

"Goodnight," he said.

"Goodnight sweetheart," she replied, and then went on to say, "Michael honey, I don't know what's going on with you, but it's God's work for sure. Still baby, be careful. Please ... for Giggy." She pulled him close one last time and added. "I love you sweetheart, sleep well and tell Tim I love him always."

An unspoken understanding blossomed between them. When she released him, she spotted a tear in his eye.

"I will Gigster," he replied, then quickly went down to his room.

After crawling under the covers, Michael found himself too tired to sleep. His body felt totally relaxed and docile, but his mind was on fast forward.

"Dad, did you hear what Giggy said about what I'm doing being

God's work?" he asked, stretched and yawned again.

'Yes sweetheart, I did. It's true that the Bible says our Lord God sent the meek against the mighty, and they were always triumphant. God is always with us. But it would be dangerous to assume his grace is behind our quest. You know the saying, "Vengeance is mine sayeth the Lord,"' answered Tim.

Slowly slipping into a pre-dormant stage of sleeping, Michael contemplated what his dad had said.

"You're right, but remember, He always used someone to administer a little justice as well, like the story of David and Goliath," he said dreamily, slowly rolling over on his side and snuggling up in a fetal position.

'More like Michael the Arch Angel,' Tim mused.

"Dad, will you tell me a story the way you used to?" Michael asked. There wasn't a response, only a soft but steady hint of breathing. The room became a temple of tranquility as one of God's precious children drifted off into a dream world where only he could travel.

◆ ◆ ◆ ◆ ◆

The sound of a huge timber slowly being dragged over the cobblestone road was barely audible over the roar from the crowd. Everywhere he looked, strangely dressed people were arguing and chanting. All Michael wanted to do is see what was going on. He tried again to push his way to the front, but failed. A funny-speaking man repeatedly shoved him back and for some reason, yelling angry gibberish at him.

Like a human tidal wave, the huge mass of people poured from the city's gate, continuing to flow as one to a small hill shaped like a skull.

The further they went, the angrier Michael became. Why was he being held back from the event unfolding beyond the wall of adults? He wondered. Pushed to his very limits, he began kicking at the rear ends of those blocking his view. A very tanned man with a dirty looking beard turned around and pushed Michael to the ground, where he landed painfully on his bottom. Then the man barked some kind of foreign command at a woman standing next to him. She immediately, and forcefully, jerked Michael to his feet, said something demandingly that Michael couldn't comprehend, then repeatedly slapped his already sore backside.

Michael stood there in shock. 'Who does this woman think she is to even consider touching me', he thought, as his anger started to boil over. That is until he saw the pain on her face and a tear in her eye. Michael loved her and didn't know why.

All of a sudden, there was a sharp clank of a hammer hitting something metal. Whatever it was, it changed the attitude of everyone. Most produced groans of disgust. A few minutes later, everything went dead silent. It was as if nothing would ever utter another peep.

In unison, everyone in front of Michael fell on their faces, finally allowing Michael his first glimpse of the reason for the gathering. There on the hill were three men on three crosses. The one in the center was bleeding from every pore of his body. He had been severely beaten by the devil himself. No human could have ever been so cruel. Plus, to add insult to injury, some demon had forced a crown of huge thorns painfully down on the poor man's head.

Through excruciating anguish, the abused man looked right into Michael's eye, and Michael understood instantly that this was being done just for him. He, too, fell to the ground and cried mournfully.

The sky turned black as coal and the earth trembled. The woman beside him kept calling his name pleadingly.

"Michael," she said. "Michael! Michael honey! Wake up sweetheart. You're having a bad dream. You were screaming baby. Wake up."

He finally opened his eyes and sat up in bed, covered with tears

186

and sweat. Seeing the welcoming face of his great grandmother, he began to cry harder.

"Oh Giggy! People are Horrible!" he exclaimed, falling into her arms where he sobbed uncontrollably.

Unexpected Vengeance

CHAPTER 12

It was too early to workout. The garage would be freezing until about noon, so after breakfast, Michael sat back down in front of his computer and booted up his search engine. His objective was to find something that would give him a current address on Otey. The man had more or less vanished after being released from prison.

Anita came down the stairs and just shook her head.

"You look like someone painted that shirt on you," she said and pulled at the sleeve to prove her point. "I'll get my purse. We're going shopping," she announced.

Michael rolled his eyes. Like most men, he hated going places to try on clothes. But then his frown turned into a pleading smirk.

"Can we also go to Toys-R-Us®?" he asked brightly.

"Why sure. We'll make a day of it," she answered with a loving smile, happy to see Michael acting eight again.

"Yippee," he yelled as he ran upstairs to get ready and grab some cash. Money would never be a problem. The estate would see to that. He removed a hundred dollar bill from his stash and shoved it into his front pocket. He also grabbed his bankcard to purchase clothes.

'Time to buy a wallet there Richie Rich,' Tim mused.

"You never know what a shop-'til-you-drop is gonna cost with Giggy dad," Michael responded.

The computer chimed to alert its user of a hit. Michael returned to look at the screen, finding an interesting bit of information.

"Giggy!" he yelled. "We also need to stop at Sports Authority."

♦ ♦ ♦ ♦ ♦

Every store they patronized was saturated with frantic holiday shoppers.

'Now do you see why I hated to go out on the Friday after Thanksgiving?' Tim inquired.

"Come on dad, you hated shopping every day of the year," Michael said with a chuckle.

It took a while, but Michael finally managed to slip away from Anita and walked to the front of the store, getting in line at the courtesy desk. The minutes dragged by as he waited his turn.

After reaching the front, the young woman behind the counter simply looked past him to the next adult. "Welcome to Sports Authority. How may I help you?" she asked in an overly rehearsed and monotone voice.

The elderly black woman behind him started to step forward, but Michael stopped her by speaking up.

"Yes you certainly may!" he said and moved closer.

Clearly irritated, the clerk huffed and rolled her eyes.

"What do you want kid? Can't you see I'm busy?" she barked.

"I'm sorry, but I was here first!" Michael informed her.

She let out a groan of displeasure.

Michael did the same, then placed his hands on his hips with determination. He read her nametag before speaking.

"Listen Julie, I'm offended by your obnoxious, unprofessional behavior." He paused and pointed to his chest. "I have as much right to courtesy and respect as any of my older fellow patrons." Now he pointed his finger at her. "It's your obligatory responsibility as a visible representative of this establishment to accommodate those of any age with professionally orientated service-etiquette," he finished, and three or four people in the line began to clap.

Showing his disappointment, Michael turned and acted as if he were going to leave. On the wall in front of him was a huge sign with a picture on it introducing the store's manager. Michael stopped and turned back around.

"In answer to your earlier question, what I want is to borrow someone's cell phone. I would like to call my uncle Mark, who just happens to be in charge of this franchise. I'm sure he'll be thrilled over your disreputable attitude! Good day!" he said with a wave of his hand, letting her know that she was unworthy of any further articulation. He felt like laughing as he turned again to leave. Many of the others in line held out their phone for him to make good on his threat.

"Hold on young man, please," Julie pleaded.

Michael granted Julie his full attention but offered no form of articulation. Instead, he crossed his arms over his chest, openly displaying frustration.

His facial expression prompted her to grovel.

"I'm terribly sorry for the misunderstanding. I only thought that you were with the lady behind you," she lied, smiling like the cat who ate the canary, letting go a nervous little laugh.

Still not convinced that he had her to the point of doing just about anything that he asked, Michael pushed on.

"So your justification for being ungracious and unmannerly was based simply on misidentification?" he inquired, slowly lowering his arms to portray an intolerable animosity. "Wow, you're really trying to insult my intelligence!" he said.

The dark skinned woman who had stood there during the entire altercation moved forward and took hold of Michael's hand.

"How old you be honey child?" she asked with a tone of natural warmth and admiration.

Michael's manners kicked in automatically. This woman could derail his plan, but that didn't give him the right to be rude.

"I'm almost nine ma'am. My birthday is February twenty-sixth," he responded politely.

"Well, I swanny! You shore nuf gots some fancy talkin' for a youngun," she pointed out. "Now don't bees letin' dis smart-aleck lil girl bees callin' no demons of anger on ya so it bees weighin' ya down baby," she advised, then patted his hand. "Do Ms. Millie a favor an' bees tellin' dis girl wat it tis you bees needin' so's I cans bees getin' on home," she suggested, releasing his hand and stepping back in line.

Julie forced a smile.

"May I please help you?" she asked so sweetly, Michael thought he felt cavities forming in his molars.

"Yes. Thank you. I need to see a "request for delivery" form. It's on numerous types of exercise equipment purchased last Friday morning. The customer name is Onezean Otey."

The clerk looked suspicious.

"Is there a problem with the order? I wrote that one myself," she admitted cautiously.

Michael smiled.

"No problems. It's so I can get an idea of what to buy my dad for Christmas. I'd hate to get him something duplicating what he just bought. I'm sure you can understand," he said as convincingly as he could.

Julie didn't bite.

"As I recall, Mr. Otey was a handsome young African-American around twenty-two years old. You're trying to tell me he's your dad?" she questioned.

Michael dropped his head like he felt shame.

"It just doesn't feel right calling him my step-dad. He's the only person who ever treated me like a son," he explained, then raised his head and his voice. "This is because he's black, isn't it?!" He almost yelled. New people started to gather around to witness whatever was going on. "Is your reluctance to provide proper service to me racially motivated?" Michael asked in an accusing tone.

Julie almost jumped out of her skin.

"No! No stop. I'll get it! I'll get it! Just hold on a second please!" she pleaded frantically while going through her on-site files.

The friendly black lady leaned forward and whispered in Michael's ear.

"Stepdaddy, child I ain't never heard the likes a' you. You bees sumpin' else I swanny!" she said.

It didn't take long for Julie to find and hand over the forms Michael requested.

Michael stepped to the side and examined the documents for any information he could use. The first thing he noticed was everything was paid for in cash.

'I guess crime really does pay,' Tim said

Michael didn't respond. His thoughts were on Onezean, and what a clever criminal he was not to leave a paper trail anywhere.

"But not clever enough," Michael mused when he finished the second page of the contract. Like most people, Onezean didn't realize that the store usually doesn't sell you the items off the showroom floor. They come from the manufacturer. The proprietor has a responsibility to insure the transport of the merchandise in case of damage during shipping and handling, the owner becoming the beneficiary. An address is a number one priority after the name or names of the buyer. "And that's how I found your butt Otey," Michael said joyfully to himself. There on the insurance form in big black letters was the address of the next creep to pay the piper.

"Thank you!" Michael said while handing the forms back to Julie. He turned and said merry Christmas to Ms. Millie, catching a glimpse of Anita standing by the doors watching him. He walked over to her side, not knowing how long she'd been there, or what she may have heard.

Anita gently took his hand.

"I don't even want to know," she informed him.

In the back of Anita's mind, she couldn't help wondering about the list of strange things Michael had her purchase, and what was on her great grandson's mind.

Keeping time with the car's wipers, they sang Christmas carols all the way home.

♦ ♦ ♦ ♦ ♦

Even though it came with numerous irritations, the cab ride was a completely new and exciting adventure for Michael.

The first problem of the day was the Hispanic driver, Blanco, who pretended to speak broken English when it suited him. The main problem was getting him to pick him up, a child, from lock-three's recreational park. The bickering got so bad that Michael was tempted to retrieve his bike from the bushes where he'd hidden it earlier and just go for a ride like he'd told Giggy he was going to do, trying again tomorrow. Or, as Jackie suggested, grab a piece of driftwood from the beach nearby and knock some sense into the Mexican's fat head. Michael didn't do either one.

'Side-kick him in the crotch, punch his lights out, do something, he's wasting our time!' Jackie screamed, sharing Michael's frustration

Almost ready to comply, Michael unconsciously moved his left foot back into striking position. In his mind's eye, the act was perfectly executed and he was sitting at home watching cartoons when the immigrant came to. However, the reasoning voice of his father cleared away the fantasy.

'Wave a fifty under his nose,' Tim suggested.

194

Michael reached into his shirt pocket following the advice.

The cabbie's dark eyes grew to twice their normal size, and his English improved drastically.

"Okay, my friend! Where do you wish to go?" he asked through a mouthful of green teeth and reached for the dangling bill.

Michael jerked it back quickly, changing the man's facial expression in the process.

"When we get where we're going. No drivey. No money. Comprendes?" Michael explained, wiggling the cash in the air, captivating the Mexican's attention.

Though it made him angry, the currency was calling Blanco's name.

"Si. Me understand," he admitted, then with a small bow, more accustomed to the orient, he motioned to the rear of his cab, stepping back to allow Michael to enter of his own accord.

After buckling himself in, Michael checked his watch, thirty minutes behind schedule.

"Let's get a move on. I'm in a hurry," he said, then leaned back to enjoy the ride. But his mind raced as he contemplated what lay before him. He removed Onezean's picture from his backpack and studied the killer's face. "Today you will pay," he whispered.

Looking up, Michael caught the cabbie's vigilant and venomous stare in the rear view mirror. He could read the man's thoughts in his eyes. Some evil plan was forming deep in the driver's mind of how to separate Michael from his money and the cab.

'I wish you'd try it amigo,' Michael thought.

At the next red light, acting as if he hadn't seen the looks, Michael reached up his sleeves and magically extracted two, six-inch throwing knives from a sheath attached to his forearms. Like a circus performer, he began juggling and twisting them around his hands masterfully. Every third or fourth move was a deadly thrust. By the time the light had changed, so had Blanco's intentions. Now when he checked his mirror, he displayed a healthy fear and respect.

The rest of the ride was peaceful and void of anything but thought.

"We are here," announced the cabbie as he pulled up to the curb.

The address of course was not the one Michael was in search of. The last thing he needed right now was to be dropped off in front of the home of a manic, one that the cab companies records could leave a trail back to him. If he was victorious in today's revenge-fueled battle, the presence of a red headed eight-year-old at the crime scene would cause him a lot of trouble. Thankfully, Paul Dickson's pride had caused him to report being beaten by a rival gang, instead of a trick-or-treater. But the police knew that Michael was there that night, and there really was no way anyone would believe in such impossible coincidences.

On the other hand, if today was a failure, it wouldn't matter anyway. That thought made him anxious.

"Is there a problem senor?" the driver prompted tentatively.

"No. No problem," Michael answered, handing Blanco the fare and the extra fifty.

"Wait here, I'll be back shortly," Michael instructed.

"Sure," Blanco replied without conviction, stopping Michael short of exiting the cab.

Michael turned back around and pulled a one hundred dollar bill from his pocket. When it had the Mexican's full attention, Michael spoke firmly.

"Take a siesta," he said, and to the astonishment of Blanco, tore the bill in half. He put one piece back in his shirt and offered the other half to the driver. "Thirty minutes max," Michael said as he left the car, the damaged bill spoke clearly in all languages.

With his pack slung over his shoulder, Michael began jogging through the yards, quickly disappearing from sight.

Five homes later, he emerged at his destination. A two-story, white square house with a flat roof that doubled as a balcony. The garage door was open and the interior was full of brand new weight lifting machines. Some barbells were scattered haphazardly around the driveway.

'Looks like our boy has been trying out his new toys. Hopefully he's worn out,' Tim said

"I hope so dad. There's over two hundred pounds on the bench press. Otey must be pretty big," Michael responded as he walked up to the house.

Thankfully, the Lord had blessed the day with sunshine and warmth, so with all the outside activities, he didn't appear to be out of place.

His scar began to itch and tingle.

"Here we go dad! Show time!" he said, scanning the area for his quarry.

The wait didn't last long. The front door opened to allow Onezean to step from the dwelling.

"Hey kid! What are you doing?" He inquired unthreateningly as he walked up, towering over his visitor like a giant. Even though it was late November, Otey wore a sleeveless T-shirt and cutoff shorts. His muscles were well defined and bulging from recent use. In one hand, he held a tiny cell phone and in the other a large glass of iced water.

"Aw nothing mister. Just looking at all this cool stuff," Michael answered as if his curiosity had justified his trespassing.

At the use of the title "mister," Onezean's chest swelled even further with pride and ego. He was obviously unaccustomed to being addressed with any respect.

"I just had it delivered this morning. Early Christmas present to myself," explained Otey.

Michael walked into the garage and whistled at the extravagance of the equipment.

"Wow mister, you must be really rich!" he exclaimed excitedly, his itch becoming an uncomfortable burn, demanding action.

"Not really. I just came into some extra cash," Otey bragged deviously. After following his uninvited guest into the garage, Onezean studied Michael inquisitively. "I've seen you some place before. But I can't put my finger on where," he said.

Michael's stomach turned sour and he pretended to be confused as well.

"Maybe around the neighborhood," he offered, shrugging his shoulders. "I bet you could lift all this weight with one hand, huh mister?" Michael added, relying on the criminal's vanity to change the direction of their conversation, which was successful.

Otey's suspicious expression turned to one of uncontrolled pride.

"Yeah, I guess I could. I bench press five hundred pounds," he lied.

Michael's eyes widened in pretend awe.

"Wow, oh man! That's as much as a truck," he said, acting like he believed the creep.

Eager to show off, Onezean set his things down on a box and pulled the bench press out into the driveway. There, he added a six-foot steel bar and four fifty pound plates. Next, he began waving his hands in the air to warm up. After that, he laid down on the bench.

Michael discretely bent down and picked up a twenty-pound dumbbell, which he carefully hid behind his back.

Otey lifted the weights from their cradle and lowered them to his chest. Blowing out forcefully, he pushed them back up until his arms locked.

"One!" he moaned, then repeated the movement. "Two!"

"I think I remember where you've seen me before," Michael announced.

"Three!" Otey called out. "Where's that?" asked the showoff. "Four!"

The reps were getting slower and his arms began to shake.

"Yeah, I'm sure I do now," Michael stated. "It was the night you shit heads robbed the arena and killed my dad."

The bar descended to the criminal's chest at the same time as the realization of what the kid said sunk into his mind, causing a pause in the exercise movement.

Michael leaned over and looked down into the man's shocked eyes.

"You remember? You hit my dad with the butt of your shotgun," he said and swung the heavy steel apparatus in his hand at the creep's jaw. "Like this!" he added.

Otey frantically tried to push the bar back up to its resting place, but three-fourths of the way, the dumbbell struck his chin, stealing all his strength. Isaac Newton's law returned the two hundred fifty pounds to his chest with a sickening crunch, expelling every ounce of his breath in a rush of pain.

Michael raised his new weapon in the air as high as he could reach and dropped it on the crook's nose. It sounded like a watermelon hitting the concrete from two stories up.

Michael's internal knowledge of the human anatomy assured him that this killer was finished. He started to leave.

A very audible gurgle of blood caused him to pause. *'Don't look back son. It's just the sound of death,'* Tim explained.

"I won't dad," Michael said and moved further down the driveway. The clank of the weights being replaced back on their hooks stopped him dead in his tracks. He spun around to find the bloody, agonizing, hate-fueled face of the killer coming his way.

Onezean had staggered to his feet with murderous intentions written on every aspect of his being. Before he could speak, he spat a mouthful of broken teeth and bloody saliva onto the grass.

"You're dead," he moaned through the pain.

Michael's new fear paralyzed him where he stood.

'Run!' Tim Screamed.

Otey continued to move in Michael's direction like a recently reanimated zombie. When he came to within five feet of claiming his next victim, Michael's cross burned like a branding iron, snapping him from the hypnotic grip of terror.

The dark blood running from the corners of Onezean's mouth verified massive internal injuries. Any normal human would've never survived the recent trauma, but the evil driving this demon wanted revenge. He seemed to be drawing power from the devil himself.

Knowing it was only a matter of minutes before the grim reaper claimed Otey's violent soul, Michael ran to the side of the house with the murderer hot on his trail. At the back of the home, a staircase ascending to the balcony-style roof, gave Michael a temporary advantage. He scrambled up them with ease while his pursuer, fighting for air, had to almost crawl.

Once aloft, Michael realized that he'd made a grave error. There wasn't another way down except back past his demonic follower.

The roof had a table and chairs for entertaining welcomed guests, some recliners for the occasional sunbather and potted bushes to give the place a natural beach look.

Michael's instincts told him to hide, but where? He was out of time. The heavy labored breathing of his walking nightmare indicated that the steps had failed to finish the job he'd started. He ran to the far side of the roof and fell to his knees behind one of the planters displaying a fake evergreen. Not to conceal himself but to buy a few minutes. He quickly removed his backpack and started rummaging through it. The second he placed his hand on the eight-inch nun chucks Anita bought him, Onezean was there. With superhuman strength, Otey grabbed and threw the huge cement pot like a paperweight. It flew all the way across the balcony before crashing into a thousand pieces.

Michael's first reaction was to attack the killer's kneecaps in a zigzag motion with the small weapon, then at the top of the man's bare feet with lightning-fast blows. The results were minimal at best. In fact, the pain it inflicted seemed to have an adverse effect, actually appearing to invigorate the maniac.

Crawling away on all fours, Michael rushed beneath the nearby table in an attempt to escape with his life. No sooner had he'd gotten under it than it too became a projectile, but this one landed out of sight, crashing somewhere below in the side yard.

Trying once again to scurry away, Michael felt an iron grip seize his belt at the rear and begin to pull. He could feel the heat from the sun as the tug of war exposed his skin. Out of pure desperation, he started kicking with all his might. The contact of each strike should have caused damage to any normal human being, but on this dark-skinned version of the terminator, it was wasted energy.

Onezean lifted Michael effortlessly with one hand like he was inspecting a lobster, honed in on his target, launching a deadly punch.

With the name of Jesus on his lips, Michael's belt miraculously broke, allowing him to slip free, which caused the projected punch to strike nothing but air. Ignoring the growing pain in his neck, he again tried coming to his feet, only just in time for

Otey to grab him by the ankle. Otey lifted Michael into the air and started swinging him violently into the furniture and railing. With every connecting blow, Michael felt himself losing consciousness. The battle was over, and he'd lost. He knew he would see his dad again soon, and that was strangely comforting. He actually felt calm.

Jackie Lee must have taken over the remainder of Michael's strength. Out of nowhere, Michael found the throwing knives in his hands, not even sure how they had gotten there. With the precision of a highly trained master, he launched both blades. The first finding its mark in the attacker's bicep. The next between his knuckles, causing the involuntary release of Michael, allowing him to crash painfully to the floor again.

After rolling over, Michael watched in horror as Onezean pulled the metal dagger from his hand like removing a ring, then from his upper arm with little more than a grimace on his blood-soaked face.

Like King-Kong, Otey lifted a nearby four-foot long cement planter over his head, intending to smash Michael like a cockroach.

Too worn out to move, all Michael could do is close his eyes and pray. He asked God to let his death be quicker and less painful than last time.

The crash sounded like two tractor trailers colliding, but distant. His prayer had been answered. There wasn't any new pain inflicted on his already agonizing body. *'Wait a minute. If I'm dead, why do I still hurt?'* He thought to himself, opening his eyes, hoping to see his dad, but found himself on the criminal's roof. The only thing different was the absence of the killer.

Michael painfully picked himself up and walked over to the edge of the roof where he could look over the railing. The driveway was littered with fragments of broken concrete from the obliterated planter.

After pulling himself up further where he could look straight

202

down, he was sickened by the sight of Onezean's remains. The lifeless body was grotesquely bent over backward where the spine had snapped from landing on the weight bar, still sitting on the weight bench. Either Otey had lost his balance or he had finally succumbed to the injuries Michael caused earlier. Part of Michael hoped the creep fell, but the vengeful side felt different. Either way, the creep was dead, and Michael was glad of it.

Fighting the urge to throw up, Michael turned away from the carnage and began retrieving his scattered weapons and backpack. Each move felt like he was still being beaten, then painfully he descended the steps, stopping in the garage long enough to pocket Onezean's cell phone. And even though dad said never to eat or drink after anyone, he turned the glass of iced water up, drinking it down in seconds.

Leaving the house, Michael made a wide path around the hideous corpse that appeared inhuman and seemed to be staring at him unblinkingly.

The sound of an emergency response team could be heard in the distance, making Michael realize he had to hurry despite the excruciating pain, and do so without being seen.

The cab was right where he'd left it, and he limped to it the best he could. To him, it was a beautiful sight.

"Thank you God," he said as he reached the back door.

After entering the car, the driver's look told Michael he was a mess.

"Couple of bullies. You should see them!" Michael explained in a way that said, "Don't ask Blanco. There will be no further elaboration."

"Back to lock three," Michael said and slid his half of the torn currency up to the cabbie.

Trying to conceive a story to tell Giggy, he came up with a bike wreck. One that he knew would mean taking a hammer to his bicycle later and pushing it off a cliff, but nothing else could explain so many injuries.

He tried not to sleep because of a possible concussion, but he drifted off anyway. Next thing he remembered was the cabbies voice informing him of their arrival, him arguing with someone, and waking up in his own bed cleaned and bandaged. The rest was a fog-filled blur.

CHAPTER 13

There was a mid-December chill in the air as Michael rolled over and reluctantly opened his groggy eyes. The first thing he detected was an overwhelming scent of pine, courtesy of Giggy's attempt to naturalize their artificial Christmas tree with a can of forest fresh spray. The smell stimulated his thoughts uncontrollably with a small spark of holiday excitement shared by normal eight-year-olds. But it also created a totally new, and unfamiliar feeling of sadness, dread, and loathing. Emotions he'd rather live without.

How unfair it felt to celebrate without dad's physical presence. Especially knowing that somewhere, two of his killers would be joyously attending family gatherings. Neither of them having any concerns over the homes they'd destroyed. Even opening gifts purchased with blood money and receiving hugs and kisses like the ones Michael could never again enjoy from his mom and dad.

Anger and frustration began to gnaw at his mind, and he allowed it to direct his attentions. He would finish this ugly, vengeful quest of his before Christmas if it killed him, temporarily forgetting the last adventure had almost done just that. The more his imagination produced a mental picture of holiday cheer in Watts and Caldrone, fantasy or not, the more enraged he became.

He threw off his covers, ready to begin his attack with the forcefulness of a charging tiger. However, the advance was short-lived. Immediately he was ordered to retreat by a bugle-call of pain shooting up his right side. It quickly joined a deep ache in his neck and shoulders.

"Aah!" he groaned, lowering himself gently back to the mattress.

Minutes later, the creaking of the staircase gave warning of Giggy's inevitable visit, robbing him of his choice to remain motionless.

Relinquishing the comfort of his Serta®, Michael forced himself to rise again, this time with respect for his condition. He knew when she arrived that he had to be fully animated, but also fully unhampered by his injuries. If not, she would insist on taking him to see his pediatrician, who would require a step-by-step explanation leading up to his trauma. The main problem with that was, he couldn't remember any of the details of the story he'd made up for Giggy. Plus, the contusions, scrapes, and scratches may, under professional scrutiny, be inconsistent with his accounts of the incident. If Anita discovered his deceit, she wouldn't let him out of her sight until he turned eighteen. And that would definitely put a hold on his deliverance of justice and a stay of execution for Watts and Caldrone.

Grimacing, Michael managed to be standing next to his window when Anita arrived. He pretended to be mesmerized by something beyond the glass.

"Morning honey," Anita said.

Michael turned as if surprised by her presence.

"Oh! Hi Giggy," he said, not showing any anguish, and crossed the room to receive his morning hug. He wanted to scream as Anita's frail arms embraced him. Although she was as gentle as a summer breeze, it felt like a two-ton bull had used him for a seat. The second she released him, he had to turn away from her to hide tears caused by the pain.

"Breakfast will be ready soon, so get dressed for church," she announced, turning to leave. "One more thing," she added. "Will you do your Giggy a favor and grab the paper out front," she asked and left the room.

Michael let out a small sigh of relief, then after catching his breath, he tenderly retrieved his suit from the closet and put it on. The movements seemed to relieve the stiffness, and he was actually looking forward to the day, with yesterday's adventure beginning to fade from his mind.

As he walked up the driveway in the crisp, fresh morning air, his mood improved with each step.

"Thank you, God," he said, as he admired the clear blue sky.

The paper hadn't arrived yet, but the delivery van could be seen slowly moving up the road a dozen homes away. Having time, Michael sat down on the curb to reflect on the beautiful morning. Becoming lost so much so that he missed the sound of the automobile as it came up next to him.

"Hey Opie! Wake up!" came the teasing voice of the thin guy behind the wheel, poking fun at Michael's similarities to a young Ron Howard.

Michael stood up and dusted off the rear end of his dress pants before approaching the van.

"Here's your paper Opie!" the man said as he handed the rolled parchment through the open window.

Michael accepted it with a smile.

"Thanks, Barney! Say hi to Thelma Lou for me," he said, returning the pun because the guy looked like the deputy from Mayberry.

For a second, the man was confused and then caught on, bursting into robust laughter.

"Merry Christmas!" he said and waved.

"Y'all too Barn and Goober says hey," Michael answered, returning the wave.

Halfway down the driveway, Michael rolled the rubber band off the fire-log-sized publication. His only interest was the Sunday comics, so he began working them out of the center of the large conglomeration of media press.

'Did you see the front page?' Tim asked.

Michael knew that he had, but only subconsciously took note.

"Not really dad. Why?" he asked.

'I think you should, however, please find a place to sit down first,' Tim suggested.

Michael's stomach filled with hundreds of spastic butterflies. His conscious mind holding back what his eyes had seen, refusing to release even the smallest hint.

After reentering the house, Michael went directly to his room and dropped the heavy newspaper on the bed face up, reluctantly forcing himself to take a quick look.

"Oh my God," he whispered with a quivering breath as he tried not to scream. Even though he'd seen it before, the shock of having it in front of him again made him weak in the knees.

'Are you going to be alright son?' Tim asked concernedly.

Michael only nodded his head slowly and ran his fingers over the page lightly as if he were reading braille. No longer holding back, he began to cry mournfully.

By the time Anita had finished preparing breakfast, she was convinced that Michael had fallen back to sleep. She quietly descended the steps to check. He hadn't fooled her this morning by pretending to be pain free, any more so than his made up bike wreck. She would wait for him to tell her the truth whenever he felt comfortable in doing so. And if she found him in bed, she'd let him sleep. His breakfast could always be reheated.

The last thing Anita expected was to find Michael sitting in the corner crying with his face in his hands.

"What's wrong sweetheart?" she asked as she knelt down, taking him in her arms, then like the baby he'd always be to her, began rocking him back and forth. Neither spoke a word. Love was speaking loud and clear for the both of them. Just like when

Tim held his boy, Anita cared for nothing else at the moment; the world would have to wait.

After a few minutes, she kissed Michael on top of his red head, then took his cheeks in her hands and gently lifted her great-grandson's face so she could see into his teary blue eyes.

"Why Giggy?" Michael asked with torment in his voice.

"Why what honey? What is it sunshine?" Anita softly pleaded.

Michael wiped his eyes with the back of his hand before answering.

"Why did they take my daddy from me?" he asked, still fighting back overwhelming emotion.

Pulling him back into her arms, Anita resumed the rhythmic movements.

"I don't know precious, I just don't know," she admitted, then started rubbing his shoulders. "What brought that up baby doll?" she inquired

Instead of speaking, Michael just pointed toward the paper on his bed.

A distant beeping alerted Anita that the biscuits were ready to be removed from the oven. Even though nothing was more important to her than Michael, allowing the house to burn down around them didn't seem wise. Reluctantly, she released Michael and got to her feet.

"I'll be right back honey. Our breakfast is going to burn," she said apologetically. Before leaving, she decided to take a quick look on Michael's bed. "Lord have mercy," she whispered to herself. All her emotion transformed into pure rage. She barely resisted the urge to tear into the paper, shredding it into a million pieces. The calling timer kept her from doing just that, knowing that the next sound would be the smoke alarm. Angrily, she gathered the parchment into a crumpled mass and left the room.

Once Anita reached the top of the stairs, she dumped the whole thing into the trash container, quickly removed the food from the oven, and went back down to the basement. She was relieved to see Michael standing at the bathroom sink washing his face.

"Are you alright?" she inquired while reaching into the closet for a clean towel for him to use.

Accepting it, Michael wiped the dripping water from his cheeks.

"Yeah Giggy, I'm fine now," he said and turned to stare at his reflection in the mirror. "Where is it?" he asked disgustedly.

Crossing her arms, she stepped a little closer.

"I threw the horrible thing in the trash. I'm sorry I sent you to get it. I feel awful. I should have gone myself," she admitted, lowering her head in shame.

This time it was Michael who wrapped his arms around Anita. The roles had reversed. He was now the comforter.

"It's not your fault. There's no way you could have known," he explained as reassuringly as possible.

Anita tried to show she was as brave as Michael appeared to be.

"I guess you're no longer in the mood for breakfast, are you?" she asked.

"Giggy, it would take a lot more than some stupid newspaper article to keep me from one of your delicious meals." He patted his midsection to indicate he needed to fill his fat belly, an action borrowed from his dad.

This show made Anita smile. She loved cooking for her baby, so she ruffled Michael's hair and turned to leave.

"Well, hurry along, it's ready. Still going to church?"

Michael smiled brightly.

"Wouldn't miss it for the world," he proclaimed joyfully.

♦ ♦ ♦ ♦ ♦

Nothing else was said about the morning attempt by Satan to ruin their day. They actually had a wonderful time at breakfast, talking about Michael's Christmas wishes.

Two things shocked Anita though. The first was the amount of food that her great grandson consumed: four fried eggs, three pieces of toast with butter, and five links sausages. She didn't keep track of how many glasses of milk the boy drank, but it was enough to satisfy a lumberjack. The second shock was Michael's pursuance of her desires for the holidays. She was always doing things for him, now he wanted to do something nice for her in return, which swelled her heart. Whenever she was convinced that she couldn't love him more than she already did, he would prove her wrong.

The morning was turning out to be a blessing. A couple of times, however, she caught Michael glancing at the trashcan with a hint of despair. It made her wish she'd thrown the newspaper into the oven while it was hot, burning the thing to a crispy piece of coal. She still fought the urge, even though it would be dangerous and messy. But no matter what happened now, she couldn't take the image from her baby's mind.

As soon as the meal was over, Michael asked to be excused and ran back down to the basement to finish getting ready for church. Anita knew he was actually headed for the toilet, and that would give her a few minutes to accomplish a task she had set for herself earlier. Even though it made her feel disgusted, she removed the newspaper from the trash can and carried it to her room.

It didn't take long to find the media giant's phone number in the advertising section. Anita dialed the digits and the call was answered on the third ring.

"Yes you can. I need to speak with your manager in sales and distribution … Yes, I'll hold, but not for very long," she said, receiving no answer. The receptionist had already transferred the call. A nerve racking music resembling vocal-less rock and roll filled the line for what seemed like an eternity, adding to her frustration.

Finally, someone answered.

"To whom am I speaking?" Anita asked and waited for a response. "Well, Mr. Jack Jones, I need to cancel my subscription immediately," she said, then conveyed her full name and address ... "No sir. The delivery has always been on time for the past twenty-five years," she started to hang up when something Mr. Jones said caught her full attention. "What did you just say?" she inquired and then listened. "Yes you can make a recording of this call for quality control. Plus, if you're unsure of what I'm saying is what I mean, you can play it again as many times as you like." She again let Mr. Jones try to save her business, and really irritating her in the process. "No! I do not wish to have a free month of service! Listen up, what I want is to never see your publication in my home again. And if I do, I'll call the sheriff! Yes, I'll give you a reason. It's your front page story today. The one of Onezean Otey being found murdered in Goodlettsville and the graphic picture of his broken body lying on that ... whatever it is ... '' she was explaining when she paused in mid sentence. The man on the other end must have rudely interrupted her with something that finally pushed her from irritated to just plain angry. "No, that is not all Mr. Smart Ass!" she snapped, her use of profanity even shocking herself. She never cursed, so she took a deep breath in an attempt to calm down, then continued more civilly. "It's the other picture that makes me as mad as a wet hornet. Under your headline of "POLICE SUSPECT MURDER VICTIM TIED TO THIS SUMMER'S HOMICIDE OF NASHVILLE DOCTOR", your paper felt the need to include a snapshot of my grandson-in-law, lying dead in his own blood, just to sensationalize your report. Those people are someone's family members Mr. Jones. My eight-year-old great-grandson got to see his mutilated father's body on the front page as an early Christmas present. Thanks a lot!" she spat angrily. Feeling herself about to start cussing again, she slammed the phone down without another word.

Anita's anger soon turned into an uncontrollable curiosity. She needed to read the rest of the story.

"A detective named Bruce Edison, with the Metro Police Department, had tried unsuccessfully to convince the locals on the scene that Mr. Otey's death was accidental. However, blood found on the roof, as well as on other types of equipment in the garage discredited his claim. He was also quoted as believing there was no possible connection to the doctor's shooting. This, too, became proven incorrect when a search of the home turned up two of the arena's moneybags and a sawed-off shotgun, which may very well be that night's murder weapon. Everything has been sent to the lab for further inspection."

Anita was thinking how stupid, or how crooked, this Edison person must be when the final line of the story crushed her heart: "Red-headed neighborhood boy seen at the home around the time of death was being sought for questioning."

Something in her brain short-circuited, and in her mind, she screamed Michael's name. Slowly she lowered the paper as the battle between her emotions and her intellect began. The truth was right before her eyes in black and white, but she refused to acknowledge it.

"He was home all day Friday. That was the day he'd wrecked his bike," she whispered, now trying to believe his story.

The memory of that day now flashed through her head like a bolt of lightning. She had told Michael that he looked like he had been fighting for his life.

'Come on Anita, there's got to be thousands of red headed boys around ... who just happened to be at the violent demise of one of Tim's killers?' She questioned herself and could feel her sanity slipping away. *'Murder, precious Michael, redheaded boy seen, bike wreck injuries, fight for life.'* The thoughts were coming so quickly, she dearly wanted to scream. To vent her

boiling frustration, Anita attacked the newspaper and started squeezing it harder and harder to quiet its relentless attempts to make her face reality.

"No, No, No ... not my baby!" she yelled, this time unrestrained, then tore the paper in half and threw it across the room. Shocked at her loss of control, Anita fell to her knees and began to pray for God's mercy.

CHAPTER 14

Even though it was the first day of winter, December 21 was warm and beautifully bright with sunshine. These two blessings made it easy for Michael to manipulate Anita into a pleasure trip to Moss-Wright Park.

With school being out for the holidays, the area was crawling with children trying to deplete their unimaginable energy. Even Michael found himself caught up in the frenzy for a while and was having a great time. There were even a few kids from his class who treated him like a long lost friend. It was wonderful being nothing more, nothing less than an eight-year-old Michael Clark.

Later that day, to his surprise, Michael ran into Jerry Cox and his little boy, who was introduced by the nickname J.J.

Michael was delighted that the three-year-old kept calling him sir and Anita said J.J. was so cute that she could bite his head off.

The city park provided swinging benches for the parents to enjoy while allowing a full view of their offspring at play. Jerry rolled himself over to one of them so everyone could sit and talk.

Anita, without hesitation, became J.J.'s playmate. Off they went, clearly pleased with each other's company.

Although bound to a wheelchair for life, the ex-policeman knew how blessed he was, and it showed in his eyes as he watched his son at play.

Because of their past, it didn't take long for the reason for their friendship to become the topic of their conversation.

"Did you hear on the news that for a while there, they thought they had caught the guy who shot me?" Jerry asked solemnly.

Michael's face turned as red as a sunburn.

"What do you mean thought?!" he responded heatedly and shocked.

Cox paused to contemplate why Michael reacted so passionately.

"No evidence to positively link the creep to the crime. They had no choice but to release him," he explained. The account of the story was so painful that he spoke barely above a whisper.

Michael jumped from his seat.

"No evidence!" he yelled, running his fingers through his hair. He looked as if he were about to start pulling it out in frustration. "What about the .38 he had next to his hand the night they arrested him? Isn't that proof?" he asked kicking at a stone. "They had it in a plastic bag with his fingerprints all over it for God's sake," he added and turned back around. The look on Jerry's face told him he'd gone too far.

"How do you know all that?" Cox asked, once a cop, always a cop. And the question sounded like part of an interrogation of a suspect.

Michael knew he'd been caught with his hand in the cookie jar.

"Oh, um, uhh, that's right! I didn't tell you. I had just happened to be trick-or-treating in that area and well, got lost, I mean separated from Giggy, and umm, by some crazy coincidence, as inconceivable as it now seems, ended up at the place where I was, um ... " He stopped trying to explain. If the story sounded half as full of bull crap to Jerry as it did to him, they were both going to need boots. "Where are J.J. and Giggy? I better run find them," Michael said unsuccessfully trying to change the subject, and slowly moving away.

Jerry's firm voice stopped him dead in his tracks.

"Not so fast," he said and pointed at the bench. "Nice try. Sit!" he ordered.

Michael did as instructed.

The ex-lawman continued.

"I guess you also expect me to believe it's a fluke that I gave you the address during one of our talks at therapy?" he asked seriously, then changed his tone. "I've got a question for you," he stated, a smile broadening his face. "How good are you with a piece of copper pipe?" he asked jokingly.

Knowing his secret was out of the bag, Michael smiled back.

"Apparently really good, if I do say so myself," he answered, making them both laugh. Using his index finger, Michael then made a cross on his forehead like the one he left on Paul's face, then pretended to pass out by rolling his eyes back in his head, throwing himself backwards on the bench.

The levity was short lived as the severity of Michael's actions sank in, aging Jerry's face with concern.

"You could have been killed. You do realize that don't you?" he asked, sounding more like a father than a friend.

Still trying to keep a happy overtone in the conversation, Michael made another futile attempt at humor.

"Killed? Been there. Done that. Hated it," he said comically. However, when Jerry failed to respond favorably to his jesting, Michael looked away. "Yeah, I know. But someone has to make those creeps pay for murdering my family and putting you in that chair," he said with tears forming in his eyes.

Jerry felt emotional as well but had an easier time controlling it.

"There's no way of knowing right now who put me in this rolling recliner. As for your mom and dad, there's nothing more I can say except I'm sorry. But this matter should be left to the police," he stated as if the case was closed.

Even though Michael liked Jerry and would do anything in the world for him, his naive statement pushed the wrong button.

"Leave it to the police?" Michael responded and stood up again.

He had a mixed expression of anger and disbelief on his face, his voice raised to just below a shout. "You've got to be frickin' kiddin' me! Leave it to the police to do what? Put them in jail for a couple measly years like the devil who blew my mother's brains out right in front of me! Yeah right, Jerry! Let's leave it to the police my ass!" He was so angry the tears now flowed for a different reason.

Jerry just sat there dumbfounded; shocked into silence.

Michael turned away to control himself. Something inside him wanted to beat some sense into his friend, disabled or not.

"How can you even think like that after the way they've mishandled your case? I was there Jerry. When I mentioned the shooting of you and your partner, believe me, Dickson's face confessed to the crime. He was even willing to risk a few more whacks from a piece of pipe just to keep that information from leaving his house," he explained, then turned back around and placed his hands on the armrests of Jerry's wheelchair, their noses only inches apart. The only emotion left in Michael's heart was rage. "He was one of the shooters Jerry! And he had help!" Michael's voice grew calmer, but deadlier. "David Watts, René Caldrone and Onezean Otey. In the end, they will all face my judgment of death," he proclaimed with undeniable conviction, then stepped back.

Jerry got a detached and faraway look of contemplation for a few seconds, then his focus returned with a new understanding, a veil of shock manifesting on his face.

"Oh my God! Onezean Otey! That was you!" he said as stating a fact.

A test of loyalty had been set in motion. The only sound was of children playing in the background like a distant storm. Michael's rage vanished.

"Now you know," he said and crossed his arms. "I'm not asking for your help, even though I could use it. But friend or foe, please don't get in my way," he said instructively, creating an awkward silence between them. Michael was anticipating a policeman's response instead of a friend's.

Jerry's dilemma was how serious to take what Michael had just said as a threat. On one hand, standing before him was a redheaded, eight-year-old boy with big blue eyes who should only be able to put fear in the fathers of the neighborhood girls. But, on the other hand, he'd seen the fury of Michael's rage on the front pages of newspapers. He placed his hands together as if in prayer, studying Michael's face for any signs of weakness and not detecting even a trace. The boy's slightly swollen black eye driving home his determination for vengeance.

"Do you know how dangerous this is?" Jerry said bluntly as a final attempt as an adult, a friend, and a peace officer, to redirect his young friend's crusade.

"I believe we've already established that fact," Michael responded unmoved.

"No matter what I say or do, you'll finish this quest or die trying, won't you?" Jerry asked as serious as he could, even overemphasizing the word "die."

Michael didn't flinch.

"As the Lord is my witness," he answered coldly. Their eyes locked on each other in a mental battle of will power.

Knowing he was defeated, Cox finally shook his head in submission.

"Okay. As the old saying goes, if you can't beat them, join them," he said, offering his hand, which Michael accepted, forming an alliance. "Although, you'll have to be Batman and I'll be Robin who has to stay in the Bat Mobile," he added and patted the chair's armrests.

"Well crap," Michael said to his bewildered friend disappointedly, then smiled, "I wanted to be Spiderman," he mused, causing them both to laugh through their anxiety. On the surface, all was apparently well while, on the inside, their hearts grew heavy with the burden of the future.

They were soon rejoined by Anita and J.J. causing the conversation to return to the joyful day, and that suited them both just fine.

Anita plopped down on the bench.

"Whew! That child is about to wear me out," she proclaimed, acting drained of energy.

Still full of energy, Jerry Junior climbed up onto her lap.

"Mown Giggy, wess pay," he whined and began tugging on her arm.

"That's enough J.J., let her be," Jerry instructed with a stem fatherly voice.

"Best stay out of it Jerry. He's called her Giggy. That's a clear sign that he's already spoiled beyond recovery," Michael said and raised his arms to block an incoming though non-existing punch, acting as if he was accustomed to being struck.

Jerry joined the laughter when Anita stuck out her tongue like a defiant child.

"See what I mean?" Michael added, and this time received a gentle smack on the shoulder by his great grandmother.

The sun began to go down and soon took along with it the warmth of the day as it slipped slowly below the horizon.

It never ceased to amaze Michael how the super-heated light from the sun could burn your skin one minute, then only required seconds to dissipate into the atmosphere after setting. A little astonishment he had shared with his father. With that thought, he realized he hadn't talked to his dad in days.

Using the excuse of needing to pee, Michael walked away from the others in hopes of finding some solitude. Once he felt sure that no one could overhear him, he spoke quietly.

"Dad, are you still there?" he asked fearfully, knowing he

couldn't face the trials ahead of him alone.

'Of course I'm still here buddy,' Tim answered.

Michael let out a sigh of relief.

"I just haven't heard from you in a while and it scared me," he admitted.

'I'm sorry sweetheart. Jackie and I went out for pizza,' Tim joked.

"I'm serious dad!" Michael shot back.

'Honey, I'll be here as long as you need me,' Tim explained.

"That will be forever dad," Michael responded.

The earlier cheerfulness of the park vanished as quickly as the heat. The place had turned into a battleground of crying, wailing and argumentative children. The patient mothers and fathers could be heard trying to reason with their little ones. Others making false threats of never returning or Santa is watching. Some more or less dragged their kids kicking and screaming to their cars, and a few of those had trouble having a seat after arriving.

"I'm glad I never acted like that," Michael pointed out, shaking his head slightly.

'Yeah right! How soon we forget,' Tim said.

"What's that supposed to mean?" Michael asked, but didn't receive an answer.

To his left stood a huge pavilion that provided a covered picnic area for large gatherings. Today, it gave host to about twenty Hispanics from different families. They were all trying to finish cleaning up their area before the dark made the chore more difficult.

A very pretty young woman's voice drew Michael's full attention.

"René, grab my jacket por favor!" she yelled across the park.

Hearing that name alone was enough to make Michael's blood boil. Following the direction of her inquiring shout, he saw the back of a dark haired man carrying a cardboard box of post-picnic goodies.

"Si mi Rosa!" the guy called back over his shoulder, putting Michael's senses on high alert.

"What do you think dad? Could it be him?" he asked uncertainly.

'There's thousands of Renés. Remember our search on the computer?' Tim said.

Relaxing a little, Michael agreed.

"Yeah, you're right. This couldn't be him, or I'd feel it on my cross," he confessed.

'This isn't some cheap novel where the author can't think of anything better than a coincidental encounter between a hunter and his prey at a city park,' Tim reasoned.

"Unless it's his first," Michael replied and began to circle around to get a better look at this René.

The night was coming on quickly, and Giggy began calling for Michael by his first name. As of yet, there wasn't any panic in her voice, so he turned and could see her walking in a semi-lighted area next to Jerry and J.J., all three headed for the parking lot.

"I'm coming Giggy!" he yelled back to keep her from shouting again. He knew next time she'd use his last name as well. If this was who Michael hoped it would be, hearing that would be devastating at best for the cause.

Fortunately, the container René was carrying had slowed his pace, allowing Michael the advantage of speed. He came around the side of a Ford Bronco with tinted windows seconds before the Spanish man reached the parking lot. The darkness and the colored glass of the four-wheel drive provided ample cover for

Michael's concealment.

At the time, there wasn't any possible way of knowing which of the many vehicles belonged to the approaching man, making Michael's chances of fleeing unseen slimmer by the second, and increasing his heart rate to that of a humming bird's.

Temporary relief came over Michael as the trunk of a blue Chevy in the next space over popped open automatically. The small interior cargo light of the compartment cutting through the darkness like a knife.

René walked into the illumination.

Michael didn't realize he hadn't been breathing until he saw the lit up face and gasped. One in a million or not, this was one of his father's killers, and his cross began to burn like hot coals.

'Now what? You can't do anything here. Go get help from Jerry,' Tim said nervously.

But Jackie's voice screamed a different tune. *'Find a board, a stick or even a big rock! We'll never get another chance like this again! Kill him quick!'*

Michael was reminded of an old television commercial where this man had a little devil on one shoulder and an equally sized angel on the other, both trying to persuade the guy to follow their contradicting advice. He knew his dad's logic was sound, but Jackie was right.

As René bent forward to lay his burden in the floorboard of the car's trunk, Michael decided to compromise. Running full blast, he threw all his body weight onto the compartment's lid, causing it to crash down on the center of Caldrone's back.

Cursing out profanities in Spanish, René quickly and aggressively tried to stand.

Once again using all his stored-up frustration, Michael slammed the trunk hood. This time, the combining forces of motion created a tremendous impact on Caldrone's head. If the sound was any indication of the damage done by the impact, Caldrone wouldn't need to look skyward in order to see stars for a long, long time. It had to have cracked the man's skull. The only problem was, it also drew the curious eyes of other park goers who now would only see an open trunk. Both Michael and René had slipped unseen into the night. The only difference was Michael was conscious of the retreat.

As quickly as he disappeared from the encounter with René, Michael rematerialized less than eight feet from Giggy, Jerry and J.J.

"Hey, what's everybody looking at?" he asked as he came up behind them.

"God only knows honey. It sounded like some poor soul's been hit by a car," Anita answered sympathetically.

Michael acted concerned.

"You want me to run over and see if they need any help?" he offered.

"No, no. Of course not. It's dark and you don't need to be running around alone. It's dangerous and someone could get hurt," she replied.

Michael wanted to laugh at how ironic that statement was, but didn't out of respect. Instead, he turned to Jerry.

"Did you ask Giggy if she wanted to take J.J. for ice cream?" he asked.

Jerry looked confused, and for good reason.

"What?" he questioned stupefied.

Michael rolled his eyes.

"You wanted me to come over and watch your new Batman and Robin movie," he said as if talking to a forgetful child and inclining his head slightly in the direction of the people gathering around René's car.

"Oh yeah! Sorry," Jerry said, finally catching on. "How about it Anita? My treat," he asked.

Before she could answer, Jerry junior became a problem. His chant went from saying "ice cream!" over and over, to "I see Batdan and Bobbin too," his bottom lip protruded.

Michael understood how that had always worked on his dad, and his heart went out to the boy.

"Now that's a 'buy-me-a-toy' face if I ever saw one. If it's alright with Giggy, J.J., I'll give you enough money to stop at Target and you can buy yourself a brand new Batman toy of your own." Michael offered, his eyes wide open to share in the excitement, but the little guy didn't bite.

Michael was trying to think of another idea when the smaller child solved the problem himself.

"I vonted Superman!" he exclaimed excitedly and swished the air with his tiny hand to indicate his imaginary toy in flight.

"Okay. Superman it is," Michael said, and handed Anita a twenty dollar bill. Nothing was said from Anita. Her love for children was forever present. There wasn't anything she'd rather do than spend time with a little one. Even if she acted to the contrary, Michael knew better.

Anita took J.J. By the hand and started to leave. She knew she was being removed from the scene, but didn't let it show.

"Alright," she said, leaned forward and kissed Michael on the forehead. "Whatever it is you've got planned, please be careful. You're all I've got," she explained, then she and J.J. walked away.

Michael felt like crap having to mislead his great grandmother again, but he couldn't tell her his plans. He didn't even know them himself.

Michael gave Jerry a quick rundown of the events that had transpired out in the parking lot.

"Oh my Lord Jesus. I better call it in!" Cox said, but after seeing the look on Michael's face, he realized how silly his flash back had sounded. "Sorry partner. What's your plan?" he asked.

Michael shook his head. "I'm not really sure. The only thing I can think of right now is to follow the creep. He should go to the emergency room, that is, if he's still alive. I got him pretty good," he admitted and smiled. "However, being criminally minded, the jackass will probably head for home, and we need to know where that is. We may never get another chance," he added.

The sound of panic is easy to recognize in any language, especially Spanish. People were gathering around where René had fallen, talking rapidly. Some woman had helped Caldrone to his feet, only to watch him crumble again. This time to the hard blacktop, causing someone to scream.

"What on earth did you do to him? He's really fu … messed up!" Jerry said after watching the injured man take a nose-dive.

But Michael didn't answer, he was elsewhere in thought.

"I should have listened to Jackie and killed the piece of trash when I had him on the spot," Michael said, thinking aloud.

"Jackie? Who's Jackie?"Jerry asked, sounding bewildered.

Michael snapped back to the real world.

"I'll explain later. Right now we need to get you loaded into the van. I seriously don't want to lose this horse turd," Michael said comically.

The van was a warm welcome from the night's chilly air. Michael and new partner Jerry sat quietly watching René's friends, or maybe they were from his family, help him into his car. Just in time too, a police cruiser made a swift turn into the parking lot. It was incredible how fast the scene changed from chaos, to tranquility, by the mere presence of the law.

The woman, who unknowingly by her request for a jacket, had put René in the hands of an uncommon vigilante, got behind the wheel of his car and peacefully drove Michael's target from the area.

The cat and mouse game didn't last very long. They had only gone about six blocks before the rodent returned to his hole.

The woman pulled into the driveway of a tiny duplex. The short trip had made the large van impossible to miss as a tail.

"I think we've been spotted. Pulling in here may be a trick to let us pass," Jerry pointed out.

It only took Michael a split second to contemplate the situation.

"Pull in behind them," he said, and crawled into the back seat. "Tell them you were at the park and wanted to help," he finished, fading into the compartment's shadows. Jerry did as instructed.

The driver opened her door and only stepped part of the way out, reluctant to fully expose herself from the safety of the car.

"May I help you!" she yelled with a tone that portrayed a no-nonsense attitude, one that also said, "There's no victims here, move on." Jerry rolled down his window, and out of habit, flashed the badge he still carried.

At the sight of the shield, the woman's defiance turned to respect or maybe fear. She fully removed herself from the car, closed the door and walked closer to Jerry's van.

Cox knew from experience that this was a trick many play in hopes of drawing an officer's attention away from their vehicles and usually something illegal within.

Rosa had no way of knowing that this particular cop was unable to get out anyway.

"Yes sir, is there a problem?"She asked.

"No problem ma'am. I saw your passenger fall back at the park and wanted to see if you needed assistance or maybe an ambulance," he explained.

"No thank you officer. I'm going to put him to bed. Too much to drink, I suppose. I'll run to Kroger for bandages afterward," she said.

"Are you sure?" Jerry asked once more.

"Yes, Merry Christmas sir," Rosa added and walked away.

"Now what?" Jerry whispered as he slowly backed out of the driveway.

"Take me to K-Mart®. I've got a really mean idea," Michael replied, sounding devious.

Once they had moved down the road a little, Michael climbed back into the front seat.

"That just reminded me of my dad and me," he laughed. "Whenever we would go somewhere together, I would have to sit in the back seat. Mother's rules. Anyway, once we were out of sight ..." he said and motioned with his hand to finish the statement.

Cox wanted to tell Michael about these actions being against the law, and how unsafe they had been, but really couldn't because like eighty percent of American fathers, he was guilty of the same crime. Just like now, he knew he had to stop thinking like a cop.

"What's your plan?" he asked instead.

Michael tilted his head slightly and a devilish look adorned his face.

"Well, did you happen to see the red crown sitting in their rear window?" It was surrounded by statues of Mary and Saint somebody," he said.

Jerry thought for a moment.

"Yes. Now that you mention it, I did. You're very observant," he said.

Michael raised his eyebrows up and down a couple of times.

"But I bet you missed the chicken bones and feathers hanging from the rear view mirror, didn't ya?" he asked knowingly.

Cox shook his head in response, so Michael went on explaining.

"Our boy is confused about faith and religion. His deity is Christ's mother, which means he prays to idolatrous images. That also tells me that he doesn't know the truth of the Bible, or the condition of the dead," Michael was saying, but then went quiet. The presence of the spirits of his dad and Jackie was also a contradiction of God's word.

"Michael, are you alright buddy?" Jerry asked with real concern in his voice. "You left me hanging there for a minute," he added.

Michael turned and watched the world go by outside his window.

"Something I need to work out on my own," he answered just above a whisper. His thoughts were drawn to the scriptures, and how the Lord said once you die, you'll know nothing until Jesus' second coming, then all will rise together. The living, as well as the dead, for judgment. He was confused. Things were not computing.

Jerry sat quietly to allow his passenger time to think, not interrupting until they reached the shopping center. Then he prompted Michael to speak.

"What about the stuff hanging from the mirror?" he asked.

At first, Michael was still lost in thought, then he focused quickly.

"Voo-doo!" he said in a spooky ghost's voice. "We have a fool who believes in carved images, the Pope as God on earth, spell cast by witch doctors and zombies," he explained, and paused to allow Jerry time to catch up. "Drop me off here! When I get back, I'll fill you in on my plan to use his superstitions to bring him down."

Cox pulled over to the curb and watched as Michael jumped from the van and entered the store. His police instincts were nagging at him for allowing a child to shop alone at night. But the only thing he could do is find a place to park.

Twenty minutes later, Michael and Jerry pulled out onto Long Hollow Pike, just in time to see René's Chevrolet parking at the grocery store. And thankfully the woman, Rosa, was alone.

Michael changed into the new suit he'd purchased and once again jumped into the front seat.

"You intend to grow into that thing or what?" Jerry asked half jokingly.

"No. I made sure it was extra large before I bought it. This way, it will look to René as if I've started to decompose. I've been dead six months you know," Michael explained as he removed a jar of white face cream from his shopping bag, then removed the cap. Using his fingers, he applied a thin coat on all of his exposed skin, making him so pale, he almost glowed.

"You're amazing," Jerry said as his young partner's plan became clear.

"Stop over there at the Publix construction site," Michael said, pointing an extremely white finger.

When the van came to a halt next to a large pile of top soil, the zombie to be got out and plunged head first into the soft dirt. While rolling back and forth, he began throwing the earth skyward so it would rain down on him. Next, he started rubbing some in his hair, then filled his pockets with a mixture of grass and weeds. Once satisfied that he was a complete mess, he crawled back into the front seat of the van.

"Let's go!" he ordered as if commander in chief.

Jerry eyeballed the filthy child sitting on his cloth upholstery.

"Was that necessary?" he inquired, clearly irritated.

Michael's head snapped around to face Jerry like a cobra.

"I've got to convince that creep that I've just crawled out of my grave! Or else he may send me there for real!" he said, sounding a lot angrier than he intended. "Listen, you're either in this with me one hundred percent, or I go it alone!" he added and was shocked at his lack of self-control.

The look on Jerry's face made Michael feel a touch of guilt, but this wasn't a game. Death itself was knocking at the door, and tonight, someone would have to answer it. The realization of that person possibly being Michael plunged them both into silence.

Slowly, Jerry reached up and levered the transmission into gear.

"Where would Robin be without Batman," he said sorrowfully. Nothing else was said between them until they reached René's home again.

Thankfully, the ride only lasted minutes because it felt like hours sitting on death row.

"I'm sorry I got so mad. It's just that this scares the crap out of me, okay," Michael confessed, then started to exit the van.

"Hold on!" Jerry said. He really wanted to try again to change the boy's mind, but he knew it was a waste of energy. "Be careful please. If something were to happen to you, the repercussions would be endless," he added with great remorse.

"I'm not alone," Michael explained. "It's cool. Beep the horn three times quickly if someone comes. And if I don't come back, just scram," he said. Before leaving, he reached into his shopping bag and removed a bottle of ketchup. "Oops, I almost forgot the blood," he added.

The dome light went out as Michael gently closed the door behind him.

Under the dim illumination of the dashboard gauges, Jerry lowered his head and was disgusted at the sight of his worthless legs.

"Why?" he asked himself as pride condemned him for not being able to go with Michael. For the most part, he knew this outing was extremely wrong. But another, equally strong, side of him wanted the sweet taste of revenge that only an eight year old was willing to provide. Here he was, willing to risk the life of a child for his own gratification. Even the realization that Michael would have done this anyway didn't help him feel less guilty. All he could do to help now came from above, so once again, he bowed his head; this time in prayer.

There is always an indescribable stillness that haunts Tennessee's winter nights. The smallest of sounds can seem to intensify a hundred times in the cool, crisp air. The gravel crunching under Michael's every step sounded to him like thunder. And because of it, he expected to see his father's killer peering at him from one of the windows any second. Even though the driveway was only about thirty feet in length, it felt to Michael like he was crossing a massive battlefield, one that kept expanding endlessly before him. The pounding of his heart also appeared to echo off the line of foliage-free, skeleton like trees marking the property.

After finally reaching the house, he pressed his back to the wall. His breathing was deep and rapid, each exhalation created its own vaporous cloud. He waited there for his vitals to return to as close to normal as possible, and to listen for any internal noises that would indicate that his presence had been detected.

"What do you think dad? Was I observed getting here?" he whispered.

'Leave!' was the only answer.

Michael shook his head.

"Sorry, not an option. I've come too far," he said.

'No you haven't. You don't even have a real plan. What are you going to do, scare him and run? Now you walk your butt back

232

up to Jerry and tell him I said to take you home,' Tim instructed.

Refusing to listen, Michael stepped up onto the concrete porch and slowly opened the dilapidated storm door. It screeched and threatened to crumble into a pile of scrap metal at his feet. Taking hold of the entrance doorknob, he slowly turned it until it made a click that to him sounded like a shotgun blast. Releasing the handle, the door swung slightly inward. A smell of cat urine, feces and putrid garbage assaulted his nose.

"Whew!" he expressed, using all his will power not to vomit.

Still determined to proceed, he took a huge breath of fresh air and stepped inside. Once his eyes adjusted to the darkness, he found himself standing in a small kitchen. A table at his right held at least three meals worth of dirty dishes, a half open pizza box lay in the floor and a basket of soiled clothes filled one of the chairs.

All of a sudden, a disinterested feline jumped from the counter top and ran from the house in a flash, scaring the crap out of Michael in the process.

"Wow! Just like in the movies. The poor thing was probably desperate to liberate itself from this overwhelming stench," he whispered.

'Just like you should be doing,' Tim pointed out.

"Nope," Michael answered halfheartedly, and pushed the door closed behind him, leaving it slightly ajar.

Before moving deeper into the home, Michael took the time to turn the stove's burners on high, and then he blew them out one at a time, the heat feeling welcome on his skin. The smell of rotten eggs joined the already foul air. The next room was the living area that was scarcely lit by a single bulb near the front wall. Its ability to shine being diluted by a dingy lampshade covered in dust.

A small hallway gave way to three doors. The first was

obviously the bathroom. It's distinctive smell a dead giveaway. Even a blind man could find it easily.

The next was a very small but empty bedroom. Michael was relieved. If it had contained any indication that it belonged to a child, Michael could not have continued on his quest. The pain that stabbed at his chest should never be felt by another young person, no matter the sins of the parents.

Coming to the final room, Michael just stood there staring at the dim light shining under the door, watching intensely for any sign of movement.

'It's not too late son. This is going to get you killed. You don't have a plan or even a weapon. Please leave!' Tim reasoned again.

"Have a little faith dad. I'll think of something," Michael responded in a whisper. He no sooner stopped speaking before Jackie spoke his opinion.

'Hurry up. Smell the gas? Let's finish this.'

Without another word, Michael quietly opened the door and entered the bedchamber of a psychopathic killer.

To his left was a small receptacle light that provided some visibility. There, stretched out on the bed before him, was René. On the criminal's head was what Michael assumed to be an ice pack.

"Aw ... does the poor baby have a headache?" he mused. His fear instantly vanished, but his scarred chest burned like a furnace.

René's slow, rhythmic breathing told of his condition. He was unmistakably in deep sleep. Hopefully from a concussion, Michael thought.

The smell of freshly burned marijuana was more than noticeable, lingering in the air.

'Perfect! Doped-up, superstitious, groggy and just plain stupid.

This may work,' Tim said.

Michael turned and held the top of the ketchup bottle tightly to his belly while he opened it to keep the characteristic "POP" of the lid from echoing throughout the quiet room. He then approached the bedside and filled both of the sleeping man's hands with the blood-like substance, then walked back to the doorway.

After taking a mouthful of the ketchup himself, Michael flipped the nearby wall switch and a blast of bright light flooded the room, courtesy of two bedside lamps. The assault on the injured man's eyes, even though closed, made him jump with a moan of pain.

"Aah!" he yelped, turning his head from the stinging rays. "Rosa, baby … please!" he begged.

Michael hit the switch again and allowed Caldrone time to relax.

"Gracias," René whispered gratefully.

Michael flipped the lights on again.

This time the killer got belligerent.

"Rosa! Damn!" he yelled, and instantly covered his face with his hands to protect his eyes. The presence of the tomato paste took only seconds to register. "What the …" he said, lowering his arms to contemplate the stuff in his palms.

The total look of confusion, and the globs of red on Caldrone's face, made Michael want to laugh, but he knew it would be a deadly mistake.

Still delirious from the drugs, the head trauma and sleep, René fell for the illusion that he was fatally bleeding. He raised his head hoping to find some comfort in the face of Rosa. However, with the recognition of whom and what stood before him, he became paralyzed with unquenchable terror, his mouth falling open in a silent scream. All the color drained from his face, leaving him so pale, it looked as if his life force abandoned him in fright. With his eyes the size of saucers, he managed to find some form of articulation.

"You ... you're d ... dead," he stammered.

This whole time, Michael hadn't moved a muscle, not even to blink. Then, as if under some reanimation spell, he slowly turned his head in René's direction. While raising his arms, palms up pleadingly, he let out a deep agonizing moan along with the now diluted ketchup. As it ran out and down his chin, he pointed his finger accusingly at the killer. Half gargling, half-whispering.

"Caldrone!"

René began to shake his head violently and scream at the top of his lungs, then he tried to escape up the wall.

Michael couldn't discern where the crook thought he was going, but he looked like a rat climbing the wall of his glass cage, going nowhere fast. Hoping to push him over the edge, Michael spoke again.

"Murderer. Return my soul or forfeit yours!" he said.

René's movements became aggressive and hysterical. He began slipping and sliding on the linen like they were made of mud. The wall started to resemble a child's enlarged finger painting or a very poorly done piece of abstract art using only the color red. In his panicked state, his legs shot out in different directions causing his feet to contact the lamps, crashing them to the floor, which threw the room into temporary darkness.

By the time Michael's eyes adjusted to the dim night light, he could see that René had settled down and was smelling the red stuff on his hands. Apparently, some of the ketchup had found its way to his taste buds, and it returned him to his sanity. The process, even in the minute illumination, revealed tremendous anger and hatred along with his understanding.

"Ketchup!" he said with disbelief and shock. He then lifted his murderous gaze to the fake zombie.

"What a sucker!" Michael taunted teasingly.

René charged like a raging bull. The only thought in his mind was to dismember the little actor, who had made such a fool out of him.

Michael pulled a handful of dirt from his pocket and threw it into the man's face. It didn't slow him down, but it did cause him to lose his concentration long enough for Michael to execute the first strike. He launched his body into the air by slinging his left knee skyward. His foot connecting under René's chin with a satisfying crunch. Caldrone's head jerked backwards, spraying artificial and real blood on the ceiling. Before René could compose himself, Michael turned and delivered a mule-kick to the criminal's mid section, sending the creep stumbling backwards, colliding with the wall before collapsing in the corner. There, on top of the broken lamp, a sharp edge must have stabbed Caldrone's rear end. He howled out in pain, and quickly lifted his bottom off the floor. Forcing himself to his knees, he studied the intruder with a newfound reverence.

"Come on turkey! Come get you some more!" Michael offered with a smile.

Instead of proving to the kid that he was a fool, René jerked open the nightstand's drawer and produced a gun.

Not wanting to hang around to see what kind it was, Michael kicked the receptacle light, sending the room into total darkness, then quickly stepped back out into the hallway, slamming the door behind him.

No sooner had the door clicked, when a large hole appeared in it next to Michael's head, sending small pieces of splintering wood flying, some stabbing into his cheek.

'Run!' Tim screamed in terror.

"No shit!" Michael yelled as he ran back through the house the way he'd came in. A large thud from the bedroom told Michael that his pursuer must have fallen in the dark.

Reaching the kitchen, Michael could hear René entering the hallway cussing up a storm. So this time, he crashed through the screen door without slowing down and high-tailed it up the driveway.

The next blast of gunfire was immediately followed by a huge explosion as the gas impregnated structure ignited. The percussion propelling Michael ten feet into the air, then painfully slammed him to the ground. His breath knocked from his lungs in one rapid exhale, and he knew he'd never breathe again.

Pieces of glass, hunks of brick and fragments of wood rained down around him and an area a hundred feet in every direction.

Fighting unconsciousness, Michael began to crawl.

'Come on son, get up!' Tim begged.

Gasping, Michael did his best to comply with his dad's instructions. The pain made him want to cry out in agony, but he had no air in his lungs to begin. His first attempt to rise, brought him back to his knees.

"I can't dad, help me!" he wheezed. The ringing in his ears threatened to drive him insane. He laid back down to give up.

'I swear to God son, if there was any way possible to be there for you, I would. However, We both know that I can never come home again. I need you to be strong and focus on how much I love you. Please don't ever give up,' Tim said.

With that, Michael forced one of his feet out in front of him. Then, through an invisible strength from the love within, stood up. Teetering from lost equilibrium, he took a small, agonizing baby step. Then, by the grace of our Lord Jesus, he dragged out another. Holding his arms out for balance, he managed to progress forward.

After the sound of the first shot, Jerry had pulled the van up to the edge of the driveway and opened the passenger door. It was less than five feet from his partner now, although to Michael, it was still a mile. Too dizzy to continue any further, he fell back to his knees once again.

Cox began to panic.

"Michael!" he yelled as he struggled to free himself from the driver's seat harness. He intended to crawl to his friend's aid if need be.

"Help," came a voice so weak that Jerry almost missed it. He looked up just as Michael's little fingers grasped onto the seat belt.

"Thank you God!" he cried, and frantically took Michael's hand, pulling him into the floorboard. He then hit the accelerator and the van shot forward, the momentum slamming the door closed.

Some gravel became tiny projectiles as the back tires fought for traction. Once they hit the blacktop, they both smoked from burning rubber, squealing like a pack of scalded dogs.

With the devastation growing smaller in the side-view mirror, Jerry's erratic driving was a perfect example of how badly he was freaked out. Every corner became a tire squealing, hair-raising event any NASCAR fan would be proud of. Plus, he had no idea where he was going. This was not the side of the law he was used to being on. Ever since he'd seen Michael running up that driveway, and that man shooting at him from the exploding house, he'd been more or less lost in panic.

"Oh my God! Oh my God!" he chanted repeatedly as he fought to keep the van between the ditches.

Michael finally moved. In a trance-like state, he rolled his head and opened his eyes.

"Jerry," he said breathlessly. "Take me home," he added, then seemingly went back to sleep.

Knowing within reason that they were far enough away from the crime scene, Jerry pulled over and tried to arouse his partner by shouting his name.

"Michael! Can you hear me?" he asked, then leaned over to feel the child's neck for signs of life. The touch made Michael jerk away from Cox's hand, but once he realized who it was, he allowed his friend to help him up into the seat. It was a very painful ordeal to say the least.

After staring at Jerry's moving but wordless mouth, Michael realized that he'd lost his hearing.

"I'm deaf Jerry!" he unknowingly yelled.

Cox got the look of a concerned father.

"I'm taking you to the hospital," he said, and pulled away from the curb.

"No!" Michael said after reading Jerry's lips. "Take me home. Doctors mean explanations, explanations mean cops, cops mean investigations and it all comes down to one conclusion. Trouble for both of us. Just take me home. I'll be fine."

Jerry wanted to argue, but he knew Michael was right.

"Point the way," he said, using as much animation as he could, hoping Michael could understand.

The comical look of the act made Michael laugh. It didn't last long, however, causing a massive pain to shoot up his side.

It only took approximately ten minutes to reach their destination. Jerry whistled at the sight of the stone mansion Michael's finger had directed them to.

"Wow! You really are Bruce Wayne," he mused jokingly, causing his partner to laugh. Cox was astonished. "You heard me!" he exclaimed.

Michael nodded his head and pointed to the rear of the house.

"Pull around to the back in case the neighbors get nosy," he instructed.

Doing as requested, Jerry parked his van under a large carport supported by four stone columns.

"Doesn't look as if your Giggy is home yet with J.J." he commented.

Michael climbed out of the vehicle and walked around to the driver's side.

"This isn't where she and I live. This place belongs to me. Dad left it to me in his will," he explained, then turned and headed for the rear door by the garage. There, he presses a series of numbers into a keyless entry pad.

The lock clicked and the lights came on. Turning back around, Michael raised his voice slightly.

"Come on in if you like. I'll only be about twenty minutes at most. I really need a hot shower. There's not much to eat or drink except potato chips and bottled water, but you're welcome to them. The kitchen is inside and to the right," Michael said, and waved before stepping inside.

Jerry worked himself into his wheelchair. He wanted to go in, not because of hunger or thirst, but plain old curiosity. He just had to check out the massive home. It was hard to believe that this place belonged to an eight year old. But nothing would surprise him about Michael ever again. Every minute he spent with the boy revealed something else incredible and awe inspiring.

At first, the cobblestone sidewalk proved to be a trick to maneuver, giving him second thoughts, but he pushed on.

The door opened up to a huge hall, running the full length of the mansion. In a wondrous gaze, Jerry rolled to the front of the estate, finding himself in a large foyer that was bigger than his apartment. A beautiful hardwood staircase coiled upward to the second floor, ending at an open balcony that surrounded the room. A brass chandelier hung like a descending spacecraft over his head. The front of the home was adorned with a set of massive oak doors that arched to at least ten feet.

Jerry wanted to continue the exploration, and wished he could climb the steps, but knowing it would be impossible, headed back the way he came. After about thirty feet, he turned left through a wide opening. The lights came on automatically as he crossed the threshold.

"Wow!" he expressed.

Laid out before him was a kitchen right out of a fancy hotel. Every appliance carried a top name brand and was made from highly polished stainless steel. The counter tops were black granite that matched the marble tiled floor. Everything else was manufactured from red oak and clear-coated so thick, the cupboard doors looked like mirrors. The only thing missing was a fat man dressed in white with a fluffy hat.

Jerry backed out to see if the lights would go out the same way they came on. They didn't, but the ones in the room across the hall did. Turning to see what had become illuminated offered the view of a gigantic, cherry paneled library right out of the movies. He half expected to hear the voice of Robin Leach say "Welcome to the lifestyles of the rich and famous."

Before realizing he had moved, he found himself deep inside the room facing a stone opening the size of a single car garage.

"Man! What a fireplace!" he said aloud, then almost jumped from his chair when it came to life in a burst of flames.

"It's voice activated," Michael said as he came up behind Jerry undetected, startling him a second time.

Cox quickly turned toward the voice to see his young friend standing next to him, drying his ear with a fuzzy yellow towel.

"What?" he questioned, his demeanor portraying guilt as if he'd been caught in the act of doing something wrong.

"The logs. They turn on and off by verbal command. You must

have said the magic word. My mother wasn't a very animated or functional person, so my dad had all these simplifying contraptions installed all over the house. I personally believe that it just made her more inactive, if that's possible," he explained, then took a seat on a brown leather, button-pleated sofa next to Jerry's chair and joined in watching the gas fueled blaze.

"Think that was cool? Check this out," Michael suggested and pointed toward the wall. "Television on, channel eight, mute," he ordered and a huge screen materialized from a hidden panel. The picture that appeared was so vivid. It gave the impression of a portal to another dimension through which a person could step, leaving this world behind. "Stereo on, surround sound," he added, kind of showing off. The room became a concert hall. The music was coming from every direction.

Michael turned to Jerry and began bobbin' his noggin' like a head banger. On about the third downward motion, something popped.

"Ouch!" he yelled as he grabbed his neck. "Crap that really hurt! Stereo off … man … that was painful!"

"You gonna be alright kid?" Jerry asked as he rolled closer.

"Yeah, I guess so. I'll sure pay the piper come morning though," Michael responded as if it were a joke.

"You're crazy, you know that?" Jerry pointed out while placing his hands on Michael's arm. "I'm a stupid fool to have gone along with your crusade tonight. It's a miracle you're still alive, and there's a bullet hole in my van to prove my point," he added.

Michael looked up with a spiritual intelligence covering his face.

"I believe everything that has happened to me since the night that I was shot and died has been under the hand of divine guidance," he explained, and was seriously considering telling his new friend all about his afterlife experience and how he'd returned possessed by his dad and Jackie. Before he could make that final decision, his attention was diverted to the television by his guests shocked face.

A special live report had interrupted the program.

"Turn up the sound," Jerry said. Michael didn't need to respond, Jerry's request was answered by the computer, the volume increasing instantly.

A beautiful oriental woman was standing in front of what used to be René's house. Red lights were flashing on the background from every direction. Two firemen could be seen carrying from the rubble a large black bag, which obviously contained human remains.

"Police are calling tonight's tragedy an avoidable accident. One that could have been prevented by an inexpensive maintenance check of the heating system prior to its use. This type of catastrophic event always needlessly marks the beginning of cold season. Fire officials want to remind home owners to please have their gas appliances serviced properly before this kind of horror is repeated," she was saying when a man from the station cut in.

"Maylynn, there appears to be a casualty. Have police commented on how many there may be?" he asked.

The woman held her finger to her ear as if to keep out unwanted noise.

"Well Tom, nothing official. However, all indications are one fatality at this time. Back to you Tom," she finished, but before she could sign off, the sound of a woman screaming drew the camera person's attention, so they focused on the source.

Michael and Jerry both recognized Rosa immediately. She was hysterical. Tears flowed down her face as she tried to fight her way past the officers, attempting unsuccessfully to reach Caldrone's body.

"Television off," Michael ordered, and the screen went black as instructed before returning to its hiding place in the wall, leaving Michael and Jerry silent with their thoughts.

Somewhere in the house, a grandfather clock chimed seven times to enlighten all within hearing range of the hour.

Cox was the first to speak.

"Do you feel as bad as I do about tonight?" he asked.

Michael looked up from couch button he'd been picking at.

"What do you mean? Feel bad about what? Seeing a piece of crap like that scumbag who murdered, or help murder my family meet his just reward? No! I don't feel any more for his life than that of a worm I'd kill by going fishing," he answered sarcastically.

Jerry looked hurt. "But we killed a man. Doesn't that bring us down to his level? I've always hoped that I was better than that," he pointed out.

Michael shook his head in disbelief.

"Just the fact that you feel something over his death shows your human compassion is far superior to his," he said, getting up and walking over to the fireplace to warm his hands. "Plus, we didn't cause his death. I might have helped it arrive early, but I didn't cause it. If you'll think about this logically instead of emotionally, you'll understand what I'm saying. He pulled the trigger that ended his life. If not for his evil intentions toward me, he could have lived to destroy someone else. Do you believe he lost one minute of sleep over devastating our families?" he added quietly, trying to suppress his emotions. Every time he had to relive his father's demise, a lump stuck in his throat as if he were trying to swallow a softball. He wiped away the moisture from his bloodshot eyes.

"I know your right as always, but the look on Rosa's face will haunt me forever," Jerry confessed, obviously feeling a lot of guilt.

Returning to his previous seat, Michael continued to convince Jerry they had done the right thing.

"Were her tears more real than mine? Were they more heartfelt than your wife and son's as you lay clinging to life on an operating table, or deeper than the ones that sting your eyes every time your son looks at you with disappointment because you can no longer do the things that other fathers can do? And how about all the other things this creep René robbed from your life?" he was saying when his emotions got the best of him. He no longer fought back the tears.

Jerry had also given in. He dropped his head into his hands and began to cry openly.

"What if they had actually killed you Jerry? Where would J.J. be now?" Michael asked through his tears. "And how about the next family that would have gotten in his way of capital gain?" he added, wiping his face with the bath towel. "The way I see it, by helping to end René's reign of terror, we've saved others a lot of agony that we're going through. That includes Rosa," he finished, touching a raw nerve of memory in both of them.

Now that the truth of their pain was fully exposed and their psychological defenses were down, there wasn't any way left to conceal reality from their hearts. Their emotions were unleashed and they both wept uncontrollably.

Michael's need to be held in times like these made Jerry a substitute for his dad, so he got up and put his arms around his new best friend. The embrace was welcomed and returned, they stayed that way for each other, a bond being formed that would last a lifetime.

The ringing of the phone interrupted the hug, and gave Michael concern. It had been months since he'd been in this house, so he had no idea who could be calling. He reluctantly picked up the receiver.

"Hello?" he said anxiously, then relaxed. "Oh, hey Giggy. How did you know we were here?" he asked. "Well, it's good to know the neighbors are watching the place for me .... I know it's the first time since, but I promise I'm okay," he explained. After a long pause, Michael's end of the conversation restarted. "Hold on, I'll ask," he said and covered the mouthpiece with his hand. "Giggy wants to know if you want her to bring J.J. here, take him home, or if she can keep him," he asked Jerry comically.

Even with the humorous remark, sadness deepened on Cox's face.

"It's my weekend. If she could please bring him here, I'd appreciate it," Jerry answered painfully.

Michael could only stare at his friend and wondered how much a man has to suffer through in a single lifetime.

"Bring him here please ... Thanks, I love you too ... bye-bye," he finished.

After hanging up, Michael lowered his head shamefully.

"I'm sorry, I didn't know," he said apologetically.

"My wife couldn't handle being married to half a man with a low income," Jerry explained, almost in tears again. Then looking for any excuse to change the subject, he added, "Your home is beautiful. You could fit my apartment in this room twice and still have room to park my van."

Michael was shocked.

"Apartment? What happened to your house?" he asked without thinking. It had been a long day and he wished he could take back what he'd just said. Jerry was already hurting and that question just added fuel to the fire.

"She got the house in the divorce. Plus, with J.J. needing a yard to play in, it was only fair because she got him as well. Hell, my disability check wouldn't have even covered the water bill. I live in a Nashville, crime-ridden, two-room place with no furnishings. That's why we were at the park. I'm too ashamed to even bring my son home," Jerry said, dropping his head.

Michael was getting angry. All this sadness, these tears, the destruction of families, the separation of loved ones and loss of limbs stemmed from one man's sin, a piece of crap that still walked the streets undamaged. Michael knew the day was coming for David Watts. For now, Michael felt he had to do something nice.

"Jerry, I need your help. I can't pay you. It will be strictly volunteer work," he said, smiling brightly.

Cox's eyes narrowed suspiciously.

"Now what kind of suicidal adventure have you got in mind this time?" he asked, raising his eyebrows.

Acting crushed, Michael pretended to have chest pains.

"Whatever do you mean? Little ole me, I'm just a mere child," he said with his belle-of-the-south accent.

"Yeah right! Like a baby cobra," he said and they both cracked up.

After a few seconds, Michael became serious.

"No, what I need is for you to move in here and keep an eye on this house for me. You know, manage the estate for oh ... the next ten years or so," Michael said.

Caught off guard, Jerry looked shocked and confused.

"I couldn't Michael. And I don't accept char ..." he was saying when Michael cut him off.

"It's either you do it, or I'll have to sell the place. I'd hate to do that. This belonged to my parents, and I'd love to be able to raise my child here. In the mean time, you can raise yours. It's paid for. There's a trust fund to cover maintenance. All it needs is a resident. Can you imagine what could happen over the next ten years to an empty mansion while it waits for my eighteenth birthday?" Michael commented.

"But the stairs and ..." Jerry tried to protest, but Michael wouldn't let him finish.

"There's an elevator at the rear of the kitchen," he explained and pooched out his lower lip. "Please Mr. Cox," he said childishly, but before Jerry could answer, Anita and J.J. Burst through the back door.

"Yoo-hoo, where are you?" Anita yelled.

"In the den Giggy!" Michael responded.

J.J. entered the room with his eyes shining like fish bowls.

"Daddy!" he exclaimed joyfully and ran to his father's lap. The little guy's mouth was in overdrive. "I haded ice twem, I got Superman's new toy, there's a fwimming poo outside and a fwing set. Who wifs here daddy? Who?"

Jerry couldn't get his son to stop talking long enough to answer, so Michael did it for him.

"This is where your dad lives J.J." he said, stifling the child's rambling.

J.J.'s mouth fell open in shock, "wheel-we?" he asked.

Cox had fallen into Michael's trap. Fighting back his emotions, he looked into his son's excited eyes.

"Yes buddy, wheel-we," he admitted.

Knowing tears of joy were on the way, Michael cut in again.

"Come on J.J. I'll show you where your dad keeps the really cool toys.

Anita understood what her great grandson had done. In pride, she leaned over and kissed his forehead.

"God bless you," she said and Jerry agreed.

"Toys ... toys ... toys," Jerry Junior kept repeating while bouncing around like a jackrabbit. "C'mon sir, toys!"

Giving in, Michael took the three-year-olds' hand and headed for the doorway, but just before stepping into the hall, he stopped and looked over his shoulder.

"One condition and it's not debatable. Your ex-wife has to pick up and drop off J.J. Right here," he said smiling wickedly. "And maybe once a month or so, we can hire a maid and a butler, then invite her over for supper," he added.

Jerry's face lit up like Christmas, "Oh yeah! I wouldn't have it any other way, except maybe sending the limo around to get them," he added, moving his head to display pride.

Michael's heart was light as a feather seeing the happiness return to his friend after being lost for so long. It was the best holiday gift he'd ever received.

CHAPTER 15

Michael lay on the bed staring at the ceiling. The patchwork pattern Tim had created while finishing the room had a mesmerizing effect on the eye. It actually seemed to trap ones attention with the same alluring power of a rainstorm, or the sparkle and dance of a campfire.

Looking at the clock, Michael became frustrated. It had been over four hours of trying to fall asleep before he finally succumbed to the reality, it just wasn't going to happen. Not only was his body aching all over from yesterday's exploding adventure, his mind was spewing thoughts as if it had a bad case of mental diarrhea. Some were pleasant while others were quite disturbing.

Knowing that he'd done a wonderful thing for Jerry and his son was cool. And seeing J.J.'s excited face as he discovered Michael's toys was priceless. But there was that awkward moment when the tour he was giving them reached the home's master bedroom and an unseen demon snatched the joy from his heart. Everyone, no matter who or what they are has a personal scent, and because of Tim's choice of soap, aftershave and cologne, his spirit was still alive in that room.

Michael half expected to see his dad walk out of the bathroom, welcoming him into his arms just like a million times before. Even knowing it to be impossible, the feeling was overwhelming, causing his heart to skip a beat and for him to catch his breath. Then suddenly from out of a horror film, Michael's photographic mind vividly displayed that picture of his dad lying on the black top, covered in his own blood. Trying to clear that thought by shaking his head proved useless, and too late to avoid the same evil from stabbing at his heart with its red hot dagger. A tear formed in the corner of his eye and rolled down his cheek.

After observing Michael's darkening mood, Jerry asked if the boy was okay, but didn't receive an answer.

Anita understood, however, because that creature of darkness had attacked her emotions as well. Stepping forward, she had taken her great grandson in her arms and held him. Nothing else was, or could have, been said.

Feeling more out of place than any other time in his life, Jerry was thinking that he could never accept Michael's offer of the home. It wouldn't be right.

Later, as they all sat in front of the fireplace, Cox mentioned his concerns, feeling intrusive, but Michael refused to let him out of their deal. And once J.J. Fell asleep under the glow of the fire, It became clear that Jerry was out numbered three to one. The home held a new family to fill its halls with love.

Before they left, Michael and Anita promised to return in the morning. She would watch J.J. while the men-folk cleaned out Jerry's apartment. They also planned to do some last minute Christmas shopping. The house needed to be decorated for the holidays, and fast. A twelve-foot, tree with all the decorations, had already been ordered for the den. Everyone was excited and joyous, even Michael.

Rolling over again, he tried to recapture some of that good cheer in hopes of sleeping. Again, it was futile. Nothing could mask the anger and frustration closing in on his soul like a fog. Here it was only four days before Christmas, and Watts still walked among the living. Plus, Michael couldn't think of any way to locate the devil. Even prayers didn't seem to ease the foreboding feelings of helplessness.

After punching his pillow in frustration for the hundredth time that night, he slammed his head into it facing the wall. In doing so, his eye caught a glimpse of something seemingly out of place. There on the nightstand was a small, wooden car that's top was open. Tim used it to collect his pocket change at the end of each day. Michael had kept it for the same reason, but hardly ever needed to use it. Tonight, it drew his full attention and made his scar tingle uncomfortably. Sticking out of it was a little black antenna about two inches long.

"Onezean's cell phone," Tim and Michael said in harmony.

"Wow! Prayers really do work. I forgot all about that crazy thing. Giggy must have placed it there the day I came home injured," Michael explained.

Throwing the covers back, he slid over to the side of the bed where he let his bare legs drape over the side. After reaching out and taking the phone in his hand, he stared at it as if it were from outer space. The night air was chilly on his exposed skin, but he didn't seem to notice, or acknowledge, the goose bumps forming on his arms like a runaway rash.

'Open it!' prompted Tim, sounding as if he too had been mesmerized.

As requested, Michael flipped back the top half and the tiny screen came to life. The sound of Amazing Grace played by computerized bells filled the room. It struck Michael as odd that a person like Otey would be a fellow Christian. Then in his memory, he suddenly recalled seeing a gold crucifix hanging from the killer's neck, and was baffled.

After the welcoming advertisement finished greeting the user, a selection of functions appeared with simple instructions for their usage. Choosing the one indicated as the directory, a list materialized like magic. It was as if the little computer had preconceived the request and had been waiting for the human element of the equation to catch up.

The data was displayed in alphabetical order and the third entry was that of "Caldrone, René". Michael thought about erasing it from the memory, like he had done to the criminal from the face of the earth, but decided to wait. The information may help later on in his quest. Just seeing it though made the room cool off a little more, sending a shiver down his spine.

The next point of interest was "Dickson, Paul". Michael subconsciously rubbed back his red hair.

"I guess I'll need to revisit him," he said, mostly to himself, forgetting that he wasn't alone.

'Yes, I'm afraid so son,' Tim responded.

Jackie also had a remark. *'Next time, we'll see to it that there are no loopholes for that maggot to crawl out through,'* he said.

Michael nodded his head in agreement.

"Edison, Bruce" was the next name to catch his eye.

"Well now, isn't that interesting that a policeman's number is programmed into the phone of a criminal. Unless it was done for illicit reasons," Michael said, sounding a little bewildered.

'We'll have to keep that in mind, especially dealing again with Paul,' Tim pointed out.

A birth of understanding over the way Dickson's arrest was handled formed in Michael's mind. This new scenario and its complications frightened him. However, if he were correct in his hypothesis, Edison would have to be added to the "to do" list.

"Come to think about it, the detective has been involved in every aspect of this story since my mother was murdered," Michael muttered aloud.

None of the other data held anything important to him, until he reached the bottom of the list. The last two entries, however, hit him like a bolt of lightning. The very sight of them turned his stomach sour. The cold room suddenly became a freezer, and his fingers began to ache from the pressure he was placing on the phone, squeezing the life out of it. The black letters on the bright blue background seemed more insidious than a rattlesnake coiled and ready to strike.

Michael pulled back his arm with the full intention of smashing the diabolical contraption against the wall, and if it hadn't been for his dad screaming for him to stop, that's exactly what he would have done.

The name "Woods, George" only gave Michael a mental pause for serious thought, but the other one choked all the goodness from his heart.

""Watts, David,"" he mumbled, and all his emotions vanished as soon as he spoke the name aloud. It was as if speaking it triggered a brain malfunction; one that resembled hearing a key word implanted by a hypnotist. Just as if a ghost had entered the room, the atmosphere turned into that of a morgue. The air became lifeless, an unmovable vapor that seemed to refuse Michael's need to breathe. His attempts to inhale proved useless.

Michael could actually see the killer standing at the foot of his bed, laughing insanely, staring with his ice-cold, demonic and inhuman eyes.

Michael started shaking uncontrollably and hyperventilating, caught in a panic attack. How long Tim had been yelling was unclear, but his voice was starting to break through. *'Michael! Snap out of it!'* He went on, and finally brought his son back to reality, helping him to regain some composure.

Michael quickly studied the room for any lasting remnants of his overactive imagination. And even after finding nothing sinister, it still took a few minutes to settle down and accept that the maniac wasn't there.

Once convinced the apparition was only part of a trance-like demon, most likely brought on by exhaustion, he relaxed.

'That's it! This crap has to stop! You've almost lost your life twice this week! And now this! It's over! Do you hear me young man?' Tim said in a way that he expected no other answer than, "Yes sir."

Michael crawled back up to the center of his bed and pulled the covers up to his chin.

"Calm down dad. You're being emotional and not thinking logically," he began. "Listen to some facts we have to face. First, we've already attacked these criminals by disposing of Caldrone and Otey. It shouldn't take long for them to realize that we've retaliated. Dickson may not be smart enough to figure us out, but Watts and this Woods guy are. And if Paul comes clean about the beating I gave him on Halloween night, it will be a red carpet to my door. Plus, we may have a cop involved. If I back off now, it will only be a matter of time before they come for me. I have to continue to strike first or I could put others in danger, especially if I allow them their choice of time and battlefields. You know, I'll never get to rest until all these scum bags are worm food," he paused to contemplate what he had said before continuing. "Sorry dad, either they die, or I do. There's no other way to end this war, and you know it," he said. His speech had started out to persuade his dad what needed to be done, but ended up convincing himself as well. Having the full truth exposed didn't frighten him. Instead, it somehow gave him greater determination and strength.

'Damn it son!' Tim said somberly.

"I know dad, I know!" Michael replied, and then, somehow, drifted off to sleep.

◆ ◆ ◆ ◆ ◆

There was a gray cast of snow clouds moving in from the north.

"Maybe we'll have a white Christmas this year," Anita said with anticipation as they drove toward the estate.

"That would be great," Michael replied, then he and his great-grandmother began to reminisce about the snow storms of the past. It was hard to do so and not dredge up sad memories. Tim always loved to play with Michael on the frozen hills. Sleds and their large go-cart were the best. Those good times were gone, but the recollection of them would always remain a treasure.

Anita was concerned that it was too early in the morning to

arrive. However, Michael insisted on going. There was a weeks worth of preparations to do and only two days to do it in. After that would be Christmas eve and there wouldn't be a logical reason for decorating. Plus, trying to shop after today would be suicidal. Her reluctance proved to be unfounded when J.J. met them at the back door, excited and full of life. Like most children, when he needed to get up, he'd fight for extra sleep time, then on days he could sleep late, he was up at the crack of dawn.

Jerry was a lot less chipper, but it was nothing a good strong cup of coffee wouldn't cure. The fact that Anita and Michael brought some with them along with donuts, made his day.

"Dood momean sir," J.J. Greeted Michael, but didn't wait around for a reply. Instead, he half dragged Giggy off to see the closet full of toys he'd found while exploring.

Cox gratefully accepted a steaming cup of java, then as directed by a silent finger gesture, followed Michael down the hall to a large office. This room, like the rest of the house, was extravagant. It resembled a high-dollar executive suite of a Wall Street tycoon. Jerry began to wonder why it wasn't part of last night's tour and the thought crossed his mind to ask, but Michael's body language made him realize that this room was a part of the past that he was not willing to share. It was clearly a memorial shrine to his dad.

As soon as Michael sat down behind the large oak desk, he reached up and corrected the angle of a wooden block adorning a brass nameplate reading, "Dr. Timothy James." The pride in Michael's young face verified Jerry's assumption. It also became clear that this office was off limits except when invited.

Fumbling around with an ink pen, Michael quickly explained the discovery of information provided by Onezean's phone directory, and his plans for implementing that data. It took a few minutes to rehearse their active parts but both soon felt confident enough to begin.

Michael picked up the desk phone and dialed David Watts' number. After an uncounted amount of rings, a man answered, then very politely informed the caller, "The Cellular One prescriber you are trying to reach is unavailable or out of the calling area. Please ..." he was saying, but Michael didn't wait for the recorded message to end, he just hung up and dialed the second number.

"Plan B," he said.

Once the connection was made, he pressed the transfer button to conference call and placed the receiver back in its cradle.

The soliciting ring was loud and clear from the tiny speaker.

"Hello," said another male voice that Michael recognized immediately.

"It's Paul Dickson," he mouthed silently, giving Jerry his cue to begin.

"Hey Paul! What's happening, my man?" he asked.

"I'm cool! Just hanging loose waiting to fly by Uncle Bruce's house for some Christmas chow. You know what I'm saying man?" Paul answered.

"Yeah dog. I feel ya. I hear Mrs. Edison can really lay out the grub," Cox replied, digging.

"No lie bro, it's killer whack!" Dickson admitted, unknowingly answering one of the important questions.

Michael was thrilled and hopeful that the bonehead wouldn't catch on until exposing even more.

Jerry took another stab. He was actually having fun.

"Where's Watts my man? I ain't laid eyes on him in a minute. Is he straight?" he asked.

"He's still running smack for Woods; low dog in the kennel. Kicking dust instead of ass like a slave puppy." Paul boasted in a way that expressed he was glad David was punked out, and it was a position he'd never be in because of his higher level of criminal attributes. His attitude changed Jerry's playful mood.

"Where is David Watts, Paul?" Cox asked again. But this time he sounded less like one of Dickson's parasitical associates and way too much like a cop.

There was a long pause as the jerk contemplated the change in the caller's demeanor.

"Man! Who is this?" Paul asked with a nervous overtone creeping into his voice.

"Tell him the truth," Michael whispered to his friend.

At first, Jerry was shocked, and it was written on his face. It also caused him to hesitate for a second, but after Michael waved his hand and nodded for him to continue, he relaxed. Jerry had learned a while back to trust the intelligence of his young partner, so he did as instructed.

"Well, you inbred moron ... this is one of the policemen you creeps used as target practice in front of your home last spring. Now answer my question. Where is David Watts?" he asked again, this time with a conviction of authority.

"You can't be for real man. Watts would cut my throat if I told you that! Don't you need a warrant or something to ask me questions, or to call my private number?" Paul asked, trying to sound tough over the phone, as most cowards will do.

"I guess I would if I were still on the force, but you and your butt-hole buddies have seen to that. Nowadays, I'm nothing more than a really pissed-off civilian with a bad attitude looking for vengeance," Jerry explained.

Paul regained his bad-boy bravado.

"I ain't tellin' you squat man!" he barked.

Cox lowered his voice to sound both calm and sorrowful.

"Well, that's too bad, and it's not the story I'm going to pass on to Watts. Let me recheck his number you gave me along with the other information. Let's see ... pushing drugs for Woods, I believe you said. And ..." Jerry paused long enough for Michael to hand him Onezean's phone. "Ahh! Here it is ... the number you gave me for David was 233-2261. Is that correct Paul?" Jerry finished with a rhetorical question.

The sound of panic was so obvious coming over the line that both Michael and Jerry could feel, as well as hear, Paul's tension.

"Dude! They'll kill me for sure man! You were a cop. Don't you care what would happen to me?" he inquired, sounding like a disgruntled child.

"No Paul. No more than you and your buddies cared for my partner and me as you pumped us full of hot lead. Run and hide Jackass! Run and hide!" Jerry said to indicate that the conversation had ended.

Dickson began to beg for a reprieve.

"Hold on man! Please! That hit was ordered on Thomas Hayes, not you. Wrong time, wrong place ... you know?" he said.

"Ordered? By who and why?" Jerry asked, sitting straight up in his chair like a statue, his eyes bulging with shock.

"I can't man," Paul whined.

"Your funeral," Cox replied uncaringly.

"Okay, okay! Man! You can't say nothin' to nobody! Swear it man?" Paul pleaded.

"It's a deal dirt bag. Now spill it before I change my mind," Jerry instructed. And like his interview with the ninja back in October, Paul became a fount of useful intelligence. He even snitched about things that Jerry didn't give a crap about.

The call lasted another ten minutes. After that, Michael pushed the disconnect button and jumped to his feet.

"Let's go!" he said.

Jerry turned to follow.

"Where we headed?" he asked.

Michael didn't stop. Instead, he spoke over his shoulder.

"Dickson's at home sitting in a puddle of his own urine afraid to fart. He knows he can't tell anyone we called, however, he may let it slip and progress things too quickly for us. You've seen how he likes to talk once provoked. So we're going to take care of this a-hole while he's in our sights," he explained.

Jerry stopped.

"We can't do that. I'll need him to testify about my shooting," he said.

Cox's comment brought Michael to a halt. He turned and looked at Jerry as if the ex-cop had gone crazy.

"You're kidding right? After all you've been through, you still believe you can go up against these people legally and win! Get a grip! There's only one justice for these creeps, and that's us! Right now, we need to administer some to Paul for his role in all this. I gave him a chance to live by going to prison, but once he refused that mercy, he lost it," he explained, then stepped over to the kitchen intercom system and pressed the call button.

"Giggy, we're off to Jerry's apartment and the stores. If you need anything, call the cell phone. Love ya!"

Anita's sweet voice came back over the speaker.

"Love you too baby doll," she replied.

Jerry tried to hide his nervousness with a shot of levity.

"I'm confused. Is it Batman, or Baby Doll?" he asked jokingly.

Michael only smiled sarcastically and pointed toward the back door like a corrective schoolteacher.

Minutes later, the van roared to life as the two unlikely vigilantes embarked on another deadly adventure.

♦ ♦ ♦ ♦ ♦

The mornings' first promised blanket of white turned into a slush-filled disaster for commuters. The gentle flakes of beauty quickly became miniature frozen missiles of sleet that clung to every surface like a clear plastic coating. If you were fortunate enough to be at home admiring the day from indoors, it was an incredible sight to behold. However, for all those who had to face it head on, it was a living nightmare.

The twenty-minute trip to Paul's took approximately two hours. The tension became evident in Jerry's white knuckles as he continuously over-squeezed the steering wheel.

The stress was also transforming Michael's character into someone he didn't recognize. He even caught himself cussing at the way people around them drove. Most acted as if it were their first day on the road and hadn't discerned the difference between the accelerator and the brakes. It was enough to make him want to cancel the trip and just kill a few of these fellow motorists instead.

Once they finally pulled up three doors down from their destination, the two found it necessary to sit quietly and calm down. The emotional roller coaster they were riding would only prove to be counterproductive in this endeavor.

A few minutes later, the wiped area of the windshield became the only view to the outside world. Everything seemed so surreal.

Michael got this strange feeling that the van was a spacecraft and they had just landed on an icy planet.

"What's next, Batman?" Jerry asked, keeping his eyes on the winter wonderland before him.

Michael turned to face Jerry as he spoke.

"Have you got your service revolver in your utility belt, Robin?" he inquired.

The mixture of his humor, and the tone in the request for a deadly weapon, caught Jerry off guard. He snapped around to see the face of the real Boy Wonder. The raw determination and maturity of the freckled child drove a stake through his heart. Michael looked more like an aged and battle-tested warrior than most veterans of foreign wars. Jerry felt his stomach tie itself into a knot and the taste of bile assaulted his tongue.

"Yes, I've got it," he answered slowly.

Michael nodded his head.

"Good. This could turn serious in the blink of an eye. They've had hours to set up an ambush," he said, then his tone changed again, this time to that of a drill sergeant. "Get it ready. I don't want us to be the ones firing the second shot! Got it?" he ordered as if Cox should have already done as instructed, and was having to be told a second time.

Seeing the look of reluctance on Jerry's face, Michael got concerned and pushed on.

"Can you kill this spawn of a dog without hesitation? If not, hand your gun to me and I'll do it," Michael said, holding out his pint-sized hand palm up, acting like a professional hit man.

The whole thing was making Jerry even more nervous. He knew that no matter who discharged his weapon, the shit would end up in his lap.

"Yeah. Of course I can," Cox admitted, but there wasn't any conviction in his voice.

Michael studied his partner through squinted eyes.

"This is as real as it gets. Someone is going to die here today. It's up to you who that someone is. I'll ask you again. Can-you-do-it?" Michael asked.

Cox pulled out his pistol and chambered the first round like a movie hero.

"As God is my witness," he proclaimed boldly.

Michael wanted to laugh at the melodramatic move, but only nodded his head in approval, then removed Otey's phone from his pocket and began dialing. It didn't take long for Paul to answer.

Cox was disappointed that they didn't still have a speaker phone and all he would hear was this end of the conversation.

"Hi Paul old buddy, it's me!" Michael started off, sounding happy. "Come on dude. Take a wild guess. Don't you recognize my voice?" he asked, shaking his head in disbelief.

"Your number? Oh, it was in the cell phone I took off of Onzean the morning I beat him to death and threw his body off the roof," he lied, then paused to listen, and while doing so, rolled his eyes at Jerry.

"You still don't know? What an idiot! I'm also the one who ended René's plans for the holidays. It was a real blast ... No? Alright Paul, last clue. I came by your place Halloween night and did some fancy plumbing work in your home. Remember the fun we had? ... Now you do ... Good boy. Anyway, ... I'm on my way over to finish our talk. Another person-to-person sort of beat- I'm sorry, I mean talk ... See you in about ten minutes," Michael said, then comically removed the phone from his ear while making a funny face. "I think he's fainted," he said to Jerry with a smile. "Hello!" he tried again.

Within two minutes, the front door of Dickson's house sprang open and Paul scrambled out of it as if the place was on fire. His coat was unzipped and flapping in the wind. He'd only taken time to put on one boot and was hopping across the porch, desperately trying to get his foot in the other one. At the base of the steps, his frantic actions caused him to lose his balance and he more or less swan dived onto the concrete sidewalk, sliding at least ten feet on his nose, plowing slush and ice with his forehead. His terrified mind must have overridden the pain because he didn't miss a beat coming back to his feet. Two steps later, he pitched forward again. This time smashing his head into a parked car.

The thud was easily discernible, even in the van almost eighty feet away.

"We may not even need to get out. This goofball's going to end up killing himself for us," Michael mused, shaking his head slightly.

This time when Paul came to his feet, he was moving a lot slower.

"Showtime!" Michael said as he opened his door and stepped out into the cold.

On the other side of the van, Jerry rolled his window down to secure a target. He aimed his gun at the center of the stumbling criminal's chest. A police academy kill shot. Even though it was freezing, he started to sweat.

Out front, Paul finally managed to pull himself fully erect by using a nearby car's bumper. Leaning there against a beat up Toyota's trunk lid, he began to gently inspect his wounds with his index finger.

Blood had already begun running from his nose and a really ugly gash on his forehead.

"Boy! That's gonna leave a mark!" Michael called out.

Dickson quickly looked up to see the unmasked ninja standing only three yards away, just standing there with his hands tucked into his sleeves like he didn't have a care in the world. Paul recalled the last time he'd heard that statement, and as before, lost control of his bladder, wetting his pants.

The steam rising from the hot urine was a telltale sign of what had occurred.

"Come on dude! That's totally gross," Michael taunted.

Back in the van, Jerry could only imagine what could have happened between Paul and the trick-or-treater to cause so much fear. One thing was for sure, he was glad the kid was on his side.

Michael walked a little closer to the pee-soaked criminal.

"Don't worry buddy, what I'm going to do to you will only hurt like bloody hell as long as I can keep you alive," he explained in an attempt to push the creep further over the edge. It worked like a charm.

Paul's focus was so intense on the little assassin that he didn't even notice Jerry or the nine-millimeter pointed in his direction. Hearing the ninja's intentions caused him to panic. Frantically, he reached inside his coat for the gun he carried. Trying to rush out of terror, his feet slipped out from under him again and he fell straight down on his rear end, hard. The impact caused his weapon to fly from his hand and into the street.

Jerry saw the punk drawing his pistol and fired his service piece. The bullet took off a piece of Paul's ear before shattering the car's rear window. The fall had saved Dickson's worthless life.

Grabbing his injury with one hand, Paul started crawling and managed to reach the driver's door, where he dove inside, just as another round was fired. This time, the headrest exploded into a cloud of white dust.

While all the action was unfolding, Michael ran to retrieve the discarded weapon, hoping to join the battle. Behind him, the Toyota's starter made a horrible grinding noise as Paul threw the transmission into gear before the engine was fully operational. A split second later, it was fish tailing up the icy street. By the time Michael reached the revolver, Paul was too far away to risk taking a shot, so he ran back to the van.

"Crap!" he yelled, slamming his fist on the dash. "After him! We can't let him get away!" he ordered, but needlessly. Jerry was already on the move. Both vehicles proved to be equals in their description of poor traction. At this point, calling this a high-speed chase would have been laughable.

At the end of Fatherland Street, Paul ignored the stop sign and turned right, sliding all the way across the four-lane, slamming into the curb violently, which in turn bent the front wheel. The damage failed to impede his forward motion.

Here on the main road, the heavier traffic helped to melt the frozen precipitation, making the chase elevate to a dangerous level. Neither driver acknowledged the red light at Gallatin Road as they shot down the ramp onto Edmonson Pike.

The little car's unbalanced front end was shaking with the resemblance of an unevenly loaded washing machine on spin cycle, and the van loomed over its rear end like a male elephant in musk trying to mate.

Michael rolled down his window and extended his arm. In his hand, he held the recently acquired weapon. The wind proved stronger than he expected, so he used both hands to take aim. At this speed, he knew the wind chill could cause frostbite in a matter of seconds, so for the first time in his life, he pulled the trigger. The recoil painfully jerked the pistol from his hand and sent it soaring into the air. In his mirror, he watched as the revolver broke into several pieces as it tumbled along the blacktop, temporarily joining the chase.

After closing the window, Michael turned to look back at Jerry, then shrugged his shoulders out of embarrassment. The expression on his face was priceless. Under any other circumstance, it would have been humorous and maybe in the near future they could laugh about it, but not today.

The right turn onto Brily Parkway almost folded the Toyota's left rim completely over. How Paul was still able to steer astounded his pursuers. As the highway opened up to six lanes, the chase intensified to a reckless speed. The telephone poles shot by in a blur like a picket fence. Finally, in front of Gaylord Enterprises, the durability of the small car met its limits. The wheel disengaged and shot out across the median like a rocket. The compact's rear end took the lead with blue smoke bellowing from the screaming tires that remained. Sparks flew in all directions like the Fourth of July as the bare metal disagreed with the concrete's attempts to grind it smooth. Then, resembling a well-trained dog, the vehicle began to roll over, exploding the gas tank into a huge ball of flames, which quickly engulfed the entire automobile.

As if in slow motion, the agonized face of the criminal came into view and reminded Michael of a Bible verse: "the angels shall come forth and sever the wicked from among the just. And shall cast them into the furnace of fire. There shall be wailing and gnashing of teeth." — Matthew 13: 49.50

The tumbling mass of blazing metal impacted the snow-covered embankment and became airborne. Like a meteorite shooting across the night sky, what was left of Paul Dickson and his Toyota plummeted to the Cumberland River sixty feet below to be extinguished in a dark and icy grave.

Within seconds, there was very little trace of the violence that had just occurred. All that was left was a small cloud of steam lazily drifting toward the heavens, and a steel-belted radial, complete with rim, standing on the side of the interstate as a memorial to Paul's demise.

"That's three down dad, and one to go,'' Michael said, then turned to Jerry. "Well, we're here at Opri-Mills, might as well get our shopping done," he suggested.

Jerry couldn't understand how easy it had become for his young friend to accept the loss of life. Paul's burning face had already started to haunt his own thoughts. Even though the dead man had taken his legs and altered his chance for a normal life, he still felt remorseful.

"Just think of it as cutting the head off a poisonous snake," Michael offered after reading Jerry's thoughts.

"You sure he's dead?" Cox asked, already knowing the answer.

Michael rubbed his chest because the truth was there.

"One hundred percent," he said, and then smiled at some inner thought. "Yes sir, I am one hundred percent sure."

♦ ♦ ♦ ♦ ♦

This part of the country is notorious for its rapid temperature fluctuations. Especially in winter months. It's not uncommon to require your car's heater on the way to work and then your air conditioner on the way home.

Michael and Jerry had finished their shopping around noon and had removed everything Jerry wanted to get from his apartment by two. There really wasn't much more than clothes anyway. The only furniture was a bedroom set that came with the place. And the television was used as payment to a young man named B.J. Collins who had volunteered to give them a hand.

The trip back to Hendersonville started out pleasant and comfortable. Both occupants of the van had their windows down enjoying the spring like air, the morning's volatile mission already receding in their memories. Truth be told, it was hard for them to believe it ever happened.

Michael's thoughts were on Christmas morning, which for him was a wonderful change of pace. And Jerry's thoughts were on that of his son's coming reaction to all the spectacular gifts that his new friend had purchased, relieving the burden he was facing over a poor man's holiday. Now he wasn't going to have to explain why his presents were miniscule and cheap.

Between the happy song of Jingle Bells blaring from the radio and their trance like thoughts, neither one of them heard the siren until the metro cruiser drove directly in front of the van and the policeman pointed over his unit for them to pull over.

Myatt Drive is a very busy and dangerous road that doesn't provide a shoulder, so for everyone's safety, Jerry turned into the Dollar General™ store's parking lot and waited for the officer who within minutes was standing at Cox's open window.

"Hello Jerry," he said while tipping his hat, a scene straight out of the old west. The movement seemed insignificant and performed out of nervousness. "How's it going?" The officer asked, trying to sound cordial but still couldn't conceal a

269

serious tone in his voice or the dislike in the slant of his penetrating hazel eyes.

"Dorsey," Jerry answered, using the officer's first name with the same unfriendly and guarded level of suspicion.

Michael could only speculate on the obvious animosity between the two men as possibly a poor history on the force together, so he remained silent and observant.

"Just doin' my job here Cox!" the uniformed man offered to maintain peace.

"I don't recall harassment as being part of the training we received at the academy. Did I exceed the speed limit or is there something else?" Jerry inquired impatiently.

"No. I didn't pull you over for any traffic violations. Seems there's been an accident and one of our detectives is curious about your location. Just make this as easy on both of us as you can, will ya? All I need to know is where you've been all day," explained Dorsey.

"Well, I really don't need to tell you a damn thing!" Cox answered rather snottily.

"Calm down, I'm not trying to be your enemy!" the police officer responded with a professional and rehearsed statement he'd learned in order to gain a suspect's trust.

Jerry knew the drill and felt insulted. But he also knew by not answering, or if he appeared reluctant to provide information, it would cause him to look suspicious.

"If it's really any of your business, my friend and I went shopping at Opri-Mills this morning, then we spent the afternoon moving my things. Can we go now?" Jerry asked, thrusting out the last part of his answer with a question that sounded more like a statement of intent, and started to pull away.

"Hold on!" the policeman yelled, obviously something had

raised his suspicion flag. "What time were you at Opri-Mills?" he asked.

Jerry clinched his teeth and stared at the sergeant with an intense hatred burning in his eyes as he slowly began to pull the pistol from the seat-mounted holster.

Michael was shocked at how angry his friend was getting. Whatever had happened between the two had obliterated Jerry's good sense, so Michael reached over with his foot and gently pushed the gun-filled hand back down, holding it there. For a second, he became the recipient of Jerry's glare.

Until now, Michael hadn't spoken. "It was around nine a.m. Officer Johns," Michael admitted.

The sergeant's eyes enlarged as he really took a good look at the passenger for the first time.

"Oh my God! Michael Clark! This just keeps getting better and better all the time. Give me one good reason not to arrest the both of you on the spot," Johns asked rather boastfully.

"That wouldn't make a lot of sense officer. What charges would you use to justify detaining an ex-policeman injured in the line of duty, and an innocent eight year old boy who only dreams of Christmas morning?" Michael asked, protruding his bottom lip and using his poor little boy look.

"Innocent my rear end! And don't give me that face bub! I might have fallen for your game Halloween night when you were supposed to have been lost, but it's not working this time copper pipe kid," the sergeant professed, adding an insinuation.

"Well, it's a good thing that it won't be you that I'll need to convince anyway. The judge may not share your insight," Michael explained, holding his chin up with pride. "Face facts here officer. You'll be easily and diplomatically out-maneuvered," he added.

Johns removed his hat and started rubbing his temples. "So let me get this straight! It's just pure coincidence that you were lost at the home of a person of interest in your father's murder the night someone beat the guy half to death with a piece of plumbing, which was found, by the way, with tiny finger prints all over it," he said to Michael, then pointed at Jerry. "This same creep turns out to be the suspect in your shooting as well. Now ... here's the two of you together. And to top it off, you're admitting being in the location where this same man was burned up before he drowned. And I'm to believe it's all by chance? Give me a break here fellas," the Sarge said, feeling insulted.

"That's right officer. It's a small world after all, and anything's possible. Just like the fact that the gun used to shoot Jerry here, as well as myself, happened to be in Dickson's possession the night he was arrested. I saw it! Then it somehow vanished into thin air. Plus, Paul's uncle, by some phenomenal coincidence, was the detective in charge of that case, and ours. Talk about a small world. I can guarantee he is the same gold badge you're following orders from this very instant. Bruce Edison if I'm correct, and I know I am," Michael explained.

At the mention of his superior officer's name, the color drained out of Sergeant Dorsey's face. Stepping away from the van, he began to rub the back of his neck while thinking. It was obvious he had some earlier thoughts concerning this situation and Michael's statement brought a new light to the subject, illuminating the truth.

"Oh my God!" he said again, but this time as if in prayer.

"You're smart enough to see what's happening here Dorsey. You could choose a side, or stand in the neutral zone," Jerry said while raising his hands in a non-caring display.

Johns just stood there staring at the back of his patrol car, contemplating his options. He was between the proverbial rock and a hard place. As more elucidations rapidly manifested themselves in his mind, a not so friendly feeling of being inadequate crept into his thoughts. His career could be over, and maybe his life as well if he chose the wrong side, and he wasn't even sure which side that was.

"Go home Jerry. I didn't see hide nor hair of either one of you. Got it? And you haven't seen me," he finally said, returning his cap to his head, making a decision to remain neutral.

"Smart move! Can we go now?" Jerry asked, still angry.

"Yeah, yeah sure. I'll see you tonight. I need time to think. Go on!" Johns said, pointing up the street as he walked away.

"What did he mean by seeing you tonight?" Michael inquired once they were alone.

Jerry looked over at Michael with a very sorrowful face.

"He'll ride over with the ex to pick up J.J.," he explained, sounding as if he were chewing on a pig's toe.

Now the reason his friend was ready to shoot the patrol officer so quickly was clear in Michael's mind, and from what little he understood about adults and love triangles, stopping Jerry from shooting Johns could have very well gotten him shot as well.

"Oh, sorry," was all he could say.

Even though the sun was still shining brightly outside, there was a dark cloud filling the van interior. The day seemed to have lost its blessings. Nothing more was said the rest of the way home as both passengers sat locked in the dead silence of personal thought.

◆ ◆ ◆ ◆ ◆

The ups and downs of the day were already proving to be mentally exhausting for Michael. He was seriously feeling like an emotional yo-yo. The warmth of the large kitchen was more than welcoming and the smell of biscuits browning added to the room's aura of tranquility. However, here it was less than five minutes since he was convinced that life was little more than a battlefield; one where only the ferocious and unscrupulous survived. Now standing in the doorway watching his great grandmother and her very young assistant preparing a meal, he was transported to a whole new world. His heart, like that of the

Grinch who stole Christmas, swelled with love and tenderness.

'Looks like the beginning of a family,' Tim pointed out compassionately.

Michael swallowed in an attempt to hold back a tear.

"That it does Dad, that it does," he responded, accidentally speaking aloud.

"What did you say?" Jerry asked quizzically.

Michael shook his head sadly.

"Nothing."

At the sound of their voices, J.J. wearing a red, child-sized chef apron Sara had purchased during one of her failed money making schemes, jumped down from his perch on a bar stool and ran to his father's side, eagerly greeting him with a chocolate covered kiss, compliments of the cake mix he'd been stirring.

"Daddy. I's cookin'!" he announced proudly.

Jerry accepted the affection, batter and all with a smile.

"I see that! Are you teaching Anita, I mean Giggy, how to cook sweetheart?" he asked while winking at her.

Ignoring the remark, Anita walked over and placed a kiss on Michael's forehead.

"I was beginning to worry about you. Did you finish him off?" she asked.

The question caught both Jerry and Michael by surprise. Their eyes enlarged on each other in shock. They resembled two small boys who were uncertain as to whether their devilish deeds had been exposed, fearing any response might entrap them, letting the cat out of the bag.

"What?! Wh.. whadda ya mean?" Michael responded, sounding panicked and obviously guilty.

Anita examined them both suspiciously.

"Moving his things," she explained. "What have you boys been up to?" she asked with her hands on her hips, giving them the "I'll know if you lie to me" look.

Jerry's face turned as red as a cheery as he struggled for an answer.

"We um, well you see, hum … uhh … " he stammered.

Fortunately, Michael spoke up.

"Giggy, it's too close to Christmas to be asking questions," he offered, causing an awkward silence between them.

"Mm-hum, sure," she said after a few seconds, clearly not buying his excuse.

Michael only shrugged his shoulders, unable to elaborate.

Anita turned her attention to Jerry who mimicked the action of his young friend.

"Well, go wash up and try to stay out of trouble long enough for me to finish supper," she ordered, returning to her work.

J.J. discovered that the mixing spoon made a better rocket than a mixing tool, so he began to fly it around the room, its jet engines roaring courtesy of his personal sound effect and lots of chocolate spittle.

"To the bat cave Robin!" Michael proclaimed comically, and pushed Jerry's wheelchair quickly out of the kitchen and down the hall.

Once they entered the office, Michael removed his coat and tossed it across his chair. Next, he extracted the concealed throwing knives from where they were hidden in his sleeves, and laid them on the corner of the desk, catching Jerry totally off guard.

"You always carry those?' he asked.

Michael picked one of them back up and stared at it

affectionately while turning it slowly to reflect the light.

"I've found them to be quite handy. And if it wasn't for Jackie Lee's efficiency with their deadly power, my little confrontation with Otey would have been disastrous. To tell the God's honest truth, he saved my life with them," he explained, speaking more or less to himself while placing the blade carefully and respectfully back next to its sister.

Jerry took a few moments to absorb what was said and to structure his response so that nothing would be condescending or offensive to his young friend.

"Michael, please tell me what's going on. You're always talking to your dad and this fellow, Jackie Lee, which is cool, but sometimes it's as if you believe they're still alive and standing right next to you, even now claiming Jackie saved your hide with these weapons," he pointed at the knives. "Seriously, it scares me and kinda freaks me out," he admitted.

Leaning forward, Michael propped his elbows up on the desk to evaluate his friend. The man had become a trust-worthy ally and seemed open to the realm of possibilities, so Michael exposed the entire story, starting from the fateful moment that hateful bullet pierced his skin with its burning desire to end a life, up until René's brown eyes turned blue. One blew this way, the other blew that way.

By the time the story had ended, Anita had sent J.J. back more than once. Each of his quoted requests for their presence at the table became a little more agitated and demanding. The last one had something to do with them going hungry while the neighbor dogs feasted like kings.

Lost in thought, Jerry still managed to turn his son back around with another promise to follow immediately. Then opening his hands pleadingly returned his focus on Michael.

"Can we discuss this further after we eat? I'm starving!" he said, and rubbed his growling belly.

Michael responded by clapping his hands together and jumping to his feet.

"Let's chow down!" he said, and started to slide the knives back into his arm sheaths.

"1 don't think you'll need those at supper. I'll make sure not to touch your plate," Jerry said jokingly.

Michael looked up with a comical display of suspicion masking his face.

"I guess I can trust you, but if you even look at my biscuits wrong, it's on baby. It-is-on!" he said, causing both of them to laugh joyfully.

After a few seconds, Cox turned and rolled himself from the room. Michael held back, deciding to hide the throwing knives in case J.J. got rambunctious and stumbled across them. He opened the lockable bottom drawer of the desk with the intentions of concealing the weapons inside. In the process, his eyes caught a glimpse of an envelope with his name written on the front, instantly recognizing his dad's scroll.

"What's this dad?" he asked while slowly removing the letter with a trembling hand.

'I'm not sure what to tell you. Open it and see,' Tim suggested.

Michael laid his new discovery on the desk planner and just stared at it.

"How come you're not sure? Didn't you write it?" he asked, but didn't receive a reply. "Dad?" he prompted.

'Open and see, son,' came the answer.

A little intimidated and uncertain if he could handle what was inside, he pushed himself back from the desk.

"I can't, I just can't!" he admitted.

'Yes you can. After what you've been through, this is a cakewalk!' Tim explained.

Michael slowly moved his hand to comply.

"Sir! Giggy sayed she ditting da hickerdy tick!" J.J. yelled from the doorway.

"Okay buddy!" Michael replied, happy for the interruption. On the way out, Michael slipped one of the knives up his sleeve, just for the peace of mind, then, apparently under orders from Anita, J.J. took Michael by the hand and lead him up the hallway.

The smell of the wonderful supper, and the sight of his new family seated around the table, pricked at his emotions. It was all he could do not to break down. Life was so much more complicated than he could ever have imagined. When asked to say the blessing before the meal, he was surprised at how easy it came. There was a lot to be thankful for, and if he had the time, would have expressed each and every one of them.

◆ ◆ ◆ ◆ ◆

If someone could capture in a photograph the feelings of joy and contentment that filled the den, they would have in their possession the design for the most perfect Christmas card ever made. The massive tree with all its sparkling glory dominated the bay window at the rear of the room. And the fireplace, even though it was still sixty outside, burned softly, adding to a calm and relaxing atmosphere.

Anita, with her unlimited supply of energy, insisted on cleaning up the kitchen.

Jerry had replanted himself into the comfort of a very large Lay-z-boy recliner and although he refused to admit it, drifted in and out of consciousness.

Like two brothers, Michael and J.J. played with the new toys that Santa had delivered early. Michael was thrilled over his assortment of Power Rangers and kept trying to pull J.J. into imaginary battle, but the younger child wasn't about to relinquish his grip on the neck of his new purple dinosaur named Barney.

The pre-holiday celebration was going perfectly for everyone, that is until Jerry's cell phone began to ring again, once more snapping him out of, as he says, "resting his eyes".

Trying to answer too quickly, Jerry bobbled the device, almost dropping it in the process.

"Hello!" he barked, once stabilizing the contraption next to his ear. "Yes, Sally. The address I gave you is for real! I've already told you three times ... I'm not trying to pull a fast one!" his voice moving up in volume along with his frustration. "I know you get him for Christmas! Pull in the freaking driveway and come to the door!" he instructed as if talking to a stubborn mule. After closing the cover with an angry snap, he tossed the phone onto the couch and started to rise.

"What's up?" Michael asked, getting up from the floor.

Jerry shook his head looking beat. "The ex is driving back and forth out front. She's convinced I gave her some bogus information in order to keep J.J. over the holidays," he explained, and once again moved as if to lift himself into his wheelchair.

"Sit. I'll handle this," Michael ordered, pushing Jerry back down into the fluffy cushioning.

The doorbell rang just before Michael reached the foyer, and then chimed again.

"Coming!" he yelled.

Michael was stunned when he opened the door. Jerry hadn't informed him of how beautiful his former wife was. Her long blond hair flowed like silk down over her shoulders. The blue of her eyes matched his and the dress she wore over her shapely figure. He found himself staring speechlessly at a button-nosed goddess and when she smiled at him with her perfect teeth it paralyzed him.

"Hello. I'm sorry to have bothered you, but my ex-husband insists that he lives here," she explained timidly.

Still at a loss for words, all Michael could manage was a non-intelligent grumbling growl.

Misinterpreting the child's reaction, Sally became angry. "I knew it! Forgive me for intruding on your home young man!" she said irritably, then spun on her heal to leave.

"Miss, all I know is some really nice rich guy lives here and sent his limo driver over to get me so I could play with his kid," Michael explained.

Sally paused and looked over her shoulder like a model on a runway.

"Well, that's obviously not my worthless ex-husband for sure," she said, still frustrated.

Her statement about Michael's good friend exposed her inner self and Michael no longer found anything about her attractive.

"If you say so. J.J. is waiting for me, so good night," he said as he pretended to close the door.

At the mention of her son's name, Sally spun back around facing the entrance.

"Did you say J.J.?" she asked. "Then my ex must really live here," she added.

Michael looked at her as if she were insane.

"Yes ma'am, I did, but the man who lives here is a far cry from being worthless. As a matter of fact, he's an ex-policeman shot in the line of duty, an exceptional father and provider for his son. Plus, you don't appear to be the heartless type who would selfishly abandon someone after they've sacrificed their legs to protect society, so I say again. Good night!" he said while resisting the urge to slam the door in her face.

Sally quickly placed her hand on the door to keep it from latching.

"Excuse me, I'm sorry," she proclaimed.

Michael locked his gaze on her hand in shock, causing her to pull it back as if the panel was scalding hot.

"What is it lady?" he asked angrily.

"Could I please speak to the homeowner?" she pleaded while batting her blue eyes.

Michael recognized the ploy. It was the same trick as his bottom lip. And under any other circumstances, it would have worked. He looked at her with contempt and acted reluctant.

"I guess so, but if it were my house, I'd release the hounds," he said, mocking Mr. Burns from the Simpsons. "Follow me," he added while opening the door wider for her to enter. After closing it behind her, he lead her back through the house without speaking.

"Mommy!" J.J. yelled. But instead of running to greet her as expected, he quickly climbed into his dad's lap, burying his face against the man's chest.

"Ready to go baby?" Sally asked meekly, her eyes traveling across the massive den, trying her best not to appear impressed or reveal the millions of questions scratching at her mind.

Jerry wrapped his son up in a bear hug and then turned his attention on the woman he still loved.

"Forgive me for not getting up dear, but as you've pointed out many times, I'm not half the man I used to be," he said, letting her own words come back to condemn her.

Michael stepped away from Sally as if she'd passed some horrible gas.

"I'll be in the kitchen Mr. Cox. Do you need me to ask your maid to bring you anything?" he asked.

Jerry smiled at the reaction on his ex-wife's face.

"No thank you, we'll be fine," he said, purposefully failing to offer his guest anything.

Michael turned to leave just as J.J. began to pitch a royal fit.

"Me not doeing!" I wivves wit daddy now!" he bellowed, clearly just getting started with his rebellion. Michael thought it would be nice to be a fly on the wall, but knew they needed to work this out on their own, so he continued down the hallway to the office. He had something private to handle as well.

The letter was exactly where he'd left it, not that he'd expected anything different, he was just kinda hopeful it wasn't real or had somehow vanished. He plopped himself down in the chair and sighed while picking up the note his dad had left him. The envelope remained unsealed, somehow making it seem even more mysterious.

"Well, here goes," he said while pulling the contents out and unfolding them on the desk. The first words crushed his heart and he wanted to stop there, but knew he'd never be able to try again, so he fought his emotions and read on through a river of tears.

> "To the love of my life,
>
> Son, the fact that you're reading this letter could only mean one of two things. Either I've passed away, or I've been forced to leave because of something beyond my control. I pray it's the first. To me, my death would be preferable to living without you. You're the reason I take each and every breath. I love you more than mere human words can express. I'd cut the very heart from my chest and hand it to you if you asked for it. Even though my family blood doesn't run through your veins, you're as much a part of me as my inner soul. If it's for the second reason, please understand it's not my choice. Wherever I may be, your memory will dwell in my every thought, and a hundred billion tears shall escape me until I once

again behold your precious face. Whatever the reason for our separation, I want you to know how proud I've been to be your step-father. You've given me the greatest joy a man can obtain. Be strong and brave my son. You're smarter than any child I've ever seen and you have the potential to become anything you desire. Whether it be curing cancer or digging ditches, either road you choose will fill me with pride over your accomplishments. And my love for you will never dwindle. As within any family, there have been times that I've crossed the line and hurt you emotionally and or physically. I beg for your forgiveness. I would rather burn in hell a thousand years than to have caused a single tear to form in your blue eyes. Sometimes as human beings, we expose our inner demons and it hurts the ones we love the most. That person for me is you Michael. Please keep faith in our Lord and Savior Jesus Christ. Live on and live well. I pray we'll see each other again in this life. If not, we shall in the second coming of the Lord. This isn't goodbye.

As God is My Witness,

I'll Always Love You Tremendously!

Dad

Slowly, Michael lowered the letter back to the desktop.

"Why didn't you just tell me what you wrote dad?" he inquired sadly, the tears still flowing down his face.

'Would you have read it if I had?' Tim replied with another question.

"I'm not sure. Maybe in ten years from now I guess," Michael answered, and they both went silent.

"Sweetheart! J.J. is about to leave honey. Come say goodbye," came Anita's voice over the intercom.

Michael got to his feet while whipping his eyes on his shirtsleeve and started taking deep breaths to calm and compose himself before leaving the room.

Once in the foyer, Michael could see his feelings mirrored in the younger boy's face. Both of them were being forced to spend their first Christmas without their fathers. The emotional pain was something that neither one of them could disguise.

"Mairdy Trissmiss sir!" J.J. said unprompted with a pout. The cute way he spoke brought a temporary smile. One that faded as the door closed behind the little fellow and his mother with a lonely click.

The three remaining slowly returned to the den.

"That was a really nice Christmas gathering," Anita said, trying to re-elevate the other's somber mood. Soon they were all talking about Jerry Junior, and it did lift their spirits.

It wasn't long before coffee and hot chocolate was offered and Anita excused herself to the kitchen to prepare the drinks. While she was gone, Michael told Jerry about the letter and how his dad claimed to be unknowledgeable of its contents.

"Maybe it's because the voice you hear really doesn't know," Jerry ventured.

Michael looked at his friend as if he'd lost his mind.

"How's that even possible? He'd have to know what he wrote. Duh!" he responded a little aggravated.

"That's my point. Don't get angry. But isn't it more probable that you want your dad with you so badly that your mind has created his voice to help you cope with his death? You were going through a very traumatic situation when this started. Stronger men would have already lost it," Jerry said calmly.

Michael knew it sounded logical, but he refused to give in that easily.

"Oh really? What about the tests I took? I'm not that smart!" he explained.

Jerry nodded his head.

"From what I've seen, you're correct. Smart is not a word I'd use to describe you. I'd say brilliant and cunning."

Michael stood up and began pacing the floor.

"How about the fighting skills, hmm? Are those also part of my imagination? And how did I recognize the gang members who were responsible for killing my dad? Answer that one Dr. Sigmund *Fraud*!" he shot back defensively.

Jerry reached out and took hold of Michael's trembling hand.

"To answer the last part of your question, you were there! And consciously or not, you saw them all. As for Jackie Lee's part, you've been taking karate most of your life. Believing Mr. Lee was in you only gave you the heart you needed to apply your skills," he explained his assumptions.

Michael jerked his hand away. His friend's logic was taking his dad away again, and he wasn't ready to bury his dad forever. The things in the Bible confirmed Cox's hypothesis, but he still wanted to fight the truth.

"No! My dad is still alive!" he almost yelled, then viciously locked his eyes on Jerry's. "As a matter of fact, he's trying to talk me out of punching your lights out right now!" he said loud and angrily, elevating the sound of his voice with each word.

The security system misunderstood him as a command and responded, descending the whole house into darkness.

The humor of the situation and a yelp from the kitchen stabilized and calmed Michael's temper.

"Crap! Lights on!" he said, laughing at himself for losing control.

Jerry rubbed at his chin.

"I know how we can test my theory if you're willing ... without killing me of course," he said half jokingly.

Michael froze as an internal battle began to rage. Half of him wanted to know, the other wasn't ready.

"How?" he asked nervously.

"Do you know the name of your dad's first love? If not, ask him," Jerry suggested.

Michael turned white as a ghost.

"Dad ...?" he asked, but didn't receive an answer. Before he could ask again, the doorbell rang.

Jerry looked around the room. "I guess J.J. must have forgotten something," he said, then turned in the direction of the foyer.

"Allow me," Michael said, running from the room, and reality.

For the second time tonight, Michael was shocked when he opened the front door. The first time was pleasant, this one was horrifying. He found himself staring down the business end of what appeared to be a cannon. Its barrel pointed directly between his eyes. Beyond that, was the demonic smirk of David Watts.

"My Christmas has come early!" the devil boasted and laughed insanely.

Michael became temporarily seized by the hellish display of his living nightmare as he stood there helplessly waiting for the bullet to enter his brain. However, the sound of the hammer clicking back jolted his need to survive and his body reacted without command by slamming the large oak door just in time. The Hardwood door absorbed the impact of the first shot and also created a momentary barrier between him and the crazy executioner.

"Hide Giggy!" he yelled while running back down the hallway. Behind him came the banging sound of the killer, kicking violently at the door, cursing with every breath.

Veering into the kitchen, Michael yelled again.

"Lights out!" Then he hit the panic button. The dark house went wild with ear-splitting alarms. Next, he flipped the automatic lighting switch off. He knew every inch of his home and moving through the blacked out rooms would be to his advantage.

A second later, the back door burst open with a cracking of wood and tinkling glass.

"Police!" someone barked.

'Easy son, it's way too early for the law to have responded.' Tim said.

Michael agreed and ran up the rear staircase looking for a place to vanish. He knew Giggy would conceal herself as well, thanks to years of hide and seek. However, his plans changed instantly when Jerry popped into his thoughts.

"Damn! I forgot him. He's a sitting duck, literally." A maniac with a gun is a lot to contend with, and there may even be two. He had to do something and quickly.

Michael made his way to the upper railing of the foyer just in time to see that Watts had gotten in and was carefully moving deeper into the house. His confidence proved that the other intruder wasn't there with good intentions either.

Slipping the knife from his sleeve, and being angry with himself for not grabbing them both when he should have, Michael tip-toed down to the bottom of the steps. There he made a quick head check down toward the criminal's path. The creep's silhouette was easy to discern next to the den's entrance. The fireplace slightly illuminated his face as he moved in front of the cased opening.

Not wanting the murderer to have Jerry as an easy victim, Michael threw his weapon at the shadowy figure with all his strength, then dove into the formal dining room.

Watts gave out a howl of pain and surprise before returning the assault with two rapid shots, tearing chunks of plaster from the wall only inches from his target's ear.

With white powder raining down on his head, Michael scurried like a roach across the room where he was able to make himself almost invisible in the dark recess of a china cabinet.

As if rehearsed, Watts appeared in the doorway at the front of the room, just as another sinister shadow emerged from the rear entrance. Whether intended or not, they had nicely trapped their victim between themselves.

"Michael ... it's me, Detective Edison. I'm here to help you. Come on out," said the dark form standing in the kitchen door. Undoubtedly, Bruce Edison underestimated Michael's intelligence and hoped his art of persuasion would provide an easy kill.

He was wrong. Michael wasn't fooled and remained as still as a corpse. Although, he couldn't believe they didn't hear him breathing because even with the clanking of the alarm, to himself he sounded like a charging rhino.

"There you are punk! I see your ass now!" Watts yelled, attempting to make his target panic, which almost worked.

'He's lying son. Don't move.' Tim ordered.

The next couple of seconds of uncertainty felt like hours. Then Watts yelled again after Michael hadn't moved.

"Come on dead boy, move!" he said, then yelled to his partner, "Did he get by you?"

"I didn't see him, but it's darker than Hades' closet in here!" Edison yelled back. "We better split before the law ...," he was adding, however, instead of finishing his statement, there came that undeniable sound of someone getting whacked over the head with a blunt metal object. The dirty cop crumbled to his knees with a painful groan. His weapon discharged into a shelf full of displayed dishes, causing most of them to shatter to the floor.

David panicked and fired his pistol at the empty doorway, hopeful to hit whoever was there. Then losing his nerve, he began to back out of the room slowly. He'd come bravely to kill a little boy and an old woman, but things had changed. His cohort was dead and someone else was in there. Someone unseen. Someone with a weapon. He could feel it and it terrified him.

Suddenly, David's fears were maximized as a large, dark figure materialized less than ten feet away and stumbled toward him. He frantically fired again, emptying his gun into the shadowy form.

The recipient of Cox's panic-stricken action slammed into the far wall with a scream, then slid down into the corner becoming still and silent.

"Your gun's worthless now coward!" Jerry yelled as he stepped around the corner. There, he was able to disarm the noisy system and flip the switch that would allow the lights to come back on.

Standing there in the doorway with a fireplace poker in his hand, Jerry looked angry and ready to rumble.

David knew his butt was finished, so he turned to flee. However, he only took one step before Anita hit him square in the face with a frying pan. Then, before he could recover, she spun her entire body and performed a perfect spinning uppercut. This time, the skillet connected under Watts' chin with a teeth shattering crack, and another satisfying gong, which sent David stumbling backwards with enough force to crash him through the large plate glass window.

Anita proudly walked over to the new opening and looked down at the unconscious man lying in the shrubs.

"You picked the wrong granny this time dirt bag!" she said, then resembling the movement of a major league pitcher, she wound up and threw her weapon of choice at the sleeping man's crotch. "And that's for messing up my baby's Christmas," she added.

David replied with an agonizing groan.

By the time Anita turned back around, Michael was by her side.

"Is he dead Giggy?" he asked, snuggling up to her.

"No sweetheart, but when he comes to, he'll wish he were!" she answered, taking Michael into her arms. "It's over now baby. You can be a little boy again," she said tenderly.

The cool evening air blowing in through the broken window caused them to turn away from their view of the busted up and bleeding creep.

Jerry was kneeling down next to the detective's body. "This one isn't feeling any pain," he said while pulling his fingers back from Edison's neck. He then stood up, wiping his hand unconsciously on his pant leg.

Michael's mouth dropped open and Anita gasped with shock.

Jerry quickly raised the poker he still held and spun around, thinking there must be another intruder. Not seeing anything alarming, he turned back.

"What?" he asked with a puzzled expression on his face.

At a loss for words, Michael only pointed and Anita held her hand over her mouth as if she'd said something hurtful.

Following the direction of Michael's finger, Jerry looked down. Before he could finish uttering the Lord's name, his eyes lost focus and he fainted.

◆ ◆ ◆ ◆ ◆

The moans David made as he rolled from the bushes were similar to those of someone being systematically tortured. The knife protruding from his shoulder screamed at him to remain dormant. But somehow he still managed to come to his hands and knees. His teeth seemed to burst into flames with every breath that assaulted with a vengeance the nerve endings of each broken tooth. In an attempt to ease the pain, he tried to draw air through his nostrils, quickly learning, that too, was useless. His nose had been crushed, and the swelling tissue sealed it. If he hadn't known better, he could swear that his heart had moved up into his face. Even opening his eye became a hellish experience as lightning flashed across his vision, leaving trails of tiny shooting stars.

Everything in him wanted to lay back down and let the world of unconsciousness wrap him in its loving arms. Looking up as best he could, he saw the back of his red headed enemy standing in the window, and his hatred of the boy gave him strength to rise. He wanted to pull Michael through the glass shards and snap the kid's neck. But knowing a man with an iron rod was still in there caused him to do one of the only smart things he'd done all night, he turned and walked away.

"I'll be back Clark. I'll see you die!" he said to himself. With each step getting progressively faster, Watts made it to the back yard. There, he broke into a run, or at least as close to one as he could manage.

◆ ◆ ◆ ◆ ◆

When Jerry first started to revive, he was so completely disoriented, he almost hit Anita with a punch intended for an imaginary attacker.

"Whoa! Calm down there big guy! You're among friends!" Michael said reassuringly.

After a few second, Jerry allowed himself to be lifted into a sitting position on the floor.

"What happened?" he inquired.

Anita placed her hand on his forehead like all grandmothers' do, checking for a fever.

"You fainted. Are you alright?" she asked caringly.

Still influenced by a fog of recuperation, Jerry analyzed his surroundings thoughtfully, trying to clarify the events that had placed him in his current condition. He wanted to make sure that what he believed had transpired had actually happened and wasn't some crazy hallucination, or part of a lucid dream.

Once Jerry became confident that he wasn't off in some artificial or parallel realm of existence, he grabbed his thighs and squeezed.

"I felt that! My God it even hurt!" he yelled joyfully and began to cry. His emotions proved to be contagious. Michael and Anita immediately joined in with tears of their own.

Cox became excited.

"I was walking wasn't I? Praise God! Michael, did you see me? Did you? I was walking!" he spat out between sobs.

"Yes, I saw you! But how? What happened?" Michael asked, sharing in the excitement.

Jerry lowered his head into his hands, still trying to compose himself and to contemplate a logical response. When he rose back up, his face seemed to glow with understanding and awe.

"Well, let me see ... I was sitting in the den when I heard that first shot, and Michael ... you started yelling. Trying to reach my wheelchair, I fell to the floor and laid there like a fish out of water. I began to curse myself for being worthless. Then came a loud crash from the back door and I saw a shadow pass by. A second later, another one was standing in the hall and then more gun fire ..." he paused and pulled Michael closer to his side. "I started to cry. I had failed to protect you, and I thought you had been killed. But then I heard Edison trying to talk you out of hiding. That told me you were still alive and I'd been given another chance. Calling out in the name of Jesus, my legs began to burn. At first I thought it was because of how close I was to the fireplace ..." he paused again, this time to wipe the moisture from his eyes. Then some inner thought assaulted his emotions further and he placed his hand over his mouth to keep from breaking down completely.

"It's okay honey. We're here for you," Anita advised softly. Cox looked up at her and then at Michael, trying to decide if they were going to believe what he was about to say. He wasn't even sure if he believed it himself.

"Well, one of them yelled something about finding you Michael. That's when my brain kinda reprogrammed itself. I got up and grabbed the first thing resembling a weapon I could find. I didn't even think twice about being unable to walk. That is, not until I knew you were safe. I love you Michael, and because of that love, I walked," he finished and hugged Michael tightly.

"It's a Christmas miracle!" Anita chimed joyously.

Michael became ecstatic and couldn't remain still.

"Get up! I want to see it again!" he proclaimed, dancing with happiness.

Jerry was reluctant. He wasn't exactly sure if he wanted to know if he could walk again, or if he could face the truth if he couldn't.

Understanding his dilemma, Anita took his hand in hers and gave an encouraging tug.

"The Lord Jesus only heals those that trust in His name and have faith. Let me quote our Saviors very words, "Rise up and walk!"" she said, now pulling on his arm as well.

Cox stood up slowly on trembling legs with his eyes closed tightly in prayer. Again, he burst into tears of joy.

"I'm doing it! Praise God, I'm doing it!" he yelled once fully upright. In resemblance to a tightrope walker, Jerry took his first conscious steps in months. His entire body felt stronger than at any other time in his life. So much so, he grabbed Anita around the waist and began to dance around. He was about to break into a tango, but the dead and still bleeding police detective at his feet changed his mind.

"I guess this time I really should call this in," he said. "Don't you?" he asked, reverting to some police jargon.

"They should have already been here. Remind me to fire the security company," Michael said as he walked back over to the broken window. Just as he arrived, an authoritative knock came from the front door.

"Never mind, they're here!" he added and then looked down to get one last view of the busted up killer of his mom and dad, only to receive a shock. "But Watts isn't!" he yelled angrily and jumped through the opening into the quickly cooling night, which caused Anita to scream loudly.

♦ ♦ ♦ ♦ ♦

At the sound of a woman in distress, the two responding Hendersonville police officers charged into the house with their weapons drawn.

Even with probable cause, the law still required them to announce their presence.

"Police!" They yelled as they entered the foyer.

The double-cased opening to the right was clear, so the lead officer pointed his revolver down the hallway as the other made a quick head check in the room to their left, and it stunned him momentarily. He wasn't ready for the scene and his heart skipped a beat in his chest.

In front of him stood an obviously hysterical elderly woman. To her left stood a white male of around thirty years of age, with a fireplace poker and a look of guilt written on his face. Behind the two lay the remains of a middle-aged man with what appeared to be large bullet wounds still oozing blood. At his feet, a dropped or discarded pistol. *Oh great! A domestic!'* he thought. The worst and most dangerous call an officer can receive.

'The male with the iron tool has to be the shooter,' the cop thought.

"On the floor - now!" he ordered, pointing his weapon at who he believed to be the perp.

Before anyone could comply, the second police officer, now overly excited, charged in.

"Freeze! Nobody move!" he demanded. Everything became a damned if you do and damned if you don't situation.

The would-be suspect knew the drill and automatically dropped to his knees, interlocking his fingers behind his head. His actions convinced the officer that the man in his sights was responsible for the crimes here and had obviously faced the law before.

The policeman kicked the weapons out of everyone's reach, holstered his weapon, grabbed the perpetrator by the neck and slammed his face into the carpet. While his partner covered him, he added cuffs, along with, in his opinion, some well-deserved pain.

The older woman started yelling again, but now her rage was directed at the officers, and that's the main reason these types of calls were so volatile. People can change sides so quickly.

"On the floor grandma!" the second officer demanded rudely.

She gave him a look of defiance and shock.

"Now lady!" the cop barked. He didn't realize it yet, but the poor fool had just unknowingly poked a stick into an angry hornet's nest.

◆ ◆ ◆ ◆ ◆

Even though the dirty water was just shy of glazing over with ice, it felt heavenly to David's broken skin. The initial shock had made him gasp and involuntarily shiver, but it also seemed to numb the throbbing around his eyes and nose. The following splashes of cold liquid prove beneficial in cleaning away most of the blood saturated soil that, thanks to a tumble down a hill, was caked into most of his facial features.

Unable to shovel the natural anesthetic fast enough by hand, Watts finally dunked his head into the stream like in the old western movies. He wanted desperately to be able to rinse out his mouth as well, but just the thought of it made the nerve endings of his new dental work scream bloody murder.

"I'll kill that old woman!" he said to himself, then spat a wad of dark red saliva on the bank along with another one of his teeth.

Tilting his head back to run his fingers through his crystallizing, frosty hair, he detected the ever-nearing sound of someone approaching. Because he had been raised by Hollywood's motion pictures, instead of using common sense, which he didn't have, he quickly decided to wade into the creek. After all, television had taught him that it was the best way to shake the police off your trail.

The slow, slushy current flowed around his ankles, chilling them all the way to the bone marrow in seconds. Nevertheless, compared to the prisons they send cop killers to, crooked or not, this was a stroll on Waikiki beach.

It only took a few dozen steps for the new pain in his frozen legs to overrule that idiotic decision. Stepping ashore, the soggy ground swallowed his right shoe, actually sucking it from his foot like a vacuum. To make matters worse, his poor choice of exits placed him dead center of a thorn patch. The added trauma to his already agonizing feet made him want to howl at the top of his lungs. The only reason he didn't was knowing that it would be the same as sending up a distress flare, bringing his pursuers on him like flies. Instead, he tried biting down on his index finger. The white-hot pain from that brain fart caused his oral cavity to explode, and he collapsed back into the darkness.

◆ ◆ ◆ ◆ ◆

Michael hit the ground rolling like a tumbleweed, the damp earth generously relinquishing some of its surplus moisture, soaking the back of his shirt and pants all the way to his skin.

Standing there in the yard with each breath exiting his body in a foggy vapor, Michael listened to the drama unfolding inside of what used to be the only place he still felt safe. That is, at least since the violent death of his parents, and when the innocence of youth shielded him from the cruelty of the real world. Now even that was gone.

Turning and scanning the neighborhood in hopes of spotting Watts, or at least seeing some clue as to which direction the creep may have gone, produced nothing remotely helpful, so Michael decided to head for the woods behind the house. Logically, it was the only ideal way for a fleeing animal to escape. The other avenues would have taken the demon into the lighted areas, increasing the risk of easy detection. Evil always lurks in the dark where it can hide its ugly head.

Crossing an embankment at the rear of the property, Michael lost his footing on the wet grass and slid on his rear end all the way down the incline. It had been a blast back when he and his dad used to do it for fun, but tonight, it was unexpected and painfully irritating. At the bottom, he came to his feet and began wiping the mud from his trousers, then flinging it from his hand. While doing so, thanks to the light from a full moon, he could detect fresh signs from someone else's inability to maneuver the saturated hillside as well. Plus, the hollowed out impressions of that person's heals betrayed the wearer's course of flight, unknowingly providing an easy trail to follow.

With a clear idea of where he was now going, Michael began to sprint. He wanted to run full blast but the terrain wasn't runner friendly and a twisted ankle would most likely allow his quarry to escape.

The evidence of Watts' passage ended at the shore of a small brook. Exhausted, Michael leaned up against a large oak tree to catch his breath and to contemplate the situation. The steam rising from a combination of his body heat and damp clothing gave him the strange appearance of being a forest spirit.

"What do you think dad? Which way?" he asked between huffs.

'I think you should go home to get warm and dry before you get pneumonia or killed out here chasing a madman.' Tim responded.

"That's not what I ..." Michael started to reply irritably when a bitter truth Jerry had voiced earlier stopped him short. "You ... you really are just a part of my subconscious, the one of reason and safety, aren't you dad?" he asked sadly.

There wasn't an answer.

"And I guess Jackie is my reckless side ... I ... I really ... I'm all alone," Michael said quietly and emotionally just before falling to his knees where he dropped his head and began to cry.

The next thing Michael realized is that the woods had become totally void of sound. He felt as if he'd somehow been transported into a sealed chamber. The water in the creek had even stopped flowing. Nothing was moving, not even the air, which until this very second, had been whispering through the treetops.

The cold hard ground and the feeling of dampness on Michael's hands and knees vanished. Somehow, he'd lost all sensitivity to the world around him. His mind raced for an explanation. Had he passed out? Or had death claimed him again? They say you never hear the sound of the shot that kills you.

'Michael!' came the crisp, clear voice that had been a part of his life since as far back as he could remember, and then it came again. *'Michael my son.'*

Michael's head lifted on its own as if someone's hand was beneath his chin, gently pushing upward the same way his dad used to do when he wanted eye contact. A feeling of inner peace wrapped its arms around him.

All of a sudden, Tim was there, more or less floating above the motionless water like a ghost.

"Dad!" Michael screamed as he stumbled in an attempt to reach the apparition that seemed to be made of little more than strips of paper and cotton.

'My precious, precious child ... You're not alone. I'll live within your heart and memory as long as you'll have me. You are everything to me son. Even death can't steal you from my heart and soul. I'm sorry for not being there for you. But my spirit will always be, for I'll love you forever and ever and ...' the specter kept repeating the last two words as it faded away like smoke.

"Dad!" Michael yelled again sorrowfully as everything returned to normal in a rush of sound and sensation.

Lifting his face from the ground, Michael realized that he hadn't moved since he'd fallen to his knees earlier. And the shock of that made him gasp for air.

The noises were not the only thing to return. Michael was cold. No ... he was freezing. He wrapped himself into a ball for what little warmth it could provide, then began rocking back and forth as he questioned his sanity.

"Was any of it real? Or could all of it had been an hallucination brought on by hypothermia? Maybe I was so exhausted, that I'd fallen asleep and dreamed the spiritual visitor." He thought of many explanations, but couldn't answer his own questions.

The only thing Michael knew for sure was that he needed his great-grandmother. Shaking like a leaf in a windstorm, he got up and headed for home. His teeth were chattering like a mariachi band, and doubt clouded his mind as to whether he was going to make it or not.

"Giggy! Help me! Giggy please!" he screamed at the night sky. The lights from his home, and the ones from the emergency vehicles filling his yard, looked to be a thousand miles away. And each tentative step he took seemed to add to that distance.

♦ ♦ ♦ ♦ ♦

After coming to, David found himself laid out in the thorn bushes, painfully receiving an unwanted session of acupuncture from the nest of nature's finely honed needles, and a chill that ran to the bone.

Close by, Watts could hear the pleading voice of his hated enemy. His first thought was fueled by blind rage. He wanted to pull the knife from his shoulder and return it to its rightful owner in a violent and vengeful way. The first touch of the weapon's handle altered that plan and almost returned him to a state of unconsciousness.

Using the overhead branches, David managed to pull himself upright. Standing there exerted a lot more effort than he'd anticipated and he teetered, while attempting to maintain his balance. He looked around trying to decide what to do. His options were limited. As much as he loathed the idea of leaving with Michael still alive, he knew killing the little shit would have to wait. His mind was willing, but his body was not.

Thorns or not, Watts was about to lay back down and give up when the sound of his salvation came in the form of a distant automobile horn.

Taxing his strength past its limits and struggling to take every step, Watts limped out into the open field, then began to run as best he could.

Behind him, David could clearly hear the punk screaming for help and assumed he must have been spotted, so he moved a little faster. Time was not on his side. The only thing that had gone right all evening was his call to George Woods. But even that blessing wouldn't amount to much if he failed to reach the parking lot quickly. When the king of Nashville said ten minutes, that's exactly what he meant.

Looking like a scene from an old horror film about werewolves, the hunched over form of a demon crossed the empty horizon in the light of a full moon.

♦ ♦ ♦ ♦ ♦

A car horn blaring from behind him caused Michael to pause

and look back over his shoulder. Off in the night, he could see a large black limousine pulling into the church parking lot out on Center Point Road. Meaning nothing to him, he turned back toward home. Then he caught a dark shape in his peripheral vision. At first, he ignored it. He was too cold to care. It felt as if his spine was going to shake out of his skin, and every muscle ached under the effort to walk.

After a few steps, Michael once again uncaringly glanced over his shoulder to watch the shadow moving toward the house of God. Still suffering from mental overload, his thoughts about the figure eluded him. He couldn't even remember why he was outside half dressed and freezing. The feeling was strange. But what was even stranger was that for some crazy reason, that silhouette of a man running across the open field, meant something ... something important ... something to do with ....

"David Watts! ... Oh my God ... He's getting away!" he yelled. The scar on Michael's chest began to burn like hell's fire and his anger along with it. "No!" he screamed, and without thinking of his condition or his safety, he sprang from the trees in a dead run.

♦ ♦ ♦ ♦ ♦

David couldn't believe he'd made it to the edge of his rendezvous unmolested. Every painful step had been haunted by the expectation of hearing the word "freeze!" His wet clothing had already began to comply with that unspoken order, and his skin wasn't far behind.

Watts knew beyond any doubt that each added second of exposure to these winter conditions brought him closer to meeting the angel of death. However, even with his ticket to warmth and freedom idling only a few yards away, it crossed his mind to give up and succumb to the elements.

'Funny how things can change,' David thought. Less than a year ago he'd been dying to get out of that devil's car. Now here he was literally dying if he didn't get in. All that stood between

him and life was a four-foot high retaining wall that he'd have to descend. Normally, he'd simply jump the short distance, but tonight, with all his injuries and the numbness in his feet, the little stack of railroad ties he was on became an elevation equal to a mountain-side cliff overlooking the Grand Canyon.

As Watts searched back and forth for an easy way down, a heavy snow began to fall. The millions of small flakes quickly diminished his visibility. He could still see the means of his salvation, but it was like watching a television show on a channel with poor reception.

The crunching sound of dry grass being stepped on startled David, so he spun around in a panic anticipating a regiment of policemen to materialize from the darkness.

After searching the blizzard for anyone lurking, he began to calm down. He couldn't see anything out of place or detrimental to his escape. Then from the flurry, came a blurred sole of a small, black shoe.

◆ ◆ ◆ ◆ ◆

When he misjudged that last step, Michael thought for sure his element of surprise had been lost, especially with his elbow ending up in a pile of dry brush. The cracking had turned the killer in his direction, and Michael could have sworn their eyes had locked for a fraction of a second, causing an involuntary gasp and a punch of fear. But he quickly realized he was wrong. The snow that was covering everything in a white blanket had actually, and thankfully, blinded the demon from the nearby administer of justice, once more proving to Michael that his quest was, as Giggy pointed out, sanctioned by God Himself.

Michael began to wonder why the creep had picked that particular spot to stop running and why he was searching the area as if he'd dropped something. The second part of that scenario raised his hackles. *'Maybe he did see me and is looking for his weapon,'* he thought. And with that possibility overriding his sensibility, Michael attacked by charging. When he'd gotten within five feet, he launched himself into a flying side kick. At the last second, his target turned to face him.

♦ ♦ ♦ ♦ ♦

Before David could react, a foot slammed painfully into his chest like a sledgehammer. The collision sent him soaring backwards with a howl, relinquishing him of his breath and his need to find a way down. His fall ended with a sickening thud. The violent contact with the blacktop was excruciating. Every existing trauma intensified harmoniously with the new infliction. Watts' mind clouded as he teetered on the edge of consciousness, then everything went black.

♦ ♦ ♦ ♦ ♦

Michael had once again run down the last of his father's killers. But this time, it had been costly. He had become victim to the natural force of gravity as well. The reason David had stopped where he had became clear, but too late.

Laying there in the wet snow, Michael began to roll around and rub frantically at his swelling hipbone, unsuccessfully trying to diminish the internal screams of agony caused by the landscaping timbers un-giving corners.

♦ ♦ ♦ ♦ ♦

George had been impatiently waiting for his insubordinate to arrive when he saw two muddy humanoids come stumbling from out of nowhere. With his visibility simultaneously being obstructed by the storm, and the car's foggy windows, there wasn't any safe way to evaluate the situation from where he sat. And until he was sure no one else was going to fall from the sky, he would remain a cautious and dormant spectator. A man didn't last long in a position like his by being careless or taking unnecessary risks. That's what he paid others to do.

"Bring those two and make sure they're alone," he instructed while pointing across the lot.

The ever-present ebony giants drew their weapons as they

exited the car as ordered. Seconds later, their large forms faded into the flurry, almost disappearing. Their first duty was to check the surrounding area for any onlookers. What may need to be done required no witnesses.

Woods barely had time to light up before his trained gorillas returned with their captives. He pulled his collar up to protect his neck from the chill that had dominated the limo's interior ever since the goons opened their doors to leave. He couldn't believe that earlier that day he'd worn little more than a T-shirt, and now this.

"Welcome to Tennessee," he said to himself, then took a hit from his cigar to set his mood before climbing out into the blizzard.

The bite from the wind was nothing compared to the sight before him. One of his men held a small boy by the collar. The kid just hung there submissive and limp like a kitten being carried by its mother. It also appeared that someone had rolled the child in mud. The thug's other hand was busy helping an equally filthy, semiconscious, blood-soaked person to remain standing. This fellow's face had been hammered beyond recognition. If it hadn't been for the earlier phone call from Watts, George wouldn't have had the slightest idea of who he was looking at. The damage looked more like the results of a bar fight with a half dozen bikers, not the work of a confrontation with an eight year old boy who looked six. Woods was thinking, shaking his head in disbelief.

Unable to look at Watts any longer, the crime boss re-focused his eyes on those of the red head.

"You must be the young warrior whose name has been annoyingly brought to my attention lately," he said as he studied Michael with a calculating stare. Then he took a long drag on his smoke and blew it into the child's face.

Michael wanted to choke but fought the urge. He wasn't about to give the creep any satisfaction. Instead, he slowly raised his head until his blue eyes were level with that of the gang leader's.

"The displeasure is all mine Mr. Woods, I assure you!" he replied bravely.

George was impressed, as well as a little shocked.

"Ah … so you've done your homework. A gold star for you. That means you should know, little man, that it's obviously very dangerous to cross me," he said all high and mighty, clearly proud of himself.

Michael's facial expression remained unimpressed and stone cold, his voice became venomous.

"Don't let my size make a bigger fool out of you than you already are!" he spat disrespectfully and was instantly rewarded by a violent shake at the end of his captor's massive arm like a rag doll. The punishment hurt all the way to the bones that felt about to snap, and elevated his anger to rage.

In a desperate attempt to free himself, Michael began kicking at the rib cage of the monster that held him. The only response he received was a deep, grizzly bear chuckle and a more aggressive shake. He intended to try again by striking at the oak tree sized elbow when the echoing "click-click" of a shell being chambered caused him to pause and re-think that idea.

Returning his attention to the thin man in front of him, Michael found the origin of that distinctive sound pointed directly at his head. Beyond that, the triumphant grin of a heartless villain.

Losing his look of victory, George lowered his gun, confused over the lack of response from Michael.

"What's with you Clark? Haven't you any fear of dying?" he asked.

Now it was Michael's turn to smile.

"Been there, done that!" he answered sarcastically.

Woods only stared with bewilderment. Using the end of his

pistol, he motioned for his goon to put the captured boy down. The giant complied by tossing his prisoner to the macadam like a discarded dirty towel, then kicking the accumulated snow off his expensive shoe into the boy's face.

George stepped over to where Michael landed and puffed up his scrawny chest to show supremacy.

"Mr. Clark, I'm going to ask you a question that will be the determining factor in whether you walk out of here tonight, or get carried out in a bag," he explained, then looked up at the falling white powder as if trying to find the right words. Without looking back down, he began to speak again.

"Why have you waged this war of yours on my organization?" he inquired and then once more returned his focus on Michael, who rolled his eyes in disbelief.

Pointing an accusing finger at Watts, Michael began to explain.

"That piece of crap killed my mother, then he and his co-pieces of crap murdered my dad and put me through living hell. That not being enough to quench their criminal lust for blood, two of the jackasses broke into my house to finish me off, on Christmas Eve of all nights." The whole time he spoke, his anger got hotter and his voice got louder until he was actually yelling. "What did you expect stupid? A holiday gift card to the mall?" he finished and began to rise. About half way up, George stepped forward, pushing him back down with his foot, causing Michael to fall flat on his back again. Before he could try once more, the criminal placed his shoe in the center of Michael's chest. A scene from a gladiator movie where the victor waited for the emperor's signal, thumbs up, or thumbs down.

Even though Woods was a thin man, the crushing force he applied to Michael's midsection restricted the boy's ability to breathe. The anguish in the kid's face seemed to please the king.

"Call me stupid one more time …!" he said violently.

Michael struggled to inhale and he could hear his breastbone cracking as he felt himself passing out. Just as he was on the verge of suffocating, Woods finally released the pressure, but the creep left his foot where it was.

"As for your parents, they were killed before Watts came to work for me! Tonight's screw-up was also none of my doings! Actually, I instructed David not to bring heat upon my head with this personal and foolish vendetta! I assure you, he will be sorry for going against my wishes!" George explained quite angrily.

Michael gulped deeply, trying to fill his aching, starving lungs.

"What about Edison?" he asked between gasps.

At first, the mention of the detective's name caused Wood's eyes to enlarge, but he quickly composed himself.

"Never heard of the man," he lied. However, after a brief pause, his curiosity got the better of him. "Why?" he asked.

"Well, your employee of the month over there in la la land emptied a gun into the man's chest. He's dead." Michael explained.

For a few moments, George was at a loss for words. A major member of his empire had been lost in the unsanctioned fiasco, and there wasn't any way to replace a crooked cop at the level of chief detective for less than a hundred grand. That's the part that hurt. To him, human life had no value, but when it came to his money, like most Americans, he drew the line.

Michael could tell that he'd hit a nerve in the criminal with his disclosure. If he pushed a little harder, maybe he could cause the creep to make a mistake. He still had to proceed cautiously, he didn't know the man or how he handled his temper. He could just start shooting. The thought was frightening, but no more than being crushed under the jerk's foot or laying in the snow becoming a strawberry-blond boy-sickle.

"How long until the cops tie that shit bag to you? Sounds like a major headache on the way if you ask me," he offered.

Woods pointed his gun at Michael's head again.

"Well, I didn't ask, so shut up!" he yelled.

'This is it. I'm dead ... again,' Michael thought. The part he'd added, "again," struck him as humorous and he giggled.

The kid's chuckle caught Woods totally off guard. Never had someone laughed at the business end of his gun. Either the boy was crazy, or the bravest person he'd ever met, or both. George's admiration for the red headed brat made him wish they were on the same team. He'd seen three hundred pounds of muscle beg under less of a threat than this, and here this little fart was actually laughing.

George moved the pistol out of Michael's face and smiled.

"You're something else kid! I kind of hate the fact that I'm gonna have to kill you," he said.

Michael's blue eyes went from the beauty of innocence, to the rage resembling that of a psychopathic killer.

"Funny. I'm going to enjoy killing you!" he replied with conviction.

As soon as the shock covered Wood's face, Michael recognized his chance and sprung into action by bear hugging the foot on his chest and rolling sideways. The quick and rigorous movement forced Woods into a painful case of the splits. Michael continued to roll, with the howling man having no choice but to follow. The momentum only slightly diminishing as George's knee struck the macadam with tremendous force. Still trapped in a high velocity descent, the criminal's arms naturally shot out to protect his body from a violent landing, the pistol slipping from his hand in the process.

Accomplishing his goal, Michael released his grip and spun on his back like a break-dancer, his twirling legs crashing into George's elbows. One second the man appeared to be doing a push-up, the next he was showing his love for mother earth by kissing the snow covered blacktop.

Everything happened so quickly that by the time the two giant bodyguards could react, it was too late. They stood there with their weapons drawn, but unable to shoot. The kid was completely covered by their boss's body, and a missed shot would cost them their bread and butter. Also, to their surprise, the red headed youngster had somehow retrieved the dropped pistol and had it pressed up against their bosses temple.

"Tell your trained gorillas to put their toys away and back off!" Michael ordered while grinding the gun's barrel into George's skin. At first, no one moved. Michael was thinking that these creeps were either shocked, stupid or they didn't believe that an eight year old had the guts to pull the trigger. Whatever their dilemma, he decided to give them a little more to consider. "You've already let my size make fools out of you once tonight. Why press your luck like your dead compadres Otey, Caldrone and Dickson did? Not to forget that steaming pile of dog crap at your feet," he said, and paused to allow them time to weigh their options.

Michael was happy to see their gears turning as all eyes fell on David Watts, whose beaten body hadn't moved since the goon dropped him ten minutes ago. The bloody snow around the downed man would give anyone second thoughts about underestimating Michael's determination.

George turned out to be smarter than Michael gave him credit for.

"Do whatever he says," he commanded, sounding defeated.

Both human mountains of muscle complied without question by slipping their weapons back inside their jackets and stepping backward.

'This short-lived Mexican standoff is over, now what?' Michael thought.

Before Michael could decide his next move, the sound of a nearby helicopter dominated the air.

"Hear that Woods? The police are out looking for me and the man who wasted one of their own. How much do you want to bet that when they get here, they shoot first, and sort through the garbage for the rotten apple later?" Michael questioned.

George knew he'd lost this round and his goose was cooked if he didn't change this situation quickly.

"What do you want Clark?" he inquired.

The question pushed Michael's button to the point he almost pulled the trigger, splattering Wood's brains all over the parking lot.

"What do I want?" Michael repeated angrily as if it were a stupid thing to ask. "I want to go home and open Christmas packages with my family like a normal eight year old! I want my mom and dad to be there to tuck me into bed at night! I want to stop obsessing over revenge. And I want to walk to the street without fear of being murdered by jerks like you. Or having to sleep with one eye open because even the security of my own home has been violated," Michael explained and began to cry, knowing these things were never going to be possible again.

George's emotions were pricked as well. The kid just wanted to be a kid. He wasn't any different than himself at that age: Parent-less, living in fear, and wishing for a family of his own.

"I'm sorry Michael," he said with such conviction that it surprised everyone.

"What did you say?" Michael asked confusedly.

Woods forced his body to relax. He wanted to express a total surrender by eliminating any form of tension between them. Some actions speak louder than words.

"I said how sorry I am, and I really mean it," he said.

Michael's common sense told him the man was lying, but his

heart didn't seem to agree. He closed his eyes trying to collect his thoughts or receive advice from his dad. Nothing came.

George knew that Michael believed him.

"I can't change the past, but I can promise you that no one from my organization will ever bother you or your family again," he said honestly.

Michael eased the gun's pressure off George's temple.

"How can I trust someone like you?" he asked.

"It's the only choice you have, other than pulling that trigger," Woods explained.

The beating of the chopper's blades grew closer and a large spotlight could be seen panning the field between Michael's home and the church's parking lot.

Woods looked up at the beam with concern.

"If that light falls on us, our lives together will have just begun. Let my men and me walk away now, and you'll never see us again," he said and started to rise.

Michael didn't stop him, but he did keep the gun pointed at one of the man's vital organs.

"Okay Woods walk. You have my grace of mercy. This time. There won't be a next!" Michael explained, sounding dead serious.

George nodded his head with understanding, and then turned toward his men.

"Get in the car. It's over," he instructed.

The larger of the two men bent over to scoop up what was left of David Watts, and Michael came to his feet.

"No way! He stays!" he said.

The huge man looked to his boss for direction and Woods waved for the monster to get in the car.

"Leave him!" he ordered. "The last thing I need right now is to be arrested for aiding a fleeing cop killer," he added and then reached out to Michael to retrieve his nine millimeter.

Michael trusted the guy, but he was a long way from being foolish.

"I think I'll hang on to this a little longer, thank you," he said.

Thinking he understood Michael's intentions. Woods looked over at Watts and then back to Michael.

"Don't let your hatred for that man turn you into him," he said like it was a road he himself traveled. With that said, he turned and walked toward the limousine. Just before he climbed in, Michael yelled again.

"Hey Woods!"

George stopped and looked back.

"Yeah kid?" he hollered back.

Michael smiled and said, "Merry Christmas."

The smile was returned.

"Yes indeed Michael Clark. Yes-in-deed!" George replied, and then entered the limo, and it quickly pulled away, leaving Michael alone with his worst enemy only seconds before the lot was illuminated as if the sun had risen. The wind from the aircraft's rotors made the already frigid night air unbearable.

"This is the State Police! Stay where you are!" came a demanding and authoritative voice from above.

Time had run out and Michael knew it. The ground unit would arrive soon and there is no way they would allow him to do what he intended.

Michael walked over to the destroyer of his family.

"Hey shit head! Wake up!" he yelled and kicked David's leg.

Watts looked up in a daze, his focus instantly zeroing in on the gun pointed between his eyes, then up at Michael.

"Clark!" he muttered.

Michael thumbed back the hammer.

"How does it feel jackass?" he asked.

David was in too much pain to show any emotion.

"Go ahead. If the roles were reversed, I wouldn't hesitate to blow you away!" he boasted.

Michael started to squeeze the trigger, but what Woods had said earlier about becoming the one you hate stopped his finger.

"Yes you would wouldn't you? And if I were to pull this trigger, I'd be just like you! No thanks!" he said, lowering the weapon and stepping out of the creep's reach.

Instead of feeling good about his life being spared, David got angry.

"Come on Clark, do it! I'd rather die here than spend the rest of my life in prison!" he yelled hatefully.

He couldn't believe it, but Michael was actually feeling pity for the man that killed his parents. Making sure that David could see what he was doing, Michael flipped a small latch on the gun's handle, and the slender clip containing the deadly projectiles slid out into his hand. Then he threw them into the darkness.

Stepping forward again, Michael held the weapon out to Watts.

"Here; I'm nothing like you! Even though you showed no mercy to me or my family, I extend it to you! There's one bullet chambered in there and the cops are only seconds away!" he was explaining, but was interrupted by the blow horn broadcasting again.

"Drop the weapon! This is the State Police! Drop the Weapon!"

Michael paused and looked up. "Unlike my mom and dad, you have a choice. You could shoot me again and spend the rest of your days behind bars for killing a child, or ...," he said, shrugging his shoulders, feeling no need to elaborate.

David grabbed the gun and spun it on Michael.

"You're a fool kid! A dead fool!" he spat wickedly.

Michael smiled at the threat. "Death no longer frightens me! Life does! Besides, I've been there. And people who love me are there waiting for my return! The choice is still yours!" he finished, then turned his back on the creep and started walking toward the approaching police cars. Behind him, Watts was yelling all kinds of obscenities, but Michael just kept moving away.

The report from the shot had the equivalence of a sonic boom in the crisp winter air, and it caused Michael to jump in anticipation of the bullet entering his back. It never came.

David's decision had been the coward's way out. And Michael never looked back. Justice had been served by the most unexpected vengeance.

The End